The Mentor

Colette Waddell

Published By Top Cat Press

Copyright © 2023

All rights reserved. No part of this publication may be reproduced or transmitted in any form or by any means, electronic or mechanical, including photocopy, recording, or any information storage and retrieval system, without prior consent of the publisher.

The Mentor

ISBN-13: 978-0-9791518-2-8

Emma Woods has retired from her university research job to take over the family farm and embrace a predictable, peaceful life. Everything changes when a mysterious envelope appears containing a safe deposit key, along with a message from her father who was deemed a traitor and assassinated by the U.S. government. Amidst the loss of everything she holds dear, and her own life under attack, Emma seeks out the help of her neighbor Anthony Newcastle. But can she trust a man who works for the very organization that appears to be threatening her?

Author Colette Waddell takes a departure from non-fiction and introduces unlikely heroine Emma Woods. With her childhood past and life experiences, Colette creates an adventure that thrusts Emma into the hands of Anthony's protégé, CIA officer David Jamison. From a small town in Oregon, to Washington D.C. and back to the Middle East where it all began, they both must dive headlong into danger, guided only by The Mentor.

For Ross

And for my Mentor
And for Matthew, the Wizard

Table of Contents

Home..1	Pulling The Thread 197
A Fresh Start 12	Dubious Allies...................................213
The Key And The Consequences 22	The Chase..221
Refuge..43	Karl's Game 232
Friends And Neighbors 51	Istanbul..237
A Watchful Eye 61	Shaking The Bushes.........................245
Voices From The Past 66	Frank 254
Digging Deeper 79	Comrades In Arms...........................264
Coming Clean..................................84	Patricia...271
The Slaughter 88	Uncle Amir..277
Old Acquaintances 94	Debra..284
Meeting With The Mentor.............100	Allison 295
Ultimate Sacrifice 112	Desperation.......................................303
The Reckoning................................117	Hostage 307
Reconnaissance...............................124	Emma's Proposal 309
Saving Emma..................................128	The Catch..315
Reinforcements...............................137	Setting The Snare 321
The Company Man.........................147	A Pause In The Madness................325
Showing Some Cards 154	House Of Cards................................333
Officer Jamison...............................160	The Takedown..................................340
Camaraderie....................................170	The Ghost..348
The Librarian..................................177	A New Life 360
Matt The Wizard 189	

Chapter 1
Home

The smooth rope and fluid zipping of the belay line felt good in Emma's hand. A breeze created by her rapid descent pushed wisps of renegade tendrils of hair from the sweat around her helmeted face. Clicking sounds of her carabiner placement echoed up the crevice wall, and she lightly tapped the toes of her climbing shoes over red rock. This brought her face to face with the petroglyph never once viewed by a white person. Adjusting her head lantern, Emma leaned in to inspect it more closely. A familiar voice sought her from far above. "Everything okay down there *Sha kiss*? It was the clipped Native style of speaking, the kind of voice that comes from the chest, not from the nose like non-Natives. "How's it looking? You gonna build a hogan down there," he giggled. "I got it, Kee," Emma replied to her old friend and guide Kee Yazzie, "It's beautiful! *Nizhoni!*" She fumbled in a vest pocket for her notebook, and frantically scribbled some notes. "Are you sure this is your last time?" Kee yelled back down, with more than a little doubt in his voice. "Yeah," Emma hollered, distracted. Then, muttered to herself, "It's the last time…officially anyway."

A ledge that once allowed the ancient artists a place to stand had fallen away long ago. Restricted access to the rock art left it in pristine condition. It was a real find for any anthropologist, and Kee had offered its secret location as a sort of going- away present. Emma felt it was a satisfying finish to a relatively successful career. She carefully copied the petroglyph in pencil onto her notebook paper. This would be her one and only opportunity to view the rock art, so sacred to the Navajo, and her last encounter with both the object and the people she'd grown to love. It wasn't that she regretted her decision to retire from her position at the university. She truly wanted to change the direction of her life and revive her grandparents' farm. Her choice to embrace such a dramatic change felt right, but she would miss the research and the friends she'd made on the reservation, not to mention the security her position offered. A steady paycheck and health insurance wasn't the only thing she was giving up. She would also lose the camaraderie of her university friends and knowing what to expect from each well-planned day.

Emma stopped for a moment to ponder how life as a farmer could possibly replace that security. Her pencil poised over the drawing she'd made, she thought for a half-second of changing her mind. Then the rope jerked and she dropped a few inches down the crevice. "Kee! What the fuck?!" She screamed up to the man she'd trusted with her life, or at least with keeping the rope taut. "Sorry 'bout that Em," Kee laughed, "I had to smack a fly outta my Pepsi." Emma furiously glared at the older man's face looking down at her from atop the butte. With the sun directly behind him she couldn't make out his features, but she knew Kee well enough to suspect an impish smile growing beneath the black mustache he'd had since he was a teenager. "For fuck's sake Kee! Are you trying to make my last day working here my last day on earth?!" She would have nothing of his usual shenanigans…not today. And she sure as hell didn't want his cavalier attitude to result in her plummeting to an untimely death. "Jeez," Kee whistled through his teeth, "I said I was sorry *bilagaana*, using the Navajo word for White woman.

"Just guide me down, okay? And try not to kill me in the process." Emma tucked her notebook back into her pack and proceeded to rappel down toward the base of the monument. Kee dutifully fed the climbing rope in a smooth fashion until she landed safely on the red dirt. Judging by the rope that dropped to the ground, she assumed Kee had begun to make his way back to her. Emma knew he had to scoot on his butt over the steeper part of the trail, and she felt a pang of guilt about yelling at him. She finished gathering up her gear, and after taking one last look at the magnificent view decided to meet her friend on the other side of the rock. Glancing at her watch, she thought he was running a little late. *'What's taking him so long,'* she wondered. Maybe he'd stopped to finish off his soda. He practically lived on the stuff, in spite of Emma's warnings that so much sugar was bad for him. She reached the place where they had parted ways that morning, but there was no sign of Kee. She thought she heard him high above her, scrambling over the top of the monolith. She was sure he was headed her way when a few pebbles and red dust showered her head. Then she heard him cry out.

"Kee!" Emma yelled as loud as she could toward the direction of his cry. Without waiting for an answer she began running up the same path her friend had taken that morning that led to the top of the rock formation. He told her then that he'd been playing on that path since he was a kid. But Emma was not familiar with it, and half way up the path vanished into a hill of crumbling shale. She stopped to listen, waiting until she heard Kee calling out to her. Following the direction of his voice she dragged herself up the embankment, using her hands to grab at the mound of broken shale until she could hoist herself to where the rock became solid again. There was one more steep section to tackle, but within this part of the rock were carved hand and foot holds. Emma could just reach each indentation she presumed had been carved by Navajo ancestors, and finally reached to the top of the mesa. She lay on the rock to catch her breath, but heard Kee call out again. "I'm coming Kee," she gasped, sucking in more oxygen before crawling, now on her stomach, toward a crevice just in front of her. Emma could now hear groans coming from between the ragged edges of a hole just large enough for someone to fall in. Still on her stomach but leaning on her elbows over the edge of the hole, she could just make out Kee's black hair.

"I'm here Kee!" she panted, "are you hurt?" Her friend managed to crane his neck and stare up at her for a moment. "I hurt my ankle going down, I think," He gasped, "and I'm kinda stuck!" Emma was doing her best not to panic, her mind racing through their options. If she left to get help it would take a good hour just to reach the family *hogan*, and that was if she was able to navigate the four-wheeler through very difficult terrain. Kee had always done the driving, and Emma wasn't even sure she had a clear notion of the best route back. "There is a way to come around on the other side of this crack Emma," Kee yelled. She could tell by his measured words that he was having trouble breathing. "Okay," she would do whatever it took to help her friend, "just tell me how to get you out of this mess."

Kee was struggling to move his hand to point out the alternative path, but it was hopelessly stuck. Instead he pointed with his lips,

Navajo style. "Go back the way you came, and jump down the first ledge on your right. That'll take you to the other side of me. It's kind of sketchy, but you can do it. We used to go that way as kids all the time." He was panting hard now, having exerted too much energy and losing precious oxygen. Emma didn't waste a minute. She scurried across the butte and retraced her steps until, half way down; she saw the ledge to her right. Under normal circumstances she would have used more caution in jumping such a distance, but she didn't have time to second guess her movements. With surprising agility, she leapt from one rock to the other, and was soon standing close to Kee's left side, while the right was hopelessly jammed into a narrow v-shaped opening.

"Hey Mr. Yazzie, I'm here," she softly said, hoping her comforting tone would mask the despair she felt over this disastrous turn of events. "Hey kiddo," Kee whispered. He was conserving his air now. "I knew you'd make it down. You're kind of like one of my goats." The act of chuckling over this idea used up more valuable air. "What happened Kee?" Emma couldn't imagine how her friend ended up in this predicament. "I don't really know," he answered with a look of embarrassment, "I've been climbing on these rocks all my life, an' I thought I knew every inch of 'em." He shook his head in wonder, "I guess I wasn't payin' attention and kind of backed into this hole here." The two friends smiled at each other for a moment, but both were evaluating the situation. Kee came up with a plan first. "You gotta get me outta here so I can breathe. And then I'll tell ya how to drive the jeep to a shortcut into town. They got a good clinic there where they can patch me up." In her panicked state, Emma was having trouble understanding exactly what Kee was asking. "Why can't you slip sideways out of the rock Kee?" she asked. It didn't look as if he was wedged in so tightly that he couldn't extract himself. If he braced his foot against the natural step to his left, he could raise himself up and out of the crevice. "Well," Kee sighed heavily, "we got a small problem." It was then that Emma saw his right hand slightly obscured by a small opening between the rocks. She could only make out part of Kee's hand by the wrist, which was badly bleeding. "Kee," she whispered, "you can't get your hand out of there?!" "Nope," he said matter-of-factly, "it ain't budgin'."

Emma's mind began to race. If he couldn't dislodge his hand then he could suffocate, or even bleed to death before she came back with help. The situation seemed hopeless, and she was at a loss about what to do for Kee now. He looked her straight in the eyes, and with a slight smile said, "you're gonna have to cut me out *bilagaana*." The words didn't register with Emma. He couldn't be serious. "Kee," she firmly said, "I am *not* cutting your hand off!" She felt sick to her stomach at the thought of hacking away at her friend's limb. Kee shook his head and laughed a little, "You don't have to cut off the whole hand bilagaana…just the last few fingers. I can feel the other ones, but I think those last three are toast. They're jammed in there so tight I couldn't use 'em again anyway. So you'd just be doin' me a favor."

Emma gave him an incredulous look. "Are you actually trying to put a positive spin on this?!" There was a telltale fear in her raised voice. Kee grimaced as he tried to reach around with his one free hand, and pointed to his back pocket. "Look, I got a real good buck knife here. Can you get to it?" With trembling hands Emma fumbled through her friend's dusty jean pocket and drew out the knife. She still couldn't believe what he wanted her to do. Kee knew it was a big ask, but it was the only way out for him. "Look *sha kiss*," Kee tried to calm her down with the Navajo word for sister, "you can do this. I'll talk you through it. It's just like butchering a sheep." Emma's stomach turned once more, "Kee, that's not a helpful comparison!" she was screaming at him now, refusing to accept the ordeal that lay ahead. "Calm down Em," Kee felt himself losing consciousness. If he was going to help her through this it had to happen now. "Now I'm going to lean forward so you can get to my hand. I just sharpened the blade real good, so you won't have to saw at the fingers too long. Try to go just below the knuckles where you can see 'em. Then, when you can pull my hand out, wrap it up in my bandana." He used his good hand to loosen up the blue kerchief, damp from sweat, and handed it to Emma.

Steeling herself for the inevitable carnage, Emma threw the bandana over her shoulder and pulled the buck knife from its sheath. "Okay. Okay," she was speaking to herself really, willing herself to forge ahead. Kee closed his eyes and pushed his body forward, turning his face away from Emma and flat on the rock. It felt cool on his cheek, and the smell of it reminded him of the summer days he played here with his friends. When he was a kid, his mother told him the monuments were made by the gods. "This is a sacred place *sha kiss*," Emma heard him murmur just before beginning her surgery, "nothing can hurt us here."

Later, she couldn't remember hearing Kee scream-sing his war song as she started cutting. She imagined that she sort of blocked it out in order to complete the miserable task of removing her friend's fingers. She had found a place in her head that switched off every sensation, and placed all of her focus on working the knife back and forth over Kee's imprisoned digits. The ability to tune out the world had served Emma well over the years. She fostered this skill during her father's beatings, as a way to ignore the pain. Her sister Leena always praised this ability. She claimed it showed courage in the face of their father's abuse. But Emma believed it was the coward's way out. By mentally going outside her body, she escaped the reality of her dad's belt against her bare backside.

She used that technique now to finish the grim task of slicing her friend's fingers free from the rock. There was no escaping the horrid sensation of blade on bone, and the sound of it made her retch. The smell of blood, dank and musky, invaded the small space where she labored. The aroma of it crept into her nose and hung in the air. Droplets of Kee's blood spattered on to the back of her hand, and when she wiped the sweat from her upper lip the coppery taste snuck inside her mouth. Emma could feel vomit rising up into her mouth, but with a hard swallow she kept to her task. Finally she felt the knife hit rock, and what was left of Kee's hand began to give way. He had passed out during the operation, but he suddenly came to, when she managed to wrench his bloodied hand from the rock.

A searing pain caused his eyes to fly open, and he let out an ungodly scream that brought Emma out of her heightened state of concentration. She fought to control the shaking that now threatened her attempts to wrap Kee's hand with the bandana. Her right hand was so thoroughly soaked in blood that the knife slipped from her grasp and plopped into the red dirt. Using her clean left hand she held the cloth over his severed fingers while she wiped her bloodied right one on her nylon hiking pants. The position of Kee's hand made it too awkward for her to tie a tourniquet. She tried to keep it elevated, but Kee brought it down and held it tightly to his chest. It looked as if he might pass out again, and Emma briefly thought all her efforts to free him were in vain.

She also recognized the dire fact that the sun was going down. She would never find Kee's shortcut in the dark. "Honey," Emma held her friend's face in her hand, slapping it gently, "do you think you can wiggle yourself out of there now?" Kee grimaced with pain but nodded. "Yeah, I think I got it in me. Can you give me a little boost though?" Emma gripped his elbow with one hand and grabbed his belt with the other. She was leaving bloody handprints all over her friend's clothing. "On three," she instructed Kee, and they both counted down. By "three" he moved up and over toward her, effectively freeing himself from the treacherous crevice where he had been wedged for what seemed like hours. He almost fell on top of Emma, but was able to right himself and lean against the rock, where she was able to tightly secure the bandana and stop the bleeding on his mangled hand.

"I'm going to have to use the rope to lower you down onto the path," Emma explained to Kee, "can you wait here a minute while I go get it?" Kee offered a wan smile, "Sure lady. I got nothin' else to do." She wasn't aware of the shale cutting into her hands as she slid down to the path. She came back with the rope just as Kee was starting to pass out again. "Hey," she urged him back to life, "you gotta help me out here friend. I can't do this alone." He shook his head in agreement and let her wrap the rope under his arms. Emma was thankful her friend had a slight build, long and lean like all of the Yazzie men. Still, it took all her strength to lower him down onto the path and half-carry him to the jeep they'd parked just off a restricted dirt road deep in Monument Valley, Utah. Kee tumbled into the passenger side, and Emma threw her gear into the back. Her notebook fell to the floor of the dirty jeep, but her research didn't seem to matter much now. She hopped in behind the wheel, started up the vehicle and thrust it into gear. "So you're going to show me this shortcut Kee," she yelled to her friend over the noise of the engine. "Okay *sha kiss*," his voice was so feeble she could barely hear it. His good hand was holding tightly to the seat, and using his damaged hand was out of the question. "Head over that way," the exhausted man yelled in Emma's ear. He pointed with his lips, Navajo style.

Their trip through the desert was a blur, with Emma following Kee's instructions and trying not to bottom out in the deep sand. He had been right about the shortcut however, and before long they found themselves racing up a rutted washboard road leading out of the tribal park. It was dark by the time the jeep lights hit upon a faded sign pointing to the direction of the clinic.

She brought the jeep to a screeching halt just in front of two nurses who gaped at a dusty and bloody Kee slumped over in his seat. "We need help!" Emma shouted at the two women. The closest one moved to assist Kee while the other ran inside, emerging seconds later with two male aides bringing a gurney. Emma saw her friend gently loaded onto the gurney and followed him into the clinic. As they pushed Kee through the doors into a treatment room one nurse held back and stepped in front of Emma. "You better wait here honey," the nurse commanded, but she gently led the exhausted young woman to a row of chairs in the center of the lobby. Emma slid into the nearest one, straining to watch the gurney being whisked away.

She didn't know how long she waited there, hugging herself and praying her friend was alright. Somebody brought her a paper cup of water and offered her a blanket. But after that, time seemed to stand still. The morning sun crept over red hills and shone into the lobby where Emma had kept vigil. When the light hit her dusty face she woke up with a start. At first, she forgot where she was. Then the previous day's event came flooding back, and she shuddered. Her hands hurt. Examining them closely she finally realized how badly the shale had cut into both of her palms.

'I wonder if one of the nurses can give me some disinfectant,' Emma thought to herself.

She remembered a nurse coming out and telling her Kee would be alright, but they might have to amputate the entire hand. The sad and horrible news hit Emma hard. She was angry at herself that her shoddy work would result in the loss of her friend's hand. Emma prayed Kee could forgive her. She didn't even have the energy to cry last night, but she started to tear up now in the lobby that was empty except for her. She rubbed the grime from her eyes and looked around. As if on cue, the double doors of the treatment room opened and a Navajo man strode out toward her. Judging by his white lab coat Emma surmised he was a doctor, and she stood to hear what she hoped would be good news.

"I'm doctor Begay. You must be the young lady who helped Kee," his tone was somber as he extended his hand and Emma's heart sank. "Is he okay," she meekly asked, trying to keep it together and not burst into tears. It had all been for nothing. She'd tried to save her friend and failed. Her dad had been right about her. She couldn't do anything right.

"Oh yes, he's fine," the doctor said with a reassuring smile. She could have slapped that smile off his face. "We got him all sewed up and were even able to save his hand."

A rush of relief washed over Emma and she let the tears come after all. Doctor Begay, who'd never had a good bedside manner, offered Emma his arm.

"Would you like to go see your friend? He's still a little sedated, but he wanted me to come get you. Actually, he insisted."

Emma gratefully accepted the doctor's arm and he led her through the double doors, down the hall, and up to a room marked with the letter B. Patting her on the back, the doctor shook Emma's hand once again.

"You do good work. He only lost his pinky and half of his ring finger. It was a good, clean cut."

She could hear the admiration in his voice, but recalling yesterday's butchering made her inwardly shudder. Doctor Begay motioned for Emma to enter room B, but then put one hand on her shoulder.

"He told me he couldn't breathe, and he didn't know how long he could last in that hole. I'm pretty sure you saved his life." For some reason, Emma didn't feel like the hero Doctor Begay was describing. She only smiled and pushed open the door.

She and Kee visited for an hour before they both felt the need to rest. As she rose to leave Kee took her hand in his good one, and gave it a squeeze.

"I owe you one *sha kiss*," he said, eyes shining with gratitude. "For a white girl you got balls." As tired as she was, Emma couldn't help laughing at her friend's praise.

"You're the warrior," she teased, "I was just doing as I was told."

They shared a smile between them and Kee patted her hand before letting go. "You sure you wanna leave this life of excitement *bilagaana*?" He asked, but he knew her answer.

"Yes my friend. I'm definitely done." She sighed heavily, "I think we're both getting too old for this stuff."

Kee grinned and playfully pushed her arm so that she stumbled a few steps from his hospital bed. "Well, *you* are anyway," he joked. "What'er you gonna do with all your free time now Miss Emma?"

He had heard all about her plans to move back to her grandparents' farm, but he liked to tease her about her so-called "retirement." He and his family had lived and worked in the Valley for generations, and he knew how hard it would be for his friend to run a farm.

"Maybe I should come with you and help. I know how to take care of animals better than you. I could do it one-handed," he said with a chuckle.

Emma shook her head, "Now, what would all your sheep do without an elder like you to look after them?" She knew that Kee, like a lot of other people, didn't think she was capable of running a farm.

She had her own doubts, but she pushed them aside. She gave her friend one last hug and made her way out the door, meeting a nurse bringing Kee his medication.

"Bye Kee," she said over her shoulder.

"See ya' later gator," Kee laughed.

The Navajo never like to say goodbye. As she walked down the hallway, Kee's nurse came from room B.

"Hydrogen peroxide," the nurse called after her. Emma stopped and turned back to the nurse. "What?" She was so damned tired she wasn't even sure the nurse was addressing her.

"That'll take the blood out of yer clothes," the Navajo nurse offered, before ducking back into her patient's room.

"Oh. Yeah. Thanks," Emma said to an empty hallway.

Chapter 2
A Fresh Start

She'd made up her mind, and there was no going back. The next day, while sitting in her coach seat on a flight back to Seattle, she thought once again of how much she would miss Monument Valley and its people. But she also felt excited about the new life waiting for her at the old family farm.

Jeremy hadn't liked the idea at first. When he and Emma started dating a year ago he was mulling over his own life changes. Working for an investment firm provided him with a good living, but not a good life. That was how he put it to Emma when she asked why he wanted to quit his job. She'd been attracted to his confidence and drive when they first met on a blind date arranged by mutual friends. The fact that they were both so ambitious in their pursuits was the very thing that led to their friends arranging the date. The expensive dinners and premier concert seats continued through the first stage of their courtship. But Jeremy soon began to discount his success and gripe about the stress and long hours his work required. Emma tried to be empathetic. After all, she was working at something she truly enjoyed. And since it was Jeremy footing the bill for their somewhat lavish lifestyle, didn't he deserve to try his hand at something less demanding?

Still, Emma was taken aback when her boyfriend announced the decision to leave his well-paying job to pursue a career in music. She'd heard him play his guitar of course, and he was pretty good. But the songs he penned and crooned for her on occasion left her underwhelmed. His lofty dreams of becoming a professional musician blossomed when he managed to form a band with other Seattle musicians. Soon Emma was spending her evenings attending gigs while Jeremy and the Harry Canaries played at various clubs and coffee houses within the city. The late hours began to affect her research and teaching at the University of Washington, and they severely affected Jeremy's quality of work at the investment firm. When he was given the choice to recommit to his work or walk away with a modest severance package Jeremy chose the latter.

"But what are you going to do!?" A panicked Emma pleaded when he broke the news over their last visit to a fine restaurant.

"I'm gonna do what I always wanted to do, what I was meant to do," her boyfriend explained defensively while stuffing a generous spoonful of pasta in his mouth. "I'm going to make music."

She could barely make out the words obstructed by penne noodles and Bolognese sauce. "But what does that even mean?" Emma didn't try to hide her confusion. "Are you going to go on the road? Are you going into the studio?" She had done the research when Jeremy first began hinting at a career in music. She knew that even well paid studio musicians could only count on sporadic work, and Jeremy's playing skills were nowhere near studio quality.

"I mean, am I going to be in charge of paying all of our bills now? Will you even be able to make rent?" Jeremy's nonchalant shrug did nothing to quell her concern.

"I don't have it all figured out yet babe," he placated Emma, "I just gotta see where things go with the band."

The band never really got off the ground after Jeremy announced to them his desire to go on the road. The other members all had day jobs, and none of them could afford to rent a studio and record their few original songs. So when Emma told him she was thinking of taking an early retirement in order to take over her grandparents' farm in Baker City, Jeremy didn't bat an eye.

"I can create in Oregon just as easily as Seattle," he assured her. "Maybe I'll use some of my severance to set up a little studio of my own."

Emma didn't really think so. He'd already gone through most of that money on a new guitar and expensive blue jeans. Her own dwindling bank account led her to take stock of things. She thought perhaps it was time for something different, something she'd always imagined for herself but never dared act upon, a life as a farmer.

Both Emma and her sister Leena knew the farm would go to them when their mother Anne died. Mom had taken care of the place after her in-laws died, but she never really took to the lifestyle. She was placed in hospice care at a local rehabilitation center when her cancer returned. The girls stood by Anne during her last days, making her comfortable and trying to recall the few good times they'd shared with her when they were young. Mom's friend, Patricia came by as much as she could, just to provide support.

Emma and Patricia had become friends when Anne moved into the old farmhouse. As the only neighbor within miles, Emma's mom came to depend on Patricia to ease the loneliness of rural life.

The day after Anne's passing Patricia pulled Emma aside. "Look sweetheart," she said in a comforting tone, "if you ever decide to come back, you can count on me for help, okay?"

At the time, this idea struck Emma as rather odd. Why on earth would she want to come back to the farm? But then Jeremy's change in fortune caused her to entertain the idea. If Jeremy could do a complete reboot of his life, why shouldn't she? Her sister Leena was all for it.

"I think a change like that would do you good Em," she encouraged her sister. They both knew that Leena had no interest in the family farm. She loved her cabin in the mountains and very clearly had no intention of giving it up for farming. "It would take a lot of work," Emma worried over their weekly phone call. The girls had always been close, growing up as allies amidst their father's violence and their mother's inability to protect them.

Leena loved her sister and had always believed she would one day return to the farm. When they spent their summers there as girls it was Emma who rose early to help grandpa with the animals. Leena liked petting the sheep and horses, but she hated the chickens. The feeling was apparently mutual as the entire flock would scurry away whenever Leena approached. Once, when she attempted to offer the feathered ladies treats, Chester the rooster even attacked her. So she never really connected to them like Emma. Emma spoke to the chickens in a soft voice, and they would surround her when she sat and sang to them. Chester even tolerated Emma holding him, emitting a low cooing sound as she rubbed his neck. Leena remembered warm summer afternoons when the girls lay on top of haystacks, telling secrets in the cool of the barn.

"I'm going to leave mom and dad and go live in the mountains just as soon as I turn eighteen," Leena promised.

"You can't leave me with them Leena," Emma whispered to her older sister, "I couldn't stand to be with them all alone."

"You could come with me," Leena offered. "We'll build a cabin and hunt for our food." But Emma couldn't imagine killing an animal.

"No," she would sigh in resignation, "I'll just come back here and live with grandma and grandpa. Maybe they'll give me the farm to take care of someday."

It was always just a dream Emma kept in the back of her mind, even after both girls grew up and attended college. Leena didn't last long at community college, and she soon quit and took on a manager's position at a popular lodge in her beloved mountains. But Emma earned scholarships and pursued her anthropology degree, eventually going on to earn her Master's degree. Leena admired her sister's intelligence and drive, but she instinctively knew the farm would be good for Emma at this point in her life. Leena cheered her sister on before ending the phone call.

"You'll figure things out at the farm, Em. You've always said you wanted to settle down there, so you may as well take the plunge."

And with that, the decision was made. Emma put in her resignation at the university and sold off the expensive furniture she and Jeremy had accumulated. They wouldn't need it at a farmhouse full of mostly antique pieces. She set Jeremy to the task of tying up loose ends, such as informing the landlord of their condo that they were leaving, and turning off utilities. She made one last trip to her beloved Monument Valley in order to wrap up the research she'd begun last term, and arranged for Patricia to meet Jeremy at the farm where he was to unload the little U-Haul trailer of their things.

"Yes," Emma mused, "this will be a good change for us." She imagined Jeremy working alongside her on the farm, pushing aside the nagging feeling of such an unlikely scenario. She'd had to prod him into packing and planning the move, but she chalked up his lack of initiative to the increase of weed he was consuming.

One month later Emma found herself knee-deep in mud, straining to inspect the hoof of one very obstinate horse. His limping would have gone unnoticed, had she not been mucking out stalls in the nearby barn this morning. Now she was hoping to find only a stray rock hindering his normally easy gait. She tried the familiar process again, of leaning into the horse, gently running her hand down the back of the beast's leg, and then firmly gripping his hoof in an effort to coax it up and away from the horse. Three times Emma tried to encourage the stubborn animal to give in, and each time Patches refused to cooperate. It didn't help that she was working in a pasture turned to sludge after days of rain and freezing fog. Her labored breathing competed with Patches' agitated huffing, and with numb hands and fingers white with cold, she gave the hoof one more determined tug. With unexpected ease the nine year-old Paint relented, as if he'd meant to cooperate all along.

Emma reached for the pick in her back left pocket, her right hand cradling the hoof before finally resting it between half-bent knees. Quickly scraping away the mud and debris lodged in Patches' shoe, she discovered a small but jagged rock wedged in his frog. With a flick it was dislodged, but the sudden release of this irritant caused the horse to take back control of his foot. He side-swiped Emma with his strong backside, and it sent Emma, ass first, into the pasture. Her hands instinctively reached back, bracing behind her for a clumsy fall into the mud. She immediately heard her father's cruel laughter, the childhood memory of it bumping around inside her head.

"You're too soft to take up farming," she recalled he once said with a sneer. "Go back to your warm bed and hide in your books."

As she felt her fingers sink into the muck, it became abundantly clear that her morning's work was done. Trying to ignore the twinge of pain in her back, Emma rolled over onto all fours and struggled to stand. Righting herself, she pulled one boot, and then the other out of the mud with a great *slorp-slorp* sound.

"Thanks a lot Patches!" she called out over her shoulder. "You're such an asshole!" Patches only gazed smugly at his owner, and resumed munching on the hay had Emma brought as a distraction.

Blue jeans stiff with clotted earth, Emma lumbered toward the farmhouse. Her Great Pyrenees guard dog, Stella, waited faithfully outside the pasture gate. Now she moved to herd Emma back home. The huge and panting dog happily licked at her owner's filthy hands. At last mommy understood the value of playing in the dirt! They went together up creaking porch stairs, past grandma's rocking chair, and into the mud room. Emma plopped down onto the old wooden bench and strained to yank off her boots. She unceremoniously tossed them in the corner kindling bin and reached for a towel to clean Stella's wet fur, matted and gray from her morning romp.

"You're a good farm dog, aren't you girl?" Emma cooed. Stella gazed at mommy in silent agreement. Emma paused for a moment, towel hovering over the dog's head as her eye caught something on the porch, just outside the mudroom door. In her haste to get inside, the small brown envelope hadn't even registered. Now she wondered how she missed seeing it earlier.

The farmhouse was a solitary place, situated back from the main road where a dented and rusty mailbox stood sentry ever since Emma could remember. Oftentimes the mailbox door fell open, and she would later come upon random envelopes or small parcels piled haphazardly against the lone oak tree just a foot away. Even though Emma knew the postal lady; had in fact attended teenage summer parties with her, packages were rarely driven up the long dirt driveway to the house. That was fine with Emma. She cherished her privacy, and even now took advantage of it by slowly peeling off her muddy jeans and depositing them, inside out, into a deep work sink. Best to give them a quick rinse before placing them into the nearby washing machine she purchased that year to replace her grandma's decrepit old model. She gave her clothes a cursory washing and squeezed the excess water out. But they still left a dripping trail as she went to retrieve the package.

Standing barefoot and in her underwear, Emma gripped the wet clothes in one hand, then kicked open the mudroom's screened door. Awkwardly, she bent down to grab the envelope and brought it to her chest. Letting the door slam behind her, she led Stella into a kitchen that was still warm from that morning's fire.

Jeremy was still asleep, of course. He'd made his usual promises to help Emma with morning chores. They'd argued the night before about his place on the farm and in her life. She should have known better than to have attempted to engage with him while he was deep in the ritual of weed consumption. He never remembered anything after seeking out the last toke of the day. Sure enough, Emma found him at dawn, sacked out on the couch, an empty bag of chips on the floor beside him and snoring loudly. Emma wondered how they had come to this point, her doing all the work while he pretended to make music that nobody would hear. The successful and seemingly ambitious man that had once attracted her seemed to have completely disappeared. Her faith that things would get better slipped away over time, and was replaced by a passive disappointment. She knew that, deep down, Jeremy felt guilty over his failed artistic attempts. It showed in the way he grew critical of her, discounting her efforts at improving the farm.

"I don't know why you thought farming was a good idea," he'd mocked her as she lay underneath the old tractor. It broke down the very first day she tried firing it up, and he leaned against it while she changed the oil. "You really don't know what you're doing Emma."

The lackadaisical manner in which he insulted her only made Emma more determined. She managed to fix the tractor, and Jeremy avoided her the rest of the day. Instead he pouted in the kitchen while she endlessly plowed the field.

She wouldn't admit to herself that she felt trapped and wanted something better. Jeremy couldn't change, and she would simply have to make do. The sound of his raspy breathing and the stale stench of pot followed her out the kitchen door.

'If it means I have to hide his pot, I'm going to make him clean up his shit this afternoon,' she swore to herself before going out to feed the animals.

She pulled an old knitted cap on top of her unruly red locks and grumbled, "My grandparents' house smells like a teenager's goddamn dorm room!" Now, as she stumbled back into the house she could still hear him snoring, and the house still reeked of weed. Sighing heavily, she let the package fall on a kitchen table that had witnessed generations of home-cooked meals, and surveyed the brown mailing envelope. There was a slightly familiar return address, and only a few lines in the center indicating who the package was for.

Emma Woods

Woods Ranch, Baker City, Oregon , the words were clearly hand printed in block letters.

'How strange,' she mused. Why hadn't she seen someone drive up the road? And how had they managed to evade Stella's super sensitive guard dog ears? "Weird," Emma said out loud, causing Stella to cock her head sideways with a questioning look. Peering out the kitchen window, Emma could see there wasn't a soul on the immense lawn surrounding the house. With a shudder, she sank into a chair next to the old wood-burning stove, grateful for the heat that warmed her bare legs. She began to tear at the brown paper, but Stella lost interest and curled her fluffy body up into her bed by the stove. She was already asleep before Emma managed to open the package.

She shook the brown envelope and felt a small object rattling within. Examining the return address Emma recognized the name and address of the attorney who read her mother's will to her and her sister the previous year. She tore open the envelope and let the object slide out. A small key settled into her cold hand. Emma dangled the key at eye level, scrutinizing it in the early morning light, and then clutched it back into her fist and looked for an explanation in the little package. A note was stuck inside, carefully folded in half. Emma pulled it out and read the few words it offered. *Dear Ms. Woods,* heralded the words written neatly in the lawyer's script. *Before her death your mother gave me very strict instructions to ensure you received this key exactly one year after her passing.*

'Good Lord,' Emma wondered, 'has it only been a year!' It felt as if her mother had died ages ago. Maybe it was because Emma had come to terms with her death when she first heard of her mom's cancer diagnosis. She'd been preparing all that year for the inevitable, seeing to her mom's care while planning the service that would take place. Speaking with the hospice workers daily and discreetly packing up the photo albums and bits of family history to put into storage. It made her feel ancient just thinking about it.

The mention of her parents also invoked feelings she'd hoped were left buried after her mom's death. Anne Woods' parting words to Emma were the shocking revelation that her father saw her as a dim witted and useless girl. Before her mother died she'd always secretly believed she was her dad's favorite. Theirs was a complicated relationship built of devotion and pain, but when he died under mysterious circumstances she felt more than a void in her life. From then on she operated amidst a sense of impending doom, as if the details of his death simmered beneath every move she made. When her mother revealed how her dad really felt about his youngest daughter, that sense of doom mingled with a hopelessness that left her devastated and insecure.

Emma swallowed hard, forcing those old feelings down, and read on.

I am not certain why your mother insisted on the delay in your receiving this key. However, she stressed that I follow her instructions to the letter, and so I am honoring her last wishes. This key will open a safety deposit box at the Wells Fargo Bank located in your town. Apparently, your father's family had been conducting their banking there for some time. Although your mother did not reveal to me what might be inside the box, she clearly believed in its importance and value to you. I wish you all the best, Charles Lansing, Attorney.

Emma carefully placed the note back into the envelope. Her head suddenly felt muddled and dizzy. This was stupid. What was the point of a safe deposit box when both Emma and her sister knew her mother had nothing of value? Anne died a few months before Emma met Jeremy and his available funds, and Leena rarely had any extra income generated from her work at the lodge. They'd inherited the family farm of course, but had not looked into selling it. Consequently, they were land rich but cash poor. It had taken both of the girls' meager savings to pay for Anne's cremation and small service. And why wait an entire year before sending a worthless key? It made no sense, and it irritated Emma that her mother was interfering with her life even now, from the grave.

'Well I suppose I have no choice,' Emma thought to herself, *'I might as well go check it out.'*

Sighing heavily she rose and wrapped an old towel from a nearby cupboard around her chilled body. She took a few steps from the wood stove, then suddenly stopped and turned back toward the welcoming flame. Then, without knowing why, she opened the stove grate and threw the envelope containing the lawyer's message into the waiting flame.

Chapter 3
The Key and the Consequences

Now, as she stood in front of the bank where her grandparents, and even her great-grandparents, had saved their pennies, Emma wondered if she made the right decision. During the entire twenty minute drive into town she argued with herself over whether she should explore the meaning of this key or simply chuck it out the window. With that key now clasped in her hand, she realized she had to know its purpose.

She thought she wanted to put the past behind her. It hadn't been easy taking care of her mother. She'd had to put aside her feelings of abandonment brought about by Anne's inability to protect Emma and her sister. Every Sunday, after church services, mom would drive them to the local donut shop. A dozen glazed donuts were all she ever ordered. The girls were not permitted to pick out their own sugary treat. Then they drove home to offer up the entire box of donuts to dad, like making an offering to a god. Except it never worked, and the two girls ended up being sacrificed. Emma never understood why her father hated them going to church. When he was in the mood he sometimes told his girls about attending church as a boy, and it didn't seem like there was anything horrible about it. She reveled in those brief but peaceful moments with her dad. He seemed like an entirely different person when the two of them hunkered over a puzzle, listening to classical music. He would tell her about the missions he flew overseas, and what it was like to be in command of a fighter jet.

"You have to remain completely aware of your circumstances, Emmers," her dad would say about his time in the cockpit, "if you don't stay focused you could lose your life."

She thought of her father as a hero during those hours of puzzles and war stories. And it was easy to forget the monster he could become.

But when her dad wasn't flying overseas on some mission, Sunday would always be a bad day. It began with him sighing with impatience as they prepared for church, each irritated breath sending its message of discontent. Emma wondered why her mom didn't just let them stay home, and just attend church when dad was out of town. But no, she insisted on going and taking the girls with her.

Once they completed that ridiculous ritual of donut offering, Emma and Leena would hide in their bedroom, waiting for the shit to come down. Inevitably, their father found something to get pissed off about, and no matter how hard Anne tried to placate her husband there would be no redemption. The yelling became louder, and when they heard things starting to break the girls headed for the closet. Dad liked to break mom's cherished bunny figurines, throwing them at her one by one until Anne ran from the room, crying.

That was when the girls knew it was their turn. Hiding in the closet was futile, of course. Dad knew where to find them, and the Sunday beating would ensue. Emma could vaguely remember her mother meekly protesting these beatings, but she never managed to stop them.

And she never packed up the girls and left.

One day Emma asked her mom why she didn't leave, and Anne confessed that she never even considered it. "Where would I go," she said to her accusing daughter, "I had no way of supporting you girls. And anyway, your father promised he'd find me and kill all of us if I tried." Emma thought it was stupid to stick around, but that wasn't the only reason she hated her mother's weakness. It was when Anne told the girls to go into their dad's study and "apologize." They were only ten and eleven years old, not even teenagers, and their father had just doled out one of his Sunday floggings. Anne collected the sobbing girls from their room and led them into the hallway.

"Your father was just angry over the way you talked back to him," she explained.

The girls looked at her as if she were insane. They'd never had the nerve to talk back to their father.

"Now you just go in there and tell him you're sorry and you love him." Emma wanted to scream at her mother just then. How could she ask them to humiliate themselves when their dad was clearly the monster at fault for all of their pain and sorrow? And yet, off the girls obediently went to their dad's study, tiptoeing along to the inner sanctum of his office where he often retreated after a tirade.

Emma could remember her father slumped in his big leather chair, head in his hands. How strange it was to see him look….what was it? Broken? The fearsome giant they'd run from just minutes ago, was he crying?! In that moment Emma felt a pang of sympathy for her father. But the sting of his last beating reminded her it was unwise to trust this man was anything but dangerous. When the girls went to their father with murmurs of apology he didn't look up. He only reached out to pull them in closer and all three of them cried together. Emma never could come to terms with how she felt about her father that day. But she knew her mother had let her and Leena down, and in her heart she carried that resentment even after her mother's passing.

The worst betrayal came just a week before Anne died. Emma brought some magazines and flowers to the hospital as a way of cheering her mother up. Anne smiled over the flowers, then began flipping through the tabloid rags she so loved. Almost to herself, her mom began reminiscing about Emma's childhood, or at least, her mother's unique memory of it.

"I like how much you're paying attention to me," her mother cheerfully said, "I suppose you're making up for the way you hated me as a child." Emma was shocked at the statement.

"I never hated you mom," she had said defensively, "why would you say such a thing?"

Her mother had looked up from her magazine and gave Emma a condescending look. "Oh, I guess 'hate' is too strong a word. You just didn't look at me the same way you did your father. God…you worshiped the man. It's strange too, because he really didn't think too much of you."

Her mother let the comment sink in, and seemed to revel in the horrified expression on her daughter's face.

"Your father thought Leena would be the successful one. He never thought you were very bright. He would always say to me that you would probably just end up pregnant and working at a Dairy Queen."

Emma struggled to make sense of her mother's cruel words. It couldn't be true! Her dad always told her she was his "bright penny," and that she had a wonderful imagination. Always afraid to believe anything but the worst about herself, Emma took her mother's words to heart. Then she delivered the crushing blow.

"Before we left for the Middle East, your daddy told me that if anything should happen to him, I should spend everything we'd saved for your college tuition. He just didn't think it would be money well spent. It's a good thing he gave me his blessing to do that too. If I didn't have that tuition money I don't know how we would've survived when we got back to the States."

Emma left the hospital room after that, with her mother calling after her, "Honey, don't go away mad! I didn't mean to hurt your feelings."

'Yes you did,' Emma thought bitterly as she walked down the hall and out of the cancer ward. Her mother had always been jealous of the bond she and her father shared over history, music and putting together puzzles. Back then it seemed to Emma that her dad preferred her company over her mother's. A tiny voice inside her head said her mom made the hurtful comments up, to sully the few good memories Emma had of her father. But the voice of doubt was stronger. Her dad didn't really have any faith in her. Hadn't he mocked her love of reading, chiding her for spending so much time with her nose in books? When she was a kid, she took his teasing as his way of saying he was proud of her reading. But maybe he really did think she was wasting her time?

Eventually, Emma let her mother's words stick to her like flypaper, and she conducted her life from then on as if they were true. She chose one bad partner after another, believing she wasn't worthy of real love from a man of quality, one who would value her. She managed to pay for college herself, never realizing her mother spent the money meant for her education. She excelled in her classes and got a job in research and teaching, effectively proving her father wrong. But that didn't seem to matter once her mother told her the truth. She wanted her dad to be proud of her, but he died thinking she was mentally weak. Emma had lived blissfully unaware of her father's disdain for her, until her mother brought her back to cruel reality. She never told Leena about the conversation, and she was glad when Anne succumbed to her cancer a week later.

It wasn't just the memory of her mother's complacent dysfunction and dreadful recollections of her father's abuse that continued to plague Emma. It was the conflicting emotion of wanting so much to be loved by her parents, and feeling that somehow she didn't deserve that love. When something triggered the bad memories it made her stomach hurt and her heart ache. So she kept it buried deep in the back of her mind and kept her memories superficial. It was so much easier to remember the few times her father had made her feel special. She tried not to think of her mother at all, and this became easier after she died.

And now, here she was, standing in front of a building she used to visit with her grandfather. That first visit, when she was only seven years old, she carried her piggy bank with her and opened a savings account. She smiled at the thought that she was now all grown up, but none the richer. The late afternoon sun was bright, but the air was cold, even for February.

'What the hell,' she thought to herself, *'finding nothing here would be the worst that could happen.'*

She pushed aside a strange sense of foreboding and stomped up the stone steps. When she pushed open the heavy and gilded door a musty smell inside the old building rose up to greet her. She'd forgotten how much she loved the nineteenth century architecture of this place, and the way the sunlight filtered through big windows casting bright rectangles of light on the marble floors. She paused in the nearly empty building to check for mud on her boots, balancing herself on one of the stuffed high back chairs, its green velvet indented at the seat from the rest of countless customers.

She was careful to wear the nicer boots reserved for her rare visits into town. But even that pair could harbor a clump or two of mud from her driveway. Seeing a fairly clean sole, she advanced to the row of caged windows that used to put the fear of God into her as a child. Even now they felt intimidating. She couldn't help but try to dress up a bit for her visit to the old bank. She'd pulled on the expensive blue jeans purchased during more lucrative days in Seattle. But the only decent shirt she managed to pull from the back of a drawer was a red flannel that was missing a bottom button. Oh well, it would have to do. It wasn't like everyone else in the bank was in business attire, not even the woman who pulled the little saloon doors from the last window at the end and called over to her.

"Hey Em," Beatrice Mulvany chirped, wiping the crumbs of a half-finished sandwich from her red flowered blouse. "I'll take ya' over here doll."

Bea had worked at the bank since Emma was a teenager, and could easily retire if she had a mind to. But then what would she do with her time?

"Hey Bea, how's Roy?" Emma asked, because she knew Bea liked to bitch about her husband. She wouldn't mind the distraction of chit-chat, and she was secretly hoping to avoid the task at hand for a while longer.

"Oh you know my Roy," Bea chuckled, "if he had a brain he'd be dangerous." The two ladies giggled like conspirators while nodding in agreement. "What brings you here on a Thursday?" Bea asked, not really expecting an interesting answer.

Emma sometimes deposited money earned from her sales at the local farmer's market. Bea suspected the Wood family farm house and land might be worth a lot of money if she ever decided to sell. But Emma's efforts to restore the farm were taking its financial toll, and she usually came in to withdraw funds. The bank clerk thought Emma might be wasting money to keep that no-good boyfriend of hers in a good supply of weed. Bea didn't approve of Jeremy, whom she referred to as "that dirty hippie."

She would never have recognized the polished, successful businessman Jeremy was in Seattle. All she knew was that he wasn't born and raised in her little town, and so could not be trusted. And it sure didn't look like he took care of sweet Emma. Bea had seen him wandering through town on occasion. She'd heard he sometimes threw back a few beers at the tavern with the local boys, pretending to be some kind of rock star. It drove her crazy thinking of poor Emma's plight.

"Have you come to do another withdrawal?" Bea asked, offering a sympathetic smile. "No, I just want to check and see if this key goes to anything here," Emma said breezily, trying her best to appear nonchalant. "My mom's attorney forgot to give it to me when she died."

She hoped the lie was convincing. "He thought it might go to some deposit box here."

Bea's eyes widened. "Well you could have knocked me over with a feather," she later recounted to Roy when they discussed the excitement of that day over dinner. "I'm sure Emma's mama never had no safe deposit box at our bank. I would've known if she had!"

The two ladies maintained eye contact as Emma slid the key toward Bea, then rested her chin in her hand as the older woman closely examined the mysterious object.

"Well, the numbering matches the boxes we have here. I'll have Mr. Beekman take you back to the vault."

In all the time Bea had worked at the bank she never called her boss by his first name. Emma wasn't even sure Bea knew what his first name was.

"Mr. Beekman, our Em needs your assistance over here," Bea hollered across the bank, making Emma cringe as the few people doing business in the bank turned their eyes on her. So much for discretion.

The portly bank manager waddled out from his office and peered at Emma over his readers.

"What's this Emma? 'You opening up another account or something? Bea can help you with that."

He still spoke to Emma as if she were the nine year old with a piggy bank.

"No Mr. Beekman," Bea corrected her boss in a voice that was still too loud for Emma's comfort, "What she's got here is what looks like a key to one of our boxes!"

Emma smiled wanly as Beekman took the key between his fingers, held it to the light and scrutinized it.

"Yes, yes. It's one of ours all right. I recognize the insignia."

Satisfied that he was correct Beekman squeezed past Bea and swung open the door to her side, beckoning Emma into the inner sanctum of the bank. Without another word he turned and shuffled toward the vault at the back of the building. Emma and Bea exchanged one last glance, and when Bea shrugged Emma obediently followed Beekman.

"We don't get much opportunity to go into the deposit box room," the elderly banker chuckled, "Sometimes just once or twice a year when ol' Mrs. Langstrum wants to look at the family jewels, heh-heh-heh."

He continued to lead Emma through the vault and to a heavy metal door with an opener that reminded Emma of a ship's wheel. He leaned over the dial so Emma couldn't see the combination he had memorized during the forty years he'd worked at the bank. He nodded after each number clicked into place, then turned the wheel and swung the massive door open wide. Theatrically bowing, he gestured for Emma to precede him into the room.

After glancing once more at the key Beekman began slowly walking down the line of safe deposit boxes, softly muttering the numbers to himself. Emma walked behind him, reviewing the ornate gold boxes and numbers framed in filigree. She could never imagine any of her family visiting this place, least of all her mother. Finally Beekman stopped in front of a corner box.

"Number two hundred and six! Here it is!"

Then sliding in the key and pulling out the box he huffed over to a waist high table in the center of the room. Plopping the box onto the table he took a step back and let out a satisfied sigh. He smiled at Emma, but averted his eyes when she didn't smile back.

"Well," Beekman muttered with a slight clearing of his throat, "I suppose you'll want some privacy."

At first Emma couldn't think of what to do next. So she just extended her hand to shake with the banker and quietly murmured, "Thank you Mr. Beekman. I won't be long."

The banker nodded and handed the key back to Emma. As he shuffled off through the vault door he murmured something about checking on other accounts. Emma watched him leave, then turned to the box waiting on the center table. It didn't look like much, though Emma really hadn't known what to expect. It wasn't large enough to hold a great deal of anything, and when she lifted the lid it made a strange clicking noise. A wave of disappointment washed over her upon viewing its contents. There was a small notebook, or address book of some sort. An envelope containing a handful of photos of people and places that Emma didn't recognize, and a cassette tape.

Flipping through the notebook brought Emma even less clarity. She recognized her father's neat and clear handwriting, but none of the names and addresses. These were not the family and friends with whom she'd grown up. These names were unfamiliar and some quite exotic, as were some of the addresses. Germany, Turkey, and Iran caught her eye as she scanned the countries in this little black book. She snapped it closed when she heard Beekman re-entering the vault.

"Everything okay in here?" he asked jovially. Emma let out a small sigh at the intrusion and began stuffing the newly discovered contents into her handbag.

"Yes Mr. Beekman, I'm all done here thank you," she tersely remarked while zipping the bag closed and heading for the door. She strode past a confused Beekman who noticed the box, open but empty on the table.

"But...what do I do with your safety deposit box Emma?" he stammered.

Emma turned on her heel to face the exasperated man. *'Poor guy,'* she thought with a momentary flash of guilt, *'he thinks I've stumbled on some embarrassing family secret or something.'*

She smiled at the befuddled Beekman and said in what she hoped was a casual reply, "You can just retire the box Mr. Beekman. My family won't need it anymore." She made to leave once more, but thought she might leave him something more, to satisfy his curiosity. "It was just some old family photos and my dad's address book. My mom must have gotten the key from him while he was traveling, and just forgot she had it." At that, she left the vault with Beekman still standing in it, empty deposit box in his pudgy hands.

Emma kept her brisk pace past Bea, who glanced up just in time to see the heel of Emma's boot disappear behind the front of the closing bank door. Emma barely registered Bea's "you take care dear" goodbye. She took the bank steps down two at a time and turned onto the street that would take her to where she'd parked her old 1978 Chevy Silverado Stepside. She stopped for a moment, just outside the candy store she used to visit with her grandma after doing "town chores." Her truck patiently waited across the street, its one side sporting the primer Emma never seemed to find time to paint over. She wondered if maybe she should look at that address book more closely. And did she put the safe deposit key back in her purse? No! She'd haphazardly thrust it into the back pocket of her jeans. She fished the key out, and in her haste, let it slip from her hand and on to the pavement.

Just as she bent down to pick up the key, an SUV, shiny and black, came around the corner, something hard glinting in the sun and pointed directly at her. Emma heard a flat, coughing sound, rapidly repeating and felt a burning sensation on her forehead just before the candy store window shattered behind her.

"Fuck!" Emma screamed.

She fell to her knees and crouched down to the point of nearly flattening her belly on the cold cement. When she dared to look up, with a squeal of tires the SUV was already turning the corner. Hands shaking, Emma gingerly checked her body for wounds. Her forehead went beyond the initial burn she'd felt. Now a searing pain was setting in and when she put her hand to head it felt damp. Pulling it away, she found it red with blood. Had somebody shot at her?! Stunned and confused, Emma managed to kneel on the pavement, but a sliver of glass from the broken window ground into her knee.

"Shit!" she yelled, picking the piece of glass from her skin. Her purse lay on the pavement, right next to the key that had just saved her life. Emma hurriedly plucked up both items, and thrust the key into a zipper compartment of her purse. As far as she could tell, nobody else had seen the crime that just occurred, but the commotion brought Bea and Mr. Beekman out to investigate.

"Oh Honey!" Bea called out, and ran toward a bewildered Emma. Her desperate embrace took the air out of Emma's lungs for a moment, until she was able to gasp out a weak,

"I'm okay Bea." But when the older woman pulled back from Emma she saw the head wound.

"God Em, you're bleeding!" Bea gasped, "Did the glass hit your head?!"

Beekman also failed to recognize Emma's wound right away. He was intent on taking in the broken glass. Then Bea's words of alarm registered, and he peered at Emma's head.

"Emma, you've been hit! It looks like something cut your head! How do you feel? Can you see me alright? How many fingers am I holding up?" The rapid fire questions only served to disorient Emma more. She felt both Bea and Beekman's hysterics were making the situation worse.

"I can see your two fingers Mr. Beekman," Emma said in a level tone, "I think I'm okay, but could probably use a band aid."

"Oh sweetie," Bea exclaimed while pushing Emma's bangs from the wound, "you're going to need more than a band aid for this! I think you might need to have that stitched up!"

Emma dreaded the idea of going to the hospital. After spending so much time caring for her mother, followed by the pain of caring for Kee, she swore she'd never enter a hospital again.

"Yes," Beekman agreed, nodding his head, "I believe we should call for an ambulance. Bea, why don't you run back into the bank and do that?"

Emma held on to Bea in alarm and gave her a wild-eyed look. "No, Bea," she begged, "please don't call anyone! Just stay here with me and help me to my truck!"

Bea looked from Emma to her boss in a panic, trying to determine whose orders to follow. Beekman regarded the two women clutching each other and decided to let things be…for the moment. Instead, he surveyed the scene and rubbing the back of his neck in confusion asked,

"What happened here Emma? Were some kids throwing rocks or something?"

Emma was confused too, but she remembered the noise and blurted out, "I heard a kind of popping…"

Before she could finish Beekman jumped to his best conclusion. "Well, could it have been a gunshot! That cut on your head sure isn't from a rock! 'Strange that we didn't hear any kind of shot in the bank though."

Seeing himself as the only person of authority on the scene, the banker decided to take charge. "Could have been an attempted robbery Emma. Maybe some kids from the city who saw you go into the bank."

Emma was quick to correct the banker. "No, no. I'm sure it wasn't anything like that! They were probably just throwing rocks." She refused to believe she was shot at. The idea was too frightening, and it made no sense at all.

Beekman placed a hand on Emma's shoulder, the only body part that wasn't now wrapped in Bea's motherly arms. "You sure you're alright Em? Other than the head wound I mean? No broken bones or other abrasions? I have a first aid kit in my office."

"No really, Mr. Beekman, I'm fine," Emma weakly answered. By this time the owner of the candy store had ventured out, mouth wide open in disbelief.

"What the hell's going on out here," he yelled at Emma, as if she were the reason for all the damage done to his store.

"Leave her alone Wilson," Mr. Beekman snapped, "It's some damn kids from the city who vandalized your window. I'm calling the cops." And with that Beekman pushed his way through the small crowd of curious onlookers who were now gathering.

"I'm sorry about your store window Mr. Wilson," Emma offered, now on the verge of tears.

Wilson then caught a glimpse of Emma's bleeding head, and sheepishly offered her the cloth handkerchief he always kept in the pocket of his blazer. In all the years he'd owned the candy store, he never found a reason to use the starched linen cloth. But it was always there. Wilson was old fashioned that way.

"Here ya' go young lady," the older man said, as he gently pushed the hanky into Emma's trembling hand. How could he have yelled at a woman who was clearly distraught? "You just keep that now. I have others."

And with that he ducked back into the candy store, emerging seconds later with a broom and dustpan. Emma gingerly pressed Wilson's handkerchief to her forehead as he began to sweep up the broken glass

Now her head really began to hurt, to the point that she felt she might pass out. The burning pulsing through her forehead was unbearable. Emma leaned against the storefront and pressed harder against pain that was so severe it allowed the nagging idea of a gunshot to creep into her mind. But she knew she wouldn't share this information with the local police. None of this could be happening to her. She was a farmer in a small town where shootings just never occurred. She felt herself slipping into a different, more reliable world; the imaginary place to which she escaped as a little girl. There she could make believe her father wasn't hitting her. She could slip away to that place of comfort right now, and pretend she hadn't been shot. She could even convince Bea and Beekman that it was all just an accident. The glass had cut her from a window that had somehow shattered behind her. Yes, that was what she would tell the police. It felt good to have that story inside her head. She was determined it would be the only story she would provide.

A series of sirens could be heard coming ever closer, and Emma wished with all her heart she could bolt to her truck and avoid speaking with the police. Down the main street raced three police cars, sirens blaring and driving way too fast on the small town boulevard. Each one of them screeched to a halt as if they'd happened upon a bank robbery. For all Emma knew, that was what Mr. Beekman described when he called in. She ducked her head in embarrassment, turning toward the empty frame of the candy shop's shattered window. Bea looked up at the three cop cars now parked strategically in front of the store. The entire police force of Baker City was clearly excited to have something to do.

"Well that's just silly," Bea proclaimed to Emma, "why do they have to act like a SWAT team? Do they think those kids are comin' back?"

She continued to stand with a protective arm around Emma as the police, two to a car, strode toward the scene, a couple of them speaking into the radios strapped to their shoulders. A shooting was obviously a big deal in the small town, but Emma thought the amount of law enforcement sent was overkill.

"Guess it's a slow day down at the precinct," she muttered to Bea, mustering a faint smile.

Bea recognized Officer Danforth. He was the senior man amongst the group of policemen approaching, all of them hitching up their belts and fiddling with the gear that never saw much use. She smiled at George Danforth, who took the lead in this group of fidgeting cops.

"Hey Georgie," she greeted the man whom she'd babysat years ago, "you putting on weight from your wife's good cooking?" Bea hoped the gentle teasing would put George off guard and make this whole thing less intimidating for Emma. Danforth self-consciously shuffled his feet, looking over his shoulder at the younger men.

"Dammit Bea, don't call me Georgie! And quit foolin' around. This shit is serious!"

"Oh fine Georgie," Bea chuckled, "but don't fire a bunch of questions at Emma. She's pretty shook up, and she doesn't need you scaring her any more than she already is!"

She let her arm slip from around Emma's shoulders and whispered, "you just tell officer Danforth what you saw honey. I'll be waiting right over there."

Keeping the handkerchief on her head, Emma protectively crossed her free arm in front of herself and watched the older woman walk over to wait with Beekman in front of the bank, which now sported a "Closed" sign in its front window.

When she looked back at Danforth she saw the officer staring at her head, but before he could question her Emma blurted out, "I got hit by some glass!" Her outburst surprised Danforth, and for a moment he was stunned into silence. He quickly collected himself and pulled out a small pad of paper and pen from his front pocket. Taking a few steps closer, he clicked the pen a few times and appeared to be waiting for Emma to offer up information.

After staring at each other for a few seconds, Danforth realized the ball was in his court. Having been trained to observe a crime scene and everyone involved in it, he took note of Emma's practical clothes and knee high boots. She'd tried to clean the mud off, but those boots had for sure seen some use in the pasture. Yeah, she was a farmer all right. He'd lived around here long enough to know one, particularly since his family was made up of the same folk.

"So can I get your full name and address ma'am?" he began, in what he hoped was a cordial tone.

There was no reason to make this feel like an interrogation. The woman looked to be pretty shook up. If he pushed too hard he wouldn't get anything out of her.

"Emma Woods," she began, but was interrupted before she had time to give her address.

"Oh hey!" Danforth proclaimed with a smile, "you're the Woods' granddaughter? I heard you came back to take care of the place! Hell, I remember swimming in the pond behind your grandpa's barn when I was a kid." The officer, a good foot taller than Emma, was now grinning and chatting her up as if they were at a high school reunion.

"How's your sister doin' these days? I always thought she was kind of cute," Danforth's chuckle over the confession was met with Emma's icy stare.

"She's fine," Emma said through clenched teeth, "so I take it you don't need my address?" Danforth could have kicked himself for the lack of professionalism he'd just shown. He shook off the excitement of rediscovering a peer, and resumed his questioning.

"Nah, I don't need your address Ms. Woods." His tone became more businesslike, "let's just get right to what you saw here. Were you involved in the vandalism that was called in?"

The other officers were now busy collecting evidence of their own. One was pulling yellow caution tape around the candy store, while another was involved in questioning Mr. Wilson. Still another was attempting to interview Bea and Mr. Beekman, but Emma judged by the shaking of Bea's head and Beekman's waving hands, they were letting him know they'd seen nothing. Her attention was pulled back by Danforth's voice.

"I mean do you believe you were targeted by the perpetrators, or was this some kind of random act of violence?" Emma tried to regain her composure and shrugged at the officer.

"I really couldn't say," She murmured, "I didn't actually see them, just the car."

Emma didn't offer information about the SUV. She couldn't be certain the person driving that car had anything to do with the broken window. And why would anyone target her? Danforth suspected she was being evasive, but he chalked it up to nerves. Probably she was just worried the gang members, or whoever these hooligans were, would come after her for revealing what she knew. Then again, it was entirely possible this woman hadn't seen a thing. Or, if she'd been traumatized by the experience, she simply couldn't recall any details.

"So what did you do when you heard the window break behind you?" Danforth felt it was his duty to at least try and get some information from Emma.

"I didn't hear it," Emma started to say, then stopped short of explaining. *'Dammit!'* She silently scolded herself for sounding so obviously evasive.

"What do you mean, you didn't hear it? You'd have to hear a window that shattered right behind you! This is where you were standing, right?"

Danforth was incredulous and slightly confused, looking back at the remnants of the candy store window. The other officers were now intent on keeping a small crowd that had formed from pushing in on the scene.

"Look, I told you I didn't see anything. I mean, I didn't hear anything," Emma stammered and did her best to steer the officer away from her previous ridiculous comment. "I guess all I remember is the glass breaking. I don't remember seeing a rock or anything. I dropped something on the ground and was bending over to pick it up. So I just hit the deck when I heard the glass break."

The words came tumbling out of Emma's mouth before she could think things through. She'd even used one of her father's Navy terms for going down in protection mode. "Hit the deck!" he would crow as he came after her and Leena with a belt. And they would dive under the bed to escape his wrath until he dragged them out by the feet, beating first one, then the other, for some stupid rule they'd unknowingly broken.

"I've told you everything I know," Emma stated flatly to Danforth, "Can I please just go?"

The adrenaline was starting to wear off now, and she was trembling. Why did she suddenly feel so cold? It seemed as if she was standing there naked in the winter breeze.

"Well, alright Miss Woods. I guess we're done here….for now." Danforth gave up in what he saw as temporary defeat. "But I'll need your phone number in case we have to contact you again for a lineup or something."

Emma didn't bother arguing once again that she hadn't seen anyone. Her story wasn't believable, and both she and Danforth knew it. She rattled off her phone number for the officer and made to leave, fishing through the handbag still clutched to her body. Where were her car keys? Sensing the excitement was over, the crowd began to disperse, and Bea scampered up to Emma, holding her sweater close around herself against the February chill.

"I'm going to help you back to your car hon," she offered, casting a scathing look at Danforth.

"Let her go home Georgie," the larger woman snapped, causing Danforth to roll his eyes.

"Please don't leave town without informing us Miss Woods," he said in a polite but firm tone, "We'll keep you posted with the ongoing investigation."

Emma wanted to tell the officer she wasn't the least bit interested in their investigation. She longed for the normality of going back to her chores on the farm. Bea kept one arm tenderly wrapped around Emma as they crossed the street. The sound of the diminishing crowd and police radio static faded behind them when they reached the truck.

Emma took the handkerchief from her head and managed to fish the truck keys from her purse. They were held together by an old nylon lanyard she'd woven as a Girl Scout in summer camp. Still shaking, she fumbled for the old truck key then tried to force it into the door lock, only to watch the whole set tumble from her hand and onto the street. Bea finally released her grip to retrieve the lanyard, and moved to open the door for her stricken friend. It made a familiar creaky, squeaking sound that brought Emma back to life. Turning to Bea she said in desperation.

"Please don't gossip about this to everyone Bea," she begged, knowing that even without Bea's blabbing it was hopeless to keep tongues from wagging in the small town.

"Well alright hon' but folks are gonna want to know what happened…" Bea began, but Emma cut her off.

"I didn't see a thing, and that's all there is to it. I was just minding my own business and some nut job threw a rock at me, or at the store, or whatever!" Even though Emma knew her explanation sounded lame, it seemed to satisfy Bea.

Emma allowed the older woman to ease her into the seat of her truck. She peered at the younger woman's head and gave a slight nod.

"I think the bleeding's stopped here Em, but you should get some iodine on it."

Emma smiled weakly at the idea of using the disinfectant that always burned when her mom used it on her.

"I'll find something to clean it Bea, back at the farm." Bea reached over for Emma's seatbelt and buckled her in.

Don't you worry about a thing Em," she said matter-of-factly, "I'll shush anyone who starts jabbering about all this. I'll just let 'em know you got nothing to say on the matter."

She patted Emma's hands clutching the big steering wheel. The poor thing was still trembling from her experience and seemed so fragile now. Emma turned the key and inwardly rejoiced at the sound of her truck starting up at the first try.

"You drive safe now," Bea calmly demanded in a parental tone. Emma looked at her and nodded numbly. It would do her good to focus her attention entirely on driving home. She slowly pulled away and drove out of town, past two more police cars heading toward the bank.

"Wow," Emma thought in amazement, "they must have called in highway patrol too!" News certainly traveled fast around Baker City. Her desire to put the afternoon's events behind her was rapidly evaporating.

Chapter 4
Refuge

  Jeremy heard the kitchen screen door slam just as he lit up a half-smoked joint. He didn't bother rising from his lounging position on the living room sofa when Emma marched past him and into the bathroom. Through a haze of marijuana smoke that curled around his unshaved face he wondered if Emma looked weird, or if he was just being paranoid.

  "What's up baby?" he blithely called after her, but she'd already shut the bathroom door. When he heard the lock slide closed on the door he lost interest. *'Probably a lady thing,'* he mused. If there was one thing Jeremy steered clear of it was any kind of "lady problem." He stretched out his skinny frame, still clothed in last night's pajama bottoms which had seen better days. In a slow and deliberate motion he inhaled yet another drag from the joint, taking comfort in the delusion that Emma didn't need him. In the relative safety of the locked bathroom Emma took stock of her situation. The shaking had stopped once she reached the farm, but now that she stood at the bathroom sink she realized she needed to clutch the cool porcelain sink just to remain steady. She didn't recognize the pale reflection staring back at her from the old vanity mirror. The wound on her head had swelled a bit, and she gingerly touched it with a bit of fascination. It seemed like a piece of glass would do less damage. She had to admit to herself that maybe, just maybe, this was something worse.

  Emma quickly turned the faucet and splashed cold water on her face with one hand, fearing she'd crumble to the floor if she let go of the sink with her other. Then, in one move she sat hard upon the closed toilet seat and made a conscious effort to slow her breathing. She cradled an aching forehead in her wet palms, placed her elbows on her knees and rocked gently back and forth. The ritual was reminiscent of another way she had coped as a child during one of her father's violent outbursts. Back then she would never have hidden in the bathroom. If she dared to hide behind a locked door it only increased her father's wrath, resulting in the door getting kicked in.

'You need to focus Emma,' she repeated her dad's words in her head and tried desperately to make sense of the last few hours. None of it seemed real, and though she didn't wish to relive it, she fought to slow her brain down and consider every moment leading up to what she now realized was a shooting.

The concept of a drive-by shooting seemed like nonsense to Emma. Even if it were possible some gang member from the city came to the insignificant town to prove himself, why would they target her? The very idea was ridiculous. And the car didn't seem right either. The shiny SUV had crept up on her from nowhere. No, this felt…..personal. It was just a feeling she had, and that same feeling told her this had to do with the safety deposit box, and by association, her father. Her mind went back to the sound she heard when she'd opened the box. Was it a clicking; a high-pitched beep?

"Hey babe, are you all done in there? I gotta pee!" Jeremy's impatient knock on the door brought Emma out of her reverie.

"I'll be out in a minute!" She hollered back. The last thing she wanted to do right now was to deal with Jeremy. And where the fuck was her purse?

Her answer came from Jeremy, whining on the other side of the door.

"Babe, if you open the door I'll give you back your purse. I won't even look inside it," he joked, though they both know he'd taken cash from her purse on numerous occasions. Emma chastised herself for being so careless.

In her confused state she must have dropped the purse on her way into the bathroom. A stupid move, she decided, due to the importance of what hid inside the handbag. She stood and took a deep breath in an attempt to calm down before dealing with Jeremy. Smoothing down the front of her flannel shirt, she reached for and slowly turned the old glass doorknob that opened the bathroom door. Jeremy peered through the cracked opening.

"Finally!" he proclaimed, and pushed past Emma, shoving the purse into her chest and making a beeline for the toilet. He hastily lifted the toilet lid with one hand while fumbling for his penis through the worn out pajama pants, then let out a steady stream of pee into the toilet. While relieving himself, he thought to look up at Emma and did a double-take.

"Hey," he said with the mildest of concern, "what happened to your head?" Emma turned away and shut the door on her bewildered boyfriend, effectively muting his other questions. By the time she walked out the front door she couldn't even hear Jeremy hollering after her. "Did Patches do that to you? Hey, where 'ya goin'?"

She needed to find a place where she could be alone and sort out the day's events. Her first thought was to make her way over to the Newcastle's place. Besides Patricia and Anthony being her closest neighbors, Patricia had been a good friend and a comforting presence in her life even before Emma's return to the farm. They had Anne in common, but Patricia had more patience with Emma's mom than most people could muster. Anne was famous for being very emotional about the most trivial things, making herself a victim in the process. She was self-centered, quick to judge others, and needy. All of the characteristics that Emma hated about her mother had been, for the most part, overlooked by Patricia. And she had been an absolute rock during her mother's illness. When it became clear that Anne was nearing death, Patricia joined in Emma's vigil at the hospital.

"How did you manage to put up with my mom for so long?" Emma asked toward the end, as they sipped coffee in the cafeteria. "I love my mom, but that's in spite of the way she treated me and my sister over the years. We had to put up with her because she's our mom, but why did you hang in there for so long?" Emma just couldn't understand how her mother deserved the friendship and loyalty of someone like the pillar of strength sitting across from her. To Emma's surprise, Patricia simply laughed and shook her head at the question.

"Darling girl," she sighed, her smile fading, "I know exactly what your mom is, and why she turned out the way she did. She had a shitty example of motherhood in her own mom. Let's just say she knew that

I was her last chance for a decent relationship, so she was always on her best behavior. I didn't mind being her friend, most of the time," she giggled.

Anne eventually passed, and Emma went back to Seattle. But the two women kept in touch through frequent emails and the occasional phone call. They quickly formed a bond that had surprised Emma at first. Besides the love they shared for art and history, Emma discovered they both had less than satisfying relationships with their parents. They would often swap stories about childhoods filled with trauma and disappointment. Patricia's mother had been the disciplinarian, while her father had been weak and unable to show the love Patricia desperately craved. Emma found it fascinating how similar their growing up had been, with only the roles of monster and coward reversed between parents.

When Emma phoned her friend with the news she was moving back to the farm, Patricia was elated.

"Oh thank God!" she squealed; "I'll have a girlfriend to hang out with again!"

Emma hadn't spent much time with Patricia's husband, but she knew he traveled a lot on business. The Newcastles clearly adored each other, but they seemed an odd match. Patricia was a very warm person and had a genuine interest in others. Anthony, who Emma learned was born and raised in England, came across as the typical reserved Brit. While Patricia was outgoing and amiable, her husband kept to himself, immersed in his books and the classical music Emma often heard in the background during her calls. Anthony's favorite thing to do was spend time with his wife, and according to Patricia he'd rather resented the time she spent with Emma's mother.

"Won't Anthony be irritated if you come to my place for girl-talk all the time?"

Emma worried. Although Anthony had a brusque demeanor, she kind of liked him, and she didn't want to annoy her new neighbor by taking up valuable time meant for his wife.

"No, no. He'll be fine," Patricia assured her, "he didn't care much for your mother, of course. But he won't mind if I slip away every now and then so he can work." Emma wasn't so sure, but she appreciated Patricia's willingness to lend an ear when she needed to complain about her workload or bitch about Jeremy.

Now, as Emma tripped over dirt clods in the huge meadow separating their two houses, she hoped Anthony wasn't home. She could barely hold herself together, and she didn't want him to witness a hysterical female's melt-down. She only wanted to fall into her friend's arms, unobserved, and sob over the day's events. It wasn't even that she sought clarity about what happened that morning. What insight could Patricia possibly provide about what appeared to have been an attempt on her life? But her friend would know just what to say, or she would instinctively know to say nothing at all. She came to the Newcastle's property from the back, and let herself in as she usually did, pushing the big green garden gate with her shoulder. The old gate made a familiar grating sound that always reminded Emma of an old man complaining about his arthritis. She'd spoken to Patricia about fixing the gate because she feared it would one day simply fall off its hinges.

"Oh, Anthony will get around to fixing it someday," Patricia remarked, although both ladies knew the repair wouldn't happen any time soon.

Trudging up the garden walkway Emma did her best not to slip on the mossy stones. A perfectly appointed English garden lay sleeping on either side of the path, dormant until the coming spring when it would burst into color. Emma stood at the kitchen door and rapped at the window. She could see Patricia sitting in the little kitchen nook, reading by a tiny fireplace where they usually had their chats. Her friend glanced up and waved to Emma, smiling as she marked her place in the book. She beckoned Emma in, and went to the stove in anticipation of starting tea.

"Hi there stranger," Patricia greeted her friend, reaching for a lighter she kept on a nearby shelf. The old stove was yet another repair waiting on the ever-procrastinating Anthony. By now, Patricia had grown used to lighting the burners manually. Emma slid into a bench seat to the left of the fireplace, garnering the maximum amount of heat. She was shivering slightly from anxiety, but Patricia mistook Emma's shaking from the cold.

"Honey, you're trembling like a leaf! I'm going to get you a blanket or something. The kettle's on so we can warm you up with some tea." Emma managed a slight smile and put up no resistance. Instead, she leaned back on the bench cushions and let her head rest against the wall. Her lids felt heavy, and she allowed them to close over eyes that had become bloodshot. It felt good to rest and think of nothing, even for just a moment.

She must have dozed off, because the whistling of the tea kettle jolted her awake. She started to extract herself from behind the breakfast nook, when the kitchen door swung open and Anthony appeared. In his robe and bedroom slippers he shuffled toward the teapot. Emma sat back down on the bench and wondered why the man always dressed as if he just got out of bed.

"Hi Anthony," she softly greeted the older man, and he turned in surprise.

"Emma! I didn't see you there dear. How on earth are you?" Anthony had always been kind to her during her visits to their comfortable country home. In spite of his gruff façade, Emma believed he was actually quite an easy-going guy with a genial nature.

"I wondered why Patricia was rummaging around in the closet. She mumbled something about being cold, but I suppose the blanket she's retrieving is for you."

He turned his attention back to the tea and began pulling cups from a nearby cupboard.

"You do look a bit peaked dear. Why don't I make you a cuppa?" He glanced over his shoulder at her. "Patricia didn't say what you were discussing. Everything alright?" Emma tried to come up with a benign answer to his question. No, everything was definitely not alright. But she didn't want to reveal what had happened that morning to Anthony. It wasn't that she didn't trust him, but she wanted to speak with Patricia first. It would be easier, and somehow felt safer.

She watched as Anthony continued to prepare two cups of tea she imagined were meant for her and Patricia. Anthony never joined the ladies for their chats. Emma thought it was sweet how he performed little tasks for his wife. Patricia bragged that, when her husband was home, he made a point of doing up the dishes or making the bed. While he never seemed to get around to the many projects needing attention on the Newcastle property, he made life as easy as possible for his wife in seeing to daily chores. Now, as he stood making tea he appeared to be completely at home in the kitchen, and not at all the savvy businessman he was rumored to be. Anthony wore his bathrobe over pleated khaki pants and a long-sleeved shirt. The sleeves were pushed up to his elbows, bunched up under the more worn out sleeves of his robe. This casual outfit was his uniform whenever he was puttering around their home. He turned back to face Emma, and she had to suppress a smile. A shock of graying hair stood almost straight up from his forehead. No doubt this look came about from the habit of rubbing his head when fully immersed in some book.

"We haven't seen you in a while Emma. What have you been up to?" Anthony's light conversation was too much to bear after her crazy day. Anthony didn't see where the bullet hit her. She had been careful to pull her bangs down and obscure the wound. She wanted to scream at him that she'd nearly been killed, that she was confused and scared and didn't know what to do. She wished with all her heart she'd never gone to the bank, had thrown the key into her wood burning stove along with the lawyer's letter. But there was no undoing the morning's events, and she scrambled to come up with an answer to Anthony's innocent question. Luckily she was saved by the return of Patricia, clutching the fluffy blanket she'd been looking for.

"I found it!" she victoriously announced. Seeing her husband attending to the tea, she warmly smiled and planted a kiss on his cheek. "Aw honey, you made the tea! You're my hero." Patricia's attention drew a blush on Anthony's cheek, but he smiled back at his wife and pointed to the blanket.

"Why did you need that particular blanket darling," he asked in an effort to steer the ladies' attention away from him.

"I wanted Emma to have the super soft afghan I made last winter," Patricia said, and handed the blanket to Emma.

"Thank you for going to so much trouble," Emma murmured, folding the soft fabric around her shoulders. It felt lovely and comforting to be fussed over. Anthony arranged the teacups and pulled out Patricia's chair for her to sit.

"I'm going to leave you girls to it," he said, kissing the top of his wife's head before slipping out from the kitchen.

Patricia focused on Emma who was quietly sipping her tea.

"Girl, what is going on?" She could tell something was off in her friend's demeanor, and she didn't intend to waste any time in getting to the bottom of it. Emma gave up any pretense of keeping her cool. She needed to unload, and Patricia was probably the only one who might make sense of things.

"Well," Emma began, "I guess I kind of got shot at..." she began.

"What!?" Patricia let out a scream. Emma realized she shouldn't have been quite so blunt, but it was too late now. "What do you mean somebody shot you?!," Patricia's voice was now panicked. "Are you okay?! Was someone on your property?! Where was Jeremy?!"

Her questions were given in the same shrill tone, causing Anthony to call from the other room, "What's going on in there ladies? Is someone getting murdered?" Both women exchanged wide-eyed looks, but Emma quickly shook her head letting her friend know to keep quiet.

"No honey," Patricia shouted back. Nobody's been murdered." Then turning back to Emma she let out a sigh and said quietly, "have they?"

Chapter 5
Friends and Neighbors

"I don't know how it happened," Emma explained to her friend. Patricia gently brushed her fingers over Emma's wound, which had turned into an angry red welt. "It didn't really hurt until I got up from the pavement. I had to pick a piece of glass out of my knee, and that actually hurt more, at first." She'd only given a thumbnail version of the day's events. The letter leading up to her visit to the bank, and the contents of the safe deposit box had left Patricia puzzled to distraction. She hadn't even seen the gunshot wound until Emma moved her bangs from her face. Her friend became so alarmed that the story of how it got there was momentarily put aside. Patricia let her hand fall from Emma's wound and grabbed her hand.

"Honey, I don't understand why you didn't go to the hospital to get this looked at. I'm going to get some disinfectant."

Emma didn't really want her friend to fuss over her, but she had to admit to herself Patricia was right. And after the day she'd had, maybe she should let someone take care of her. Jeremy certainly wasn't going to. She watched Patricia leave the kitchen to fetch first aid supplies, and decided she would be completely honest with her friend when she returned. Then she heard whispering in the hallway. James [*Anthony ?*] was being informed of her situation.

Instantly, the kitchen door swung open, and in two quick strides Anthony was facing Emma and surveying the damage done by the mysterious bullet. He didn't say anything to Emma, and moved with an uncommon familiarity around her. She thought he was acting as if he were inspecting a strange insect, or peering under the hood of a car in need of repair. She wasn't used to this kind of attention from Anthony. He examined her wound in a clinical fashion, then stepped back from Emma and scowled.

"Why didn't you have that looked at by a doctor?"

She suddenly felt like a small child being reprimanded by a schoolmaster. Anthony's tone had a sharpness that she didn't recognize. In the past, they had always exchanged pleasantries and kept their conversation friendly and superficial.

"I...I just wanted to get out of there," Emma stammered. She was put off by his demeanor. It left her feeling somehow exposed. Maybe she should have gone to the hospital, but it seemed more important to simply flee the scene as soon as possible. She didn't want to admit to Anthony she'd been too afraid to do anything else. "I really didn't think the cut was that bad...."

"It's not a cut Emma," Anthony interrupted, "it's a bullet wound, it will continue to bleed, and it could easily become infected. It was foolish of you not to seek out medical care."

She self-consciously shifted on the bench and put her hand up to cover the laceration.

"Don't touch it!" Anthony admonished a now truly rattled Emma, "you'll infect it for sure if you haven't washed your hands after the accident."

Accident?! Maybe Patricia hadn't completely informed her husband about the true nature of her wound? Emma wasn't sure at all about what had happened a few hours ago, but it sure as hell hadn't been an accident.

"I did what I felt was best Anthony," the pang of anger she felt over being misunderstood allowed Emma to gain some composure. "I didn't want to hang around the crime scene when I could be safe at home." She had no trouble referring to the incident as a crime now. She wasn't going to fool herself that this was some kind of fluke. The sudden realization that she was in danger fell over her like a cloud and the sense of dread must have shown in her face. Anthony grew quiet, folding his arms over his chest and shaking his head. Emma could almost hear him thinking *'tsk, tsk, you poor stupid thing.'* Instead, he turned and opened the kitchen door to call for his wife. "Patricia, do you need help finding the bandages?" Gone was the cool and abrupt man Emma had just witnessed. He was back to being an attentive husband.

Patricia entered the room seconds later, and Anthony stepped aside so she could treat Emma's wound. She dabbed at the red gash with a cotton ball soaked in alcohol.

"I think I can fix you up, but it's going to hurt," Patricia said almost to herself. She continued with her nursing and didn't see Emma and Anthony exchange glances. Emma glared back at her neighbor believing she had been right to avoid a visit to the hospital.

For just one brief moment a shadow fell over Anthony's face. Emma couldn't quite place it. It wasn't so much a look of disapproval, as one of repressed anger, almost contempt.

"Well, you seem to have this under control my dear." Anthony made the confidence he had in his wife quite clear. "Do keep an eye on that Emma," he tersely remarked, pointing to the wound, "it looks rather deep for having just grazed you."

And with that, he walked out of the kitchen without so much as a backward glance. Emma could hear his concentrated footsteps going down the hall, presumably back to the study where he read while listening to music. Patricia pulled out a large, sturdy adhesive bandage and fixed it onto Emma's wound. The "butterfly" effectively stitched the jagged flesh together.

"There," her friend announced, gathering up the cotton balls while studying her work, "I think it's pretty safe from infection now." She had sensed a change in the atmosphere when she first entered the kitchen, and she wondered what had transpired between Emma and her husband.

"Did you tell Anthony what happened honey?" She silently hoped so. Anthony would know what to do in this situation. He was worldly and connected in ways Emma couldn't imagine. Patricia felt sure her husband could get to the bottom of all this. It was strange how he acted when she filled him in on things in the hallway. He hadn't been surprised by the fact that their friend and neighbor had been shot. *'Well,'* she thought to herself, *'that's just his way. Nothing fazes him.'* She knew her husband well enough not to read too much into his supposed nonchalance. With Anthony, still waters ran deep.

Emma sat back and placed both hands around her teacup. It was no longer hot, but it felt warm enough to help settle her nerves. Anthony's behavior had been unsettling. Why had he seemed so angry with her? It wasn't as if she intentionally put herself in harm's way.

"I really didn't get a chance to tell your hubby anything," Emma explained, "he was busy giving me a dressing down for not going to the hospital. Honestly, he appeared very disappointed in me." That was putting it mildly, but she didn't want to hurt Patricia's feelings by criticizing her husband.

"I'm sorry honey," Patricia said, shaking her head, "he gets impatient with people sometimes. Please don't take it personally. He was just concerned."

She decided to switch the conversation over to what was really important.

"Do you have any idea why anyone would want to harm you? I mean, otherwise this whole thing seems so out of the blue."

Emma couldn't agree more, but she still had no clue as to what triggered the obvious attempt on her life. "This entire day started out in such a strange way," She mused, "first with the letter and the key, then going to the bank. It seems like a whole chain of events led up to getting shot at."

Patricia nodded in agreement, "yeah, the stuff you mentioned in the safe deposit box sounds kind of weird too. Can you show me what you brought?"

Emma had almost forgotten that she was still carrying the items with her. Eager to share this mystery with someone she could trust, Emma swiftly lifted the purse strap from around her neck and dumped the contents on the kitchen table. Both women gently raked their fingers over various photos, picking them up one by one to more closely examine them. Quickly losing interest in the unfamiliar photos, Patricia flipped the cassette tape over with her index finger.

"We'll have to find something to play this on," she commented. "I think Anthony keeps an old tape player in his study. He would never let me throw it out, even though we don't play cassette tapes any more. I don't think we have any in the house!"

Emma was only half-listening. She was intent on thumbing through the address book, now noticing that some names offered addresses, and some only telephone numbers. Coming to the end of the Z section she found just one name scrawled in….Zanders, and a number after it. The inside of the notebook cover wasn't faded like its cover, holding the gloss of black leather and still shiny from lack of exposure. It was then Emma saw the edge of what looked like notepaper tucked into the back cover flap.

Using her nails to grasp at it and gently tugged at the paper's edge, she drew the paper out. It was soft and fragile with age, and she cradled the folded square in the palm of her hand. Patricia looked up from her study of the tape, and took notice of her friend's new found clue.

"Where did that come from?" she asked Emma, who was now beginning to carefully unfold the paper.

"It was tucked into my dad's address book," Emma softly said, "at least I'm assuming it's his, because I recognize his handwriting." Both women leaned in over the words revealed on the small sheet that had been precisely folded in half. Emma's heart jumped at the sight of a long-forgotten pet name given to her by her father.

Dear Emmers,

If you're reading this, I assume any number of things have happened. I imagine I might be dead, or have disappeared from your life some time ago. I struggled over whether I should place these items in your care, but ultimately decided you could handle it, that you might even relish the challenge. You must know that, by being in possession of what I've left, you are in danger. You could destroy it all and relieve yourself of the burden, or use this information to serve your country, as I have tried to do. It's entirely up to you Emmers. If you choose to dig deeper into my past, be assured that dangerous people will soon come after you. They may have already. But you're a smart girl and very brave. I know this, because you always stood up to me. Follow the clues I've left you, and hopefully you'll find a way to avert some of the damage I have already seen take place. It is why they are after me, and the enemy is within, so be careful who you ask for help. Look for NEQUITIA.

Love, Da'

Da' was Emma's nickname for her dad, when she wasn't afraid of him. She'd read a book about a poor Irish family when she was a kid, and the father was referred to as "Da." The father character was a kind and gentle country farmer who loved his family. Emma liked the idea of having that sort of father, and her dad didn't seem to mind when she started calling him Da' in a cautiously playful way, even copping an exaggerated Irish accent. It was impossible for anybody outside of her family to have known how Emma and her dad addressed one another.

"Well, it sure seems like this is from your father!" Patricia exclaimed, as if reading Emma's mind. "But what did he mean about his disappearance?"

Emma cringed at the idea of having to explain her father to Patricia. She had intentionally avoided the subject when they first began their friendship, wanting to put the ugly past behind her. Her mother steadfastly refused to speak of her father, and would certainly never share the details with Patricia, no matter how close they became. Now Patricia would expect an explanation that could be nothing but complicated and painful.

"He died when we were living overseas, in the Middle East," Emma was still doing her best to say as little as possible. "At least that's what we were told. My mom didn't get much information from the company he worked with, and she didn't like to talk about it with me and my sister." She hoped this was enough to appease Patricia, but she needn't have worried. After reading more closely the message from her dad, Patricia snatched the paper from her hand.

"Shit Emma!" her voice was raised in alarm, "he predicted the shooting that happened today! It's right here! *Dangerous people*! That's fucking insane!"

Emma put a hand up to quiet her friend. She had also wondered about what her dad's note meant, but she certainly didn't want Anthony to hear his wife yelling about the whole creepy situation. Emma sensed it would be best to keep this information between the two of them, at least for the time being. She needed to think, and she needed Patricia to help her do so.

"Don't jump to conclusions lady. We need to chill out and look at this objectively."

Her father had been right. Overriding the intense fear Emma had about pursuing this crazy game was a desire to unravel the puzzle her dad had presented. This was quite unlike the puzzles over which she and her dad had bonded. This one seemed far more complex, inherently dangerous and with a lot more at stake.

And there was something more, something that motivated her beyond the curiosity of an unsolvable puzzle. By leaving her the note, Emma's dad had shown confidence in her. He presented her with a challenge knowing she could take it on! For the first time, Emma began to doubt her mother's account of how her dad viewed her intelligence. If he really thought she was incapable of delving into the mystery of his death, why would he leave the note for her to find? For that matter, why would he have even trusted her with the contents of his safe deposit box? She speculated that Anne hadn't known what was really in the box either. Her mother had dutifully made sure Emma received the key, but not until she'd been dead for a year. Maybe her mom had a feeling there were things left by her father that could dispute what she'd told her daughter? Emma wasn't frightened anymore. Now she was angry. Angry at her mom's vile jealousy, angry at her father's untimely death, and especially angry at the people who were trying to stop her from getting to the truth!

Patricia was looking at her friend as if she were mad.

"How the hell can you sit there and not see the meaning behind all of this? I mean, at the very least look up that word Nequitia! What the hell does that mean? It sounds like some kind of code." She wanted to shake some sense into Emma. If she didn't realize her life was in danger, it would be impossible for Patricia to protect her. She decided to play along with her friend as a way of steering her toward the safest route.

"Okay," Patricia agreed in a quieter tone, "let's just assume that what happened to you today is completely unconnected to your dad's note."

Feigning calmness she didn't feel, Emma was folding the note back up to place back in the address book flap.

Patricia continued, "What do we know for sure? We can be reasonably sure that note came from your dad, right?" She practically willed Emma to nod her head in agreement. "Right, so we can also be sure that, even if that bullet wasn't specifically meant for you today, your dad has sent you a warning, possibly from the grave. Agreed?" Emma placed the little book back into her handbag and began to gather up the rest of the items on the table. She could almost ignore Patricia's condescending statements by focusing on this mindless task.

But Patricia was not letting it go.

"Listen honey," she pushed at her friend, "even if you look at all of this objectively, you have to connect the dots and know you're in some kind of danger." She put her elbow on the table and placed chin in hand, pondering the words in that note.

"There's something I don't get about your dad's warning."

For Emma, there were more things than one she didn't get, but she turned her eyes to Patricia to hear her out. She wanted to depend on the older woman's common sense. For the first time since her visit to the bank she didn't feel so alone. Patricia dutifully laid out her hypothesis.

"Your dad said that people would know you were digging into things. How would they know? I mean, you get this key out of nowhere. It's been moldering in that attorney's office for two years. You could have just thrown the key away, but your dad is betting that you'll check out the safe deposit box."

Once again, Emma wished that she had thrown that key in the fire.

Patricia went on, "so you make the arbitrary decision to go to the bank and get the box. There's no way these bad guys, or whoever they are, could have known you went to get the box, right? I mean, what could have alerted them?"

Emma struggled to relive every moment of that horrible morning. She could see herself opening the attorney's letter, and then throwing it in the fire. She retraced every movement she made at the bank, and suddenly it hit her.

The strange clicking noise of the box opening nudged its way back into her mind. It had barely registered with her then. She'd never been in the bank vault, and so she imagined the click was part of the box's structure. But what if it were something else? She certainly couldn't go back to the bank and ask Mr. Beekman to open a different box, or could she? Patricia was now looking very closely at her friend's expression.

"What are you thinking Emma?" she asked, sensing a revelation had occurred.

"It's nothing," Emma said with doubt in her voice, "I just thought I heard something funny this morning when I opened the safe deposit box."

The sound kept running through her mind, click, click, click. The memory of it played inside her head and danced around with the sound of the gunshot that grazed her. The stress and trauma of it all was taking its toll. She put her head on the table and began to weep.

"Oh sweetheart," Patricia wrapped an arm around Emma's shaking shoulders, "you must be exhausted from all of this craziness. Why don't you lie down upstairs for a bit, and we can talk about this later. We'll sort it all out."

Emma nodded in agreement and allowed Patricia to lead her out of the kitchen and up the stairs to the spare bedroom. *'Yes,'* she told herself, *'we'll sort it all out later.'* It was soothing to believe that Patricia could help her, even though deep down she suspected it would take more than that.

Chapter 6
A Watchful Eye

Anthony went into his study and started to close the door behind him. He stopped midway, and listened for the women talking down the hall. His wife's voice could be heard over Emma's, and he had to smile. That was just like Patricia, always trying to help, always seeing the good in people. He never had that quality, but he was grateful his wife accepted his skepticism, loved him in spite of it in fact. He strained to hear Emma's halting words, but the girl was speaking too softly.

'Oh well,' Anthony gave up and shut the door, *'it doesn't matter anyway.'*

Swiftly crossing the room to his stereo, he flipped the power switch. The Yamaha N503 MusicCast turntable hummed to life. It was always such a satisfying sound to him. Forgoing his usual ritual of inspecting the needle, he pulled a record from its sleeve and placed it on the turntable. It bothered him not to swipe the LP clean with a special anti-static cloth first. But he didn't have time for that. With the first strains of Albinoni's Adagio in G minor following him, he headed to the large mahogany desk in the center of the room.

'Yes,' he mused in delight over one of his favorite pieces, 'that is just loud enough.'

Anthony reached into his bathrobe pocket for a small key. He used it to open the bottom drawer of his desk and fished out a mobile phone, one of several that were piled up in the drawer. Staring at the phone, he waited only seconds before it rang, and a familiar voice came on the line.

"What have you learned?" asked the voice coldly. If Anthony didn't know better he'd have thought the person on the other end really wasn't interested. But he had been waiting for this conversation just as much as the caller who was, in fact, intensely interested.

"I know very little at the moment," Anthony sighed heavily into the phone. This wasn't entirely true, but he'd learned one should never be completely honest with Theodore Alberts.

"She came over directly after the bank visit. My wife is looking after her." Anthony could feel the anger rise up in him now, and tried to control his voice to match Albert's cool tone. "She was shot at. By some miracle the bullet only grazed her head, but it could have been deadly. You had absolutely no clearance for that sort of action Teddy."

"We had nothing to do with that!" He could hear the irritation in Albert's voice. Anthony knew his colleague detested being addressed in such a casual manner, which was precisely why Anthony did so.

"Come on Teddy," he continued to goad the caller, "nothing happens without you having a hand in it. You've seen that girl as a possible threat from the very beginning. Just admit your ridiculous paranoia got the better of you."

He wasn't concealing his anger now. Albert's had crossed a line, one that had been very clearly defined and respected…until now.

"I'm not going to defend myself to you Anthony," Alberts said, with just a hint of malice in his voice. "We followed procedure exactly as planned and you'll simply have to take my word for it." Despite the fact that he never believed a word Alberts said, Anthony let him continue.

"I don't know who shot at the girl. Perhaps there are other players in the game, or perhaps someone went rogue." Anthony allowed himself to consider Teddy's words, but said nothing in response. Better to let the vain man ramble, possibly giving up more information. He was notorious for talking himself up, and it always led to him showing his cards. Alberts didn't disappoint.

"When I created this project I was very careful to choose just the right people."

Anthony knew this was a lie. It was Albert's superior who had come up with the idea to keep an eye on Emma. Teddy had only been added to the crew at the last minute. A junior officer at the time, the ambitious Teddy had been dying to have a hand in the operation. He was furious when the baton was ultimately passed to Anthony. Alberts continued to spew what Anthony believed was utter nonsense.

"Someone else must have given up information about the girl's father, maybe for financial gain."

Anthony could hear in Teddy's voice that he was feeling cornered. He wouldn't get much out of him now. He would have to do his own research.

"I don't think this is the right time to discuss it further," Anthony let the disapproval in his voice hit home, "if there's been a leak, it needs to be addressed and dealt with immediately. I don't want the girl harmed, not unless it's absolutely necessary. Even if that comes about, there are alternatives, and procedures to follow."

He heard the sneer in Albert's voice, "well my friend, that's rather up to you isn't it?" Anthony ignored the implied threat. "You know very well what I'm saying Teddy," he bristled at the idea he had to remind his colleague of the rules, "she's to be protected while under surveillance. If she's taken out of the picture we have nothing to go on."

Alberts offered a menacing chuckle, then gave Anthony one last jab. "Don't worry Newcastle," he chided, "we'll make sure nothing happens to your girl." Anthony ended the call and thrust the phone in his robe pocket. He would dispose of it later.

'My girl,' he thought with exasperation, *'he means my problem.'*

Emma made her way slowly back to the farm, crossing the field that lay between her place and the Newcastle's once more. All that had happened that morning seemed like a lifetime away. Only the dull throb of her head wound reminded her of the day's drama. She'd promised Patricia she would ask for Anthony's help, but she wasn't ready yet. His surly behavior toward her wasn't the only thing keeping her from opening up to him. There was something else. The easy going man she'd known since becoming friends with Patricia had changed before her eyes. Even if it was just for a moment or two, Emma didn't like this other side of him. He was careful to keep his anger tightly under control, but it most certainly was there, lurking beneath the pleasant façade he'd presented to her ever since they first met. Emma recognized the fury that percolated within her once-benign neighbor. She had seen it too many times in her father. She wondered if Patricia had ever witnessed the sudden transformation. Certainly, after so many years of marriage he must have revealed the whole Dr. Jekyll/Mr. Hyde thing. If that were true, why hadn't her friend warned her of what might set Anthony off? And why suggest she seek his help if her husband had this hidden volatile side? The very idea of an open conversation with Anthony about her fears seemed far too risky. She was going to do some poking around on her own, using the items her father left as clues.

Emma was met by the stench of pot smoke when she let herself into the back kitchen door. She put the bundle she'd been carrying on the kitchen table, and headed for the living room. The smoke was thicker there, and it wafted through the air as she stomped through the house looking for Jeremy. She found him upstairs, in the bedroom, apparently napping. Judging by the amount of smoke still swirling around the house, she figured he'd only just laid down. Maybe he saw her walking back through the field and decided he didn't want to deal with her nagging.

'Oh well,' she thought with a mental shrug, 'what difference would my nagging make anyway?' If he wanted to fake sleeping it only made her work easier downstairs. She didn't want to share any of the day's drama with Jeremy, and she sure wasn't in the mood for a lot of questions. She left the room, quietly closing the door behind her.

Back in the kitchen, Emma unwrapped the old cassette tape player Patricia had bundled up for her. She claimed that Anthony didn't raise an eyebrow when she asked if she could borrow the dusty and neglected equipment. Emma would have preferred her friend snag the player when her husband was out of the house, but she didn't want to wait. Patricia pleaded with Emma to include her. She was dying to know what was on the tape.

"And wouldn't it be safer if we listened to it together?" She reasoned. "After all, two heads are better than one, and if something else happens to you…" her voice had trailed off, but Emma caught the implication. If someone tried to take her out again, then at least Patricia would have some kind of lead. But no, Emma wanted to hear what was waiting on the tape by herself. If there was a message from her dad it only seemed right to keep it private.

Chapter 7
Voices from the Past

Emma placed the tape player on the table, untangling the cord and plugging it into the wall socket. Pulling the purse from around her neck, she groped around for the solitary tape resting in its plastic case. Examining the yellowed label she could make out her father's writing. FARSI LESSON #7, it read. She remembered her parents studying the Middle Eastern language that sounded so strange to her young ears. Her parents sat in the kitchen for hours, repeating the words and phrases recited to them by a teacher hired to give the crash course needed for them to effectively function in Iran.

"Your father has accepted a job in Iran!" her mother had told her girls, trying to get them excited about yet another move, to another country no less. "We'll live in a big house surrounded by a walled garden, and you'll go to a fancy International school with kids from all over the world!"

Emma and her sister knew they had no say in the matter, so they tried hard to appear eager for the move. They spent the next few weeks helping their mother pack, while their dad disappeared into his study "to work." Evenings after dinner were devoted to the language lessons, and the girls were put to bed early. Emma didn't like the man who came to teach her parents. He always wore a black suit, and was skinny. The language instructor never smiled, and his eyebrows slanted up at the ends making him look diabolical. She couldn't remember the teacher's name, but she remembered being confused about how her father treated him, like a respected elder instead of just a language teacher.

The girls may as well have stayed up and taken the lessons themselves. The sound of their parents incessantly repeating the dour teacher's commands floated up through the stairs and into their bedroom. Lying wide awake in their twin beds, they heard first the teacher, then dad, then mom answer back in an attempt to mimic the exotic words. Now, when Emma popped the tape into Anthony's recorder, she realized she was actually dreading the sound of her parents' voices painstakingly going through yet another lesson. With her finger hovering over the play button, she recalled the lessons didn't really help much. Her father seemed to barely get by with his clumsy Farsi, and her mother never could get a handle on the difficult language. As soon as Emma hit play she could hear embarrassment in her mother's voice. She was stumbling over phrases used in the marketplace, where Emma imagined she would be expected to purchase groceries. Anne was having a hard time repeating each word the instructor launched at her like grenades. Her father's impatient sighs could be heard in the background. Only a few minutes into the lesson, the instructor suggested her mother take a break and fetch a glass of water for herself. Emma could hear the door open and close, and after a brief pause, the two men began to converse with each other in lowered voices.

Emma turned up the volume as far as it would go, and could make out a conversation that, at first, came across as predictable.

"I'm sorry Mr. Ahmadi, I just don't think my wife has the mental prowess needed to learn a new language," her father said apologetically. His tone made Emma feel sorry for her mom. Carter never did have much faith in his wife, and Anne knew it. Lacking any confidence, it was no wonder the woman cowered in her husband's shadow.

"Yes," the language instructor agreed in a condescending tone, "she doesn't appear to have the aptitude for grasping even the most rudimentary phrases."

'Fuck you Mr. Ahmadi,' Emma thought to herself. At least now she had a name for this asshole. She silently congratulated herself for telling off the man she'd never liked or trusted. It was then that the conversation took a turn.

"Carter, I wonder if you've given my offer any consideration." Why did this Ahmadi guy address her father by his first name, while in supposed deference her dad referred to him by his last? Emma didn't have time to consider this strange relationship before her father spoke.

"I have given it some thought," Carter's tone had changed somewhat. It was familiar but guarded at the same time.

'What's going on here?' Emma wondered. And what was "the offer" they were talking about?

Her father continued, "I'm afraid I'll have to beg off. Not that I don't appreciate the offer, of course. I just don't believe it's worth the risk." Emma now sensed some tension in Ahmadi's voice.

"There's no need to be coy Commander Woods. I see very little risk involved. If you truly have no interest in helping us, then by all means say so." Now this man was using her father's title acquired as a Navy pilot! But he'd retired from the Navy by the time this conversation took place. Was Ahmadi being sarcastic, or had her father maintained his status as a commander?

"Supplying intel to these people for money is dangerous, Ahmadi. I'm not playing games here. We both know I have a lot to lose if your business deal goes south. The mere fact that you felt it safe to even approach me with the offer speaks volumes. If you believed I would so easily flip on my own team, then others might also be suspecting as much. Jesus, they may have already given the information up to the highest bidder, either in Iran or right here at home."

Emma's stomach turned at the cold way in which her father now spoke, and the thought of him being tempted by this man and his nefarious offer. She still didn't understand. What "intel" were they talking about? They couldn't possibly mean some kind of intelligence. Dad was a retired fighter pilot, and jets were his expertise. Could this man be offering some kind of deal in exchange for what her dad knew about jets? The idea seemed crazy, and Emma didn't want to believe her father rubbed elbows with criminals.

Suddenly she heard a door open and her mother's voice.

"Honey," she softly implored, "can we reschedule the lesson tonight? Leena is throwing up."

Ahmadi didn't miss a beat. "Of course, Mrs. Woods," there was that condescending tone again. "Your husband and I are all finished here…for the night."

Her father's voice was terse, "Go take care of her Anne. I'll be right up."

Emma could remember the night her sister was ill. She'd had the flu, but was so hungry after days of not eating, she attempted joining them for dinner. Unfortunately, on the menu that night was mom's spaghetti. Emma slept on the sofa downstairs until the room stopped smelling like regurgitated tomato sauce.

On the tape she could hear the door clicking closed, and what she imagined Ahmadi pushing his chair back and gathering his things off to leave.

"I don't know if we'll need your services any longer Mr. Ahmadi," her father said in a dismissive way.

In fact, Emma remembered another man coming to their house for language lessons after Leena was sick. This man was fat and had a ready smile. He gave the girls butterscotch candies and even seemed patient with their mother. Ahmadi seemed to want the last word.

"The offer remains on the table Carter, unless we find someone else. I should make you aware of the fact that we plan to approach one of your colleagues. Mister Nirody might not be as squeamish as you've proved to be."

The name sounded vaguely familiar to Emma. Had she heard her dad complain about him to her mom? She couldn't recall exactly. Maybe she should call Leena and see if she remembered.

"I wish you luck," was her father's only reply.

It sounded as if the horrible language instructor, or whatever he was, made to leave. Seeing the tape nearing its end, Emma moved to turn off the player. Ahmadi could be heard stopping at the door and gave a warning that gave Emma chills.

"For god's sake Carter, the tape has been running the whole time! Pull the fucking thing out and destroy it!" Only then did the tape run out, causing the machine to automatically click off.

Emma listened to the ring tone, praying that her sister would answer. After nine rings she was ready to hang up, but Leena answered at ring number ten.

"Hey Em," came the always cheerful voice on the other end of the line, "my caller ID hasn't shown your name in a long time!"

Emma had to laugh. "Oh come ON!" she giggled. "I call you practically every week!"

The sisters loved each other, and they made a point to connect often. The miles between Leena's cabin in the mountain town of Packwood, Washington, and the Woods' farm in Oregon, never deterred their efforts to stay in constant touch. In spite of the lingering hurt fostered by Emma's mother, that their dad preferred Leena, the two remained close. With all that had been going on however, Emma had indeed let the week pass without calling her sister. And Leena had noticed.

"Are you okay sissy? I was going to call and check on you today anyway, so I'm glad you beat me to it. What's been going on that you don't have time for your sissy? I know for sure the farm ain't that exciting."

Leena chuckled and Emma let the gentle digging go. She knew her sister couldn't pass up an opportunity to tease her about returning to the small town. Leena actually admired her sister's ambition to restore the farm, but it was her duty as an older sister to give Emma shit now and then.

"Honey, this time you couldn't be more wrong." Emma spent the next half hour telling her shocked sibling all that had happened, doing her best to play down the shooting. She didn't want to worry Leena, and she definitely didn't want to hear her sister's predictable solution to her scary situation. She heard it anyway.

"You need to pack up and come up here to stay!" This was Leena's advice whenever Emma had a problem. She had suggested a visit when their mother died, and again when Jeremy was causing problems. She loved that her sister always wanted her there. The girls looked out for each other, and Emma appreciated her sister's protection. But she knew that running to her sister's isolated cabin in the woods wouldn't solve her problems.

"I love your place Leena," she admitted, "but I can't leave right now. There's some stuff I need to figure out."

"Well, why don't you show that Anthony guy everything dad left you." Leena's tone gave away her frustration. Why couldn't her younger sister see the sense of coming up to stay in the safety of her beloved mountains? "That way you're not hanging around where people you don't even know can shoot at you."

Emma knew it wasn't that simple. "See, that's the thing sissy. I don't think this was something that happened by chance. Patricia doesn't either, and I guess that's why she suggested her husband look into it. But he won't be any help, because he doesn't know anything about dad. And I think that's where all this is coming from. You should have heard dad talking to that creepy language teacher on the tape. It sounded pretty sinister."

There was a pause on the line before Leena answered, "Yeah, I never trusted that Arab." Leena had lived amongst the conservative mountain population for so long she'd started to pick up the rather narrow views of foreigners.

"He wasn't Arabian honey," Emma corrected her sister, "he was Iranian."

Leena forged ahead, "yeah, yeah, whatever. The point is he was evil, and we knew it as soon as we met him, remember? I'd say even as kids we had pretty good instincts. Is that what you're going on now? Because sticking around there based on a hunch seems kind of dangerous, Em."

Emma felt the direction she was taking to find out more was more than a hunch. But she needed to build on the thread of tantalizing information she'd received from the tape.

"Sissy, do you remember when we moved to the Middle east, dad had a couple of guys who worked with him?" "Oh yeah," her sister agreed, "They all kind of hung out together. I remember mom freaking out over having to host dinners for them and their wives. There were like four or five of them."

Emma and Leena didn't much care for the dinner parties their parents were required to put on. The girls would be trotted out in their little military style dresses, gold buttons and all. Introductions were made, and the girls dutifully shook the hands of every smiling but disinterested attendee. Then, after helping to serve hors d'oeuvres, they were excused to have dinner up in their room and put themselves to bed. The sisters fell asleep to the sound of grownups laughing and cocktail glasses clinking.

"There was one man that Ahmadi dude mentioned toward the end of the tape," Emma pressed on. "His name was Nirody. Does that name ring a bell?"

"Yeah...." Leena's voice trailed off as she thought for a moment. "Hey! Wasn't he that uptight looking guy with the buzz cut? He always wore a bow tie and seersucker suits, remember?" Emma could picture him, now that her sister jogged her memory. Every time she shook his hand it felt damp, and his lips were thin.

"That's right," she knew Leena would come through. It was ironic that, for someone who didn't like to live in the past, she had an excellent memory. "He was super uptight! Remember when mom made fun of him in the kitchen?" The girls were now having fun sharing memories.

"Yeah," Leena laughed, "she called him a square!" Both women were laughing now, and Emma almost forgot why she was asking her sister about this "square."

Settling down, she asked Leena softly, "Honey, do you think there's a record of the guys dad worked with? Maybe I could find out if this Nirody person is still alive. I might even track him down and see if he knows what really happened to dad."

"Not if he took that creepy Arab up on his offer," Leena scoffed, "if he did, then trying to speak to him would be super dangerous, Em. He probably wouldn't tell you anything about dad either. I don't think he and dad really liked each other. That's the vibe I got anyway."

Emma mulled the idea over for a few seconds before Leena broke her train of thought.

"Sissy, mom told us that one time what happened to dad. He got killed because he was doing something wrong. Something illegal, she said. And what difference does it make now? He's not going to come back from the dead and say who's shooting at you. You don't even know for sure that it wasn't some psycho kid trying to be a gangster."

'Sweet sister,' Emma thought to herself with a small smile, *'always the pragmatic one.'* Leena never liked delving into the past to relive their awful childhood. She lived for the moment, and was happy to be holed up in her quiet mountain home. For a moment, Emma wished she could be like her sister, but right now the need to understand her father was stronger than the dream of a peaceful life. Maybe, deep down, Emma had always known that curiosity would drive her.

"I'm going to try and find Nirody, or at least find out if he's alive," she told her sister. "What harm could it do just to poke around?"

Leena sighed on the other end of the line. "If you're determined I can't stop you, that's for sure," she said with resignation. "Just promise me you'll be careful, okay sissy?" An image of their father came to mind at the phrase. "Don't make promises you can't keep," he used to say.

"I'll do my best," was all Emma could offer, before hanging up the phone
    Jeremy came down from his nap just as Emma said her goodbyes to Leena.

"Jeez Em, you gotta call your sister when I'm not in the house. You guys are so loud I can't sleep!"

She looked at him wearily and rolled her eyes.

"Gee, I'm sorry, love of my life," she said, hoping the sarcasm wouldn't be lost on him. "I'm not used to living in a house where people sleep during the day."

Jeremy shrugged his shoulders and turned to the refrigerator. Opening the door, he bent down to stare at the contents.

"You got anything good to snack on in here?" he asked, and began rummaging around in an effort to stave off the munchies.

Without a word, Emma got up and headed for the stairs, grabbing the stepstool they kept in the pantry on her way out. When she reached their bedroom door, she placed the step stool directly under a long string hanging from the ceiling, took the two stairs required for her to reach the string, and pulled down the little trap door that allowed access to the attic. She unfolded a neat set of collapsible stairs that came to the floor, and carefully took them up to the warm and funky smelling room filled with boxes and old furniture.

She found where she'd placed her mother's things easily enough, and the two boxes of her mom's paperwork yielded a worn address book Emma remembered from her childhood. The yellow daisy print had long since faded, and the 1970s style lettering she once thought so cool now seemed outdated. It was the only address book her mom ever used, and she relied on it to send out Christmas cards every year. The whole family used it for years, and she'd even seen her dad refer to its pages in order to make a call to friends and relatives. She was certain she'd never seen the one from the safe deposit box, not even the few times she crept into his study, looking for the chocolate bars he sometimes kept in his lower desk drawer. She flipped through her mom's old address book, dog eared in some places for reasons unknown. All the names and addresses were written in her mother's familiar scrawl, the different colors of ink an indication of Anne's habit to grab whatever pen was available at the time.

Not really expecting to find anything, Emma turned to the section of names starting with the letter N. And there, unbelievably, was the name of Charlotte and Frank Nirody. Emma nearly dropped the book in surprise. A black diagonal line had been drawn through the address.

Mom stopped sending Christmas cards to the people with lines drawn through their names. Emma assumed these people had simply moved, or her parents no longer associated with them. Maybe the line had been drawn when mom came back from Iran, the widow of a disgraced man.

The address was listed in Long Island, New York. Emma remembered her dad traveling out to Long Island from their home in San Diego, California. Carter Woods and his family stayed in San Diego after he retired from the Navy. Emma remembered it was the longest they had lived anywhere, and she was miserable at the thought of moving away from the friends she'd made, in order to travel to what she imagined was a land of deserts and camels.

Dad began working for Grumman Aerospace almost immediately. Mom said they offered him a job because of his experience with flying the F-14 Tomcat in Vietnam. The leader of Iran, a man her mother called "the Shah," purchased a lot of those planes from Grumman, and he needed people to teach his pilots how to fly them. Emma hadn't given a shit about the Shah and his airplanes at the time, but her dad sure seemed happy with the possibility of moving somewhere he could still fly. He was fun and played with his daughters when he returned from his trips to New York, so Emma believed the move would make all of their lives easier. If her dad was happy, the whole family was happy.

Emma noticed her mom listed the woman's name first whenever she wrote in the information for a couple. *'How funny,'* she thought, *'maybe this was the only way she could make women come first in that male-dominated world.'*

She squinted to read the tiny numbers of the Nirody's home telephone. There was no listing of a work number. (613) 494-9500, she jotted down the number, and then decided to write the address down as well. It was highly unlikely she would be traveling back east to find Frank Nirody, but you never knew. Without bothering to put her mother's boxes away, Emma hopped down the attic stairs and folded them back into the ceiling's trap door.

"What's going on up there Em?" Jeremy's voice came from the living room.

'Good!' Emma thought. 'I can use the phone in the kitchen.'

Jeremy had shown very little interest in her since the morning of her bank trip. "What happened to your head?" was all he asked the night of the shooting. While preparing to wash her face before bed she had pushed the bangs from her forehead, revealing Patricia's neat butterfly bandage.

"Patches kicked me," was the only explanation she could come up with on the fly.

It made no sense at all, of course. Anyone with the slightest bit of horse experience would know a horse like Patches wasn't likely to kick unless under extreme circumstances. And his hoof certainly couldn't reach as high as her forehead. Jeremy was satisfied with the lame excuse, however. It was almost disappointing that he took it for granted that she wasn't lying to him.

"Man!" he smirked, "maybe it's time to put that nasty horse down!"

Emma hated him then for the ignorant and cruel remark, but she was pleased not to have to answer any more questions.

On her way to the kitchen, Emma passed Jeremy who was seated in front of the television, making fast work of a sandwich he'd managed to pull together. His eyes riveted to yet another episode of NCIS, he hardly noticed Emma. That was fine by her. She wanted to keep Jeremy in the dark about what had happened in town, and her efforts to discover what was behind them. She had never shared the stories about her dad with him. She felt that, even if her boyfriend knew the details behind her father's death, he wouldn't have grasped their importance.

He wasn't a bad man, really. Just wrapped up in his head, and focused on his own life. By now Emma realized Jeremy had empathic failure. He loved her. She was sure of it. But he didn't have it in him to support her emotionally, or even understand what she was going through.

Arranging her notes on the kitchen table she felt sure it was best to keep her sleuthing from him. She reached for the avocado green phone that hung on the wall by the kitchen table. It had served the Woods' family for many years, and when Emma moved to the property she decided to keep the old land line, for nostalgia's sake. With fingers trembling slightly she dialed the number she'd jotted down, then turned to sit at the old Formica table, allowing the long and coiling phone cord to wrap around her.

At least the phone was ringing. She'd expected to hear a recording stating the number had been disconnected. It rang five times before an elderly woman's voice came through, soft and uncertain.

"You have reached the Nirody residence. Please leave a message."

Emma panicked when she heard the beep indicating her message was recording. She hadn't planned on leaving a message, and she didn't have time to compose something appropriate now. Instead of playing it safe and hanging up, she impetuously dove right in.

"Heh-hi," she stammered, "my name is Emma Woods and I'm trying to reach a mister Frank Nirody." She sounded like an idiot, but dove right in. "I think Frank worked with my father, Carter Woods. If this is his number, could you please have him call me at…." She rattled off her number far too quickly. Afterwards she issued a shaky "thank you."

Hanging up, she let out a big sigh. She hadn't even made it clear what she was calling about. And why didn't she say that anyone with information could call? If Frank was dead, then that was probably his widow on the recording. She couldn't expect a lady like that to call back a stranger about her deceased husband.

Certain she had squandered an opportunity; Emma sat and thought about what other options lay before her. What if she started looking into her dad's history before things got weird? She'd never heard

76

anything but praise for his military career. Maybe the people to search for were the ones who recruited her dad to work for Grumman?

Emma grew up hating the name of the aircraft company. They had meted out a measly portion of the pension promised in dad's contract. Claiming they couldn't release confidential information the government used to block further compensation. That left next to nothing for Anne and her kids to live on. They'd had to move in with Carter's parents and rely on them for support. Her father was tried and convicted in absentia for crimes Anne never fully understood. To Emma and her sister, the people at Grumman had royally screwed the Woods family, and she was glad to hear the company closed most of its factories after The Cold War ended. Since then, the company had merged with Northrop.

Still, there had to be some record of former employees. If she could get into their archives somehow, she might at least find out what her dad had been accused of. She would have to find the number for Northrop and see if she could somehow get a look at those records.

"Hey babe," Jeremy called from the living room, "can you bring me a beer?"

Emma ignored him and made plans in her head to visit the local library. They might have information about Northrop there.

"Babe?"

Jeremy's pleas interrupted her thoughts, and she tucked her notes into the binder she'd purchased to place all her gathered information.

"Get your own damned beer," she hollered back, "I'm busy!"

"Oh come on Em," Jeremy was relentless, "don't be so grumpy."

She glanced at the clock on the wall and was shocked to realize it was already five o'clock. Where had the day gone? It might be a good idea to put all of this aside for the night. She grabbed a beer from the refrigerator, thought for a moment, and then grabbed one for herself.

"I'm coming," she yelled in a gentler tone, "what's Agent Gibbs up to now?"

Chapter 8
Digging Deeper

The librarian stared at Emma for a moment, digesting her questions, and wondering why the young farmer was making such an odd request.

"I'm sorry dear," the middle-aged woman looked at Emma with confusion, "what is it you're researching?"

Emma had anticipated this response. The small town library probably didn't get a lot of folks looking up information on Northrop. She tried again to make herself clear.

"I want to find out the contact information for Northrop Grumman Corporation. They make jets. I think they're based in California somewhere, but I don't know for sure. I need the company's address and even a telephone number if that's available."

The librarian, pleased with the idea of finally testing her skills, sprang into action. If this girl wanted information on some big company she was going to help her find it!

"We'll have to look in one of the indexes located in the back. I think that'll be more helpful than the card catalog.

Encouraged by the term "we" used by her new cohort, Emma followed the woman down the aisles of shelved books and toward the back of the building. They passed a few kids on their way, sitting at tables in the center of the room and heads bent over schoolwork.

The librarian stopped at the closest shelf where indexes were stored, and reached for the most recent book listed under the letter C.

"We'll look for corporations, and that should take us to any magazine articles or books about your company." Emma smiled. It wasn't "her company", but she didn't want to waste time correcting her ally while she was on a roll. Before long, the two women were flipping through a Forbes magazine with a story about the merger.

"Okay, so in this article they're talking about why they acquired Grumman, so maybe at the end they'll list a location." The librarian was as excited as Emma now, and intent on solving their shared mystery. An address and phone number were in Emma's hands within minutes, and she shook her new friend's hand on her way out of the library.

"Thank you so much for your help, Clara. I couldn't have found this stuff without you."

"No problem," Clara said with a shrug, "it was fun! Hey, why do you want to contact that big company anyway?"

She'd been dying to ask Emma ever since they started their quest.

"Oh, I'm just looking for somebody who used to work there," Emma replied. It wasn't a lie, but she felt bad leaving a very disappointed librarian without a juicier story.

Clutching the index card, Emma made her way to a pay phone on the other side of the street. She'd told Jeremy she was going out to shop for food. She would make the call before purchasing groceries. That way he wouldn't ask why she'd been gone for so long. The accordion pay phone door opened with a squeak, and Emma didn't bother shutting it behind her. She propped the card on top of the black box, fished out coins for the long distance call, and punched in the numbers.

She had to go through three different recordings in order to finally get a real person on the line. The woman from human resources confirmed they did have access to information pertaining to former Grumman employees. But she would have to find someone to go through the files in the basement, and it would take some time.

"What was the name of the employee you're searching for? And I'll need to know the purpose for your search. Are you doing a reference check on this person?"

Shit! Emma hadn't thought to come up with an excuse for her digging. She'd have to think fast.

"Yes, it's to confirm the employment history of a person trying to rent from me."

The lie would have to do, and it worked. Human resource lady took down the name of Frank Nirody and the general dates of employment while Emma fed more coins into the phone.

"I'll get back to you as soon as I can," the woman on the other end of the line promised, "is there anything else I can do for you?" The name of Zanders came to mind. Maybe she should ask if this man, and she assumed it was a man, had worked for Grumman as well. Why else would her dad have his name in the notebook? Instead, her desire to know more about her dad took precedence. On a whim, Emma decided to take a chance.

"I wonder if you can look up one more name. Mr. Nirody lists a coworker as a reference, so I thought I might as well confirm his employment at Grumman as well."

Wow! She was getting good at this thinking on her feet game.

"Okay," the HR lady said, "Can you give me his full name?"

"It's Carter Woods. No relation to me." Emma quickly added. She wasn't sure the HR lady would believe this, but she was too far in to care. "He would have been working for the company at the same time as Mr. Nirody. Thank you for your time!"

Emma hung up, pleased with her success, and stuffed the index card in her purse. She slipped from the phone booth and gave a slight smile to the man who had been waiting to use the phone. She didn't notice when he began to follow her, several steps behind.

Emma pulled a cart from a row of several lined up in the grocery store entrance and pushed her way to the produce section. Her plan was to buy fresh fruits and vegetables that would replace the usual junk Jeremy craved. She'd been attracted to his slender and athletic physique when they first started dating. But his efforts toward a "musical career" seemed to have increased his pot smoking, and the pounds had crept on. She was going to try and be more encouraging, and maybe stop berating him so much for help around the farm. Maybe if she lightened up he would take the initiative to be a more willing partner. She would get some quality, organic greens and sauté them up with olive oil. They always had nice salmon at the meat department, and with wild rice it would be the perfect meal for them to reconnect.

She pushed aside bunches of collard greens displayed at the front, and sought out those tucked in back with greener leaves. She sensed somebody standing behind her, and tried to decide quickly on a decent batch.

"It really is a shame," the voice behind her said. Without turning, Emma selected the best looking collards and shook the water from its leaves.

"Yeah," she agreed with the stranger, "they always rotate the older stuff toward the front...."

Her voice trailed off as she turned to face the stranger. It was the man who had been waiting to use the phone booth! Why was he here now, right behind her, apparently shopping for the very same thing? Emma knew the stupidity of the question, even as she thought it. The man offered a slight smile that didn't reach his eyes. She hadn't noticed his clothing before, but now she took in the white tee shirt and blue jeans that looked stiff and new. Medium build, brown hair, and brown eyes that had been covered with sunglasses when he was waiting by the phone booth, the word that came to mind was "nondescript." As the locals liked to say, he didn't look like he was from around here.

"I wasn't talking about the produce." Placing between them the small grocery basket he carried, the man reached past Emma, still uncomfortably close. Locking eyes with her, and without looking at the greens, he took the yellowed bunch from the front. Her heart was beating fast now. The full realization that this man was a threat washed over her like a big, cold wave. Yet, she could do nothing but stand, frozen and staring.

"It's a shame you couldn't leave things alone. You had a nice life here. Now it's too late."

His words were measured, and delivered as if he were discussing the weather. Emma tried not to breathe, as if the man's very presence was toxic. Maybe if she stood still she could disappear, and the man would go away.

'Please go away,' she thought to herself, hoping he couldn't see her fiercely beating heart beneath her own, not-so-white tee. He placed the greens in his basket, and carefully regarded her. It seemed he was enjoying playing this game, scaring the shit out of her in such a calm, deliberate manner. For Emma, it felt like hours passed before he stepped away from her and gave her the same, rigid smile.

"You should think about it," he said quietly, almost under his breath. "If you let things go, we might do the same. Then you wouldn't have to wonder."

Anger stirred in Emma's stomach. In her gut she knew this guy had been sent by the same assholes that shot at her. It pissed her off, and she wanted to slap that smug smile off this stranger's face. She knew he was waiting for her to respond, and she couldn't help herself.

"Wonder what?" She took the bait, but in a voice so loud it made a few of the other nearby shoppers turn to gape at them. The man cocked his head and looked at her as if the answer was obvious.

"Wonder what might happen next. You never know who might get hurt, and it would be your fault, of course." And with that he turned and walked out of the grocery store, leaving his basket with the yellow greens to rest in a bin of apples.

Chapter 9
Coming Clean

Jeremy was sitting on the front porch swing, strumming a tune when Emma drove up the dirt road to their house. The big wheels of her truck kicked up rocks and dust that settled on the vehicle once she suddenly braked to a stop. The cloud of dust reached Jeremy, causing him to cough and wave his hand in front of his face. Emma threw open the truck door and hopped down into the still-settling dust. As she reached the porch, Jeremy stood to give her a hug, positioning his guitar strap so that his instrument moved from his front to being slung over his shoulder.

"Welcome home baby," he cheerfully greeted her, but she ignored his outstretched arms and walked into the house, slamming the screen door behind her.

"Jeez, another bad mood," Jeremy muttered to himself before following her.

"Honey, what is it this time? I thought you were gonna bring back some groceries!"

Emma went straight to the kitchen and set her purse down on the table.

"Nothing's bothering me," she barked, and reached into the refrigerator for the bottle of chardonnay that had stayed there, unopened, for almost a month.

"Here," her boyfriend offered, "let me open that for you."

He took the cork screw from its place on top of the fridge and began the uncorking. Emma pulled a wine glass from a nearby cupboard just as Jeremy popped the cork. He handed the bottle back, and Emma poured the light gold liquid with hands so shaky it made tinkling sounds on the glass. Jeremy observed his girlfriend with a dubious look on his face.

"Baby, don't lie to me. Sure as shit something is wrong. Why don't you just tell me? Maybe I can help!"

Emma sat down hard at the kitchen table and took a healthy gulp of wine. Looking up at him she could see he was genuinely concerned, and it made her feel awful for lying to him all this time. Well…not actually lying to him, but definitely keeping him in the dark.

"Okay," she sighed, and motioned for him to sit down. He took his guitar from his shoulder and propped it against the wall, then pulled up one of the old mismatched chairs and sat, staring at his girlfriend intently.

"I think I'm in trouble," Emma began, and told Jeremy a condensed version of all that had happened that week, including her recent encounter with the stranger at the market. She left out her call to the Nirody residence and her research at the library. Jeremy rubbed one hand across his eyes and reached the other out to grab Emma's.

"Aw man! How could you not tell me all of this before?! Babe, I hope you know I would kick the shit out of anyone who tried to hurt you. You were shot at?! Seriously?!"

It was all too much for him, and Emma felt bad about dumping the whole matter on him at once.

"I'm sorry," she said gripping his hand, "I should have told you everything from that first day. I really didn't know what I was dealing with, and I thought I could handle things myself."

"But you told Patricia," Jeremy said in an accusing tone.

"That's different," Emma shot back defensively, "she's a girlfriend I've always confided in. And I didn't want to worry you."

"And now some goon walks up to you at the store and threatens to kill you? What the fuck Emma?! You gotta go to the cops."

This caused Emma to look up, wide-eyed, and shake her head furiously. "No Jeremy! No cops! They wouldn't be any help, and it might set these people off, whoever they are. For all I know they've been watching me for days! They'll know if I go to the police, and then my dad's trail will go completely cold."

Her boyfriend looked at her like she was insane, and maybe she was. But she couldn't find out what happened to her dad if the bad guys covered things up. And she was certain they would do just that if she alerted the local police. Jeremy grabbed his girlfriend by the shoulders.

"Emma, will you listen to yourself? These people are dangerous! They've proven it by taking a shot at you, and they told you they'd do it again. You are not going to keep poking around about your dad if it's going to get you killed. What the fuck happened to him anyway? How come you never talk about him?"

It was true. Emma still hadn't completely filled Jeremy in on how her dad died. She'd only skimmed over the details of what she'd found in the safe deposit box. She just wasn't ready to share everything with him, and now he knew. He knew she didn't trust him.

"You don't think I can help you either, do you?"

He delivered the words more like a statement than a question, pulling his hands away from hers. It made her sad.

"Jeremy, I just need some time to think things through. Maybe I need to talk to Anthony about this, like Patricia said. Maybe he can help me find stuff out in a way that these weird guys won't know. I just have to try."

Jeremy got up, and with resignation retrieved his guitar. He walked to the door leading into the living room and stopped, hanging his head down.

"You'll talk to Anthony. You'll tell Patricia everything. But you won't let me help you."

He turned to face her. "Have you told Leena? Have you told your sister?"

Emma avoided his gaze and took another, tentative sip of wine.

"Only a little." Jeremy sighed and headed to the living room…defeated.

"Well, you just let me know when you need me babe, if the time ever comes." He took two steps and turned to face her once more. "Oh, I forgot to tell you. Some old lady called for you. It sounded like it was long distance. She said to call her back. I wrote down everything and put it there." He pointed to the kitchen counter. She hadn't noticed the piece of paper with Charlotte Nirody's number.

"See," Jeremy said with a hint of sarcasm, "you can trust me to do some things right."

Chapter 10
The Slaughter

Emma lay in bed, staring up at the ceiling. It was just past dawn. She needed to let the chickens out of the coop and feed all of the animals. She hadn't called Charlotte back last night. She decided it would be best to wait until morning. Calculating the three hour time difference from Oregon to East Coast time, she figured the elderly Mrs. Nirody would probably be asleep if she called after getting the message from Jeremy. This was what she told herself, because she didn't want to admit she was afraid.

The man in the grocery store had clearly been following her, but for how long? Did he know where she lived? And he seemed to know she was looking into her father's death. He'd warned that more hurt was imminent if she continued to poke around. He had used the term "we." Did that mean there were possibly a good number of people who wanted her dead? Wouldn't it take a concentrated effort of organized creeps to not only track her movements, but to come after her again? She could go to the police of course, but what would she say? She had zero proof she'd been targeted, nor could she prove why anyone would want to hurt her. It would be impossible to explain about her father, because even she didn't have any details surrounding his death. For all the cops knew, she was just some crazy lady making up stories about guys in the grocery store threatening her. Maybe it was time to take Patricia's advice, and speak with her husband. But would Anthony Newcastle believe her? He didn't seem real keen on taking her seriously about the shooting.

She sighed and tossed grandma's quilt off her side of the bed, smothering Jeremy who slept through the assault. He was still miffed at her for keeping him out of the loop until yesterday. They went to bed angry, which Emma had heard was bad for a relationship. But she'd gotten so used to their constant bickering it didn't really seem to matter anymore. She had become convinced this kind of fractured relationship was all she deserved.

Emma pulled on jeans from yesterday that she'd left on the floor, and tugged on a sweater. She would call Charlotte Nirody today for sure. It was just a phone call to one of her parents' old friends. What harm could there be in that? Stella hopped onto the bed and settled into the warm spot abandoned by her mommy. The big dog snuggled in next to Jeremy, and after pushing her nose under his arm, fell instantly back to sleep.

Emma gathered the special oat breakfast she gave her chickens every morning, and in the mud room pulled on her mucker boots and a light jacket. She caught the screen door from slamming so as not to wake Stella, knowing that even a tornado wouldn't stir her boyfriend from his deep sleep. Stepping onto the front path she began the familiar trip out to the barn and surrounding pastures. There was no wind, but a thin layer of fog hung over the grass. It reminded Emma of the cotton candy her grandpa used to buy her at the county fair every September. She paused to breathe in the cool air, and listened for the usual morning sounds. She was met with an eerie silence.

Why didn't she hear Buddy, the rooster crowing? It didn't even have to be completely light outside before he started his usual territorial proclamations. And why didn't she hear the goats? Not one tiny bell announced their presence in the field behind the barn. Emma broke out in a cold sweat. Something was very wrong, and her mind went back to the strange man in the grocery store. "You never know who might get hurt next..." He had been outside the phone booth when she made her call to Northrop Grumman. Did he hear her asking about Nirody, and her father? Was another warning already coming? Her legs felt stiff with fear of what she might find as she continued down the path and toward the barn.

The silence was broken by the bleating of one goat. It sounded like one of the babies, and it was positively mournful. She picked up her pace as the kid's cry became more urgent. The animal was clearly in distress, and its solitary bleating filled her with dread. "A noisy farm is a healthy farm," she remembered her grandpa telling her whenever she complained of the rooster waking her up early in the morning. She would have to check on the chickens next. She stepped around the corner of the barn and was met by a gruesome scene. Seven of her goats lay dead and bloody, strewn about the pasture. The lone kid wandered from one carcass to the other, sniffing at a bloody heap before moving on to find life elsewhere. Emma stifled a scream, holding her hand to her mouth and trying to take in the carnage. Disbelief turned to confusion as she tried to make some sense of the heartbreaking display of butchered animals. This had not been an animal attack. This was a concentrated effort to slit the throat of every animal, the baby perhaps surviving by out maneuvering whoever performed the atrocity that was now making her feel faint. Emma fell to the damp grass and began to weep uncontrollably. Who could do such a thing? Why would anybody want to harm defenseless animals?

What was even more terrifying was the fact that the slaughter had to have taken place late last night, after she and Jeremy had gone to bed. How could anyone create such carnage without a sound? The image of someone holding closed the mouths of her goats as they suffered was unbearable, and Emma collapsed in the field, surrounded by the animals she'd loved and cared for. The one surviving kid stumbled up beside her, butting his head against her in desperation. She turned toward the kid and attempted to comfort it by putting her finger in its mouth. He suckled her thumb for a moment, but then turned away from her to resume crying.

She couldn't bear to stay there, crouched on the grass with her goats growing stiff around her. She felt sick from the smell of blood, the faint copper aroma haunting her once more from the memory of Kee. She'd managed to save him, but she hadn't been here for her goats. It was because of her they had been killed in such a gruesome manner. People had performed this insane act just to get her to stop....what? She'd made a phone call for Christ's sake! And to go to such lengths to quietly kill her entire herd, for her to find them this way, just because of a phone call? Nothing made sense, and her head was swimming. She forced herself to get up and walk away from the scene, leaving the kid to continue wandering from one fallen goat to another. She would take care of it later. Right now she needed help. Unfortunately, the only help available was Jeremy.

When she arrived back at the house she found Stella standing vigil by the door. Her dog began to whimper upon seeing mommy, and when Emma opened the door she had to push Stella back with her knee to prevent her from running out. Stella must have sensed something was wrong, and Emma didn't know how she'd react to the dead goats. Her instinct to guard them was strong, and Emma wondered if her dog would feel guilt, just as she had, for not being able to protect them.

"That dog of yours has been crying for a good ten minutes," Jeremy muttered. He was standing at the bottom of the stairs, rubbing his eyes with both hands. "She woke me up!" he complained, while Emma just stared at him through her tears. He walked in his bare feet to the kitchen.

"Want me to make coffee? I didn't smell any cooking when I came downstairs. You're slacking off Em." Jeremy chuckled over his own bad joke.

Emma followed him into the kitchen, with Stella on her heels. "Jeremy," she murmured in a shaky voice, "something's happened."

Her boyfriend was intent on rummaging through the cupboards, looking for the coffee. "Where do you put everything Emma?" He asked, not realizing he couldn't find the coffee because he never made it.

Emma walked over to Jeremy and put a trembling hand on his arm. He looked over his shoulder at her with a smile that soon faded.

"What's wrong Em?" he asked, seeing the pain in her face. "Are you okay?"

Emma found her way to the nearest kitchen chair and landed in it with a thud. "The goats…they're all dead." It was all she could say before tearing up again.

"What!" Jeremy knelt next to her and grabbed her shoulders. "What are you talking about?" he screamed, the reality sinking in. "Are you sure? How can that even be possible?! What happened?"

Emma knew he didn't want to believe the awful truth, and she couldn't blame him. But she had to calm him down if he was going to be any help to her. She'd have to snap out of it and regain some control.

"There's only the baby left," she explained in as calm a manner as possible. "It must have been too fast for them." This bit of information sent her boyfriend into another tailspin.

"Emma! What the fuck are you telling me?! That they were deliberately killed? By the freaks you told me about? The ones you're afraid of?"

"I'm not afraid anymore." The words came out before she had time to think. She should have been afraid, terrified over the menacing message left by the slaughter. However, the injustice of it all, not only the senseless loss of her animals, but the attempt on her life and the treats that followed, had resulted in the exact opposite of what those people intended. Now Emma was simply pissed off.

The realization was empowering. She was going to fight these assholes in whatever way she could. "Jeremy," she placed her hands on his face to get his attention.

"The goats all had their throats slit. It was done last night while we were sleeping, and it was done quietly. They wanted me to find them like that. They want to scare me so that I'll stop trying to find out stuff about my dad."

Jeremy regained enough composure to contemplate what she'd told him. Then he tried to fix things. "Well then you'd fucking better stop trying! Jesus Emma, what's it going to take for you to back off? What fucking difference does it make how your dad died? It's not worth it if it gets you killed!"

Emma had to get through to him. She needed him on her side. "Jeremy, honey…if my poking around led to this, then that means there's something to hide! It means that maybe my dad shouldn't have been killed, and that he was innocent of whatever the government tried to pin on him."

Her boyfriend held firm. "You can come up with whatever crazy reason you want to keep this shit going Emma. It's not gonna keep you safe from these people. These are crazy fucking people! If you don't go to the cops I will."

"No baby," Emma went on, trying to get him to understand. "I'm going to let them think they've won. And that will get them to stop. But I have to keep looking at what happened to my dad. I'll be careful, okay? I'll find a way to do it quietly, without them knowing. But no police, honey. Not yet, anyway. You have to promise me, Jeremy."

She was determined to do things her way. Jeremy knew her well enough to see that. When Emma got like this arguing with her was useless, even if they both knew she was wrong. He shook his head, and pulling her hands from his face held them tight.

"Girl, I'll do whatever you want. But if something else happens we're done, okay? I'm going to the police, and I'm getting you out of here."

The idea of him whisking her away from danger seemed so out of character for her musician boyfriend. It was the strongest she'd ever seen Jeremy. And in that moment she was proud of him.

"Alright honey," she agreed, "I'll be super careful, you'll see."

He walked to the sink and grabbed the rubber gloves lying by last night's dirty dishes. "I guess you need help cleaning up the goats…gross."

She smiled after him, grateful and surprised that, after all this time, maybe she'd finally found a decent guy. Jeremy stopped at the kitchen door and looked back at the woman he loved.

"I sure hope for my sake these crazy dudes don't find out you're fucking with them Emma, 'cos I don't wanna lose you." He walked out the door and, she assumed, to the dreadful task of hauling away the goats. She heard him call from out in the yard.

"You're coming, aren't you?"

'My hero,' she laughed to herself, and made her way out after him.

Chapter 11
Old Acquaintances

The phone was ringing on the other end. Emma tapped her pen on Jeremy's scribbled note while waiting for someone to pick up on the other end.

"Charlotte Nirody called. Call her back tonight. She says you have the number."

His scrawling failed to answer the questions burning in Emma's mind. She primarily wanted to know if Frank was still alive. She struggled with the notion of discussing Frank's death with his widow. If he had passed on, would Charlotte be willing to fill Emma in on the details? It all felt so awkward, and she still didn't know how she'd broach the topic when someone answered at the other end of the line. It was the same small voice she'd heard on the voice machine.

"Hello?" answered the elderly woman. Emma did her best to sound polite.

"Hello. This is Emma Woods. I'm returning Charlotte Nirody's call back to me. Am I speaking to Charlotte?"

The woman's voice remained feeble, but clear.

"Oh yes, this is she. I understand you're one of Carter's girls? My goodness, you must be all grown up now."

Emma smiled to herself. This woman had the same timid way of speaking she remembered when she first met the Nirodys. It brought on an unexpected wave of nostalgia.

"Yes Missus Nirody, My sister and I are both in our thirties…" She wanted to steer the conversation toward Frank, but Charlotte interrupted. "Well that's just wonderful dear, and you can call me Charlotte. So, how is your mother?"

Emma swallowed hard. She really didn't want to relive the pain of her mother's illness, or the horrible statements about her father's opinion of her. It would only distract the older woman from speaking about Frank.

"Unfortunately, my mother passed away some time ago."

"Oh I'm so sorry honey," Charlotte broke in, "was she ill? I hope I'm not being too personal."

Emma wasn't going to get any answers this way. She would have to move things in the direction of Frank.

"She died of cancer, but we got to spend time with her. In the end she went very peacefully."

It wasn't entirely true. Anne was sick and in pain for weeks before her passing. And of course, she'd planted the idea in Emma's head of her dad's total lack of confidence in her. But why upset the old lady about that? It was better to get right to the point, just rip the band aid off that threatened to mire her entire investigation. "And how is Frank, your husband?"

The question might have come across as blunt, but she didn't want to waste time if Frank was dead, and therefore useless to her. Emma held her breath and waited for Charlotte's answer.

"Oh he's fine dear," the woman seemed somewhat taken aback by the sharp change of subject, but she didn't sound offended. Emma felt an instant sense of relief. Now she could speak to Frank about whether he'd been approached by Ahmadi. Would he be honest with her, or deny any involvement? The latter seemed more likely, but she had to try.

"Is there any way I could speak to your husband Missus Nirody?" She thought for a second and offered an explanation. "I found some old photos of my dad and Frank when I went through things my mom left me. There are just some old F-14 Tomcat patches dad kept and things like that. It brought back memories of living in Iran, and I thought maybe your husband would like to reminisce."

It was a terribly contrived and badly worded attempt. She really would have to start coming up with believable stories before dealing with people.

Charlotte appeared to accept the explanation, and went on pleasantly.

"How interesting," she said, "I'm sure that Frank would really like that. We haven't spoken about those days in Iran for so long. After we moved back to the States it felt as if it had all been unreal, like a dream; all that hobnobbing with Iranian officials and trying to keep up with their wives. I'm afraid it was a bit much for me. Your mother was better at entertaining, although she did have trouble learning Farsi. And then, of course everything changed when your father..."

Charlotte abruptly stopped speaking. No doubt she was remembering the conditions under which the Woods family left Iran.

"I'm sorry dear," she continued in a contrite tone, "that must be a painful memory for you, your dad gone and leaving so suddenly and all."

Emma wanted to argue with her that the past was the very thing she wanted to bring up. But she got back to the subject of Frank.

"It's okay Charlotte. I forgot a lot of what happened…because I was so young you understand? Anyway, is your husband available? Now, I mean?" She didn't want to appear too eager, but she had to get Charlotte to hand the phone off to her husband, if he was willing to talk.

"Well, I wish that were possible dear. But he left the day you called." Emma's heart sank.

"Oh, did he go on a trip? I could call back later."

Was it already too late? Had he gotten spooked by her phone message? Charlotte unknowingly answered her question.

"I don't know when he'll be back. He said he had to go visit a buddy of his who got really sick, somebody he used to know in

California. He used to spend time out there, fishing and camping. He went out there a lot after we got back from Iran, but then I guess the traveling got to be too much for him. He must've really liked this friend, because Frank really didn't care for the outdoors. I think he just went with this man because they had been college buddies, or something like that…" Emma pushed ahead.

"Was he there when you received my message?" She had to know if he'd bolted after hearing the mention of her dad on the message machine. The specter of Carter Woods brought to life by his daughter may well have caused him to panic, if he'd had anything to do with her dad's death.

"Well, we were out when you called, and when we listened to your message, well I thought it was so fascinating that we heard from you! But Frank said he didn't like to be reminded of the past. He didn't really like his job with Grumman and he didn't like Iran one bit. I remember thinking it was so exciting and exotic, but Frank always said it was just hot, dry and dirty."

Emma made a mental note of this information, but it wasn't helpful at the moment. "So he went out of town? How long do you think he'll be gone?" She hoped Frank really was visiting "a friend in California," but it didn't ring true.

Well, there's no telling how long he'll be gone Emma, since he said his friend had cancer. He didn't say what kind, but he told me it was bad, and that he had to help his friend tie up loose ends. Those were his exact words, so I'm thinking he'll be in California for a while. He told me he'd call once he got settled, but I haven't heard from him yet."

Charlotte went on, but by now Emma was only half-listening.

"He did say I should call you back though." Emma snapped back to attention.

"He did?"

"Yes," Charlotte liked how this young lady was so interested in what she had to say. "He said I should find out how you're doing and if you need anything. It's strange that he would say that. I mean….what could you possibly need from two old folks like us?" She giggled at this and Emma felt she might lose focus again.

"Did he seem upset, Missus Nirody?" She gave it one last attempt. "Did it seem like I brought up bad memories? If he didn't like his experience in Iran then I'm awfully sorry I reminded him of it."

She wanted desperately to ask Frank about those bad memories. She was pretty sure they had more to do with her dad than the climate.

"He seemed okay to me dear," Charlotte blithely went on, "Just in a real hurry to leave. I can bring it up when he gets in touch with me."

Emma believed this would be the very thing that put the nail in the coffin for Frank opening up to her. "No, no Charlotte, please don't bother him with it. He's got so much else to think about, with a sick friend and everything."

She was wasting valuable time with poor Missus Nirody if Frank had already vanished. She would have to politely wrap things up with her.

"Well, let's keep in touch, okay?" At least she was being honest about that.

"Oh, I would like that, Emma," Charlotte sounded genuinely excited about the idea. "I would like to hear what you and your sister are up to. You were both such charming little girls, and you know your dad was especially proud of you!"

Emma paused. "He was?" Her heart skipped a beat at the thought.

"Oh yes," the woman gushed, "he went on and on about how smart you were! But he also claimed you were quite stubborn," she chuckled, "I have to be honest about that."

'Well, what do you know about that?' Emma thought to herself.

"Thank you for sharing that with me Missus Nirody. My dad wasn't one to hand out compliments, so I take it as a real gift. I promise to call back soon, and feel free to give me a ring if you'd ever like to chat."

"I will dear," Charlotte was beginning to sound a little tired from the conversation. "And I'll be sure to tell Frank we spoke. I'm certain he'll want to be in on our next phone conversation. Goodbye."

A thought struck Emma, and she caught Charlotte before hanging up.

"Mrs. Nirody, you never told me the name of your husband's friend, the one who's dying in California."

"Oh…I didn't?" Charlotte sounded momentarily confused. "I could have sworn I mentioned the man's name."

Emma waited, and Mrs. Nirody chirped, "Andrew! That's his name. Frank never called him Andy, which I always thought was funny."

Emma started to say goodbye and hang up, until she heard Charlotte finish her thought.

"Yes, such an interesting name."

"Andrew?" Emma asked

"No dear, his last name is interesting. Zanders."

Chapter 12
Meeting with the Mentor

Emma and Anthony sat across from each other in a booth at The Greasy Spoon. Emma always thought it was a poor choice for the local café. Practically no one in the little town caught the irony of such a name, and unfortunately it was a fitting moniker for this particular establishment. The food was dreadful, but The Spoon was the only game in town and so everyone simply went there for their coffee and eggs. It was originally Patricia's idea that Emma come completely clean with her husband about her experience at the bank.

"Anthony knows about such things," she assured Emma. "He works sometimes with shady people."

Emma wondered then why Anthony's work in exports would require him to deal with anyone shady. She kept Anthony in the back of her mind even after her encounter with the threatening stranger. Ever since the slaying of her goats, however, the idea of speaking with Anthony grew stronger in Emma's mind. She wasn't sure she should tell him everything, but she had to find a way to keep up her investigation without riling up the people who'd threatened her. Maybe Anthony could connect her with a private investigator or something. He must have his finger on the pulse of other movers and shakers like him. Patricia certainly implied he did, so she called her friend and asked if Anthony was free to meet up with her.

Hearing the name of Zanders invigorated Emma. At last there was something, just a tiny thread that seemed to link one of her dad's clues to a living person. If Frank's "friend in California" was the Zanders from her dad's notebook it must mean something. Emma had to agree with Charlotte, Zanders was indeed a very interesting name.

Charlotte's words about her father echoed in her ears. "Your dad was so proud of you!" This bit of information, from an objective person; a virtual stranger really, was yet another key to validating Emma's memory of her father. It was also further proof of her mother's betrayal. Why had Anne felt it necessary to shame her daughter into thinking she was nothing in her father's eyes? It seemed so petty. Emma knew her father could be a monster. She felt so sorry for her mom whenever he unleashed his wrath on her. Maybe Anne believed Emma's love for her father was misplaced, or even dangerous? Loving a monster could be tricky. You never knew when the monster might turn on you. But her dad was long gone by the time her mother sullied Emma's memory of him. The only motive for her mom's lies seemed to be jealousy, and that felt downright sad.

  Now Emma had to find a way to track down Frank. In spite of Charlotte's assurances, there was no way he would be returning home soon. She was sure she'd scared him off, and poor Missus Nirody would be left waiting and wondering. Then there was the possibility Frank would indeed call Charlotte back. He might ply his wife with questions about Emma, and about her motives for contacting him. Would that drive him deeper underground? She would just have to do more digging. She would ask Anthony for help, and she wouldn't be intimidated by him this time.

  He was grumpy when she arrived, five minutes late.

  "I took the liberty of ordering a coffee," he chided her, a "harrumph" barely suppressed in his delivery. "If you want my advice you should at least be on time for our meeting."

  Emma wasn't in the mood to be treated like a child, but she offered an excuse anyway.

  "Sorry I'm late. I had to put Jeremy in charge of feeding the animals, and he had a lot of questions."

  Anthony had met Jeremy a handful of times, and wasn't impressed with the young man. He carried the ever present stench of pot, and his half-closed eyes indicated the young man had a bit of a problem with the substance.

  "Yes, I suppose his brain doesn't retain instructions very well," he offered. Emma let slide the criticism of her boyfriend. She wasn't here to defend Jeremy. She needed a game plan for survival if she was a marked woman.

"Anthony, I think someone was trying to kill me that day at the bank."

It was a start, telling him everything from the beginning. How else would he know how to help her?

Her neighbor didn't react to this statement with surprise or concern. He merely concentrated on pouring cream into his coffee and giving it a stir with his spoon.

"Now Emma, let's not get hysterical. Why on earth would anyone want you dead? Yes, it is indeed strange that someone was brandishing a gun in our little town. Whoever they were, they most certainly weren't from here. I think, however, that perhaps the shooter was aiming at the window, and you simply got in the way. There's no real proof you were specifically targeted."

Emma became visibly upset at this.

"No, you don't understand Anthony," she argued, now near to tears.

'Oh God,' he worried, *'please don't begin crying.'*

He hated drama of any sort, and the last two weeks had been quite enough for him. Emma continued to present her case.

"I would have been hurt much worse if I hadn't dropped the key! And that car didn't look anything like a local's vehicle. It was brand new and shiny. It looked like something a secret service guy would drive."

This was a topic that interested Anthony.

"What was the make and model?" he pressed. "Was there more than the driver and shooter in the car?"

He felt strongly that the car was one clue as to who was targeting the girl. Particularly if there were more than two people involved. That would put to rest Teddy's suggestion that some officer had gone rogue.

"I don't know. It all happened so fast. I couldn't tell you exactly, but it was some sort of SUV, and it was definitely a newer model. I didn't see how many people were in the car, but there had to have been at least two, because the shot came from the back window. That's what I picture in my mind anyway."

She cut to the chase.

"Patricia said you might be able to help me with some problems I've had since the thing at the bank."

Anthony's blank stare prompted Emma to be more articulate. "She thought that, since in your line of work you deal with a wide range of characters, you might be able to direct me toward some kind of private detective."

Anthony let her ramble on and studied her face for a tell. Civilians usually let their face give away any deception. He already sensed that Emma was withholding information. Curious things had been going on at the Woods place. He was in town early yesterday morning, running an errand for Patricia. When he drove past Emma's farm on the way home he saw her and Jeremy standing by her truck, shedding sweatshirts and rubber gloves. He couldn't make out what was in the truck, and his wife was equally baffled.

"I thought I heard Emma out there crying, it was right after you left. But then I saw Jeremy walking out there with her and figured everything was fine. It was kind of nice to see him helping her for a change."

"Did you see what they put in her truck?" Anthony didn't want to alarm Patricia, and tried to sound nonchalant.

"No sweetheart," she answered, distracted by the photo albums she was finally organizing. "But she did ask me about meeting with you, something about needing a professional for help. She didn't say what kind of professional. She just wanted me to talk to you, and then she hung up. I think that shooting really got to her, or maybe she wants help with what she found in that safe deposit box. You should help her honey. I think that whole thing is just weird."

"What was in the safe deposit box that got Emma interested in her father?" He tried not to sound too interested. "You never told me."

"It was just some old photos and a cassette tape. She wouldn't let me listen to it, but that's why I borrowed your player. It's back in your office now. Oh, and her dad left a really strange note. I was sure it was meant as some kind of warning, but Emma played it down. I hope she's reconsidering getting some kind of protection. I'll bet that's why she wants to meet with you. Help her out if you can, okay sweetie?"

Anthony would do anything for his wife, but agreeing to meet with Emma was a selfish decision on his part. In the past, he was able to keep tabs on her in a cursory fashion. Even after the shooting, he felt confident about monitoring her effectively without becoming obsessive. Following her to the library allowed him to understand what she was thinking in regard to her father. Now he wasn't so sure. He'd only taken his eyes off the girl for a moment, and in that moment he was certain he'd missed something. If she wanted to open up to him this morning he'd encourage it. Better to let her unload so he could find out all she knew. Still, he needed to be cagey so as to not appear too willing to help.

"Emma I really don't know if I can assist you," he lied. "I do business with a few men of dubious intent, but they're not the type of people who go around shooting one another."

Emma wasn't getting through to him. Maybe Patricia was wrong. Maybe Anthony didn't have the connections she needed.

"No, that's not what I'm asking Anthony," her frustration was showing. "I'm just wondering if you know of anyone who investigates people…for a living I mean. Like a professional. There's…there's been some more threats on me."

Anthony paused over his coffee at mid-sip, and looked over the rim of his cup with eyebrows raised. She now had his full attention.

He carefully placed his cup down and asked, "What sort of threats Emma?"

She would tell him everything now, as if her life depended on it.

"Well, to begin with, there was this creepy guy who followed me into the market the other day."

That brief moment he let her out of his sight. Dammit! "Were you approached by this man?" He felt like a fool, leaving her exposed to the very people he suspected were targeting her.

"Yes," Emma continued, "he came up behind me in the produce section. He let me know I was being watched, and I believed him! He basically told me to stop researching my father or suffer the consequences. I mean, he didn't actually mention my dad, but what else could he mean? He said if anything happened it would be my fault."

This was not good news to Anthony. Whoever they were, they were going at Emma hard.

"Why do you suppose this man was threatening you Emma?" It was a question he had asked himself. Carter was long gone, and therefore incapable of exposing anyone. Anthony had to find out what was in that safe deposit box. That was where all of this began.

As if reading his mind, Emma gave up the information.

"I think it's because I followed up on some things my dad left me at the bank. There was some stuff about the company he worked for, Grumman. We lived in Iran for a while, when he worked for them. But he got killed there, doing something illegal. At least, that's what they told my mom. But I never believed it, and the things my dad left for me sort of pointed to that. There was a note from him saying that if anything happened to him I should look into it. He left me some clues…oh it's all so complicated! Can't you just help me find a PI? I don't want to just grab some guy from the phone book."

Anthony looked at the exasperated woman sitting across from him and quickly started piecing things together. Both his people and those coming after Emma had been alerted to the box's sudden activity. That meant the would-be assassins were embedded in the Company, or at the very least had connections there. He had to be careful.

"I suppose I can find a reputable person to further investigate your father Emma. But do you really believe the man who spoke to you in the market is dangerous? Certainly you could continue your research without him knowing."

He hated the way he sounded, minimizing her fears. But it was the only way to get more out of her. He had to know exactly what she was afraid of.

"It's not just one guy." She was almost ready to give up on Anthony. "And they've already made good on their threat."

Anthony held his breath a little, waiting for the rest.

"I looked up Northrop Grumman at the library and got through to their Human Resources department. I put in a request for information on my dad, and a guy he worked with. They found out, and sent me another message."

"And what message was that?" Anthony asked.

"When I went out to feed the animals yesterday morning I found all of my goats dead." She blinked back the tears forming in her eyes. "Their throats had all been cut…during the night….without a sound. So yeah, I'm thinking there's more than just one guy, and they mean business."

Anthony put his hands over his eyes. He rubbed them hard, and then ran his fingers up to his hair where they remained while he let out a weary sigh.

Bringing one hand down to place on Emma's he gave it a squeeze. "I'm sorry dear. I really am." He truly felt for the girl. The fact that her animals were so brutally killed, and done so quietly, was deeply disturbing. This was indeed a well-trained group if they pulled it off without being discovered. Did they know who he was, and that he was in charge of watching her? This was no longer a wait and see operation. This was personal. He had failed her.

"Emma, I think you're right. This is a dangerous group of people, and they are sending a clear message. You need to stop asking questions about your father, at least for now."

He saw the disappointment in the young woman's face, and felt just a moment of sympathy. Perhaps he should offer her some hope?

"I do have a number of colleagues in certain government circles who owe me a favor or two. I could ask them to do a bit of research into your father's....situation."

Emma's expression brightened at this, so he went on. "I'll need some information from you first, of course." Emma nodded and he continued with caution. "What else did you learn from the clues your father left? Were you able to contact anyone from his past?"

"Well, there was this one guy mentioned on the old cassette tape. His name was Nirody, and I was able to find his number in my mom's old address book."

Anthony felt a flush of pride for the girl. She was turning out to be quite resourceful.

"I spoke to his wife, but she told me her husband left after hearing my message. That seemed strange to me, like he ran off because he knows something." Emma didn't know why, but she left out her discovery of Zanders.

Anthony was pleased that she was finally opening up to him. He had been listening to her phone conversations for some time, so he knew what Charlotte had said. He didn't mind that she went into detail about what she'd discovered, so long as she ended up telling him what he needed to know. How, for instance, had she gained access to the safe deposit box in the first place?

"Go back to the very beginning Emma," he ventured, "What led you to visit the bank the day of the shooting?"

When Emma told about the envelope she received from her mother's attorney, Anthony was taken by surprise. Nobody in his team would have guessed that Carter would entrust his meek wife with a key to the box. The only reason they booby-trapped the box in the first place was in case he'd involved another officer.

They knew Emma was special to Carter. That's why they kept her under surveillance all these years. Anthony considered it a babysitting job and it bored him. Such an easy gig wasn't his usual cup of tea, but once he met Patricia he intentionally allowed his caseload to taper off. The assignment was only made tolerable by his wife's overtures of friendship. It made keeping tabs on Emma much easier. Patricia unintentionally fed him information about Emma's life without his ever having to ask. And so he had resigned himself to dealing with an unexciting assignment, because he never really expected Emma would become mired in her father's past. Now, here she was, revealing to him some very unfortunate developments. Emma had become quite ambitious in her desire to know more about Carter. And somebody besides the CIA didn't like it.

Her information did little to shed light upon any possible suspects. He would have to do some digging on his own, and keep the girl out of trouble while he did so.

Believing Anthony's long silence meant he was losing interest, Emma pulled out her father's note.

"I brought my dad's message with me," she explained, pushing the creased paper toward him. She'd read and re-read the letter, unable to see any real "clues" for her to follow. Anthony pulled the paper closer and examined it. Two things immediately struck him as important. "The enemy is within," and the word NEQUITIA. This was a code word he'd heard before. But the case had long been put to rest, or so he'd been told. Emma studied Anthony's expression for any sign he could help.

"What do you think of that word?" she asked hopefully. "Is it Spanish?"

Anthony shook his head. "No, it's Latin. It means trickery, or fraud."

"You understand Latin?!" This surprised Emma more than the word's meaning. "I didn't think anyone spoke Latin anymore."

Anthony slid the paper back to Emma. He'd seen enough. "I learned it a long time ago. I find it's very helpful in translating different languages."

Emma took the paper back, disappointed that Anthony didn't seem interested in it.

"Well, I just thought this might hold some clues, but I guess if they're in there I don't see them."

She folded her father's message up and tucked it into her purse. "I was just hoping you could help me somehow."

"Well, it means nothing to me," Anthony lied, "but that doesn't mean we can't explore it further. He tried to reassure her. "I'll make those inquiries with associates in an agency with which I'm familiar. They might have the means to investigate your father. However, it seems very strange that anyone would carry a grudge against him so far as to hurt you. After all, your father died so long ago. Still, I suppose it couldn't hurt to ask."

By the look on Emma's face, Anthony could see she was dissatisfied with his offer. But it would have to do. Pushing away her untouched coffee, she gathered her things and scooted out of the booth.

Anthony seemed to believe her, but she wasn't sure he was actually on her side. She was backed into a corner. If the guys making her life miserable ever got wind about her continued crusade for the truth, then she could expect more retaliation. If she went to the police about any of this they would think she was crazy, and probably shut her down completely. She and Jeremy had already hauled away the evidence of her slaughtered goats. Anthony was right. There was no way she could prove to the police she'd been threatened. She felt helpless and defeated.

"Well, I guess you're doing more than I could have hoped for."

Her lack of appreciation annoyed Anthony. What on earth had she expected from him? But deep down he knew he was irritated with himself. In his early days with the Company he'd been considered one of the best. He never would have allowed what was happening to Emma. It could have been avoided, if he'd been paying attention. Now he wanted to look into the Nequitia case and see if there was some connection to what was happening to his charge.

When she made a turn to leave, Emma thought better of it, and moved to extend her hand to her friend's husband.

"Thank you for doing your best to check into this Anthony," she said with some relief. "I know it all sounds strange, and I know it's strange that I don't know much about my father. I just know there's some sort of connection with the items that he left me with all that's happened."

Anthony took the young woman's slender hand and returned a firm grip. "Why don't you bring those items back to our place Emma? We can look at them together. I'd also be interested in any response you get from the people at Northrop." His renewed interest caused Emma's expression to brighten. He'd thrown her just enough rope to hang on without revealing much about himself.

"Don't worry about any of this dear," Anthony tried to sound upbeat instead of dismissive. Go back to the farm and undo all the damage Jeremy certainly has caused. I'll be in touch."

Emma smiled a little. Would she be safe on the farm? She used to think it was the safest place in the world. Now she wondered if she should purchase a firearm. Anthony misread the look on her face as fear. He didn't know the wheels were turning in her head. She was trying to remember where her grandfather put his shotgun. She would look in the root cellar when she got home. She pulled open the café door, a little bell at the top ringing her departure. Anthony stopped her with one last order before she stepped outside.

"Don't leave the farm without telling me Emma."

In answer to her puzzled look, he explained, "If I find anything out I want to be able to tell you straight away." His mind was already working out a plan as his eyes followed her out the café door.

Chapter 13
Ultimate Sacrifice

While Emma met with Anthony, Jeremy did his best to care for the animals. They'd found a new home for the baby goat; giving the orphaned kid to a local girl in the 4-H program. But there were still the chickens and horses to feed and look after. That morning Emma had reminded him how to feed the chickens, but he forgot how much hay he was supposed to give the horses. Now he stood in front of stacks of alfalfa and tried to recall what she told him last night when she let him know of the meeting she'd arranged with their stuffy neighbor.

He was scared shitless by the way her goats had been killed. Now, more than ever he wanted to bundle her up and move back to Seattle. It made him feel a little better that Em was going to Anthony for help. He'd wanted to join her, to make sure she told the whole story. If she wouldn't go to the police, then this Anthony guy seemed like the next best thing. But she insisted on going alone. Jeremy knew Anthony disapproved of him. He could feel it the few times he met the old guy, probably judging him for his hair that he'd let grow long and now wore in a "man bun."

'No way did Anthony or Patricia get high,' Jeremy thought. 'Shit, they probably didn't even drink anything but tea.' He told himself he didn't care what Anthony thought of him, pushing back his own insecurities over the failed music career. This morning he was determined not to let Emma down. It had been awful gathering up the dead goats. They had started to grow stiff, which helped when they worked together putting them in the truck. But Emma cried the whole time and he didn't like the wild look in her eyes when she talked about "the bastards" that did the killing. When the goats weren't accepted at the food bank they'd had to leave them at the county dump. That's when Emma really lost it. Jeremy wasn't fooled by her brave statement that she'd get Anthony to help her find and turn in these assholes. She was really messed up and needed him now. It was nice to be the strong one for a change.

He repeated back in his mind the different ways she had told him to measure the flakes of hay. Did she say to use his hand? Yeah, that was it! He put his hand against the open bale and yanked out a flake about six inches wide. It seemed to pull apart from the bale perfectly that way, and he congratulated himself on getting it right. Grabbing two more flakes for the other horses, he stacked them into a wheelbarrow and made his way out of the barn and toward the waiting horses.

They stood in the pasture, snorting in anticipation of their late breakfast.

'I guess she just throws the hay over the fence,' Jeremy speculated, and hurled the first flake over, narrowly missing Patches' nose. The hungry pony didn't seem to mind the assault, and he began ripping into the hay just as soon as it hit the dirt. Pleased with himself, Jeremy tossed the other two flakes to the waiting horses, and then checked the water in their buckets.

"Looks a little low," he said out loud to the horses, who ignored him in favor of the alfalfa they finally had in front of them.

"Jeez," he spoke to them with indignation. "You're lucky I remembered to look. I'll refill your water now, your royal majesties!"

He chuckled to himself and plucked up a hose lying in the grass, thrusting it through the fencing and deep into the plastic water tub. He turned on the spigot and watched absentmindedly as the tub began to fill. Maybe life wasn't so bad here after all. He liked how he felt when he got up early, and he hadn't even missed his usual morning joint. Emma barely gave him time to pull on a pair of jeans and sweater before ushering him outside to chores. He felt sort of bad that she had been doing all this every morning since they moved to the farm. He stopped wondering why she never told him about her dad, and he tried not to take it personally that she hadn't confided in him about the shooting. He realized he hadn't exactly proved he could be relied upon, but that was going to change, especially now that all this weird shit was happening. Maybe he would offer to do the morning chores from now on, just to give Em a break.

"You guys are kind of cute," he spoke gently to the horses, feeling a sudden rapport with them. Patches looked up with soft brown eyes, acknowledging what Jeremy took as acceptance of his presence.

It made him understand Emma's love for her animals just a little bit more, and why the loss of the goats had been so hard on her. Maybe they could both run this damn farm together? He could learn from her and make the place really pay off. He'd help her plant more vegetables to sell at the Farmer's Market. Heck, he'd even start eating veggies himself, instead of giving Em a hard time about forcing them on him. The idea made him think of the carrots Emma said she kept in the barn for the horses.

"You know what?" he asked his new found friends, "I'm gonna spoil you ponies!"

They ignored him as he walked up to the barn and into the adjacent tack room. There, in a barrel marked Horse Treats he found the bag of large, organic carrots.

"Man!" he said out loud, "she feeds those horses some expensive snacks!"

Jeremy grabbed three carrots from the bag and placed the lid back on the barrel. Then he heard the horses.

The sound of snorting and thudding hooves confused him. *'That's weird,'* Jeremy thought, *'nothing could distract those ponies from fresh alfalfa.'* Something was definitely wrong. He headed out of the tack room just as he heard one of the horses cry out. *'Can horses scream?!!'* Jeremy knew it was crazy, but that's what it sounded like to him. It gave him a sick feeling. Dropping the carrots on the ground, he ran for the barn door just as he heard a shot ring out.

The sound of it made his ears ring, and stumbling from the barn he stood frozen, trying to take in the scene before him.

The splashing of water overflowing from the horse's trough broke the silence. Staring back at Jeremy was a group of men huddled by the corral. There were five of them, three just within the enclosure, and two outside the fence. They were of various builds, but all very fit, muscles showing through white tee shirts. To Jeremy, they had a forced casual appearance. Even their jeans were crisp and clean. One man stood uncomfortably in the coral holding a lead rope, and another was nursing his hand, alternating between shaking it and holding it between his thighs. Jeremy had apparently caught them in the act of wrangling the horses. He saw two of the frightened animals galloping to the top of the pasture, but one burly looking man was kneeling over something, his gun still smoking. It was Patches.

Blood poured from the animal's forehead where a single shot had been delivered. The soft brown eyes of the fallen horse stared up at Jeremy for the last time, breaking the failed musician's heart into a million pieces.

"No!" The word caught in Jeremy's throat as an unanswered prayer, and he ran toward the man guilty of taking the gentle horse's life.

The man pointed his gun at Jeremy, gripping Patch's halter with his other hand. In a flash Jeremy remembered that Emma had asked that he take off the halters before feeding the horses. It was the one thing he'd forgotten.

Jeremy didn't see the gun pointed at him. All he saw was the horse he had bonded with not five minutes ago. He wanted to lie down next to the animal and stroke its warm coat, breathe in the horsey smell of the sweet beast and say he was sorry. He felt something stop him from reaching Patches. The force of it hit his stomach and instantly spread a horrible burning throughout his body. As he fell to the ground Jeremy thought, *'these are the guys…these are the ones who want Emma dead.'*

The pain was overwhelming, and he rolled onto his back clutching the wound in his belly. The sky above him was bright blue, and the sun felt warm against his face. Gasping for breath, he saw the man who killed Patches stand over him. He had a thick neck, and sweat was beading on his forehead, some dripping into black, unfeeling eyes.

Jeremy felt himself fading out, and he welcomed the darkness slowly wrapping around him like a blanket. He turned his head away from the man's voice, barely cutting through the fog creeping into his brain. "Sorry buddy," the man said in a way that Jeremy knew he really wasn't sorry. "We had to do it, 'cos we knew that one was her favorite."

Jeremy was floating now. He would go find Patches. Maybe the horse would let him hop on for a ride. That would be wonderful. He smiled at the thought, and heard the man's last words to him.

"We weren't expecting you. You got in the way."

Then there was another shot.

Chapter 14
The Reckoning

Emma let the screen door slam behind her as usual when she entered the house. By now, it was a way of alerting Jeremy of her presence. It gave him a little time to attempt cleaning up whatever mess he'd made during her absence. Glancing around the house, she saw no sign of him, or even of the breakfast he would have made himself by now. He couldn't possibly still be out tending to the animals? Even Jeremy wasn't that slow. With a shrug, Emma went to the sink to wash up the pile of dirty dishes left from last night's dinner. She'd been too exhausted to tackle the heap after eating. Pulling together dinner had been a welcome distraction from the day's chaos. And it helped to avoid Jeremy's questions about what had happened. But by the time they finished the mac and cheese with hot dogs she hit a wall. With barely enough strength to set the dishes in the sink she'd trudged off to bed, leaving Jeremy to enjoy his nightcap of weed before joining her.

Now the food was crusted stubbornly onto her grandma's old plates, and she turned the water to full hot in an effort to get them clean. A disappointing trickle was all that greeted her, and she swore in frustration. The farm had a pretty good well, but if something had been left running it went dry and would need at least fifteen minutes to build back pressure.

"Dammit Jeremy," Emma said to the empty kitchen, "what have you done now!"

She turned off the faucet and wiped her hands on her jeans. She would have to track him down and find out what he'd left on. Maybe he'd taken a smoke break in between feeding the animals. Assuming he worked at morning chores in a weed-induced haze, it didn't surprise her that he'd left the water running somewhere. Out through the back door and into the nearby pasture, she could see nothing out of place, but for the second time this week, something didn't sound right. Instead of the usual cacophony of animals she heard only the wind in the trees.

With her hand raised to unlatch the gate, she glanced furtively around the property. Where were the horses? They normally came to the fence looking for treats whenever someone even came close to their pasture. She placed one foot on the bottom rung of the fence and boosted herself up to survey the entire field. There they were! She could see Bandit and Wildfire huddled in the very top corner of the pasture. Patches must have lingered over any alfalfa left over from this morning. He loved to glean the few strands of hay the others overlooked. Emma wondered why they were grazing in the corner of the field. It was not their place of preference due to the lack of grass there. She looked closer and saw they weren't really grazing so much as nuzzling each other. This was how they comforted themselves during times of stress. But what had stressed them out so much? Emma called to them with the enticing shout of "treats!" This normally brought them running. Her horses only looked up at her for a moment and went back to their nuzzling ritual. She sighed and hopped down from the fence, deciding to check on the chickens instead.

Striding through the knee high grass she thought of what Anthony had said. Would he really ask his government friends to help her? Did they even exist, or was he planning on going to the police himself? It was so hard to read that man, and she began to think that even Patricia didn't know him…not really. He did seem to feel bad about the loss of her goats, and he'd agreed the people who killed them were dangerous. But he had no idea who he was dealing with, or what motivated their scare tactics. And she was equally incapable, just a retired anthropologist trying to be a farmer. The feeling of helplessness threatened to take over, squelching the determination she'd felt while talking to Anthony. She sighed and tried to lighten her mood with a song her dad used to sing to her. It was rather a maudlin lullaby he would hum while patting her back. "Go tell Aunt Rhody. Go tell Aunt Rhody. Go tell Aunt Rhody…the old gray goose is dead."

Emma laughed a little, looking down at her feet to avoid squirrel holes. When she reached the chicken yard and glanced up she saw that not one chicken was scratching or pecking in the fenced run. Where was everybody? Looking over at the coop, she could see her rooster, Buddy, standing guard in front of the little wooden ramp that led to an open coop door. He stood silently, turning his head with jerky motions to survey the yard, before focusing back on her. Behind him she could make out the hens, milling around inside the coop, but having the sense to stay put as Buddy obviously intended. He must have rounded them up at the first sign of trouble, and kept them in the coop away from danger.

Whatever spooked the horses had freaked out her rooster as well. That familiar feeling of dread came over Emma. "A noisy farm is a happy farm." Her grandfather's words came back to haunt her once again. She quickened her pace. "Good boy Buddy!" Emma yelled back to the rooster, who carefully regarded her departure, rising up on his talons and flapping his wings in defiance of whatever posed a threat to his flock.

Sweating anxiously and trying to breathe, she continued to make her way to where the hay was stored. She came up short when she saw Patches at the fence line of the horse corral. He was laying down, his head turned away from her. She had seen her horses laying in the field before, sunbathing in the cool grass on warm spring days. Patches didn't look like that.

She held her breath, trying to stay calm. Maybe he'd eaten too much, and was colicky. She took a few tentative steps toward her favorite horse, the one she always rode in the hills beyond the pasture gates. The one who liked to lean his head on her shoulder as she rubbed behind his ears. As she came closer her foot slid on something wet. Looking down she saw a patch of grass matted down with blood. Something got hurt here, but where was it now? Had an animal gone after Patches? She couldn't think about that now. She drew closer to her horse, looking for the rise and fall of his big, brown stomach. Patches lay perfectly still, and he wasn't breathing!

Emma ran to the gate, but couldn't open it. Her hands were clumsy with fear. Finally she lifted the latch and hurled herself on to the motionless horse. He was still warm, and she desperately wanted to believe he would shudder at her touch and rise up on steady legs, shaking the dust off his coat and becoming her beloved pet again. The first sobs were quiet, and they only wracked her body, convulsions of disbelief and sorrow. Finally she let out a wail that echoed through the pasture and floated on the wind, causing Buddy to cock his head and listen.

She didn't know how long she lay there, next to her horse, crying her heart out and rubbing her face against the animal until her nose was raw. She placed her hands on Patch's mane, stroking the dark coarse hair. Feeling something slick, she pulled her hand away and found it covered in blood. It took a few heartbeats for Emma to realize her horse had been shot in the head. She stumbled back, kicking her feet away from the atrocious sight of the once beautiful animal, now staring and bloody. It wasn't Patches anymore. It was yet another warning, and it was all her fault.

Dragging herself to the fence, she let herself out of the corral and somehow managed to latch the gate behind her. She'd lost her favorite horse; she sure as hell wasn't going to lose the other two. She numbly remembered that she must turn off the water, which had slowed to a trickle. Taking several steps back toward the hose, she found herself up against the old barn. Still sniffling, she leaned on the warm, rough wood. Reaching for the spigot that had been left on, she turned it all the way off. *'Jeremy must have left it on,'* she thought.

Jeremy! He had been here, feeding the horses! He'd given them water and….and what?! She quickly glanced around the yard. He wouldn't have let anyone hurt Patches. He knew how much she loved that horse. He would never have let her discover her horse in such a way. Unless…she couldn't bring herself to imagine what happened here while she'd met with Anthony. She remembered the blood on the grass, and started to shake.

The barn door was closed. She'd been so distraught over the death of her horse she hadn't noticed. But the two huge wooden doors were held together with a sliding slat that always made the doors crooked. It wasn't very effective at keeping the old barn entrance closed when the wind picked up, so she'd always left it open. It made hauling the hay from inside easier, and Jeremy certainly would not have bothered closing them. But they were closed now.

Emma stood at the doors for a moment, not wanting to look inside the barn, but knowing she had to. With one swift motion she pulled on the wooden slat so hard several splinters rammed their way into the palm of her hand. The big doors fell open, creaking and groaning from years of use. They rocked back and forth, swaying in the breeze as if inviting Emma in. She drew a long, jagged breath, and walked halfway in so that she could stand in the center of the old structure, with stalls on either side of her. She looked around blindly until her eyes adjusted to the darkness of afternoon shade within the barn. Nothing seemed out of place.

"Jeremy," she called out. It felt wrong to hear his name bounce off the walls of the barn. She stood a moment longer, scanning the closed stalls until she reached the open one holding stacks of hay. Her eyes fell on something bundled up on top of the closest bale. It was a gunny sack that once held grain, and Jeremy's sneakers were sticking out of the bottom.

She didn't remember running to him, or pulling off the sack that covered his face. She only remembered the familiar, coppery smell of blood. This time she threw up.

Wiping her mouth with her hand she made herself look at the man who tried so hard to help her. She had the crazy notion that he looked almost content, with a slight smile on his face. She would have thought he was sleeping, were it not for his eyes. They looked beyond her, dead and cloudy. Emma felt raw from emotion. The loss was too much to bear. She couldn't process it, and she slipped into denial. This wasn't happening.

She rolled Jeremy's body to the side and started shaking him. It was a stupid thing to do, she thought later. But she desperately wanted him to break out laughing, teasing her that he was just pretending to be dead. A bad joke played as a way of getting back at her for having to do chores. She grabbed his shoulders and lifted his slender frame up to her chest, and the tears finally came.

"Wake up Jeremy! Wake up!" She sobbed uncontrollably. His head fell back and tilted in an awkward angle. She could see the bullet hole at the base of his skull, and she retched again as the memory of her operation on Kee came flooding back.

"You can't do this to me," she screamed at the dead man, "you were supposed to stay here and help me! You promised! You told me you'd try!"

There were no apologies coming from her boyfriend. The whole world stopped. Everything disappeared around her as she sat there holding him, hiccupping through sobs and putting her hands over his eyes in an effort to close them. When her arms began to shake with fatigue, Emma gently lay him back down on the hay. "What happened babe?" She asked the corpse, gulping back tears. But she knew she'd never get an answer. She would never hear Jeremy's voice again. The thought of something so awful and final made her move mechanically up and away from the body of her boyfriend. What should she do now? She squeezed her eyes shut to erase the images of all that had been taken from her. Then she opened her eyes with a start, one thought coming to mind…Stella!

The big dog hadn't greeted her at the door when she came home, and she assumed she was with Jeremy. Stella actually seemed to love him, and she liked to follow him around the house, sniffing at his heels. With a panic that shot through her shaking legs, Emma raced toward the house. Had Stella been killed too? She would have barked at an intruder, and possibly even attacked any stranger who came on the property. Unless….unless Jeremy left her inside! Emma practically tore the screened door off its hinges as she crashed into the house, yelling for her dog.

"Stella! C'mere girl," she choked out the words, fearing the worst. There was no sign of her in the worn and clumpy bed set beside the wood stove. Emma took the stairs, two at a time, up to the bedroom.

"Stella," she cried out, "where are you girl?!" She heard a whimper in the closet, and fumbled at the closed door. A brisk breeze whisked through the bedroom, and Emma realized the door had blown closed on the poor dog when she was in her second favorite sleeping spot.

Yanking the door open, she saw Stella, making herself as small as a big dog could, curled up and shaking in one corner of the closet.

Emma knelt down and wrapped her arms around the traumatized dog and hugged her hard, ignoring the fluffs of hair tickling her nose.

"Oh girl, oh girl," she kept cooing, as she petted the dog's velvety ears, "you're okay girl. Mama's here."

Stella must have heard what was happening outside. How helpless her dog must have felt! Locked in the closet she couldn't come to Jeremy's rescue or defend the animals. For a guard dog, the feeling of guilt and failure must have been immense.

"It's okay Stella," Emma comforted the shaking animal, "you didn't do anything wrong. You're a good girl. Good girl."

She was so intent on soothing Stella she didn't hear footsteps coming up the stairs. She only became aware of someone standing behind her when Stella pulled her head up and barked a hello to their neighbor.

Chapter 15
Reconnaissance

As soon as Emma left the café, Anthony went to work, driving to the storage unit Patricia rented when they first moved to Oregon. He opened the combination lock on his unit in a few quick motions. He didn't have much time if he wanted to return home and look after Emma. The small, cramped room smelled musty, and Anthony thought back on the last time he'd entered the concrete space, devoid of ventilation and somewhat claustrophobic, it was meant to keep the boxes of records and personal photos temporarily, while they got settled in. Somehow, Patricia got around to bringing the photos back to their home, where they remained for months afterward. She kept meaning to place them in fancy photo albums she purchased just before the move. But the family pictures remained on the dining room table, while the empty albums languished in her office, gathering dust. She finally began work on the project yesterday. But as Anthony surveyed the unit he realized she'd left the boxes open, lids askew and stacked in a corner. He never planned on his own boxes to go anywhere else. There was never a doubt in his mind that the confidential records he had in his possession were unsafe at home. The unit in Patricia's name was an ideal hiding place for the old case files.

Anthony moved aside several cardboard boxes and pulled forward a smaller one made specifically for files. Pulling a pocket knife from his vest, he cut the brown tape that kept the box closed ever since their move. Deftly flipping through the manila files, his hands landed on one in the middle. It was labeled **IRAN INVESTIGATION/CARTER WOODS**, and it was a thick file. As Anthony recalled, much of the information was redundant. He impatiently turned each page of typed data and marveled at how archaic this kind of report seemed now. There were photos as well, all of them having been closely examined by Anthony years ago. But he was viewing them in a different light this morning. The photography was grainy in some of the images, but clearly the subject of each picture was Carter. There he was meeting with a supposed arms trader. Here he was speaking in an alley with what was assumed a revolutionary soldier, plotting with others to overturn the Shah. All of it was conjecture at the time, but it had raised warning flags amongst those working to provide Iran with weapons and fighter jets, particularly the F-14s that were Carter's specialty.

Of course, the officers in charge of this case knew the Grumman employee had been approached. That was why he had the photos in the first place. Carter Woods had been followed and photographed even before the Boeing 747 carrying him and his family touched down in Iran. Anthony was informed of the surveillance, but they had been largely unsuccessful in pinning any evidence of treason on the retired pilot. Anthony came across one photo that seemed out of place.

It was of Carter lounging poolside with his family at the Intercontinental Hotel in Tehran. Because it appeared to be simply a benign family photo, he'd never given it much attention. Now he peered closely at the other hotel guests in the background. A man wearing a suit caught his eye. He was the only person not dressed in bathing attire, but there was something else. His suit was of obvious quality, tailored to fit the man's thin frame precisely. Holding the photo in one hand and digging through the box in his other, Anthony fished out a magnifying glass, the kind used by professional photographers wishing to survey magazine layouts. He pressed the glass to his eye and brought the photo closer to his face. Yes, there was no mistaking it. That man had impeccable taste in clothing. The real question now seemed to be, what was Teddy doing there?

Anthony snapped the folder closed and threw the glass back into the box. Rapidly placing the lid back on and piling Patricia's memorabilia on top, he put things in order and locked the unit up tight. Driving back home, he noted that a mere thirty minutes had passed since he said goodbye to Emma. Not bad, but still plenty of time for her to meet with some trouble. By the time he pulled into her driveway he knew he'd arrived too late. He could hear Emma crying somewhere upstairs in the old farm house. Other than that, the only sound was the eerie crowing of a rooster, off in the field somewhere. And where was Stella? The big dog always came bounding out to greet or to bark at visitors. He put the car in park and shut off the ignition in one swift movement. Reaching under his seat for the reliable Glock 20 he always kept there, he stepped out of the vehicle and took measured steps toward the house, holding the weapon at his side.

The door was unlocked, as usual. The fact that Emma never bolted her door irritated Anthony, even though he benefited from this lax habit. Her false sense of security made it easier for him to riffle through her mail and check her computer on numerous occasions. Once he'd even nosed around while Jeremy was sleeping, not giving a second thought to what sort of explanation he'd give if discovered by her useless boyfriend. He simply had no intention of ever being found out. Now he was certain an explanation of his presence would be unnecessary. Judging by Emma's sobs, everything had changed. It was time to move things into a more defensive mode. He was mentally working up a strategy even as he took the stairs to the room where he knew Emma and Jeremy slept. The crying came from inside the closet, and Anthony pocketed his gun. Emma's cries were not of someone wounded, but by the sound of things she was clearly in a bad state. He hoped it wasn't the dog, as he rather liked the shaggy beast.

Standing in the threshold of the closet, he was met with a pathetic scene. Emma lay curled up beside her dog, whose whimpers matched her mistress's sobs. Once she sensed Anthony's presence Stella gazed up at her neighbor and gave a happy bark. He had trained the dog to accept him by giving her treats every time he did reconnaissance on Emma. Now Stella tore away from her mama and bound up to Anthony, just as she would to an old friend. Emma turned to look up at him while Stella nuzzled her wet nose into Anthony's waiting hand. Disappointed at finding no treats, she padded back to Emma, plopping back down as close as she could against her mistress. Emma looked at Anthony in confusion. How long had he been there? She hadn't even heard him come up the stairs, and Stella hadn't barked. She brushed her questions aside.

'I'm not thinking clearly,' she told herself.

She focused her red eyes at Anthony, and with a trembling mouth could only say, "Jeremy's dead."

"Is that so?" Anthony exhibited his usual calm, but did seem surprised at her statement. If she hadn't been in shock his demeanor would have puzzled Emma, but her head was still reeling.

"Are you hurt?" Anthony's question didn't register with Emma for a moment. What did it matter if she were hurt? Why did anything matter other than her boyfriend and her Patches were gone? She gave no reply, and Anthony knelt down to examine her head wound. Finding Emma unscathed he placed a hand on her shoulder and tried to get the girl, traumatized yet again, to come back to reality.

"Emma, where is Jeremy?" She came out of the fog of grief threatening to overwhelm her, and pointed to the window.

"In the barn, on the hay bales." She hated saying the words. It made everything more definite. But she had to let Anthony know what she'd done. All of this death was her fault.

"They killed Patches too." It was all she could muster, and she hugged Stella harder as a way of alleviating her pain and guilt.

Anthony stood and walked to the window. Pulling aside the curtain, he took in the evidence of violence below. He put a hand out to Emma and said "stay here." He didn't yell at her, but it was a definite order. She wrapped her arms tighter around Stella and nodded. Staying put sounded like an excellent idea at the moment. Maybe she would stay there on the closet floor for the rest of her life.

Chapter 16
Saving Emma

Anthony examined Jeremy's wound; a clean shot, at the base of his skull, very professional if one were to overlook the messy stomach wound. He turned Jeremy's body over onto the gunny sack, the way he'd found it. He considered asking Emma if she found her boyfriend face up, but decided to leave it alone. She was still reeling from the discovery of her boyfriend's dead body, along with her cherished horse. She wouldn't remember how she'd found him, and it seemed immaterial now. The damage had been done.

Looking over the scene in the pasture Anthony surmised the horse had been the intended target. These people were ratcheting up the pressure on Emma by moving ever closer to the things she cared about most, her animals. Jeremy appeared to be collateral damage. If they wanted Emma to back off on her investigation by killing her boyfriend, there would have been no need to shoot her horse as well. However, he had no doubt that Jeremy would very likely have been next in line for elimination.

It was very clear that the hit was well executed and meant to send a message. Somebody wanted Emma to stop snooping, somebody besides the CIA. He knew this deep in his bones. The agency, for which he had worked for years, would never have any need to issue a warning, not to a civilian. Even if the threat had been a known adversary, a hit certainly wouldn't be done in such gratuitous fashion. It must have been quite the struggle, and he was relieved his wife hadn't been nearby during the killings. This being a Tuesday, Patricia attended her painting class held at the local YMCA. But the idiots who did this wouldn't have known this…or would they? Perhaps they were watching his house as well.

At any rate, Jeremy's death alone could have sent the intended message quite easily. Why kill Emma's horse as well? It felt….vulgar. He walked back to the barn and again studied Jeremy's bloody form. Anthony felt a pang of sympathy for the young man. Judging by the half-eaten flakes of alfalfa one could see the young man had successfully fed the horses. At the café, Emma revealed she'd told

Jeremy everything. She was pleased that he'd willingly agreed to take care of the farm while she was in town. How unfortunate that, seeing his woman in need, Jeremy had finally risen to the occasion of pulling his weight, only to be cut down in the act?

Pulling out a small camera from his coat pocket, Anthony took photos of Jeremy, then covered his body with the gunny sack as best he could. He went out to Patches and took more photos, including the overflowing water bin. Looking at the slain horse, he thought of the senselessness of it all. What a waste. Tucking the camera safely back in his coat Anthony guessed he would have to call the Y from Emma's phone to keep Patricia there. He didn't want his wife involved in this, lest she become a target too! He would have to call in for a cleanup, before she came home.

He began to formulate in his mind how best to inform his superiors of this debacle. They hadn't been convinced that Emma was being targeted in any serious way. Now the entire plan had to change. He certainly didn't want to alert the police and have them poking around with questions. His people would have to send out a team right away to spirit the boyfriend's body away. He knew Jeremy had no family that would expect to hear from him. The horse was also a concern. That carcass was heavier and far too awkward to simply be whisked away. It would be better for Emma if she didn't have to deal with that unpleasant business. Emma! He would have to convince her that her boyfriend's death must be kept quiet for her own well-being. He would take her to a safer location, and then think up his next move.

'I'd better go check on her,' Anthony thought, cringing at the idea of having to actually comfort her. Empathy was not an emotion with which he was familiar. His wife relentlessly chastised him about his inability to show emotion for another's plight. It was one thing to demonstrate love and support for Patricia. She made him a better man in every way, and he was devoted to her. But he kept the rest of the world's population at arm's length. He didn't have the time or energy for other relationships, and keeping to himself had always seemed the safer way to go, particularly in his line of work.

He quickly made his way up to the farmhouse, dreading an encounter with Emma that was sure to be exhausting. The house was quiet, so at least she'd stopped crying, probably in shock. When he reached the top of the stairs he heard only Stella whimpering. He pushed the bedroom door open, and the squeak of the hinges caused the big dog to look up at Anthony. Emma kept her face buried in Stella's fur, and didn't release her grip on the dog. When Anthony stood next to them the dog nuzzled his hand again, begging for treats. He patted the anxious animal on the head and placed his other hand on Emma's shoulder. He had never touched her before today, and he was surprised at how fragile she felt now. Until recently, she had always come across as a very strong young lady. It wasn't only her lean and sinewy physique, brought about from doing farm work. In all the time he'd known her she hadn't really shown any form of weakness. Now she remained huddled against her dog, refusing to budge or even acknowledge his presence. It was unsettling, and Anthony was at a loss over how to get her up and out of that house.

He knelt down beside her and pet Stella on the head at the same time. "Look Emma," he began gently, "I know you've endured a lot, but you have to pay attention to what I have to say."

Emma could barely hear his words. They came to her from far away. The last image she had of Jeremy, lying dead and staring at her, made everything else incomprehensible. The only thing that felt real was the tactile comfort of her dog. Still, Anthony's voice was drifting in and out, nagging at her to come back to the horrible real world where Jeremy no longer existed, and her sweet Patches would never again run in the field. "...get some of your things....find a place that's safe..."

The voice was relentless, and she could no longer avoid it when she felt Anthony's hands grip her shoulders. He pulled her from Stella, and she was forced to look into his cold eyes.

"What did you say?" she mumbled.

Anthony was pleased to see she was coming out of her stupor, *'at least she's hearing me now.'* He pulled her to her feet and gave her a little shake.

"Emma, you don't have time to mourn. I'm sorry, but the people who did this will come back. We have to go now, and sort things out later."

She was a bit wobbly, and kept looking down at Stella.

"But what about Stella," she asked, still not comprehending the danger. "And my other animals? What about…" she stopped for a moment to think.

There was something else, something important, that needed attention. It came to her in a horrible flash.

"What do I do about Jeremy? And poor Patches is just lying there! What if the crows show up and….?" The reality that her boyfriend and beloved horse were both growing rigid in the field outside was too much to bear. Her eyes welled up, and she began to shake. 'Oh fuck,' Anthony was losing patience now. He knew if he allowed her to take in the whole rotten mess they'd never get out of there.

"We can't stay here Emma. Grab some clothes, about three days' worth. Where do you keep your bags, or even a backpack?"

She absentmindedly drifted over to a dresser by the bed, and began pulling out underwear.

"My suitcase is on the floor of the closet, next to…" *'Christ! Don't say it,'* Anthony thought he'd lose her entirely if she had an opportunity to say Jeremy's name. Instead, he distracted her.

"I'll get it and you start getting your things together. I'll have Patricia come take care of Stella and your chickens."

This seemed to satisfy Emma. She nodded and continued to the next drawer where she kept her sweats. It was better to sleep in sweat pants if you were in a strange place. You could run away faster wearing sweats, if you had to. It felt good to consider practical things like this, and she was suddenly glad that Anthony was there, telling her what to do.

Anthony could see she was still very much out of touch with reality. He needed her more than coherent now. In order to be any help to him at all he needed her to be angry. Better still, he needed her to be fierce.

It was the fear that threatened to cripple her, and he had to snap her out of it. Perhaps he could stoke her anger over the injustice of all the needless killing? That would surely get her moving. He grabbed her suitcase from the closet and threw it on the bed. Emma bumped into him when she tried to lay out a dress on top of the quilt. *'Jesus,'* Anthony thought, *'what the hell does she need with a dress?'*

Throwing the garment on the floor he grabbed Emma by the shoulders once more. Looking her in the eyes he again tried to get through to the fragmented woman.

"The people who did this Emma, they were trying to send you a very clear message. They didn't like that you ignored the slaughter of your goats. They went after Patches because they knew you loved him. They weren't expecting Jeremy, and my guess is he tried to save your horse. They weren't ready to kill someone; they had to in order to remain undiscovered. That means they might not be as organized as you thought."

A look of wonder crossed Emma's face. If Anthony was right, that meant these horrible people were capable of making a mistake. And if that were true, then they might let their guard down. She could find out who they were, and what hand they had in her father's killing. Now she was certain they, whoever they were, had somehow been involved.

By the change in her expression, Anthony could see he was making progress. "Think of it Emma. These people wanted to hurt you by killing the things you loved. It would have been easier to just take you out, but they failed to successfully shoot you. If it was so important to kill you, and then to try and scare you multiple times, well, that means you're onto something."

Emma stopped shaking, and felt something creep back into her body. She thought about how her mother dismissed the only good memories she had of her father. She realized now that her mother had lied to her. She was jealous of the bond she had with her dad, and in her final days she'd sought to destroy that bond. Emma wasn't stupid. She had her father's desire to know more. To unravel mysteries and solve puzzles. How could her mother have been so cruel?

"Do you think that if you stopped looking into your father's death they'll leave you alone?" Anthony went on. "They'll only wait for you to let your guard down, and then kill you anyway. They can't afford to take the chance of you being out there, knowing what you do."

The anger Emma felt was building to rage now. They wanted to ruin her life just to keep whatever dirty secret they'd tried to bury? Well fuck them.

"Don't let them do it Emma….." Anthony felt himself getting caught up in her fury. These people had come after a person he was supposed to protect. And it was possible the danger was coming from people within his own organization. This wasn't just about Emma. Now he might be in danger too.

"Don't let them scare you off," Anthony was leaning in close to her ear, whispering now. "Don't give them what they want. Come with me, and let's figure a way out of this together. I can help you Emma. But you have to trust me. And we have to leave….now."

Emma thought of her father, placing the strange items in that safe deposit box, counting on her to find them, and to ask questions. She couldn't let him down now. She had to find out how he died, and who had turned on him. If those mother fuckers thought she was done they had another thing coming.

She returned Anthony's determined gaze. "What do you need me to do?" The resolve in her voice was all he needed to hear.

"Right! You finish packing. We can purchase whatever you forget if necessary. I'll call some people to take care of both Jeremy and your horse. I know a very good group of folks who can come right away. I have to use your phone downstairs to call Patricia. We don't want to leave Stella alone."

He wasted no time heading back down the stairs, and reaching for the green kitchen phone. He dialed the number he had memorized for the YMCA. It didn't take long for Patricia to get on the line.

"Anthony? What's going on?!" He never called during her class. He knew she enjoyed the few hours the painting class offered to create something all her own. If he was calling, something was wrong.

"I don't have time to explain darling," Anthony said in a steady and direct voice, "but there's been an accident here at the Woods place."

His wife cut him off. "Oh my god! Is Emma okay? I thought she was with you this morning! Is it Jeremy? What's happened?!"

Anthony loved his wife, but being honest with her would only put her in danger.

"Emma is fine dear. I'm taking her somewhere safe. Jeremy isn't here, so I need you to come take care of Stella. Could you bring her over to our place?"

Patricia sensed her husband wasn't telling the whole story. But she knew he was a solid force during emergencies, and she trusted him to take care of whatever had to be done.

"Alright," she agreed, "I'll leave right now."

Anthony would need more time. He should have contacted his people first. Damn! All this concern over Emma meant he was losing his touch.

"No," he told Patricia a little too sharply, "there's no need to leave straight away. Give me a few hours to pull things together here." The pause at the end of the line indicated Patricia was confused.

"There are things I need to take care of that I don't want you to deal with," he said quickly. Patricia knew he was being evasive, but didn't bother asking what "things" he was talking about.

"Alright honey. I'll wait here for a while okay? I love you."

Anthony felt his heart beat a little bit faster. Patricia was the only one capable of bringing on such a reaction from him.

"I'll call you when we land somewhere. Oh, and sweetheart, there's also the chickens. I imagine you'll have to feed them and whatnot," He wasn't sure if Patricia knew how to care for chickens, but he couldn't have Emma explain the process.

Too much time had passed already. He had to get going.

"I think they just need food and water. And you might want to close up the coop at night, alright. I'm sorry to leave you with all this."

His heart swelled once more when she answered. "It's okay honey. I'll take care of everything. Just let me know you're okay when you can."

"I will, and I love you too," he said, and hung up the phone. He left the kitchen, meaning to go back upstairs for Emma. But she was standing right outside the kitchen door, suitcase in hand and Stella at her side, panting.

"Why did you tell her Jeremy wasn't here?" she asked with almost childlike innocence.

For a moment, Anthony felt cornered. If he let her wallow in the dismal reality of her boyfriend's death they would get nowhere. They had to keep moving.

"Because he isn't Emma. Jeremy is not here. Leave Stella with me and get in my car. I'll be along, shortly."

Emma did as she was told, kissing her dog on the head before going out the screen door, letting it slam behind her out of habit.

Jeremy wouldn't hear it anymore. Anthony went back to the phone and dialed another number committed to memory.

His call was immediately answered.

"Yes," in a crisp voice he gave his code name, "this is Jupiter. I need a cleanup at the Woods place."

He paused while the person on the other end spoke. Stella looked at him, head cocked in curiosity.

"No," he continued, "I don't have time to explain, but I need you out here immediately. You only have about an hour's window. There's one fatality and some livestock damage. That's right, a horse to be exact. It's a bit of a mess I'm afraid."

Stella lumbered to the window to look out at her human. She began to whine when she saw Emma get in Anthony's car.

"No," Anthony continued, "there's no problem with the fatality. There's no surviving family, so just put him on hold. Maybe you could bury the horse somewhere nearby. There's a tractor in the barn, and a man's body on the haystack. Yes, quite bizarre, but I can explain later. Thank you."

He started to hang up, but thought of one more very important detail. Even with Patricia going directly to the coop to care for the chickens, she might not avoid seeing the killing field entirely.

"Make sure the blood in the surrounding area is cleaned up as much as possible, alright?" He ended the call and gently rubbed Stella's head. She looked up at him with soft eyes.

"You keep an eye on the place girl," he murmured to the dog in a soothing voice, "Auntie Patricia is coming for you." Stella watched as the man who usually gave her treats left, closing the door behind him.

Chapter 17
Reinforcements

Emma hated flying. It was scary to be so out of control. As the plane lifted off the tarmac she felt her stomach drop to her knees. She looked over at Anthony, sitting next to her, cool as ice and reading some kind of document. She tried to catch a peek at the print, but he held it just far enough away from her view. At least they were in first class. There was more leg room, and Emma accepted the champagne Anthony encouraged her to have.

"It will calm your nerves, dear," he said, "and perhaps help you sleep." They were on the redeye flight, and half of the passengers were already asleep.

She was just beginning to feel the warm glow brought about by the champagne, which tickled her nose when she drank it. Emma couldn't remember the last time she enjoyed so much luxury. Indulging herself had never been a priority in her life, and she became quite frugal after taking on the farm. She was uncomfortable with being comfortable, especially when she thought about the conditions that brought her here in first class. 'Lose your boyfriend and quiet life for flying first class…what a lousy trade off.'

She glanced again at the curious man sitting beside her, engrossed in the document, report, or whatever he was reading. How did this man manage to get plane tickets in such short notice, and in first class no less?

He and Patricia certainly didn't come across as poor, but neither did they have an opulent lifestyle. Maybe Anthony was able to pull their trip together because he was on some sort of frequent-flier program. He did travel a lot after all. She was trying to think about what she'd packed for their trip. She didn't care about toiletries or clothes. The most important thing was the notebook. The scribbled clues and addresses she had jotted down were tucked away into that binder, and they were essential to Emma learning more about her father's past. Anyway, she didn't have time to further speculate once the plane dipped to the right, giving her a view of the pastures below.

She wondered which field they would crash into, and if any farm animals would be taken out in the process. She thought of her goats, which led to her thinking of Patches. It made her heart ache, and she closed her eyes tight against the memories. Who cared if she died in a plane crash? What difference would it make now? The life she tried so hard to create on the farm was over. She wondered what people in town would think about how she left the place, with most of her animals mysteriously gone and her disappearing into the night? Yes, dying in a plane crash would eliminate all of her problems. The locals would say what a shame it was, what happened to Emma and Anthony. And they would wonder why the two of them were traveling together, and where they were going. Patricia and Leena would get a phone call about the tragic accident. How awful.

Anthony broke through her reverie by placing a hand on hers. "Are you alright Emma?" He asked, and when she opened her eyes she realized the grip she had on the armrest was making her arm ache. She blinked and nodded to her travel companion.

"Yeah," she said, knowing she wasn't going to convince him, "I'm fine. I was just thinking." Anthony looked at her and raised his eyebrows as if questioning what she could possibly be mulling over in her tortured head. How could he not understand that she had a lot to think about? There were the events of the last two weeks, the calamity and death that followed those days of chaos and confusion, the fact that she was traveling to an unknown destination, with a man she really didn't know. Yes, she had a lot to think about.

Anthony only patted her hand, and offered her a sympathetic smile.

"Try to avoid any thinking right now Emma. The plane is leveling off, so you should be able to sleep. Put the headset on that the flight attendant gave you." He then went back to his reading, and Emma decided to take his advice. She quickly tore the plastic off her sealed headset and plugged it into the socket just below her armrest. Pressing the dial until she found a classical station, she leaned the seat back and tried to focus on the strings playing a Mozart tune. Within minutes she was sleeping soundly.

Anthony pulled his eyes away from his paperwork, silently regarding the young woman beside him. Her head was turned toward the window, but the rhythmic rise and fall of her chest indicated she was out cold. He leaned his ear closer to hear the tune faintly playing through her headset. *'Hmmm, a fan of classical music,'* he thought. It felt strange to him, but having this in common gave him pleasure. She was sleeping, that was what mattered. It came as no surprise, considering the stress she'd been under. The champagne helped of course. And the mild sedative he slipped into her drink did the final trick. Anthony felt a pang of guilt about drugging the girl, but it was necessary. Not only did she need the rest, but he wanted to focus on the journey that lay before them.

Victor Tarlino, his contact at headquarters, wasn't pleased with how things had played out. "Disastrous" was the word used during their brief phone conversation. And Anthony was faced with explaining how things had gone so wrong. Then there were the incessant phone calls from Teddy, which he ignored. As a member of his team Teddy must have felt he was owed an explanation of recent events. But Anthony now viewed him as a possible connection in the death of Carter Woods. So it made perfect sense to circumvent Teddy and contact the lead man directly. He wouldn't mention his discovery of the photo in the old case file, not until he had time to do his own investigation on whatever role Teddy played in Carter's situation. "The situation" was how the lead referred to Carter's case, never acknowledging the man's guilt or innocence, but simply implying it was old news and not worth following up.

This struck Anthony as odd, considering the recent turn of events. No one on his team had any constructive ideas about who had taken a shot at Emma. They were late in upping surveillance on her. The alarm triggered by movement of the safety deposit box caught them all by surprise. Even Anthony, who knew her daily and weekly routine, was caught off guard. He assumed she went to the bank to withdraw cash, just as she had every month or so when things got tight. Everyone grew less interested in Emma as the years ticked by.

Carter was known to have obtained the safety deposit box before his move to Iran. His wife Anne paid a visit to the vault as well, once she returned from the Middle East as a widow. But it had been impossible to know what was placed into the box on either occasion. The agency knew that someone like Beekman, a younger but just as serious man back then, would never allow an opportunity for even a government agent to inspect a customer's safety deposit box. Orchestrating a break in would have been easy enough, but might have drawn too much attention.

Ultimately, an officer by the name of Simms had been assigned to compromise the safe deposit box. Simms was positively gleeful in describing how he'd gone about it. He was able to attach a micro transmitter, not much larger that a matchstick head, with a battery able to last for years, as it only worked when activated, and then relayed a signal to a transmitter nearby. The device was actually a kind of micro leveler. If the box was disturbed, the mercury within the device moved and sent a signal back to headquarters. All it took was slipping a wad of cash to Mr. Beekman's young employee, Joshua Miller. The young man had been excited to give the officer a tour of the bank, believing the man wished to open an account, and specifically a safe deposit box. Once inside the vault, Officer Simms had a private chat with the wide-eyed employee.

"I have a small favor to ask you Joshua," Simms had said while flashing his credentials. Upon glancing at the officer's badge Joshua became flustered. He was immediately swept up in the idea of assisting a government agent. "Sure," Joshua excitedly agreed. "How can I help?"

"It's nothing really," Simms said with a shrug. "We have reason to believe one of our own is up to no good. He owns a safe deposit box here, and we just want to keep tabs on it. All you need to do is look up the number of a box under the name of Carter Woods. You can stand right here while I check it out"

Joshua hesitated. Mr. Beekman had gone home sick. He never left the bank unless absolutely necessary, certainly not under the care of such a novice employee. But he'd caught some kind of flu, and had no choice but to leave the inexperienced Joshua to mind the bank. Mr. Beekman would know what to do about this stranger's request.

"Can you come back tomorrow?" Joshua pleaded. "The bank president could probably help you more than I could."

Officer Simms smiled at the young man. He couldn't be older than his mid-twenties. "Oh I don't think that will be necessary Joshua. I trust you, and I know Mr. Beekman would want you to help us." As Joshua wondered how this man knew the name of his boss, the officer went on. "We're willing to compensate you for your trouble, of course."

At this, Simms pulled out the cash and slipped it into Joshua's coat pocket. Joshua shook his head and moved to pull the money back out, but Simms stopped him, placing his hands on the kid's shoulders.

"Now there's one-thousand dollars your government is giving you for your assistance. There will be no trace of that money going to you, because this is a top secret operation." Simms knew that appealing to the younger man's sense of adventure would be a good move. "Mr. Beekman doesn't need to know about our little transaction. Just point out Carter Woods' box so that we know it's here. You don't even have to open it up. I'm only confirming that it exists."

Defenseless against the officer's suggestion and official bearing, Joshua had done just that. After looking at the vault register he had the officer follow him to the spot and pointed to the box. Officer Simms appeared to only brush the number with his hand, but the gesture allowed him to stick the device under the number plate. He turned back to Joshua. "Thank you for your service, your country appreciates it," Simms said dismissively.

Before Joshua Miller could respond Officer Simms was walking out of the vault and exiting the bank building.

Whatever rested in the safety deposit box did so quietly for many years, until it became unimportant to the CIA team assigned to Carter's case. When the outdated alarm, dormant for so long, was finally triggered by Emma, it sent the team scrambling. Anthony was immediately contacted, but he really should have known something was amiss before then. That was what was implied by the lead, who was his boss in a sense. Anthony had seen team leaders come and go, and he'd become used to handling things without too much interference or feedback. But the new lead didn't like how things had been recently churned up, and Anthony was left to feel he'd dropped the ball somehow. Sending Emma home while he checked into her father's file seemed prudent enough at the time. Nobody anticipated another attack so soon after the last one. Hell, they'd barely recognized the shooting at the bank as a genuine attempt on her life. After he whisked his shell shocked neighbor away on this flight to D.C., he swore he'd never let his guard down again.

What really angered him was the criticism he'd received from the man currently heading up his team. Victor Tarlino was one of many top guys rotated on and off the case, and he seemed to be a satisfied cog in government machinery. A heavyset man with a sloth-like countenance, Tarlino was only a few years younger than the man he replaced. Anthony had liked working with the other man, who gave him little trouble and allowed him to manage things on his own. However, when that lead retired, Tarlino was assigned as a replacement, and Anthony was immediately put off by his new boss's dismissive manner. Until things heated up, Victor couldn't have been less interested in the Carter case. When Anthony encouraged him to review the file Tarlino's response was irritating. "It's all ancient history," had been his answer to Anthony's suggestions, "what's the use of reading through a file that is of no consequence?"

Once Tarlino sensed trouble was brewing, and that it could reflect badly on him, he began barking like a junkyard dog. "How could you allow this to happen," he screamed at Anthony when the cleanup team reported back to him. "You were supposed to be keeping an eye on the girl!" Anthony resisted hanging up on his boss and ending the useless conversation. "I was instructed not to increase my surveillance even after reporting the shooting," he had answered Tarlino in an even tone that was absolutely meant to further infuriate his current boss.

"I believe I made it clear that there could be another party involved that fostered negative intent."

The rest of the phone call proved to be uninteresting to the seasoned officer, and Anthony put Tarlino off with the promise he would be contacted once he and Emma reached a safe place. He didn't bother letting the flustered man know they were headed to D.C., Anthony wanted to get Emma there in a quiet fashion, and settle her into his favorite safe house while he met with someone he could trust.

That man would be Jamison. He had taken David Jamison under his wing some years ago, mentoring the younger man in small ways that helped the recruit advance more quickly within the agency. They had met during one of Anthony's visits to the academy. He occasionally dropped in on a former colleague there, and usually managed to do a bit of scouting at the same time. Lately, Anthony had been entertaining the idea of taking time off, maybe do some traveling with Patricia. The job wasn't as satisfying as it used to be, and had even become boring. He wished to someday retire, but not until he found the right person to take on the job of watching Emma. He was proud of the way he kept an eye on her, and he didn't want the Company to hand off the case to just anyone. The day he was invited to watch the cadets train he noticed David right away.

The young man navigated a very challenging obstacle course with ease, and he was an exceptional marksman. After following his progress further, Anthony saw that David exhibited superior computer and technical skills, but was by no means an introverted geek like Teddy in the early days. His fellow cadets admired David because he was a reliable team player, a natural leader, and confidant without a speck of arrogance. To Anthony, he was the perfect replacement if the young man could be convinced to take on the job of looking after Carter's daughter.

He and David spoke briefly about the possibility of coming on board after graduation, but David didn't give an immediate answer. Ultimately, he was snapped up by the CIA and put in charge of his own operation almost straight away. Recognized as a shining star, David quickly advanced to more senior positions until landing a job last year as Deputy Chief of Station in Geneva. Anthony had kept in touch, and the two developed a friendship based on a mutual respect for one another. Now of course David wouldn't be interested in taking on the Woods case. He was far too busy in his new position. Even before the opportunities presented within the CIA, the young up-and-comer must have viewed the prospect of looking after Emma Woods as rather tedious and unexciting…up until now. With the new and troubling developments, Anthony was hoping to connect with David and get his take on things.

As it turned out, David would be in Washington this week, taking meetings at headquarters. He'd left a cryptic message for Jamison just before boarding the flight to D.C. Without revealing too much over a line that might not be entirely secure, he informed David that he was headed his way, and would be accompanied by "the subject" they discussed the month just before his graduation. That seemed so long ago now, but he tacitly referred to it in their conversation, and David implied he remembered the case. "Things have become more interesting David," Anthony said as a little tease, "I think you might be able to help me work out some kinks that have recently occurred. I'll call when I've landed." He knew David loved a challenge. He wouldn't be able to resist the chance to untangle the mess his case had become. Anthony would reveal his suspicions to the one person he could trust, and perhaps together they could get to the bottom of what was happening to Emma, and how her father tied in to it all.

Within the paperwork in his hands was an answer to a request that he be phased out of all his other assignments. Even before the troubles started, Anthony had made it known he wanted to devote all his attention on Emma Woods. With an eye toward retirement this would serve him well. After such a varied and intense career Anthony felt ready to slow things down. Looking after Emma was child's play and it would have meant less travel and more time with Patricia. His request for a lighter workload had been denied twice, but when this business with Emma started his request was reconsidered. Victor Tarlino may have been a lazy piece of shit, but he seemed to recognize the need for Anthony to focus all his energies on the Woods case. How ironic that the one operation he felt would free him up turned out to be the one that threw him back into the fray. The request for any new information on his solitary case had produced very little. This didn't surprise him, as data dried up shortly after Anne took the girls back home to the states. The case seemed to be as dead as Carter Woods was until now.

What really interested him was the background report on David Jamison, as it afforded him a closer look into the younger associate's past. He and David shared stories about their various assignments, and David was always particularly interested in hearing of Anthony's adventures during his early days in the CIA. But his friend rarely spoke of his own past. Perhaps he was the sort of person who preferred living in the present. The Company seemed to breed that kind of officer. But as their friendship grew, Anthony became all the more curious about David and wondered if he was hiding anything. He was able to obtain Jamison's dossier that held information collected when he applied for service with the CIA. To Anthony's pleasure it turned out that David had absolutely nothing to hide. For one thing, the recruit came from a very stable home with zero baggage. His parents were both retired Navy, father a pilot and mother a nurse. Better still was the fact that David's father went on to work for the CIA. He was retired now, and Anthony had never met him. But it seemed his son wanted to carry on in the trade, and it was yet another quality Anthony factored in when considering the young man as a possible alliance.

The coincidence of growing up with a fighter pilot dad was not lost on Anthony. David would have the background needed to understand Emma's own childhood experience. Perhaps he would even provide the empathy that Anthony never could. He also had a limited amount of serious relationships, one girl in high school and a longer stint with a young lady he met in junior college. That relationship had petered out once David joined the Academy, as long distance lovers often do. David Jamison was capable of forging a meaningful bond with someone; he might even become a family man at some point. But he wasn't ready to settle down yet. He was at the perfect place in his life to help Anthony with a case that had just recently sprung back to life, a case like Carter's. David was tailor-made to assist him because of his Middle East experience as well. After being snatched up by the Company, he was sent to Iran to take part in some lower level covert operations.

His Non-Official Cover was that of a language teacher providing instruction in English to residents in the Middle East. He was connected to a nonprofit that provided educational services to some of the poorer villages within Turkey and Pakistan, eventually finding work in Iran. Teaching as an American would have brought far too much suspicion. The decision was made to have him pose as a volunteer teacher from a school in Ireland. That meant a stint at the agency's language school in Monterey, California. Once David had acquired a proper Irish accent, and the papers proving his new identity, he was on his way to the Middle East.

He exuberantly expressed his interest in the Middle East to Anthony from the very beginning.

"It's a fascinating culture," the young man gushed. "Too many people imagine that part of the world as backward and full of Muslim zealots. But the reality is much more nuanced, I think. It would be interesting to really become immersed in a place like Afghanistan or Iran."

David got his wish, and appeared to have done quite well in his work in the Middle East. It was one of the reasons he'd advanced so quickly and was now Deputy Station Chief. No doubt he still had his finger on the pulse of that region. His connections in Iran could prove very useful to Anthony…and Emma. He sighed. What to do about Emma? She was a problem he'd pushed out of his mind while they were escaping Oregon. He wondered if she was up to the task of staying focused and following directions. She had surprised him up to now. In spite of all she'd been through she had remained very brave. Perhaps it was her anger that kept her going.

Chapter 18
The Company Man

Emma shifted in her seat, muttering something indiscernible in her sleep. Anthony watched until she settled down again, and he wondered if she was still keeping something from him. He was aware of her conversation with Charlotte Nirody. Emma's phones had been tapped long ago, with very little to show for his efforts. Anthony suffered through the boring jibber-jabber between Emma and her sister more times than he cared to remember. But Emma's tentative prodding into Nirody's whereabouts was a real red flag. What did this man have to do with Carter?

Of course, he'd also known she visited the library. He had followed her there and waited until she reappeared an hour later. While she crossed the street, presumably to reach the grocery store, Anthony ducked into the library. It didn't take much for him to glean information from the librarian. After identifying himself as Emma's uncle, sent back on behalf of his niece, Clara was only too willing to get her research written down once more. His overworked and overwhelmed niece had lost the note card full of information he told Clara, shaking his head and rolling his eyes. When he exited the library, Emma had disappeared, and Anthony assumed she'd finished her shopping and gone home. But he hadn't really seen her leave. Now he knew, that was when she'd encountered the man in the store that threatened her, who no doubt had been following her, along with a team of others. He wondered how many were in this marauding team. Not knowing who he was dealing with made him uneasy. Believing they might be somehow associated with the agency he'd been proud to serve made him physically ill.

After a long career that involved reading people, he knew instinctively Emma was still holding back. He would have to pull from her whatever she was hiding when they settled into the safe house. He went back to reviewing the documents listing David Jamison's impressive test scores.

      Emma was walking in the pasture. At least, she seemed to be in the pasture, though it was a deeper green than she remembered, and she was gliding more than walking. Her precious goats grazed happily, the three horses alongside them doing the same. 'Who had let the horses in with the goats?' she wondered. A soft breeze stirred the grass and blew hair into her eyes. She pushed it aside so that she could view the rest of her property. The barn wasn't in the right place. It was up on a hill she couldn't recognize, but this didn't concern her. She felt something soft brush against her legs, and when she looked down she found a few of her chickens were walking/gliding with her, and Stella was following close behind. *'Aw Stella,'* she thought, *'what a good girl! You're not chasing the chickens like you usually do.'*

She would go check on Jeremy now. He would be up by the house, playing some awful song on his guitar. He was waiting for her, she was sure of it. Somehow, just by thinking about it, she was instantly standing on the path leading to her porch. Just a few steps would take her there, where Jeremy's guitar rested in the porch swing going back and forth. Was the wind blowing it? And where was Jeremy? Every step she tried to take toward the porch seemed to push her further away from it. She was no longer gliding; more like swimming through mud. The animals had disappeared, and the sky was getting darker. The soft breeze turned to a cold wind, and rain began to pummel her face and bare arms. But she could see someone coming from the house. It was Jeremy! He walked onto the porch and picked up his guitar, only he wasn't going to play. Instead he turned to walk back inside. She tried to call him.

'Jeremy! I'm here!'

She was certain she was yelling, but she couldn't hear herself. Jeremy turned around and cupped his hand to yell back at her.

"I did it right Em," he was trying to shout at her, but it came to her like a whisper.

'What are you talking about?' Emma yelled back, or was she just thinking the words?

"The horses," he said with a smile, "I took care of them just the way you wanted."

Then he pointed behind her, so she could see the good job he'd done, she guessed. Emma turned to look back at the pasture, and saw all of her animals laying in bizarre positions amidst pools of blood, with Patches crumpled up at her feet, a white heap lying next to him that she realized was her dog. Every single animal she owned was dead, even the chickens…even Stella! 'No!' she tried to scream. Stella couldn't be dead, too! She tried to look through a cloudy haze back at Jeremy, but he was lying on the porch stairs, just as she'd found him in the barn that horrible day. His eyes were open, staring at her without blinking, and he had that serene expression on his face as if everything was just fine.

'This isn't real,' Emma thought to herself. *'None of this can be real!'*

She had to wake Jeremy up, and then everything would be okay. But she still couldn't reach him. No matter how hard she tried to run to the porch stairs, they remained just out of reach.

'Jeremy!'

She yelled harder this time, so he could hear her, but nothing came out.

'Jeremy, wake up! Let's get out of here!' "Jeremy!"

This time the words came out so that she could hear them. Bolting upright, she realized she was still on the plane, drenched in sweat and wondering if she'd really screamed Jeremy's name out loud. She soon understood that every passenger in first class had heard her doing just that. Emma was horrified to see so many bleary eyes staring at her in confusion. Worst of all was the way Anthony was regarding her. His withering look made her shiver, and she sunk back into her seat, wrapping her sweater over her shoulders like a safety net. Anthony blinked once, and the angry look was gone.

"Ah, you're awake," he flatly stated, as if she hadn't just made a complete fool of herself.

"Yeah," she murmured, looking around in embarrassment at the other passengers. "I guess I had a bad dream." This explanation appeared to satisfy everyone, though a few stole worried glances at her. Anthony ignored them and began to pack up his briefcase.

"We'll be landing soon. You might want to gather up your things."

Theodore Alberts was not a happy man. Not that he ever felt truly happy, or even close to content. Most of his days were consumed with determining who had slighted him, and how he could seek revenge against them. He hadn't always been so bitter. Long ago, when he first joined the Company, he'd been hopeful of accomplishing great things, things that would get him attention and allow him to move ever higher up in rank. He even dared to dream of one day running the Company himself. However, little by little something, or more specifically, someone, would get in his way. His performance would be given a poor rating, or someone would be promoted over him.

One such person who always seemed to thwart his progress was Anthony Newcastle. And it was this man who was leading to Theodore's unhappiness at the moment. Indeed, it seemed as if Newcastle frequently got in the way of his success within the Company. Theodore had been overlooked back in the seventies when the operation involving Carter was first developed. He was sure that he was in line for the promotion that would put him in charge of the entire team. But somehow Newcastle wormed his way in, leaving Theodore once again merely part of the team. His latest bid for advancement had foundered when he expressed interest in the position of Deputy Director of Operations. It would place him over Anthony in glorious fashion, but that job went to Victor Tarlino.

A poorer excuse for a man Theodore could not imagine, and Tarlino certainly did not deserve the DDO spot. The only advantage of having this man as a boss was that he was an approved member of one of the larger schemes Theodore became involved in long ago. This made it easier for Theodore to call the shots whenever that very clandestine operation was threatened. It gave Alberts a comforting sense of power to be in control of keeping that operation quiet, and in certain cases, Tarlino kept his nose out of what those shadow teams were doing.

This served the seasoned officer well, who was now intent on skirting the usual pathways to the top. Over the years Theodore managed to build alliances of his own, most of them unapproved and unknown to his superiors. But they had helped him to build a network of his own containing men who would do his bidding. Work that, if discovered, would more than sully Theodore's reputation. It would completely dash all of his ambitions to advance in his field. He'd almost been caught a few times by Anthony, and he knew there was no trust between the two of them. Anthony often did whatever he wanted without so much as a memo to Theodore. Well, Anthony's days of going over his head were done. He would make sure of that.

Yesterday's visit from Lewis was the final straw. Lewis "Lou" Anderson was a newer member of this particular team. Only brought in five years ago when another member went on medical leave, Lou was good at the administrative side of things, filling out reports and following orders. But Theodore saw he lacked the imagination and ruthlessness needed to be of any service to him. A personable and chatty man, he always seemed to connect with other officers. In this respect Theodore found him useful in keeping tabs on what everyone else was up to. Lou popped his head into Theodore's office yesterday afternoon while the older man was wrapping up reports of his own.

"Hey Theo," Lou chirped, "how's it hangin'?"

Theodore hadn't answered, or even looked up at the intrusion. He hated the shortening of his name just as much as he hated being called Teddy. He also detested the manner in which Lou simply burst into his office, interrupting his work in order to engage in chit-chat. He almost ordered the annoying officer out of his office, until Lou shared his latest tidbit of shared information.

"That's some pretty freaky stuff goin' on over at the Woods' place, right? You gotta wonder what's happening with that Emma girl."

Theodore paused at his computer and felt his shoulders tighten up. Any mention of Emma Woods was cause for concern in Theodore's mind. He didn't like to admit his lack of knowledge regarding anything involving Carter's case, but he guessed he didn't have the time to delicately extract from Lewis what he knew.

"Sorry Lewis, I've been working, and know nothing about anything "freaky" that occurred at Miss Woods' farm. Perhaps you could fill me in."

Theodore's sarcasm was lost on Lou, who was pleased to share the news.

"A cleanup crew was called out there yesterday. There was one civilian to pick up, but that wasn't a problem, cos' the guy had no family. The problem was trying to find a way to haul off a dead horse! They had to use a special winch and a tractor to dig a hole for it and everything. Newcastle called it in. 'Just gave the order to get rid of all the evidence and then disappeared. Can you imagine the balls of that guy?!"

Lou laughed at his boss's audacity, but Theodore was not amused. Anthony had done it again. Not one word to him about something he had every right to know. Of course, some of it he was already well aware of. That wasn't the point. Newcastle intentionally kept him out of the loop, and somehow Victor Tarlino had allowed it. The doddering fool probably didn't even know Anthony was breaking from his team. But Anthony seemed determined to handle the Woods case on his own, and Theodore needed to know why. And who was the "civilian" who apparently got caught in the cross hairs? This went beyond petty annoyance. He had too much at stake and he couldn't let Newcastle stumble onto anything incriminating. He looked at Lewis, still casually perched on his threshold and looking at him like a dolt.

"Lewis, did Anthony say where he was going? Did he give any details as to what happened out there? It seems to me he should have given us his destination at the very least."

Lou shrugged and shook his head. "Nope, not a word. But you know how Newcastle is. He's always acting like he's got better things to do than work with us, you know?"

Lewis didn't realize how much in agreement Theodore was with this observation.

"Yeah," he drawled with a disapproving look, "He's never been a real team player. And we all suffer as a result."

The comment didn't seem to register with Lou. He pushed himself off Theodore's door and turned to walk back down the hall. Theodore stopped him. "Lewis, what about the girl?" The question was forefront in his mind, but he didn't want Lewis to know that.

"What girl?" Lou gave him a confused look that infuriated Theodore. *'What an idiot!'* he thought, until the junior officer offered one last detail.

"Oh! You mean the Woods girl! Yeah, Emma is gone too."

"You mean she's been killed?" Theodore tried to control the twitch that began in his left eye. If Emma was dead that ruined everything.

"No! No she's not dead, man. She's just gone. Anthony must've taken her somewhere."

And with that, Lou turned on his heel and headed back down the hallway, whistling to himself.

Chapter 19
Showing Some Cards

Emma sat in the passenger seat of the Ford Taurus Anthony had rented for their stay in D.C. She'd wondered why they were headed for the nation's capital when Anthony handed her a ticket in the Baker City Regional Airport. Anthony must have anticipated her question, because he explained as they made their way to the gate.

"There are people in D.C. I've known for years. They're the ones I was speaking of when you and I met in the café. I believe they'll be very helpful." Emma left it at that, but quietly started to look at Anthony in a different way.

The questions continued to swirl around her head even as they drove away from the Dulles Airport. Why was Anthony now so keen on helping her? Was it simply because he could now see how much danger she was in, or did something else motivate him? He was always nice enough to her when she came to visit Patricia, but he never seemed particularly altruistic. Other than his obvious devotion to his wife, he came across as a loner. Not self-centered exactly, but distant, off in his own world with very little patience for other people. And ever since she'd let him in on what was happening to her, he seemed downright angry! She thought that anger was directed at her, for being a hysterical woman, or a careless one. She wasn't sure he even liked her. But when he talked her into leaving with him, the anger was gone. Suddenly he had become her champion, and now she wondered if his anger was actually directed toward someone else, some unseen enemy they both now shared. Even so, she kept her notebook a secret. There wasn't much Anthony didn't know about her circumstances, but the few things she'd held back felt important to her now. She hadn't told him about Zanders, and she wasn't sure she would repeat to him anything she learned from Northrop Grumman. The meager snippets of information held in her notebook were her ace-in-the-hole, just in case Anthony ended up letting her down. Or worse, betraying her altogether.

And who were these people in Washington that he'd known for so long? Did he used to work there? Patricia never spoke about where they lived before moving to Baker City. It just never came up, and Emma assumed they'd always lived in Oregon. There was one thing of which Emma was certain; there was more to Anthony's job in the export business. When he found her huddled in the closet with Stella, and then learned what happened to Jeremy and her horse, he handled everything with a coolness she'd never seen in him, or anyone else for that matter. He moved mighty fast for a typical businessman, and the sight of death brought about by violence hadn't fazed him a bit. No, there was something more to Anthony Newcastle, a lot more.

She turned her head to watch the man who was taking her god knows where. He maintained the calm he'd displayed from the day before, and he drove as if he hadn't a care in the world. Making his way from the airport and then through the streets of Washington without so much as glancing at a map, he obviously knew where he was going.

Anthony felt Emma's eyes on him, and decided it was the ideal time to tell her a few things, though not everything of course. This conversation would be best while they were alone in the car.

"Are you tired Emma?" He wanted to make sure she was emotionally strong before launching into the explanation she was waiting for.

"I'm okay, just a little groggy," Emma said softly, turning her eyes back to the road.

"You'll feel better after getting some rest." He tried to sound reassuring. "We'll be staying at a friend's house in Georgetown. You can nap for a bit and then we'll have dinner."

Emma looked back at him with concern. "I haven't packed anything nice. I mean, I was just throwing things in my bag, so I really don't know what I have."

'Just like a woman, to panic over what to wear,' Anthony thought smugly, though he knew Patricia would have chastised him for being misogynistic. "Oh, we won't be going out. I can make dinner where we're staying. We'll have company, however, one of the people I think can lend us a hand."

Emma tried to picture Anthony cooking a meal. It didn't seem likely he was any good at it, but one never knew. She loved the idea of a nap, but wasn't looking forward to meeting anyone. Her nerves were still ragged from yesterday's events. Had it only been yesterday? She shook her head to clear the memory of it.

Anthony misread the gesture. "It's alright Emma. The person you're meeting won't expect you to be well-dressed. He won't even wish to engage in sparkling conversation. He'll be there solely to discuss your situation."

His words helped to set her mind at ease. At least this was a step forward in the quest for answers. Plunging into the unknown with Anthony may have been a reckless decision, but she felt it had been the only path she could have taken. Now they were on their way, toward something. "Something is better than nothing at all," her dad's words drifted into her head. It was one of his favorite sayings. Well, anything was better than staying in Baker City surrounded by bad memories.

Anthony's next statement startled her. "I think you need to know something about me before we proceed any further."

Emma said nothing. She just stared straight ahead at the traffic, waiting.

"As you may have guessed, I don't work in the export business, not exclusively anyway." He looked over at her for a moment, wondering how much to disclose, and deciding the less he told her the better, for her own sake.

"I'm not at liberty to say what exactly I do for a living, but I can assure you that it's legal, and I've been doing it for some time. I do it quite well, and that's not vanity on my part but simply the truth." He waited for a reaction, but received none. So he went on.

"The upside of this is that I'm in a unique position to help you Emma. I normally wouldn't put myself out for someone in this way, and I admit I have my own reasons for wanting to help you. But if you do as I say, and remain brave, then I'll do my best to look more deeply into your father's death, and hopefully prevent your own, in the process."

Emma turned to him with a look he could only decipher as one of suspicion.

"And how, exactly, am I supposed to accept what you say as the truth?" she shouted [demanded]. "Yes, Anthony," she went on, "I figured out you were something more than just a regular businessman. I'm not stupid, and I'm not going to just follow you like a dog as you pull me along in this fucked up little adventure we're having."

Anthony hadn't been prepared for this kind of pushback. "I never said you were stupid..." he began.

"And if you think I'm going to be a brave little girl while bullets fly and everything I care about is taken from me you've got another thing coming! I never asked for your protection, and it's a good thing, because so far it seems like you're not very good at providing it. I just needed a little help in understanding why people are trying to kill me. If you know something about all this bullshit you better tell me right now. As the one they're trying to kill, I think I have the right to know!"

'Oh god,' he thought, 'I've released a hornet's nest now.' "What is it you need to know?" He kept his voice calm and his eyes on the road, but inside Anthony was seething. Hadn't he saved this woman's life? She had no idea how easily she could have been taken out if not for him.

"I want to know whatever it is that connects you to this situation, and to me. What do you know about my dad? How can I even be sure you won't just abandon me somewhere?"

This was not the response he was hoping for. Deep down Anthony couldn't blame her for the lack of trust she had in him, or for anyone for that matter. Maybe if he filled her in on at least some of the details she would be more agreeable.

"Alright," he proclaimed, "let's start on my connection to you. The people for whom I work have had your family under surveillance ever since it was suspected your father had been led astray. I was assigned to keep an eye on your mother before you returned home, and after she passed away I was responsible for looking after you. Well, not exactly looking after you, but watching to see if anything came of your father's alleged treason. I say *'alleged'* because I've recently come to believe all is not as it seems regarding his case. That is why I'm helping you, because I feel we've both been duped. I don't know if your father was falsely accused or not. But someone doesn't want you to look further into it. They may know by now that I'm helping you, and that muddies the waters considerably. Still, I don't want my record sullied by letting you get in harm's way."

He went on, not wanting to give her false hope. "We may not learn anything, you understand? I can only quietly investigate on your behalf. I don't want to compromise my position, or draw any undue attention to myself, because that would lead to you. Since I can't be certain of who's after you, I can't leave you exposed. For all I know, the very people wishing you harm are doing their best to find you now."

This brought on a look of apprehension from Emma, and he regretted saying it, true though it might be.

"I don't want to alarm you. I was very careful to see that we left quickly and without a trace. But we must be proactive, and remain one step ahead of these people. Are you hearing me?"

"And that's all you're willing to tell me? It's not much if you want me to trust you," Emma said, though the doubt was beginning to fade from her eyes.

He made one last attempt at gaining her confidence.

"You'll have to trust me Emma. I know that's not easy for you, especially now. But I have an idea on how to help you, and I'm willing to try. It will have to be enough for you." Why was he sticking his neck out, he wondered? It wasn't as if he could be certain this had anything to do with him. He was working off a faded photograph and a hunch. But his instincts usually served him well, and like Emma, he had quite a lot to lose, if he was right.

The two of them rode in silence for a while, until Emma softly spoke. "Anthony?" It was almost a whisper.

"Yes." He answered, trying to anticipate what was coming from this girl.

"Can you tell me one thing?" She couldn't read his face, so she asked the question that had been in the back of her mind.

"Can you at least tell me if you're working for our government? You're not some kind of foreign spy or something, right?" She knew it was a stupid question. Why would he admit to such a thing? He could be just as bad as or worse than the people that were after her. But she had to ask.

He considered her request. Of course she was doing her best to protect herself. Why not give her an honest answer?

"Yes Emma," he flatly stated before turning into the driveway of a red brick, two-story home, set back from the street.

"I work for the United States government. Let's get you inside."

Chapter 20
Officer Jamison

David was going to be late. Not that Anthony would mind. His friend knew how needlessly long and drawn out meetings could become at headquarters. They both detested the bureaucracy that creaked along, hindering officers in the performance of their duties. David had hoped his scheduled appointment with the Chief of Station would yield solutions to some of the problems he was having in the field and with recruiting from his base in Switzerland. But he was met with budget issues, and demands that he provide more complete reports. What a waste of time. If it weren't for the opportunity to see Anthony he would have considered the entire trip a flop.

He enjoyed his time with Anthony Newcastle. The man never failed to provide an interesting point of view on the latest international goings on. And the stories of his past adventures were delightfully entertaining. More than that, David felt he had found a trusted confidant in the older and wiser officer. He didn't see Anthony as a father figure, not exactly. He was more of a mentor than anything else, and he had entered David's life when he'd needed just that. As a young recruit, David felt unsure about the direction his training would take him. The work of an officer appealed to him, and he'd even considered Anthony's offer to eventually take his place in the Woods case. But he wanted more. Even Anthony had to admit the young man was better suited to more challenging work, and he encouraged David to aim high.

"You can do anything you set your mind to," his friend advised. "Don't limit yourself to a menial desk job. You need something that will keep you on your toes, and stimulate you on a daily basis."

Anthony had been right, of course. He'd been right about many things, and David appreciated the help his friend offered in navigating the Company. When he was offered the job of Deputy Chief he immediately called Anthony.

"A plum position young man!" the seasoned officer cheered, "definitely a job you can sink your teeth into. Well done!"

David had to admit that he was pleased with his friend's reaction. He didn't purposefully seek Anthony's approval, but he liked the sound of pride in Anthony's voice when he learned David would be moving to Geneva.

It was well past six by the time he pulled into the driveway, and dusk was darkening the stately old home he knew so well. He and Anthony had both used the house as a sort of base whenever they were in D.C. It was owned by a friend of Anthony's wife, Patricia. She and the woman attended Bryn Mawr together, and the friend had married well, then divorced and moved to Europe. She offered Patricia use of the house, and carte blanche in deciding who else bedded down there from time to time. It was luxury compared to the places CIA employees normally stayed. Best of all, nobody else within the Company knew of it, so it felt a little like a hideout to David whenever he flew in from Geneva. He knew Anthony was holed up there for the time being, trying to decide what to do with Emma Woods.

Once they'd landed and made their way to the car rental desk, Anthony called David. Emma hovered nearby, trying to catch snippets of Anthony's side of the conversation. He gave David a brief outline of what had occurred out in the wilds of Oregon. David knew his friend had been winding down his work in other operations. He couldn't imagine the once, very active officer settling into such a dull existence. Sure, Anthony still went abroad on various missions. But it wasn't anything close to what he'd been doing when he was David's age.

Patricia was, no doubt, the motive for his desire to slow things down, and David couldn't blame him. She was good for him, keeping him grounded and happy for the first time in his life. That's what Anthony had said, and David was a little jealous of how content the man obviously was. Everything apparently went to shit when the Woods girl got in trouble. He wasn't exactly sure how the daughter of a traitorous ex-Navy pilot could become a moving target. But according to Anthony, she'd managed it, and possibly put Anthony in a bad position along the way. The dinner invitation from Anthony came with the caveat that David lend him a hand in some way. He would hear his friend out, but what could he do? He was leaving first thing in the morning to head back to Switzerland.

David parked his rental out of sight behind the garage, and walked quickly through the arbor that led to the side door. He tapped on the door as a courtesy. Both he and Anthony had a key to this place, but to use it would have been rude. His knock was immediately answered by Anthony, wearing a chef's apron and holding a wooden spoon with something dripping off of it and onto the side entry floor.

"Good, you're here!" Anthony gave his friend's shoulder a jovial punch before turning back to his project at the kitchen stove. David followed him into the kitchen where two pots were cooking on the stove top, one bubbling furiously. Anthony dipped the spoon into the other one and tentatively sipped some brown liquid. The younger man pulled up a chair from the wooden trestle table to watch. He slouched with his arms crossed, long legs stretched out before him, carefully regarding his mentor. As ever, Anthony was full of surprises.

"I didn't know you could cook." It was almost a question, because although his friend was indeed cooking, that didn't necessarily mean his efforts would produce anything edible.

"Yes, I can cook!" Anthony responded defensively. "Patricia has been teaching me. It didn't seem fair that the job should always fall upon her."

David smiled and nodded. He admired the way Anthony put his wife first in just about everything.

"What are we having? I wouldn't think you'd have time to get groceries if you just came from the airport."

Anthony didn't turn around, but kept stirring the sauce. "I'm making a béarnaise sauce for some steaks you had in the freezer. I found some potatoes in the pantry as well. I hope you didn't have any plans for the steaks."

161

"Not anymore." David teased. He liked having supplies on hand at this place. His per diem stretched much further when he purchased groceries instead of going out to eat all the time.

"I'm sorry I'm late. My meeting ran long."

Anthony's spoon hovered briefly over the sauce, dripping into the pot while he wondered if he should confide in David about the Carter case. Was it possible something might slip in any conversation he had with the Chief of Station? Stirring the sauce once more and pretending only a mild interest in David's meeting he asked, "Does the COS have any questions about your current work"?

David shifted in his chair, already bored with the topic. "No, I mean he's aware I'm responsible for a number of clandestine operations, but they're all kept in very small compartments. There's only one project, code-named Dark Whisper, that we're wrapping up and involved budget restraints."

Anthony gave a knowing look over his shoulder. "The meeting was not fruitful I suspect?"

"Nope," David answered with a shrug. "Damn COS talked my ear off and didn't let me get a word in."

Anthony shook his head over a thickening sauce. The Chief of Station was known to hijack conversations. The younger officers were often too intimidated to interrupt.

"Just talk over him, when you have to," Anthony advised, "I know that gentleman pretty well. He won't take it personally."

David said nothing, lost in thought over how to make his trip count for something.

"Hey," he realized why his friend called him. "How did you get the Woods girl here? And what's with all the secrecy? Sounds as if you don't trust your own team."

Anthony turned off the flame from under the finished sauce. "I trust all but one. Theodore Alberts."

David recognized the name. Anthony had told him more than one story about Alberts and his attempts to wrestle control over his colleagues' assignments. He seemed to have a real competitive streak when it came to Anthony. "Oh god, that guy?! He's always giving you shit. What's gotten up his ass this time?" Anthony turned down the potatoes and came over to join David at the table.

"I think I'd better start at the beginning and fill you in, before Emma comes down.

Hopeless. Her hair was hopeless. She woke up feeling refreshed, just as Anthony said she would. The shower had helped too, but all she found in the bathroom were men's products, and no hair dryer. She let her hair air dry while she unpacked, but that always made her curls go crazy. Damnit, she looked like a wild woman. At least she'd been able to procure a dress from her bag, slightly wrinkled from being hastily thrown in during their frantic departure. The only thing that closely resembled presentable shoes was a new pair of Keds, never worn and still lily white.

'Oh well, it'll have to do,' she thought to herself. "It's not like I have anyone to impress."

Anthony's tap on her door an hour ago drew her out of a deep, but thankfully dreamless sleep.

"Emma, dinner will be ready in an hour," she heard him say through the door. "You might want to clean up a bit as we're having a guest."

She supposed his guest would be someone much like him; an older, sort of schlubby man who "worked in the government." She didn't care what he looked like. She wouldn't even care if he was perpetually grumpy, as Anthony always seemed to be, as long as he could help her.

She finished dressing and tried running a brush through her hair, to no avail. Grabbing a sweater she began to leave the room, but stopped and pulled the notebook out of her suitcase. Looking around for a good hiding place, she decided on the bed, and slipped the thin book under the mattress. Adjusting the covers back and giving the bed a pat, she made her way out of the room, down the stairs and through the fancy dining room that looked like it could easily seat fifteen people. Even though Anthony said this guy could help her, she dreaded meeting him.

She didn't know what her mysterious neighbor was cooking, but it smelled wonderful! Emma's stomach growled, reminding her she hadn't eaten in quite a while. She longed to sit down and enjoy a hot meal, but the voices she heard in the kitchen stopped her. She stepped closer and leaned one ear against the door, trying to make out what was being said.

"You can come in now Emma. Dinner's ready." Anthony's voice made her jump. How did he know she was standing there, eavesdropping? Embarrassed, she gently pushed at the swinging door and walked in, blushing.

Anthony was standing at the stove, serving up food while wearing an apron that had the words "Fuck Off. I'm cooking" emblazoned in red on the front. Emma blinked at the sight, and then noticed a man sitting at the head of the table, half-reclined in one of the chairs. He was good looking, but not chiseled and perfect, like those annoying models in the Abercrombie & Fitch posters. This man was handsome in an effortless way, blond hair slightly tousled as if he couldn't be bothered to comb it. His suit fit him well, but was a little rumpled, the tie loosened and askew. He seemed to have been in deep conversation with Anthony until she walked in. Now he met Emma's gaze with green eyes and took in her thrown-together look. The dress was slightly creased, but he thought the blue set off her eyes. Were her eyes blue, or gray? Whatever the color, they weren't enhanced by a speck of makeup, and he found this refreshing.

Emma noticed him looking at her dress and self-consciously smoothed the front of it over with her hands.

Oblivious to her discomfort, Anthony continued to stir, only nodding toward the man. "I'm sorry dear, I haven't introduced you. This is my friend David. David, this is Emma Woods."

Gracefully pulling his legs in and standing, David turned and extended a hand toward Emma. "It's a pleasure to meet you Emma," he said with a disarming smile. "Anthony was just telling me about your farm in Oregon."

David had become skilled at making people feel at ease during the first introduction. They were more apt to let their guard down, allowing him to detect any insecurity or quirks that might later serve him. With a pleasant demeanor and subtle charm, he could easily mask the fact that he was sizing people up. It was a habit he found useful whenever he encountered strangers.

Emma reached across the table and returned his handshake. He seemed nice enough, though his easy going manner felt somewhat rehearsed.

"I made steak with mashed potatoes Emma," Anthony announced. "But the only vegetables I can offer are frozen peas." He finished serving up the food and walked past the two younger people with a plate in each hand, placing the dishes down on the trestle table that was nicely set with matching place mats, napkins and silverware.

"I thought it would be cozier eating here in the kitchen. The dining room can be a bit drafty. Emma, please have a seat," he offered. "I'm sure you're starving. Both you and David can start eating while I fetch my plate."

Emma moved to sit at the chair closest to her, while David sat back down in his.

"Anthony tells me you've retired from teaching, in an effort to manage your family's farm," David said conversationally. "That's quite an abrupt change. How are you adapting?"

Emma allowed herself to revel in the brief moment of simple conversation. It had been too long since she'd actually exchanged pleasantries with another human being, and she liked the normalcy of it.

"While I had the chance to do it, I really loved farming," she answered his question, though she imagined he was only asking out of politeness. "I don't think I've had a moment to even worry about my animals. Anthony, have you been in touch with Patricia? Do you think she needs help?"

Anthony took off his apron and hung it in the pantry. "I thought it best to keep my contact with her to a minimum for now," he answered. "I'll contact her soon, but I'm sure she'll manage just fine. David, there's a nice bottle of cabernet in here. I'm sure it would go nicely with the steak. Does that sound appropriate?"

"Yeah, great!" David said over his shoulder but never taking his eyes off Emma. He was watching for signs of fear or uncertainty. In spite of the concern for her animals, she appeared relatively steady. He would have expected someone far more unglued, having been through all she had. Was her desire to investigate her father so deep that she'd been able to rise above it all?

"I understand you've been dealing with some frightening events," he ventured. I hope you don't mind Anthony filling me in. I'm sorry your life has been so violently interrupted."

Emma suppressed the urge to cry. The farm, and all of her plans surrounding it, seemed like an impossible dream now. David's kindness made her loss more acute. She felt sorry for Jeremy, for Patches and her goats, and mostly for herself. As she thought of how unfair it all was, her simmering anger returned. All of the pain associated with her father had to count for something. She needed to know now if this man could help her. In an effort to change the subject, she turned the conversation back to him.

"So how did you and Anthony meet? Are you in the same line of business?" She didn't mean the export business, and she hoped David would clarify how his job in the government might help her get some answers.

Just then, Anthony popped open the wine bottle and smiled. Emma was being nosy, no doubt trying to veer the conversation toward the issue of her father. Now wasn't the time.

"We can discuss all that later," he declared, and poured a healthy portion of wine for Emma. After serving himself and David, he took his seat at the head of the table.

"Cheers!" Anthony proclaimed with a smile, raising his glass and waiting for his guests to raise theirs as well. They dutifully did so, and everyone took a sip.

"Um, good wine," he murmured, before attacking his steak with knife and fork. All three silently ate for a moment.

Emma wasn't about to be put off. She had to be sure she wasn't wasting her time with this stranger. She tried to draw him out once more. "So what is it exactly that you do David? Are you some sort of politician or legal aide?"

Anthony remained focused on his steak, and David balked at revealing too much of his connection with the agency. This woman was determined, and he had to admire her tenacity. To brush off her questions would seem rude, but he was uncomfortable with talking about himself. That wasn't how he played the game.

The problem was her hair. The unruly auburn locks had been hastily thrown up in some kind of ribbon. The way it fell over her eyes was very distracting. He looked to his friend for an out, and receiving none he answered her original, and far less probing, question.

"Anthony and I met while working on similar projects." He fudged the facts to keep from lying outright. "We have mutual acquaintances, but we're both easily bored with most social gatherings. I guess that's why we always ended up huddled in a corner, discussing history."

Anthony laughed in agreement and reached for the béarnaise sauce. He poured a liberal amount on his steak before offering some to Emma.

"You must try the sauce Emma," trickling the rich sauce over her steak before she had a chance to decline. "I'm really very proud of how it turned out."

David avoided further questioning by Emma. "Everything is delicious Tony. It's impressive what you did with whatever's on hand."

"Tony?!" Emma couldn't believe she'd repeated the astonishing nickname out loud. She looked at David and then Anthony. Never once had she heard anyone call the proper British man anything but Anthony, not even Patricia.

"Yes, well I don't mind David calling me Tony," he said gruffly before taking another bite of steak, "so long as the term doesn't gain popularity."

He glowered a bit at Emma, causing her to look down and tend to her own plate. Taking a bite of the steak, she let the perfectly thickened sauce slide down her throat. Her empty stomach leapt for joy, her questioning of David temporarily discarded.

"This is really good Anthony," she said through a full mouth.

Anthony smiled, and took another sip of wine. "Well, finish up and then we'll discuss your recent troubles Emma. We'll want David to give us his full attention."

Chapter 21
Camaraderie

After dinner they all sat down in front of a roaring fire in the living room, finishing off the bottle of wine. Anthony rehashed Emma's dilemma in a way that kept her somewhat in the dark of his own place in the picture. What he did reveal to her was his concern that her attackers might be connected with people working within his "government organization." David was surprised to hear even remotely refer to his association with the agency, and wondered if it was his way of upping the stakes. Anthony knew David had a special distaste for dirty officers. Maybe by laying those cards on the table, in front of Emma, he hoped to draw the younger man in.

He prodded David into entertaining the idea of helping him. "I felt that, with your connections in the field, you might be able to scrounge around a bit, see if you can discover more about the situation with Emma's dad." Anthony could be very persistent, and it wore on David. He owed it to his friend to at least listen, but it was all such a complicated mess, and he couldn't detect even a thread of a lead anywhere.

"Look," David said matter-of-factly, "even if I did manage to find out anything about Woods, wouldn't that bring attention to me, and consequently point back at you? If you believe these people are working from within our organization, then they'll figure that out and eventually come after you, just to find Emma."

He pointed to Emma who sat quietly in an armchair close to the fire. She hadn't said much, but David got the feeling she wasn't missing a thing. Anthony and David exchanged a knowing look. If Theodore Alberts was somehow involved, then the people coming after Emma already knew by now she was hiding out with Anthony. The older officer continued to pressure his friend to come on board.

"Unless we get information about what's motivating these actions against Emma, we're screwed anyway, David. She can't go back home where they'll be waiting for her. I'm fairly certain they don't have the ability to track me. But you have more ability to maneuver quietly within the company. You won't attract any attention if you're careful."

Emma listened with increasing alarm. Was he only "fairly certain" they weren't being followed?!

Anthony continued, "I don't mean to put you in a bad spot, my friend, but if there's something nefarious going on amidst our colleagues, then we both have a duty to weed it out, wouldn't you agree? David sighed. There was no getting around Anthony and his plans.

"I'll consider it and call you once I get back to Geneva, okay?" It was a signal that he wanted to wrap things up. He had an early flight tomorrow morning. He rose and extended a hand to Emma who was looking at him in a curious way.

"It was a pleasure to meet you Emma. I'm sorry I can't offer you more help, particularly while you're dealing with so much loss right now. It must be heartbreaking." He sincerely wished he could help her, but it was out of the question. Emma tried not to show her disappointment. She had decided she liked David, but it sounded like he had no intention of taking on her problems. She couldn't blame him, but she was tired of dicking around. She accepted his handshake with a tired expression. "Thank you Mr. Jamison, I appreciate the kind words."

"I'm going to see David out Emma," Anthony said. "Why don't you go up to bed, and we'll talk in the morning." The two men made their way to the side door as Emma retreated to her room. At the threshold, Anthony put a hand on David's shoulder and frowned.

"I was rather heavy-handed with that request, David. I hope you know I wouldn't ask for help if I thought I could do this on my own."

David looked down and shook his head. "I see your point Tony. And I admit I'm intrigued with the whole thing. I just don't know if I can infiltrate such an old case. I mean, shit, half the people involved must be dead by now."

Anthony decided it was time to reveal what he'd been stewing over since his first meeting with Emma.

"David, there's something more I need to tell you. When Emma showed me the note her father wrote it not only referred to officers who turned bad. There was a code name placed at the end of his writing that I recognized. I was briefly read into the case at the beginning of my career. But just as quickly, the case was shut down. I was simply told '*Nothing came of it*', and assigned other work. The trouble is, the person who redirected me to another case might have been part of a cover up. I just don't know. But it's strange the name should come up from Emma's father, what with him then taken out of the picture. It means that Carter had his doubts as well."

"Well, that does make this whole thing much more complicated," David agreed.

"What was the case name, if I may ask?"

Anthony studied his friend, wondering if it was worth getting him involved in something that could damage the young man's career.

"Nequitia," he answered after a moment's hesitation. "It's Latin…."

"Yeah," David nodded, "it means trickery."

"You understand Latin?!" Anthony was impressed.

"You forget I studied foreign languages as part of my training," David laughed. "They made us bone up on Latin. It gave us a foundation to learning the other languages."

Then he shook his head. "I don't know Tony. I won't be able to find out anything without getting caught looking. Maybe if you could somehow provide a reason for my fishing around? What was the basis of the investigation anyway?"

"The activities and movements of revolutionaries working against the Shah," Anthony explained. "We were trying to find out if we could work with any of them, just in case they were successful in toppling the government we were supporting at the time. It seemed like a legitimate course of action, and to this day I don't know why I was pulled off the assignment."

Anthony patted David's shoulder and smiled. "I know it'll probably lead nowhere. I'm just asking you to try kiddo, just try."

David was done arguing with Anthony. He couldn't say no to the man who had done so much for him. "Okay, I'll see what I can do."

"Excellent!" Anthony exclaimed, and opened the door for David to leave.

The younger man took a few steps out, then turned to Anthony with a pained look.

"Hey, you might have told me she was pretty."

Anthony cocked his head, confused. "Who? Emma? Is she pretty?"

He glanced in the direction of the second floor where she was secured in the guest room. "I don't suppose I've ever thought about it. Why would her looks matter one way or the other?"

David thrust his hands in his pockets and shuffled his feet nervously. "I don't know. I might've been more prepared. She wasn't what I envisioned…as a farmer from Oregon I mean."

He didn't really understand why the Woods woman bothered him, but she did.

Anthony put his hand to his chin, thinking. "Well," he said before closing the door, "I don't think you're what she expected either."

Emma stood at the window, trying to hear what the two men outside were saying. Her window was cracked open, but if she tried to move it any more, they were sure to realize she was eavesdropping again. And why shouldn't she? This all had to do with her, and she had every right to know if they were discussing her dilemma. All at once a thought came to Emma. Maybe this wasn't about her at all? She still believed that delving into her father's death had triggered the violence against her. But Anthony seemed to be going to great lengths to help. He was even dragging in this David character, who he obviously admired. What was all this "government" shit about anyway? What did they mean when they talked about "the organization" and "the company?" She was going to ask Anthony a whole lot of questions in the morning, and she damn well better get some real answers.

Right now she was feeling weary from taking in the evening's conversation, and trying to translate what was really being said between the two men. She turned off the light and crawled into bed, closing her eyes against the image of David Jamison. She'd caught him staring at her while Anthony spoke about the death of her boyfriend. He probably felt sorry for her, and that was nice. It would be even nicer if he actually found something out about her dad. What kind of job did he have that gave him access to information like that? This would be another question for Anthony. She fell asleep listening to David Jamison's car pulling away from the house.

David drove back to the hotel. Tony had taken on the problem of the Woods woman, but he didn't want to be involved. Staying at a hotel made it easier to distance himself from whatever trouble this might lead to. As he drove, his mind went in myriad directions. He didn't have time for this, pure and simple. His work involved recruiting and running assets, and it kept him plenty busy. They had recently put him in charge of covert operations in Iran as well, a position he was excited to pursue. In that respect, Anthony was correct in his assumption that David might reasonably request information on Carter Woods. But if he wanted to advance within the Company he had to stay in Geneva and do his job.

Working with Anthony on a case that had been effectively dormant a month ago was completely impractical. He felt badly for the guy, now that the Woods case had blown up as it had. But what could he do? This was what he tried to get across to his friend. But no, Anthony had talked him into joining forces, and that was that. Now he wondered if the information about Emma's dad was right here in Washington. He thought again about the woman with the auburn hair. Damnit, he would have to cancel his flight.

The next day Emma woke up early. Fully prepared to hit Anthony with questions, she found him in the kitchen finishing his coffee and preparing to leave. Appearing to be in a hurry, he'd barely let her get a word in.

"Good, you're awake. I have to leave for a bit to take care of some business. Please help yourself to whatever's in the fridge. I'll try not to be gone too long." He grabbed the car keys and headed towards the much-used side door.

She couldn't believe he would abandon her here, defenseless in a strange place.

"But Anthony, I need to talk to you about last night. I want some answers…"

He cut her off by putting his hand up. She thought he might as well have put it over her mouth.

"I don't have time right now Emma. We can talk when I get back."

He gave her a hard look, and his demeanor became no-nonsense.

"Listen, I want you to lock and bolt the door behind me. Don't answer if anyone comes knocking, and don't pick up the phone. I've locked the windows down here and drawn the shades. It's just a precaution, but I want anyone driving by to believe this house is unoccupied."

Emma's fear quickly turned to anger. She'd had enough of him pushing her around, expecting her to do whatever she was told without question. Her tone was accusatory. "Anthony, what's with the precautions if it's supposedly safe here? Am I supposed to hide under the bed while you're gone?"

He turned and considered this for a moment. "That might not be a bad idea," he said, as if it were a legitimate option.

He started back toward the door, but she wasn't going to let him off that easily. "Are you fucking kidding me?! This is bullshit! Can't you at least leave me a gun? Why can't I just go with you? You said you were going to protect me!"

The last sentence stopped Anthony in his tracks. He slowly turned and fixed his gaze on her once more.

"My dear, if I gave you a gun you'd probably end up shooting either me or yourself. I wouldn't be leaving if it wasn't important, and I cannot take you with me."

She stood in silence, wearing an expression of despair. He pulled on his coat and opened the door. "Please know this, I am protecting you." And with that remark he was gone.

Chapter 22
The Librarian

It was early morning and still dark outside. David sat in his car mulling over the conversation with Anthony. He knew he should be making his way to the airport to head back to Geneva. If he were being practical, he'd abandon the idea of helping his friend out altogether. His other assignments were time consuming enough without throwing this Carter Woods thing in the mix. But something tugged at his conscience, nagging him to make an effort, no matter how small, to look into it further. He needed advice, and he knew just where to get it. He pulled out his phone and dialed his parent's home number, knowing his dad would be awake and reading his paper. His father never changed his morning routine, ever; not even after retirement. He begrudgingly left the Agency after his wife insisted that, at the age of seventy, it was time. David knew his dad enjoyed his time as a CIA officer, and he approved when his son voiced an interest in a similar career. Not one to express himself emotionally, his reaction to David's advancement in the field was restrained admiration. He liked when his son called for advice about the job, but he would never show it.

Sure enough, his father picked up on the second ring. David dispensed with the usual pleasantries.

"Hey dad, it's me. You got a minute?"

"Sure son," his father answered. "What's going on?"

"Well," David continued, "I'm considering taking on some research independently…for a colleague of mine. Actually he's a good friend. I haven't really decided yet, so I'm keeping it sort of on the down low. I'll explain later, but I wonder if you have any idea about where I might find records on a case involving a former Grumman employee. He was working in Iran back in the early seventies. The official word is he got caught stealing or selling arms, and they had to take him out. Any ideas?"

The silence on the other end didn't bother David. He knew his father was thinking back on his days in the company. He waited for him to mentally look through everything stored in that encyclopedia of a brain he'd relied on for so many years.

"Are you in D.C.?" It was the kind of short and to-the-point question for which his father was famous. "Yeah," David answered, "I took a meeting here yesterday, and I was going to fly back to Geneva today, but thought I'd hang around a bit to help this friend out, just to see if I can come up with anything on this other project." There was another long pause, and then his father sighed. "Son, you'll never get to that kind of information at Langley, not now anyway. What you need to do is go to Hampstead." David pulled the phone away in disbelief. "Hampstead?!" He exclaimed back into his phone. "Where the hell is Hampstead?" He could hear his dad laughing softly. "It's in Maryland, about an hour's drive from Langley. A former colleague of mine lives on a farm out there. Her name is Harriet Whaley, but we all called her KT. If you drop that name to her she might not threaten to kick you off her farm. She might brandish a gun, but she won't shoot you."

David tried to hide his impatience. Sometimes his father liked to play games. "Okay dad, so what can this Harriet person do to help me?" He could hear the kitchen chair creak under his dad's weight as he settled in. "She used to manage the records department while I was working at the Agency. That was when they kept hard copies of everything of course, the dark ages before computers and floppy disks and all that. Harriet was not only a whiz at organizing every piece of data; she also had a photographic memory. I think she helped them with the transition from hard copy files to digital, just before she retired. She might even have access to some of the older stuff. We still exchange Christmas cards, Harriet and me. She moved into an old Victorian house to pursue her hobby of making puzzles." "Puzzles?" David asked in confusion, "Who makes puzzles?" His father laughed again. "She's really good at it. She comes up with the design and everything, carves 'em out of wood. It's truly an art form. She even makes money selling them. She's a pretty unique individual. I should warn you though; Harriet's as patriotic as they come. She won't give you anything unless you can convince her it's for the good of the country." His father paused, then asked, "Is it, David?"

A few seconds of silence hung in the air between them while David considered the question. Was this project for the good of the country? He couldn't be certain, of course. But he thought of Emma, living under the shadow of her own father's presumed treason and death. If Carter Woods had been set up by someone inside the Agency, then it sullied the entire organization. "Yes dad," David finally answered, "I believe finding answers about this particular case are for the good of the country." Deciding on this suddenly made him feel more committed to discovering the truth about Carter Woods. "Okay then," his dad said calmly, satisfied with his son's answer. "Go for it, and good luck."

"Thanks dad," David said, indicating he had to sign off.

"Don't you want to ask about your mother?" It was his father's question every time David called.

"Yeah, sure dad," David played along, "how's mom?" This was a formality they performed with every call, even though both of them knew mom was fine.

"Well, I don't know," his father said gruffly, "I think she's trying to kill me with this goddamn salt-free diet." David smiled to himself. Some things never changed.

"Give her my love dad. I gotta go."

He began to hang up, but kept his father on the line with a question.

"Hey dad, what's KT stand for anyway?"

"Keeper of the Tablets," his father said in a voice that sounded like this should have been obvious. "It's what the ancient Greeks used to call librarians back in the days when records were carved on tablets. Sometimes it seems like things haven't advanced much since then."

David laughed, "Yeah, I guess not. Thanks dad. Love you."

He didn't wait for his dad to uncomfortably respond in kind.

Now, after passing a sign heralding his arrival in Hampstead, David briefly took his eyes off the road and glanced at the piece of paper where he'd jotted down directions for Harriet's place. "It's just outside town," his father told him, "but the driveway is easy to miss because it's not marked. Look for the mailbox with a little American flag on it." David hadn't asked how his father knew the details of a former co-worker's address, but he made a mental note to bring the question up on his next visit home. After rounding a bend on the solitary country road he caught sight of a mailbox fitting his father's description. He slowed the car to a stop and peered down the long, tree-lined driveway.

Taking a deep breath, he eased the car down the shady road and followed it to its end, where a green and white Victorian house stood elegant and dignified. Although it was clearly in need of a fresh coat of paint, the old girl looked sturdy and its surrounding lawn well-managed. David parked his car directly in front, so as to be seen by anyone inside the home. He walked up the front porch and reached for the brass lion's head knocker that beckoned on the front door. But his hand paused when he heard music coming from behind the house. Curious, but keeping in mind his father's warning of a gun-wielding Harriet, he followed a path that took him to what appeared to be a ramshackle workshop located in back. The shop door was open, and what David now recognized as folk music came flooding out. Birds in the nearby trees sang along, while within the shop, a diminutive woman bent over some kind of wood cutting apparatus.

"Excuse me," David called out, hoping he wasn't mistaken as an intruder, "are you Harriet Whaley?"

The woman looked up in surprise, and then reached for something out of sight. To his dismay, David immediately recognized the SIG Sauer P238, one of the few handguns women prefer due to its size and weight. This one was pointed right at him. "Who wants to know?" Harriet asked in an even tone. She didn't appear to be at all rattled, but she definitely meant business.

David put his hands up and tried to calmly explain. "My name is David Jamison. You were referred to me by my dad, Ben. He was a co-worker at the Agency where I'm working now. He said to ask for KT."

Immediately the gun went down, and a smile broke across Harriet's face. "You're Ben's boy?!" She exclaimed as she set the firearm back on the table. "C'mon in honey! Let me take a look at you!" David approached, too slowly for Harriet who gathered him into a tight hug. He was surprised that such a small woman could administer an embrace that left him gasping for air. "Dad says hi, and that it would be okay to look you up," David wheezed. Harriet pulled back from him and smiled again. "I can't believe that old dog shared the KT nickname with you," she chuckled. "How the hell is he?" She led him into her workshop as she talked. "He's good," David said, relieved to have won her over with the mere mention of his dad. "He said you're into making puzzles now that you're retired. Is that what you're doing in here?" He was genuinely curious; examining the machinery Harriet had been working before threatening his life.

"Oh yes," Harriet said with a sigh, touching the machine lovingly. "It's a hobby gone out of control I'm afraid. But I do love it." David bent to look at the sliver of a blade she had used to cut a design into a thin piece of wood. "That's the thinnest blade you'll ever see in your life," Harriet remarked. "It's almost as thin as a human hair, and it's the only saw that won't tear up the wood I use to make the puzzles. It cost a pretty penny, but it allows me to do fine work that sells." She regarded David warmly.

"Your dad has one of my puzzles. He's really the only one who knows the little secrets I build into my puzzles." David's eyebrows rose in surprise. "What kind of secrets?" He asked, intrigued by Harriet's playful tone. She smiled and pointed to the work currently being crafted using the expensive machine. "Some pieces, not all you understand, but a few in every puzzle, bear a shape that alludes to one of the cases I kept filed for the Agency. It could be a dove, or a dragon, or any number of shapes that were used to label a certain mission or operation." She gave David another wicked smile. "Nobody would ever notice it unless I pointed it out, of course. Your father was delighted when I let him in on my little game. You should have him show it to you."

David looked up in surprise. "I will!" was all he could muster. Harriet sat on a shabby sofa and offered him a place next to her. "Now," she let out another sigh, "what can I do for you young man?"

David took his place next to her on the sofa, turning toward her in earnest. "Well, like I said, I'm working for the Agency now, and have been for some time. I had a meeting in Langley, and was going to return to my station in Geneva when an old friend asked me to try and research an old case on his behalf. He's an officer as well, and struggling to get information that could help him provide better protection to a subject under his care. My father said to *'ask KT for help'* in a tricky bit of research I'm doing. I don't even know if any records exist on this anymore."

Harriet's face lit up at the mention of her old nickname, "Oh Ben! He was such a nice man, always so polite, but very funny."

"He was?" David wasn't certain they were talking about the same man. Clearly his dad displayed a different personality at work.

Harriet wiped a bit of sawdust from the apron she wore at her waist. "I don't know if I can help you though. I mean, I'm not working at the Agency anymore. What are you looking for in particular?"

David paused. What exactly was he looking for? Best to start with what he knew based on Anthony's information.

"I'd like to learn about anything you have on individuals working with Grumman Aerospace in the early 1970s. We sold a lot of advanced weaponry to the Shah, who was in power at the time."

Harriet scrutinized David anew, clearly evaluating his motives. "Well, I still have access to some of the older files on my computer," she said guardedly. "They're piling up a bit, while in the process of transferring things from microfiche to digital. But David, that information is still compartmentalized. If you haven't been read-in, even to an old case, I can't in good conscience bring it up for you. I couldn't let you see anything without clearance from the people that headed up that case. If you can get them to read you in on it, then that's a different story. You understand my position, right?"

[handwritten margin note: Top secret info on a home computer? Unlikely.]

This was what he'd been afraid of, and what his father had warned him about. Still, if he could convince Harriet that what he was doing was for national security, he might still have a chance. "That's the problem, Harriet," he explained, "the very people I would approach about this matter are the ones I suspect had a hand in wrongdoing. I don't like that I can't trust some of the people I work for, but there it is. Now, I know it's a big ask, maybe even a risk for you to help me. But if I'm right, then it's our duty, both yours and mine, to get to the bottom of this."

He held his breath, waiting to see the doubt slowly ease from her face. "Of course," David spoke with as much dignity as he could muster. "I understand I've put you in an awkward position."

Harriet cocked her head and seemed to ponder his request. "Who's in charge of the case now?" The question took David by surprise, and he had to think back to his conversations with Anthony. "Carlino?" he ventured, then corrected himself. "No, it's Tarlino, Victor Tarlino I believe." Harriet scoffed and shook her head. "Yes," she answered, recognizing the name, "Tarlino always played fast and loose with national security. He always seemed a bit too self-serving for my taste."

She put her hand on David's shoulder. "Your father is a good man, and I trust him. So I'm going to trust you. Come with me." She led him to the back of the shop, and pressed on a wood panel that appeared no different from the others. Magically, a door swung open to a cubby where a computer had been set up on a small desk. Harriet turned on the computer and hovered over the keyboard. "I'll need you to avert your eyes while I enter my password. And David," she looked over her shoulder at the Officer, "if you're lying to me, I will kill you." David nodded and turned his back to the woman as she entered her information. After some typing he heard a beeping sound and Harriet's computer sprang to life.

"Okay," she tapped his shoulder to get his attention, "we're in. Can you repeat the information you gave me? I'll need to hunt around a bit. The older stuff is in disarray from the transition." David repeated what he knew about Grumman and Carter and watched as she deftly entered every word. There was a long pause, and then another number of beeps. "Alright, I think I'm in the right place, but I'll need to scroll through a bit. We'd better sit down." Harriet took the desk chair while David pulled up one made of teak, that looked as if it had spent years in the sun before ending up in her shop. It was too small, and he sat uncomfortably while Harriet continued to read through the various files on her screen. "What more can you tell me about this case David?" She asked this while continuing to look through paragraphs of unending text. "Any little thing would help in pulling out the information you need."

'Like pulling on a thread' David thought, and really, that was all he had. He pulled out the small notebook he'd used to take notes from Anthony. "I'm trying to find something about the specific allegations against Carter Woods," he shared with Harriet. "When my friend took on the case, it was a given that Woods was caught red-handed selling arms to Iranian rebels. He was told Woods was shot dead before they could interrogate him, so it was presumed any other players in his deals got off scot free. This was why his family remained under surveillance. If Carter's wife suddenly began making large purchases, his team was directed to investigate; follow the money if you will."

David glanced down again at the notepad and continued to read off the known facts. "Carter Woods, retired Navy fighter pilot, had been under the employ of Grumman, a company helping to provide, amongst other weapons, F-14 fighter jets to the Iranian government. Along with a group of technicians, administrators and government officials, Woods traveled to Iran with the intention of training the Iranian pilots how to operate the jets he'd flown in several missions during the Vietnam War. The Nixon administration had arranged $15 billion worth of arms to the Shah, with Grumman being one of the largest providers of weaponry, in the form of fighter jets."

Harriet nodded and clicked into a different file. He could tell by the diligent way she worked that she was getting caught up in the mystery as well. He decided it was time to share what he'd been thinking. "What's curious to me, is how Carter Woods had been enticed by rebels who surely couldn't have met the amount of money he was being paid by Grumman. With such a lucrative contract there would have been no real incentive for Woods to stick his neck out, especially since the rebel forces didn't appear to have similar financial backing. It makes no sense, but according to my friend, no one involved in the case appeared to have come to the same conclusion." Harriet kept typing, but a smile began to play upon her lips. "It's as if puzzle pieces were being forced to fit where they could not, and everyone pretended the puzzle was complete," she said so softly, it seemed she was actually speaking to her computer.

David shot his new comrade-in-arms a look of admiration. "Exactly!" he whispered back. A silence fell between them while Harriet worked. Her furious typing was the only sound reverberating through the little shop until, finally, she stopped. "Got something here," she announced proudly, leaning back so David could view the text. He rose to stand over her and they both began to read. A title sat clearly at the top of the microfiched page.

Rogue Activities of Officers under N.O.C.

N.O.C. stood for Non-Official Cover, a CIA term given for individuals intentionally placed in positions where they might have an opportunity to gather data or conduct surveillance in a clandestine fashion. Harriet moved her cursor past the title page until she landed on a tidy list of three names, their cover jobs typed adjacent to each name. Carter Woods was the second name down, and he was listed as a flight instructor.

"This is interesting," David spoke quietly to Harriet. "It looks like the CIA had placed some officers of their own in the Grumman program. So Carter Woods had been an inside man." Harriet looked up at him in curiosity. "You didn't know that?" she asked. "No," he answered. "My friend had never been informed that he was maintaining surveillance on the daughter of a fellow officer. Carter Woods may have been just a lower-level officer, but he was clearly trusted enough to have been embedded in the Grumman program."

Harriet shrugged. "Well, wouldn't it make sense for the U.S. government to have some of their own people secured in a project, if just to keep a close eye on things?" They both redirected their attention to the list. The name above Carter's was a man named Andrew Zanders, whose cover was Director of Finances. The last name was that of Frank Nirody, also listed as a flight instructor. This was a name David recognized. It had been mentioned on the tape Carter left for his daughter. Anthony had filled him in on the details of the recording, as well as the bugged phone conversation between Emma and Charlotte.

"Do you mind if I write some of this down?" he asked, reaching for his notebook. "I'll do you one better," Harriet answered, "I'll print it out for you." She flipped on the printer located behind them on a separate table. David looked on in shock. "Are you sure?" he asked with concern in his voice. "I don't want you to get in any trouble. With a few clicks Harriet had already begun the process. As the printer began spitting out papers she turned back to David and rolled her eyes. "Sweetheart," she laughed, "I'm probably already in trouble. This way, if they come looking for me, I can say someone broke in and held me at gunpoint." They both smiled over the irony of her story. "Anyway," Harriet sighed as she gathered up the papers, "I don't think it's wise for me to read any more of this. It would be better to remain ignorant and let you unravel this mess." She pulled a brown bag down from its shelf and dumped the contents onto her desk; half-finished puzzle pieces that somehow hadn't worked out. Slipping the stack of papers into the bag, she folded the opening over twice to secure the package.

She handed the bag to David and pushed him toward the door. "Go on now," she said firmly, "get out of here before I change my mind and turn you in myself."

David turned at the door to shake her hand. "Harriet…KT, I'm glad I got to meet you. I hope I didn't interrupt your schedule too much."

"Oh, I don't mind," she laughed, "it's nice to have a visitor every now and then. It can get pretty lonely out here in the country. Even though I like retirement, I sometimes miss working for the Agency. Things were pretty exciting at the end there, when I was helping to transfer records with one of the younger guys."

David looked at her in surprise. "There was just one tech person helping you? Certainly there were officers coming and going with that much work to be done."

"Oh I was lucky just to have Matthew, and even he only came down a couple times a week," she laughed. "I think it was a budget issue, but switching over the whole department to digital created kind of a mess. Mathew made the process fun, and he was so patient."

She rolled her eyes. "It took time for me to learn the computer stuff. I couldn't have done it without Mathew Kealty. He's our resident computer nerd."

David flashed a smile. "Matt Kealty? Hey, I know him! We graduated from the academy together! Where's he working?"

Harriet was pleased to have a friend in common with the young man. "He's up in DS&T, that's where they're getting all our data entered and organized. At first, Mathew insisted on handling it alone. Now he heads up an entire team of nerds, but he told me he wasn't happy about it. He didn't want anyone else messing it up. And that wasn't the exact word he used."

David beamed, same old Matt! "Yeah, he's a stickler for working alone. Computer geeks are like that I guess. Do you think he's up for a visit? I'd love to drop in and surprise him when I get back to D.C."

Harriet told him the floor and office number, which David wrote in his notebook. He tucked it back in his jacket and they walked together toward his car.

"Thanks for letting me know where to find Matt, Harriet. It'll be fun to reminisce with him about our crazy school days."

Harriet smiled and gave him one last hug. "Tell your dad I said hello," she said with a twinkle in her eye. "Tell him I miss his brand of humor."

David shook his head in wonder. His whole life, dad had never shown a talent for any kind of humor.

"I'll let him know," he promised. Then he winked and said slyly, "I'll have to ask him for stories about you."

She lowered her head, and David detected a slight blush rising to her face. "I really do have fond memories of him," she giggled.

David ducked into his car and rolled down the window before starting it up. "Thanks again KT," he said with a wave. "You take care of yourself David." Harriet's parting words followed him down the driveway.

Chapter 23
Matt the Wizard

He drove as far as the outskirts of Langley before pulling his car over in a secluded spot. He was anxious to take a look at the papers Harriet printed out for him. He read past the N.O.C. information and scoured the next pages. There were a few that detailed each man's credentials; Carter's being the largest since it listed his military experience. He also appeared to be the only one bringing a family to Iran. Nirody brought his wife, Charlotte, but under Zanders' name there was nothing referencing a wife or children.

Of course, the best officer for an overseas mission such as this one was one without ties or encumbrances. David wondered if Carter gave a thought about how he put his family in danger. Anthony's description of the man, obtained through Emma, was that of a cold disciplinarian prone to angry outbursts, at least in front of his family. He thought back on his meeting with Emma. If she had grown up fearing her father, why was she so driven to discover how he'd died? Would she feel differently if he told her that she and her family were possibly nothing but another convenient layer of cover?

He came to a copy of an eight by ten black and white photograph. The photo looked as if it had been copied from a smaller one and enhanced. The resulting image was grainy, but clearly showed a burned out car with a charred body beside it. Beneath the photo someone had handwritten "Body determined to be Carter Woods, Tehran 11-22-72." Carter Woods, who was supposed to have died in a shootout, was somehow found burnt to death in a car accident. "What the fuck…?" David whispered the words as he took in the image. It was a graphic and sickening photo, and he shuffled it underneath the other pages. He eagerly flipped to the next page, expecting to find a report on Carter Woods that explained how his dealings with Iranian revolutionaries led to his death. But within the pages there was no mention at all of any such activity. The information stopped suddenly, as if a large chunk of it had been intentionally excluded. Frustrated, David moved to the last section of the thin stack. At the top of this page there was another copy of what appeared to be the original and smaller photo showing the end of Carter. Once again, he was met by the horrific sight of a charred body, lying on worn cobblestone next to a burned out car. Half way down the page the details of Carter's death were typed out almost as an afterthought.

In an attempt to apprehend, Officer Woods was followed while driving in a gold Plymouth.

Contact with Plymouth was briefly interrupted after turning a corner, whereupon the car was discovered overturned and in flames. Single body identified as Carter Woods.

Death listed as result of pursuit.

David shook his head in amazement. This would be a revelation to Anthony, who had been very clear during their fireside conversation that Carter had been shot. It was believed by everyone on his team that Carter was assassinated while in the act of handing off compromising information to an Iranian rebel. It was never clear how this accomplice had somehow escaped capture. Emma had even winced at the idea of her father not only being discovered as a criminal but suffering a swift and brutal end because of his actions. It was yet another inconsistency David wished to mull over with Anthony when the two got together again. He would call his friend this afternoon and arrange a meeting. He suddenly realized he'd have to reschedule his flight yet again. He couldn't go home knowing there was so much ambiguity in the Woods case. This was just the kind of thing David lived for; a puzzle, seemingly unsolvable, begging for resolution.

He shuffled back through a few cursory pages of follow up on Nirody and Zanders, but there was no further mention of Carter Woods. Zanders was listed as having left Iran after the Grumman project ended. Nirody appeared to have transferred to a position back in the States, only eight months after arriving in Iran, then quit the agency entirely citing "financial difficulties." Anthony's words came back to David, "follow the money." It nagged at him. If Nirody was having money problems there was motivation for committing the very crime of which Carter was accused. It occurred to David that whoever was behind the assault on Emma must be indirectly involved with the Woods affair, and would want his actions to remain hidden from fellow officers. That would explain the extreme measures used to steer her away from exploring her father's past. Would these people, presumably working within the Agency, catch wind of his latest discovery? If Harriet's research on his behalf put up a red flag in some way, had he then endangered her life as well?

"Shit!" David swore out loud. He wished Tony hadn't involved him in all this, but now it was probably too late to back out. He felt as if he'd been led to a cliff. He could either turn around; leaving the Carter shit far behind, or take a leap of faith with the possibility of falling deeper into trouble. He slid the pages back into the brown bag and tucked it all away into his satchel. Starting up the car he let it run a bit before putting it in reverse and heading back to CIA headquarters. He would surprise his old friend Mathew Kealty and feel things out with him. Now that he had something to go on, Matt might be able to find some of the missing pieces of the Carter Woods puzzle.

It was just past noon when David pulled into the headquarters parking lot. He found a spot close to where the cafeteria was located. The food there was notoriously awful, but he'd grab something to eat and visit Matt afterwards.

Entering through the side entrance close to the cafeteria, David once again presented his credentials and found his way to the sandwich and salad bar. This was a safer bet than the prepared meals dished out by servers wearing what looked like shower caps on their heads. They always reminded David of the cranky cafeteria ladies at his high school. He carried his turkey sandwich and carton of milk to a table in the corner and glanced over the scribblings in his notebook while eating. He dared not look through the papers Harriet had provided. It made him nervous just having them in his satchel which he kept around his shoulder. He believed his paranoia was justified.
    Having possession of this compartmentalized information could implicate him in all kinds of wrongdoing. Besides costing him his job, it could land him in jail. He thought again of the possibility that someone had been notified of Harriet's inquiry this morning.

David finished his mediocre sandwich and gulped down the rest of the milk. Tossing the used packaging into the trash he walked toward the elevator, riding it two stories up to the Directorate for Science and Technology. Here he found rows of cubicles filled mostly with men, lots of them wearing glasses and all of them either pounding away on computer keyboards or peering at their screens. Not one of them looked up as he made his way down the rows and found Matt Kealty's office. Gently tapping on the closed door, he was met with a gruff "What?!" from the other side. Swinging the door open, David leaned in, leaving the bottom half of his body in the hallway.

"Dude," he smiled at his old schoolmate, "ya' gotta get your head out of that screen."

Mathew Kealty pulled his eyes from the large monitor in front of him and looked up wide-eyed.

"Ahhhhh Davy!" he yelled and rose up to greet the familiar face. "What the hell are you doing here?!" The two embraced in a guy's hug, and Matt gestured to the seat at the side of his desk. David sat and shook his head, smiling at Matt.

"I should've known you'd land a job that fed your obsession," he laughed. "How's it going? Are you heading up the department, or on some kind of special project? Our friend Harriet says you're revolutionizing all the old data."

Matt's face lit up at Harriet's name. "How'd you cross paths with Harriet?!" he asked in a booming voice. "I miss her!" David shifted his satchel from shoulder to lap, enjoying his friend's confusion. "She and my dad are old friends. He hooked us up so she could help me on a little solo project. She said you were doing some exciting work." Matt leaned back in his chair and crossed his arms over his chest. "Yeah, she's a sweetheart. But I don't think what I'm doing is all that exciting, just modernizing what I can. I feel like I'm dragging these people, kicking and screaming into the 21st century. My tiny crew of dorks have labeled me BOFH."

David gave him a quizzical look, and Matt explained. "Bastard Operator from Hell," he let out a snort, "it's a term used by this Travaglia guy. He calls users who ask him for computer help "lusers." It's pretty funny if you're into that kinda stuff."

Matt was a beefy man compared to the rest of the computer nerds stationed around him. He had the same pallor that came from constantly working indoors, but he wore the familiar wool cap at a jaunty angle that became part of his uniform back in their youth, and he was now sporting a goatee. Tattoos crept out from beneath his short sleeves, decorating big biceps with color and black cursive writing. It all gave him a rebellious flare that David appreciated.

Reaching for his mouse, he made whatever was on his computer morph into an Escher screensaver, then turned back to his friend. "What's up with you these days? I heard you got a gig in Geneva, hit the big time."

David looked down and put his hands on his hips in a self-deprecating way. He didn't like to talk about his work or rapid advancement with anyone other than Anthony.

"Deputy Chief, yeah it's interesting, but I'm staying here a couple extra days doing some research for a friend." He had a thought, "Hey, since you're in charge of organizing the library, would you have access to all the old cases? I'm looking into one from the seventies, and I think something's gone missing."

Matt raised his eyebrows and put his hand to his chin in a mock pondering gesture.

"Hmmmm, somebody filched it huh? Intriguing!" Swiveling his desk chair back to the computer he began drumming the keys like a concert pianist. Then he suddenly froze. His fingers suspended over the keys, he turned and looked over his shoulder at David, and with one eyebrow raised, murmured, "We're working on something you're allowed access to…right?" David smiled slyly and placed a hand on Matt's shoulder. "C'mon buddy, you were never a stickler for rules. Where's the renegade genius I know and love?" Matt shook his head in surrender. "This better not get me in trouble Davy. I like this job and I want to keep it." He turned back to his computer and resumed typing. David patted him on the back in assurance. "Like I said, it's an old case, and you're not likely to find anything I don't already know."

"Sure, sure," Matt grumbled, but his fingers continued to fly over the keyboard. Almost immediately a program popped up that showed a massive list of numbers and letters denoting various cases from the past. Speaking over his shoulder again, Matt asked, "Throw me something for a reference. I need a name, company, date…whatever ya' got."

David had kept his notebook handy and flipped to what he'd compiled from the information gathered from both Anthony and Harriet. "Try 1974, Grumman Project in Iran."

Matt's fingers resumed their work across the keyboard even as David spoke. Text immediately filled the screen. "Bingo," his friend proclaimed. David leaned over Matt's shoulder to view the text. It was much of what he'd already seen this morning.

"Can we narrow it down a little?" He asked. "Sure," Matt said with a shrug. "Lay it on me."

"How about Carter Woods," he thought for a moment. "No, try termination of Carter Woods."

"Termination," Matt spoke the word as he typed it. "So the guy was fired?" Matt asked.

"No," David responded, not taking his eyes from the screen, "termination as in dead."

Matt looked back at David in surprise. "What kind of crazy shit are you having me pull up buddy?"

David gave his friend a smile, "don't worry about it."

Matt scoffed and went back to work on his computer. "Yeah, right, if you say so. I'm serious. I better not get smacked down for any of this."

Typing in David's request Matt hit the enter button, and the screen went momentarily blank. Then the dismal words of "data not found" appeared in the center. "Bummer," Matt said in disappointment. In spite of himself, he had been caught up in his friend's research.

David felt stuck. He'd just hit another wall. "Why would a big chunk of file just disappear?" He asked Matt. "It's like an important part of the case was just deleted."

Matt shook his head, staring back at the screen. "Could be anything, my man. My best guess? It just hasn't been downloaded yet. I mean, the dudes working under me aren't doing the actual processing. They're just collecting and sorting stuff. I'm doing all the programming and that's a lot for one person."

David let out a sigh, and Matt turned back to his friend. "Sorry dude. Anything else you need?"

David wasn't ready to give up just yet. "Can you ask for data on another Grumman employee? The name is Frank Nirody."

Matt once again consulted his computer, and this time he was rewarded with text. It was more than David had seen in the papers now burning a hole in his satchel.

Matt read it out loud for both of them. "Major Frank Nirody resigned from Grumman Project October 18, 1974, citing wife's ill health. Forwarding address for W-9 given as 3895 Beach Drive Sagaponack, New Jersey."

"Weird," David whispered.

"Why is it weird?" Matt asked. But David stood and readjusted his satchel. "No time to go into it buddy, but I appreciate your help."

Matt pushed back his chair and dramatically threw up his hands. "Davy, you can't just leave me hangin' like that! What did you see?"

Just then the office door opened and a pale, young man wearing thick black-rimmed glasses poked his head in. "Sorry boss, I knocked but I guess you didn't hear me."

"What is it?!" Matt shouted, a little too irate David thought, for a mere interruption.

The young man stepped in timidly, and nodded briefly to David. "Excuse me, but we're having problems sorting the data you assigned yesterday. We think someone got a port cross-connected and it created a packet storm. And for sure one of the switches in the IDF closet is faulty…"

Matt cut him off. "…The stuff from yesterday?! It still isn't done?! Who the fuck installed that switch, Moses?!"

David flung the strap of his satchel around his neck. He raised a hand to his friend and began edging his way out behind the now terrified underling.

"Davy, don't go," Matt pleaded, holding up his hand, "I can fix this in a minute." The young man looked from David to Matt in confusion.

David grinned at his friend, "No, I'm good. Thanks again buddy. I owe you one."

Matt made one last attempt. "Aren't you going to tell me what we found?"

David looked directly into the widening eyes of the young man. "If I told you, I'd have to kill you," he said with a smile. He walked past the cubicles of gaping computer geeks followed by the sound of Mathew's continued swearing.

Chapter 24
Pulling the Thread

He met Anthony at their pre-arranged location right on time. David didn't like cemeteries, and he thought it not only morbid, but also rather cliché that his friend suggested the spot. But Anthony insisted it was ideal, in that they would have both privacy and security at Arlington National Cemetery. The spacious lawn dotted with headstones gave them a good vantage point to survey anyone following them or coming too close. David followed his friend's directions to the headstones belonging to soldiers who died during the Vietnam War. He pulled up to a large elm tree under which Anthony stood, wearing a long, black wool coat; no hat or gloves. Glancing around the cemetery, David had the fleeting thought of where Carter Woods had finally been interred. Certainly not a place like Arlington, and for sure Carter's body never made it into the cemetery of his home town. He would have liked to at least see a headstone, just to confirm the man had once walked the earth, and that someone actually cared enough to properly lay him to rest. He made a mental note to ask Emma if her mother ever asked for the body of her disgraced husband.

Anthony sauntered up to the car and pointed to a parking space where David could place the car relatively out of sight. Getting out, David locked the vehicle and joined Anthony on a serpentine path that skirted the headstones. He had been right about the cemetery. Very few visitors ventured into Arlington during the chilly month of February. The men walked side by side, their breath creating vapor clouds as they spoke.

"Have you left Emma alone at the house?" David asked Anthony. "Do you think that's wise?" David's concern over a woman he'd only just met mystified Anthony. "Yes," he answered, somewhat offended at the implied lack of trust. "I couldn't very well bring her along. I'm sure she's perfectly safe, but I have another errand to run after our little rendezvous here. I was wondering if you could look in on her. I imagine you've canceled your flight?"

"Yeah," David said, trying to understand the bewildering sense of anticipation he felt at the thought of seeing Emma. "I actually rescheduled my flight for tomorrow, but after my visit to headquarters I believe that will change."

This information seemed to please Anthony. "Good, good. Now tell me what you've found." He was once again enjoying the thrill of his job. It felt good to work with a younger, capable officer who displayed some initiative and energy.

"Well," David began, "I realized I couldn't get access to anything in the Agency records department." Upon hearing this Anthony scowled. "Yes, I was afraid of that." He sighed and threw up his hands. "Well, you understand we had to try…" David cut him off. "No, wait. I did get something, but it wasn't exactly…it was through a former employee of the Agency, someone who worked in records but just recently retired." In answer to Anthony's look of doubt, David explained, "She's a friend of my father's. I managed to convince her that my motives were honorable. Well, she almost shot me, but then I convinced her."

Anthony's eyes grew wide in alarm. "David, are you saying a former colleague of your father provided you with compartmentalized information? Just like that?! There's no way your activity wasn't flagged."

"That's what I thought too," David said, exasperated, "but I believe it was worth it. And trust me, it wasn't all that easy getting my dad's friend to help." He pulled out papers from his satchel, now liberated from Harriet's brown bag and presented it to Anthony. While his friend and mentor began reading through the papers David continued. "If my inquiry was flagged and somebody currently working the case learned about it, maybe it would sort of shake the bushes a bit; bring them a little more out in the open. It might lead us to someone who has something to gain by providing more information. Offering a dirty officer's exoneration if he turns could work to our advantage."

Anthony remained doubtful. "Dear boy," he said with a frown, "that's a very clever, but Pollyanna concept." He thought for a moment, rubbing his chin. "You may be right," he agreed reluctantly, "however, if you're not, we both could be thrown under the bus just for launching our own investigation into this."

He turned his attention back to the papers, and David pointed to the first page. "This was lifted from a file regarding Grumman activities in 1974. Look at the heading for Officers under N.O.C working in the Iranian project. There's three listed, and Carter Woods is one of them. Were you aware our man was a fellow officer?"

Anthony gave a startled look that turned to anger. "No, I most certainly was not aware! That seems a rather unusual detail to leave out given my involvement in the operation."

David nodded knowingly. "Well, it gets worse. Carter Woods was not shot while attempting to sell anything to revolutionaries. He died in a car wreck."

He pulled the copy of the photo from the stack of papers and presented it to Anthony. Bringing the photo closer for inspection the older man shook his head. "Yet another fact one would assume a team member needed to know. Why keep it secret, I wonder?"

David presented the last page to Anthony. "There's the original photo with the report detailing what happened. The whole thing just stinks Tony. That's why I think any notice we're unearthing this information could actually be beneficial. We already know someone is afraid this will come to light. Our inquiries might suggest the truth is bound to come out. They would willingly flip if they don't want to get burned in the process." Anthony nodded as he read the report. David went on. "There must be more information on officers like Carter who went rogue, but like I said, I couldn't get access to it. As you can see, the papers given to me go on to list the end game for the two remaining men. One simply retired, while another quit within the year, citing financial concerns. That man was Frank Nirody. Didn't Emma tell you she heard his name on the tape her dad left for her?"

"Yes," Anthony stopped to face David, and rubbed his hands against the cold. "I had her give me everything from the safety deposit box. We can listen to the tape together, if you like. The man soliciting Carter indicated he'd approached this Nirody as well. Emma managed to track down his wife, but Nirody disappeared afterwards. I had a feeling there was a connection but didn't have the chance to follow up. That's when everything went to hell and we flew out here."

David crossed his arms in an effort to stay warm. His own leather jacket offered little in the way of comfort. He hadn't packed for an extended stay and never imagined he'd be standing in the cold for a long conversation. Still, he was excited to be sharing what he'd found with his friend.

"Here's the thing, Tony. I discovered I have a former school friend working at DS&T. Lucky for me they put him in charge of digitizing everything in the basement." Anthony gave the young officer a look of admiration. "Well, you certainly have been a busy beaver!" David ignored the playful jab and went on. "Even my buddy in DS&T came up empty when we looked for the missing section of that file. But what he did find was follow up information on Nirody. Instead of listing financial issues as his cause for bailing out early, he now claims his wife's ill health was the problem."

Anthony was listening intently, pondering this new development and wondering how he could go about finding Nirody. David now dropped the final piece of information he wouldn't share with Mathew.

"Nirody left a forwarding address for bookkeeping. Want to know where he and his sick wife are living now?" He didn't wait for Anthony to answer.

"Sagaponack, New Jersey. It's a nice little town next to Sag Harbor."

Anthony raised one eyebrow. "Not far from the Hamptons, I believe."

David nodded and rubbed his thumb and forefinger together. "I guess Frank's financial issues went away once he split from Grumman."

"Follow the money," Anthony said with a smile.

It was getting dark outside and still Anthony had not returned. Didn't he say he'd only be gone a few hours? She couldn't remember now. All that morning and into the afternoon Emma stayed inside the house, contemplating what she should do next. She played with the idea of leaving the house and striking out on her own. But the danger that came with jumping ship, without Anthony's protection, seemed both risky and ineffective. Even though the protection Anthony offered seemed minimal at best, it was better than nothing. Most importantly, she had nothing to go on if she went her own way; no direction and no real leads. At least with Anthony and his supposed connections she was moving toward something.

She wasn't sure what to make of David Jamison. That particular connection of Anthony's had her baffled. He annoyed her at first, but in the end he appeared to be a steady kind of guy, very much unlike the other men she'd met in her life. And he had been kind; not the obligatory kindness of someone who pitied her situation, but honestly moved by it and empathetic. This was another quality Emma had found lacking in the dismal line-up of men on which she'd wasted her time. Not that she would ever consider David as boyfriend material. She didn't even know if he was single. But he might be a person she could someday call a friend, and she'd never had any guy friends.

By the time four o'clock rolled around Emma had grown sick of sitting around waiting for Anthony. What if something bad happened to him? The idea of being left clueless and vulnerable clouded her mind and made her stomach hurt. Instead of thinking about that, she dug out the notebook and found the page with the phone number for Northrop Grumman. She sat on the edge of the bed she'd made that morning. All that day she fostered a strange combination of boredom and anxiety, so she did chores around the house to alleviate it. Now she turned on the bed stand lamp and began doodling on the notebook page, using a blue pen she'd found in the drawer to draw circles around the number. It would still be early afternoon back in California. Staring at the outdated Princess phone that graced the upstairs guest room, she remembered how she'd always wanted a pink one of those in her room when she was a kid. Her mom said they couldn't afford it, of course, and she smiled now thinking about how her dream had finally come true.

Maybe she should call and see if any record of Frank Nirody had turned up. There was little else to do, so she picked up the phone receiver and dialed the number, tapping on the book with the pen while waiting for someone to answer. A person picked up on the other end almost immediately, and Emma asked for Rene, the woman who had promised to look into Nirody's work history. She attempted a breezy tone once Rene got on the line.

"Hi Rene, we spoke several days ago about a former Grumman employee Frank Nirody."

"Oh yes," the woman perkily replied, "I remember you. I tried to call you yesterday, but no one answered. I figured you'd call back."

Emma imagined the phone ringing in the old farm house, empty except for bad memories.

"Oh, I'm sorry," she explained. "I had to go out of town." She tried to downplay how badly she needed anything Rene found.

"It probably doesn't matter anyway. Mr. Nirody hasn't gotten back to me about the rental. But I figured I'd follow up just the same."

There was a pause on the line. "Well, I do have some information on him if you're interested." It sounded as if Rene was eager to share.

"Sure," Emma replied, "did he work for Grumman like his application said?"

"Yes, he was with the company from 1973 to '74. His work history indicates he was employed as a flight instructor training pilots of the Iranian government. That was when Grumman had a contract providing them F-14 fighter jets."

'So far, so what,' Emma thought, and waited for Rene to go on.

"It looks like he left the company halfway through the project. He gave financial issues as his reason for quitting. But it's kind of funny…"

Emma sensed a note of curiosity in the woman's voice. "How is it funny?" she asked. "You mean strange?"

"Yeah," Rene said, "well, I probably shouldn't tell you this, but this is super old information so I don't think it's a big deal. When you look at what Mr. Nirody was earning as a flight instructor, it's pretty substantial. If he was having financial issues on that salary, then he must've had a gambling problem or something."

Ahmadi's voice came back to Emma. "Mr. Nirody might not prove to be as squeamish as you proved to be." The promised payoff to her dad must have been a big deal. Would it have been enough for him to put his career and reputation on the line? She still wasn't convinced her dad ultimately took Ahmadi up on his offer, but maybe Frank couldn't resist.

"Are you still there?" Rene asked on the other end of the line.

"Oh yes, I'm sorry." Emma wondered if there was more. "That is kind of weird, isn't it? Did you find anything else? I mean, anything on Mr. Nirody?"

"No, sorry," Rene said, "that's about it. But I did get something interesting about the other man you brought up. I believe it was a Mr. Woods?"

Emma's heart skipped a beat. She'd been so caught up in Frank's history she'd almost forgotten about her dad's.

"Oh right," she responded, not expecting any revelations. "Carter Woods, I think that was one of the references Mr. Nirody gave me." This time she'd thought through how she would respond in advance of her call. She hoped the lie sounded believable.

"Well, there is record of a Carter Woods working at the same time, also as a flight instructor. But there's nothing more in his work history I can tell you."

"Oh, okay," Emma said, not bothering to hide her disappointment, "well thanks so much for all your efforts. I really appreciate it, Rene."

"No," Rene came back, "what I'm saying is, there's absolutely no other information on Mr. Woods; no termination date, nothing about if he retired, no forwarding address, nothing."

Emma tried to remember what the company told her mother regarding her dad's death and consequential suspension of all benefits that might have helped to support the family. All she could recall was the shame and sense of utter loss brought about by Carter Woods' actions. Her family received a small pension from Grumman, but they were never given her father's body to properly bury. Her mom's only explanation being that his remains were being held as "evidence."

Rene was speaking again. "I've never seen employee history just end like this. It's as if Mr. Woods completely disappeared."

She took Emma's silence as license to continue. "Mr Woods is the only person in the entire Grumman employee history to just….vanish." She paused again, and then asked, "You're not really checking on these men because of a rental application, are you?"

After hearing what Rene had to say about her father, Emma decided there was no point in lying. "No," she admitted, "not really. Carter Woods was my dad."

Rene sounded truly sad for Emma. "And you don't know what happened to him? That's awful." After a moment passed, she said, "I wish I could tell you more."

A tiny glimmer of hope began to kindle in Emma. If there was no record of her father's alleged criminal acts, not even in his work history, then maybe that was the thing these people were trying to hide. Why else would they attempt to erase his very existence?

"It's okay, Rene," she said gratefully to the woman in human resources, "you've gone out of your way to help me, really."

"I hope you find what you're looking for," Rene replied, "good luck."

Emma moved to hang up the phone after hearing Rene disconnect. Holding the phone slightly from her ear, she heard an additional click. "Oh shit!" she wondered in a panic, "was someone listening in?" She swallowed hard and sat perfectly still, until she heard a noise downstairs. Then she reached to turn off the bed stand lamp, cloaking the room in darkness.

Chapter 26
Hunter and Prey

David took the expressway exit that would lead him back to the house in Georgetown. In spite of the cold, he rode with the windows down. He liked the feel of bracing wind in his face. It helped him think. The sun was just beginning to set, and he sped up a bit in order to make better time. He promised Anthony to get there before dark, and it looked as if he'd be cutting it close. It was a good meeting with his friend and mentor. They were both excited about what David had unearthed, even though it brought about more questions.

"The money is definitely part of the equation," Anthony instructed him on their way back to the parked cars in Arlington Cemetery, "but I've a gut feeling there's more to it."

"Are you referring to your friend Theodore?" Anthony had shown him the old poolside photo of the impeccably dressed officer Alberts, lurking in the background while Carter, Anne and their daughters posed as the happy 1970s family. David was struck by how different Emma looked as a little girl, an expression of sheer joy on her face as she sat with her family, her arm around her sister who was making a face at the camera.

"Teddy never once spoke to me about having contact with Carter before the attempted arrest, not to me or anyone on our team. He's a narcissist, and as such would have gloated about that connection the very minute our team was pulled together. And he wouldn't have been in Iran unless there was something in it for him, some way of advancing up the ladder, authentically or not. There must have been an awfully big carrot dangled in front of him that suddenly got whisked away. Otherwise, he would have a position well above mine."

David was accustomed to working with fellow officers in the Middle Eastern theater. That was a world he could understand and comfortably navigate. What Anthony was implying was complicated. If the people pulling the strings in the Woods case were some of the higher ups they were supposed to trust, well that made things a whole lot more sinister. The line between what was accepted as company policy and criminal wrongdoing could get slippery.

"So, we just have to figure out what the carrot was?" David asked. The idea of someone in the Agency being so corrupt made him sick to his stomach.

"And who was dangling it," Anthony quipped. "Not only that, we also have to find out if Carter was purposefully eliminated because of something he discovered, and who the other players were. This Nirody has to be tracked down before those others find him and take him out as well."

David shook his head as he drove up the street to the Georgetown house. Anthony's warning had been grim.

"We have to do all of this….without the other players finding out how close we are."

Anthony agreed to meet him back in Georgetown later that night. "Please go directly to the house once you leave here," he'd directed, "I told Emma I'd be back before dark, and she'll be getting worried."

As David pulled into the driveway he thought of the stress Carter's daughter must be feeling. He would put her mind at ease by hinting at some of their latest developments. He reached to turn off the headlights then realized he'd never turned them on. It was only just getting dark. Switching off the ignition he moved to open the car door when he heard something, a dull thud that came from the house. David noticed that Emma had drawn the shades just as Anthony instructed, but it seemed odd that she didn't have at least one light on now that evening was falling. He quietly opened the car door, slipped out, and softly closed it again. Quickly making his way to a garden behind the house, he found a wooden stairwell that reached the second floor. Reaching for the gun he always kept in a shoulder holster, he quietly advanced up the stairs.

When he came upon the upstairs landing, he crouched down to avoid the door window that looked out on the back yard. From his jacket he fished around for the extra house key Anthony gave him long ago. He felt the cool metal in his hand and quietly slipped it into the door. With one turn he was inside and creeping down the hallway toward the guest room where Emma was staying, hanging back in the closet doorway where he remained obscured in the dark. As his training kicked in, he remembered to breathe and evaluate the situation. Gun held straight down but steady, he waited. He knew it wouldn't be long before the intruder made his move. Sure enough, he heard a creaking sound. That would be the fourth step from the top, just five feet from the guest room door. Anthony never wanted it fixed, "because it's an organic alarm system." Once again, his friend was right.

A figure appeared, dressed in black, his own firearm at the ready. David prayed Emma wasn't in the guest room, sleeping. His mind raced as he calculated the physics behind eliminating the intruder before he could shoot her, should she be in the bed. The minutiae of every object in that room flooded his brain, and in a split second he was behind the dark figure who was turning the doorknob to enter the room. David pressed his gun into the back of the man's head and drew back the hammer with a decisive snapping sound. The figure stopped, standing rigid and alert. No words were spoken. David would not hesitate in delivering the kill shot, but did the intruder know that? A decision was made, and the dark figure attempted to reach behind his shoulder for David's gun while thrusting his elbow back, aiming for the ribs. David anticipated the gesture. While training at Langley his peers were creeped out by this "sixth sense" he seemed to have, but it always served him well. He took a half step back, avoiding both the man's elbow and his reaching hand. Adjusting his aim for the man's back he squeezed the trigger and felt the bullet leave his gun and enter the man, all in what seemed like slow motion. The force of the shot caused the man to involuntarily throw up his arms, and then fall forward onto the guest room floor. David reached for the bedroom's overhead light and switched it on, kicking the man's dropped gun away and into a corner of the room. The sound of his own gunshot ringing in his ears, he scanned the room, but Emma was nowhere to be seen.

The fallen intruder moaned, and in his stupor, began crawling toward the closet door, left slightly ajar. David followed him with the intention of keeping him alive just long enough to pull answers from the dying man. Intercepting him just before the closet door, he bent down to turn the man over and begin his interrogation. But the closet door came rushing out to slam into the side of his head, knocking him to his knees and causing him to nearly fall on top of the intruder.

"Shit!" David cried out, reaching with his hand to block the door from doing further damage.

"David?" Emma asked in a shaky voice.

Temporarily deaf from firing his weapon, David couldn't hear Emma. It was only when she peeked out from behind the door that he realized she'd effectively hidden from her assailant.

"Emma, come on out, it's okay," he answered while nursing his head.

Wide-eyed and nervous, Emma cast a glance at the unmoving figure on the floor.

"I heard him come in," she told David. The gunshot had affected her hearing as well, and she was shocked to discover she couldn't hear her own words.

"I'm sorry, I can't really hear you," David yelled.

They both looked at each other, confused, until David decided they had to move…fast.

He felt for a pulse, but it was too late. The man was dead. Frustrated, he began looking through the man's pockets. "How did you manage to hide in the closet?" He asked Emma in a loud voice, who was watching him intently.

"I was on the phone with the people from Northrop, and I think he was downstairs listening." She yelled back, shivering at the thought. She looked closer at the man dressed in black. In the commotion it hadn't registered that the man was dead, and David had killed him.

Though she felt queasy and lightheaded, she was very much aware that something had gone wrong. "Where's Anthony?"

David looked up from frisking the man, and stared straight ahead, conjuring his next move. Anthony would be on his way to the house to meet them soon. Yet, this place was no longer safe for any of them. He'd have to hide a message for his friend and get the hell out of here. He only hoped there wasn't more of this dead man's team on the way as well. Digging into the man's coat pocket he found a small radio, not the type used by police, bulky and awkward. This was a piece of equipment he recognized, standard issue for field officers, with a tiny green light at the bottom, flashing.

"Emma, we have to get out of here, now. You don't have time to grab anything but a coat." Coming to her senses, Emma plucked up her jacket from where she'd dropped it on the floor and headed toward the door with David.

"Wait!" she yelled, and turned back toward the bed. Reaching under the mattress she pulled out the coveted notebook. It was the only thing of value to her now. To her dismay David yanked it from her hand and flipped to the back. He tore out the last, empty page and felt in his coat for a pen. "Here," Emma said, and produced a pencil from one of the desk drawers. Using the notebook to lean on, David hastily scribbled something on the paper. When he handed the notebook back to Emma, she felt a rush of relief. He wasn't going to try and steal the precious few pieces of information she'd kept to herself. Maybe she could trust him.

Quickly folding the paper David grabbed Emma by the arm and hurried her out the door. Neither of them looked back at the dead man on the floor. Slipping out of the back door, David hustled Emma down to the garden. She felt as if David was almost carrying her, hardly allowing her feet to come into contact with the stairs. David stopped once they reached the garden, taking only seconds to slip the piece of paper he'd written on under a small cherub statue nearly obscured by hedges. Then they were off again, David steering Emma toward the car and unceremoniously dumping her in the passenger seat. She snapped her seat belt in with trembling hands just as he started the car and pulled out. Emma gripped the armrest on the door as he jerked the car out of reverse, and her head hit the head cushion when he accelerated, taking them down the quiet neighborhood street way too fast.

"Jesus David," Emma yelled, "Be careful! You're going to hit someone!"

"I know what I'm doing," David replied calmly under his breath and looking into the rear-view mirror. The headlights he was expecting came up fast behind them. Time for plan B.

"Hold on," David commanded, and Emma clutched the armrest tighter. Pulling the steering wheel hard to the right they cut into an alley that ran horizontal to the stately neighborhood homes. Emma didn't know the alley was there, and believing they were going headlong into the corner house, she screamed. For a moment, the headlights behind them vanished, then flashed through the rear window once more in a staccato motion. The people pursuing them didn't have the territory memorized like David did. He could lose them completely with a little luck and a few more turns. They must have guessed as much because they started shooting.

"Get down!" David pushed Emma's head to the seat, muffling her continued screams. Gunning the car, he raced to the next hidden turn that he knew would take them to the expressway. This time his erratic turn went to the left, just as a bullet pierced the back window. The sound of glass breaking filled the car. Emma was crying now, terrified, but remaining face down on the seat. She covered her ears and tried to keep from being thrown to the floor in the lurching car. The headlights behind them disappeared once more, and David rapidly glanced right, then left, for oncoming traffic as they emerged from the alley. They narrowly avoided a minivan full of kids, and he maneuvered the car toward the two-lane onramp. A semi-truck entering the expressway threatened to block his progress, and he was forced to slow down.

He sensed the pursuing car before he saw it, and pulled his gun from its holster for the second time that night. Reaching over his left arm that was holding fast to the wheel, he steadied the firearm on the door and waited for the other car to gain on them, pleased with himself for his preference of driving with the window down. Over the sound of the wind blowing through the car David yelled instructions to Emma once more.

"Whatever you do, Emma," he said with authority, "do not raise your head."

They were coming up on the truck now, and as David slowed his vehicle, the car on his left inched closer. He looked straight ahead, but he knew there would be a gun pointed at him in seconds. All he needed was good timing. His training went into overdrive, and he counted down the calculated motion of the two cars aligning, three… two… one. Emma screamed when he shot, but she remained face down on the seat, hands over her ears. He never saw the shooter's face, but he felt exactly where it was and how close they were to being taken out. After taking his shot, he hit the brakes just long enough to fall behind the shooter's car, which was now beginning to spiral out of control. It spun onto the grassy border of the onramp, and flipped to one side, wheels still turning but going nowhere. David accelerated again, passing the semi and leaving him just enough room to enter the expressway. He kept to the speed limit, no longer concerned with the wrecked car he left behind.

Chapter 25
Dubious Allies

They drove to the airport in silence. David was lost in his thoughts about the next move. Emma gathered her nerves, but her ears were still ringing from the sound of the gun blast. To drown out the noise in her head, she began to formulate questions.

The trick was knowing what to ask David, first. What the hell kind of government job did he have that he could kill so easily? How did he know someone had broken into the house in the first place? What made him believe there would be others following right behind? In the back of her mind she temporarily shelved their adventure in the car. She would think about that later. Compartmentalizing was quickly becoming a handy coping mechanism. A steady wind blasted through the smashed rear window, but she felt more numb than cold. She wondered why this man had shown up and saved her life. Was he going to help her after all? And what had happened to Anthony? She was afraid if she asked the wrong question, he'd realize she was nothing but trouble, and dump her off on the side of the road. She would be on her own, with the same people after her. Only this time they would be successful in killing her, or kidnapping her, or whatever they had in mind. Just as she gathered the courage to ask him about Anthony, he pulled into the airport lot and parked the car at the very back of the garage. Turning to face her, he put a hand on her shoulder and asked his question first.

"What were you on the phone about back at the house? What do you think that man heard?"

Sensing that time was not on her side, Emma didn't hesitate in answering. "I spoke to the HR woman at Northrop. They purchased Grumman a while ago, and I had them look up my dad and Frank Nirody's employee history. Frank had some kind of money problems, and all the information about my dad is just gone."

Emma and David stared at each other, both coming to the same conclusion, but it was David who said it out loud. "They wanted your dad to disappear."

Emma asked about the one thing that had been burning in her mind since it all began. "What do they want with me?"

David looked away from her and out the window, scanning the garage for anyone who might do them harm. It was a reflex reaction, but he was incapable of letting his guard down. He felt protective of Emma now, and he wasn't used to taking care of anyone but himself. It was a strange sensation. He would have to be honest with her. "I don't know for sure how you play into all of this Emma. I think if they wanted to kill you they would have by now. No, they want you alive, but under their control. That's why they tried to scare you into leaving things alone with your dad."

He directed his gaze back at her. The blue-gray eyes didn't show fear, and it surprised him. She even managed a little smile. "So, I've got them worried."

David smiled back. "Yeah," he agreed, "and we've managed to stay one step ahead of them, until today. Anthony sent me back to check on you just in case, but he didn't really believe you were in danger at the house. Nobody knows about that place except me and him."

He rubbed his hand over his mouth and up through his hair in an agitated gesture. "These people are aware of your connection to Anthony. I know that now, and I left a message for Tony telling him the same."

Emma suddenly realized David hadn't said anything about what he may have found out about her father. "Did you check your resources, or whatever it was you were going to do? Did you learn anything more about my dad?"

"Yes," David didn't see any reason to keep her in the dark. If she was going to be part of the team, he wouldn't have her flying blind. "It looks like your dad was an officer. He, Frank and another man were embedded in the Grumman project, toward what end I'm not sure. But Frank bailed under suspicious circumstances and your dad was labeled as an officer who went rogue. The details behind all that are unknown because, surprise, surprise, that information was taken from his file.

It was a lot to take in, and David's response only created more questions for Emma.

"What do you mean my dad was an officer...an officer for what?"

David realized just how little this woman was aware of what was happening all around her. *'Damnit Tony,'* he thought, *'how am I going to do this?'*

"Have you heard of the Central Intelligence Agency?" It wasn't really a question, but he wanted to ease her into what her father had clearly kept secret from his family.

"The CIA?!" Emma asked incredulously, "Oh come on! My dad was not with the fucking CIA. He was too unstable for something like that. He had a temper you wouldn't believe. And he could be mean. I can't even tell you how brutal he could be. I loved my dad, but he was abusive, David. Why would the CIA trust someone like that as an officer?"

David thought Emma was being understandably naive. Sometimes that was exactly the kind of man the agency recruited, depending on the need. He wasn't going to tell her that, however. "Look, I don't know exactly what kind of work your dad was doing for the Agency. His duties could have been very limited. But if the files indicate he was an officer, then that much can be considered accurate. The fact that details have been erased means someone from the inside was, or still is, pulling the strings. From what I see, or actually what can't be seen, it was truly rotten how things went down with your dad." He thought of the photo within the file, showing the burned corpse that was supposed to be Carter.

"Emma, did your mom ever have a burial for your father? I'm sorry if this is painful, but did they send back his remains?"

Emma looked down and hugged herself. It wasn't the cold inside the car, but the memories that gave her a chill. "No," she said flatly, "they told my mom they had to keep his body for evidence."

'Why keep a body for evidence if it was burned beyond recognition?' David wondered. "Did they give you information about how he died?" He remembered the shock on Anthony's face when told about Carter's supposed car accident.

"Yeah," Emma felt so tired, going through all the awful details about her father. "They said he was shot while trying to run out on some arms deal. It sounded like bullshit, then, and it still does. But on the tape he left me, I know he was approached about something like that. He turned them down though, or at least he did on the tape."

David listened to every word, storing it away for later consideration. Gathering up his things he made his way out of the car. He moved to the passenger side and opened Emma's door, offering a hand to usher her out. Pressing the clicker to lock the car seemed pointless to Emma, considering the condition of the back window. David did it anyway and led her toward the airport terminal.

"Where are we going?" Emma asked, surprised that she wasn't dreading another flight. After what she'd been through, air travel felt far less frightening.

"Geneva first, that's where I'm based. I have to get some things there and let my people know I'll be away for a bit, on other business."

He quickened their pace, and Emma had to catch little gasps of air between words. "How did you unearth everything about my dad, David? And what about the guy who came after me in the house? All that shooting, the crazy driving; you're CIA too, aren't you?"

"Yes," he desperately hoped Tony found his note. The secret place for emergency communication they came up with long ago, but would there be others who stayed behind at the house, to retrieve their fallen colleague? Were they lying in wait for Tony right now? Either way, David knew that taking Emma away from D.C. was the best move. He needed time to think and formulate a plan. With any luck Tony would catch up with them.

"Both of us have worked within the Agency for some time," he said. "Tony has been there longer, of course."

They were almost at the section of the terminal for international flights.

They were walking too fast for Emma. Even in her Keds, she could barely keep up. "David," Emma panted, almost out of breath. "Where's Anthony?"

He placed his hand on the small of her back, pushing her through the sliding glass terminal doors.

"I honestly don't know," he said. He was wondering the same thing.

At noon, Victor Tarlino blew his nose loudly into a tissue, then tossed it into the wastebasket positioned at the side of his desk. It joined an ever-growing mountain of similarly soiled tissues begun only this morning. He had a cold. The red, puffy eyes and sallow skin of his face only contributed to his typically unkempt appearance. Those who knew him frequently described Victor as slovenly behind his back, but today he practically oozed the term, as a stuffy nose caused him to suck in air through his gaping mouth. It made focusing on the papers in front of him even harder than usual. He hated his job, and detested the chore of acting like it meant anything to him. He saw it only as a stepping stone toward the moment he would become financially secure, and ultimately escape on any cruise ship that offered the best buffet. He'd sampled more than his share of them already. This was evident by the strained buttons on the front of a shirt that once was white but was now yellowed by overuse and neglect.

The knock on Victor's door didn't surprise him. He'd arranged for the meeting just as soon as he got to work, making a point of scheduling during the lunchtime hour, when his administrative assistant would be out. "Come," he grunted, before reaching for another tissue.

Alberts walked into the office with an air of insolence, closing the door behind him and taking a seat in front of Victor's desk without waiting for an invitation. Victor ignored the implied disrespect. He was accustomed to Theodore's antics, and he had bigger problems on his hands today.

Victor finished wiping his nose while Alberts regarded his boss with a look of disgust. "I do hope you're not contagious," Teddy said while pushing back his chair, distancing himself from any possible virus.

"Don't trouble yourself Alberts," Victor replied with a sniffle. "I'm on the mend, and anyway, what we must discuss can't wait. Otherwise, I wouldn't have come in today."

Theodore had no doubt about that. Tarlino took any excuse possible to avoid real work, and everyone knew it. He crossed his legs and flicked off an imaginary bit of lint from his finely tailored slacks. "I told you before Victor, I'm keeping an eye on things, so you have nothing to worry about."

"The hell I don't!" Tarlino grumbled. "You've botched everything from the very beginning and only made it worse. There are people who are very unhappy with how you've handled this. They don't like your style, and they're getting worried."

Theodore's face burned, yet he refused to share his own feelings of failure. If he appeared weak in front of Tarlino, he stood the risk of being replaced, and that was unacceptable.

"I would like to have seen you come up with a better way of intimidating the Woods girl. Any other civilian would have either stopped snooping, or gone to the police, who would naturally label them as crazy or paranoid. How was I to know she'd receive help, and from Newcastle no less. May I remind you that I was not the one who chose him to head up the operation?"

Tarlino dismissed him with a grunt. He knew Alberts had wanted the job, but it was believed he would have been too obvious in his actions. With an eye on retirement and no apparent interest in the case, Newcastle was considered the perfect lead. He was a warm body going through the motions of watching Carter's daughter, until the bank visit threw everyone off. As if reading his mind, Alberts drove home another point.

"And who could have anticipated Miss Woods would somehow come upon new information on her father, as if he were reaching out from his goddamned grave? Anyway, I tracked down where Newcastle took the girl, so you can thank me for that. The team I dispatched should be contacting me shortly about how things went when they extracted her from Anthony's hiding place. As for him, he appears to have abandoned the woman and disappeared. I'm assuming Officer Newcastle didn't have the stomach for all the trouble she's turned out to be."

A menacing smile crept up on Victor's face. Alberts didn't know, and he would have the pleasure of telling him.

"Your team failed miserably Theodore. You're down one man, and the girl has, once again, gone missing." He waited for the news to sink in, delighting in seeing Alberts' haughty expression turn to one of confusion.

"Newcastle may have fallen off the map, but he put someone else in charge." Tarlino went on. "We have our suspicions about who that person might be, and if we're right, then our job just got harder."

The two men scowled across Victor's desk. There was mutual hatred, but they were stuck with each other until they could wrap up the Woods business.

Theodore scrambled to save face. "I've been at this a hell of a lot longer than you have Victor. And, I dare say, I have more skin in the game."

"Yes, yes of course," Tarlino said condescendingly. "Your work in the past was sufficient. But things are different now. It's no longer 1974, my friend, and there's so much more at stake. There has been talk amongst the bigger players of replacing you. They have a lot riding on this, so I'd watch my step from here on out."

A knot was forming in the pit of Teddy Alberts' stomach. There was a way he could remain a major player in all this, though he hadn't wanted to reveal that plan just yet. Luckily, he'd already set part of his survival plan in motion. Now he would have to carefully dance around Tarlino's threats without showing all his cards.

"You can tell the suits I have no intention of bowing out. And if they decide to take matters into their own hands, I have in place an incriminating trail of crumbs that would lead right back to them." It was a very clear threat, and when the blood drained from Tarlino's face, Theodore knew it hit home.

"Nobody's said a word about replacing you Theodore," Tarlino said with an aggravated cough. "But they want the Woods girl found, and they want to be informed about all she knows, and I mean everything. If you have to achieve this through drastic measures, then do it discreetly. Her involvement could upend key factors in our current endeavor, and they want her out of the picture." Theodore glared at Victor, saying nothing.

"And for God's sake Teddy," Tarlino said with disdain, "cover your ass." Alberts stood and brushed the neat crease on his pants back into place.

"I always cover my ass," he shot back as he headed to the door. "I suggest you do the same."

Chapter 26
The Chase

Emma stood with David under a big blue screen listing the departure and arrival of the day's various flights. David scanned the screen intently, while Emma blithely focused on the people passing by. It seemed a good way to clear her mind, wondering where everyone was going, and what ordinary story was behind their travel plans. Business trips and family vacations were blissfully boring adventures, compared to a journey laden with danger and uncertainty. David must have found an agreeable flight, because he clutched her arm and moved her toward the United Airlines ticket counter. They avoided the long line of people checking in and went to the counter reserved for frequent fliers. Emma reasoned that, like Anthony, David must travel constantly. Putting in that many miles must come with a few perks. The woman on the other side of the counter looked up and smiled. "Hi, can I..." David didn't waste any time. Pulling a ticket from his coat pocket he slid it toward the attendant. "I'm already booked for this flight, but I need to add my wife if there's room." He squeezed Emma's hand so hard at the word "wife" she didn't have time to react to the term.

"Oh, certainly sir," the counter lady answered, instantly adapting to David's business-like demeanor. Her fingers worked the computer until she paused to scan the screen. "It looks like you're in luck," she said with a cool smile, beginning the process of pulling together an additional ticket. "There are still several seats available on this flight. May I have your wife's name? And I'll need some ID."

Emma recovered and pulled her wallet from her bag. "Emma Woods," she told the ticket lady, and held the wallet open to show her driver's license. Shooting a look at David she explained, "I kept my maiden name."

The counter lady was too busy issuing the ticket to see the smiles exchanged between the two supposed newlyweds. She stapled Emma's paperwork together and handed it to her while David offered up his credit card. "I'm afraid you won't be sitting together during take-off," she told Emma apologetically. "But maybe you can exchange seats with someone once you gain altitude."

David snatched Emma's ticket and recovered his credit card. "Thank you," he snapped to the woman. "Don't you have any luggage?" she asked. But he'd already begun to steer Emma away toward their gate.

"We have just enough time to stop at the gift store so you can get a few things," he said to Emma, who once again was having trouble keeping up with him. "If we have time, why are we walking so fast?" She panted.

"Better safe than sorry," David muttered, glancing over his shoulder. They found a gift shop close to their boarding gate, and David stood by while she picked out a toothbrush, toothpaste and deodorant. It was only a few things, but she grabbed a large tote bag to use as a carry on, thinking she might buy a few pieces of clothing at their next stop. Other than the basics, she was at a loss for what else she'd need. She plopped the items by the register and began to pull out her wallet again.

"Wait," David told the startled black man working the register. He flipped through a nearby rack of tee shirts, and plucked a brown one with the word "Super Girl" printed on the front. Adding it to the toiletries he nodded at the man who began to ring things up.

"Brown is a good color," David said, smiling at Emma. "It doesn't show as much if you get it dirty. You're a size medium, right?"

Emma returned his smile, impressed by the thoughtful gesture. Then, looking at the writing on the shirt she gave a slight wince. "Super Girl?" she asked dubiously.

"I thought it appropriate," David remarked, once again using his credit card for the purchases.

Before Emma could argue over his paying, he'd pocketed the card, grabbed her bag of items and ushered her out of the store and toward their gate. People were already queuing up to board, but David slowed their pace so that they lingered at the very end of the line. Emma thought he looked preoccupied but busied herself with thrusting her newly purchased items into the tote.

"Let's sit down for a minute," David suddenly announced. Emma looked at him in surprise. "But everybody's boarding. Shouldn't we get on and find our seats?" She was already anxious that they wouldn't be sitting together. Why, she wondered, was he complicating things further? "Just for a minute," he quipped, and pushed her into a nearby row of seats.

Grabbing the tote from her hands, he placed it under her seat, then grasped her arm as if he was afraid she would bolt at any minute. Emma looked at him in confusion, and he returned her gaze.

"I'm going to say and do something that you won't understand," he whispered. "Just go along with it and stay quiet, okay?"

Emma felt the now familiar ache in her stomach that indicated something awful was about to go down. *'Not again,'* she pleaded with her eyes. But David squeezed her hand and offered a smile. "It's going to be alright. We can do this…together." Then he stood, bringing her up with him. When she moved to collect the tote from underneath her seat he kept her arm firmly in his grasp. "Leave it," was all he said, and led her back into the line of passengers.

Their moment in the waiting area resulted in giving them a place at the very end of the line. Emma surveyed the people standing in front of them, scanning each face to find evidence of malice. Only a young couple turned to look behind, a man and a woman, perhaps in their thirties. They seemed harmless enough. The woman caught Emma's eye, smiled, then turned to speak with what she assumed was her husband or boyfriend.

Emma and David presented their tickets to a flight attendant manning the door to the plane's gangway, and then proceeded down the long shaft to the plane. Emma's heart was beating hard, and she could feel the dampness of a nervous sweat enveloping her body. When they stepped into the airplane another flight attendant greeted them with a slight nod. The passengers were performing the usual preflight shuffle of finding seats and storing bags in the overhead. Emma checked the paper she had clutched in her hand, looking for a seat number, but David was whispering in her ear again.

"How well can you do crazy?" he asked. Before she could respond he turned to the flight attendant behind them, standing with her hand on the airplane door lock.

"Miss," he quietly and politely said to the attendant, "we have to go back out."

Both the attendant and Emma regarded David in stunned silence.

"I'm sorry sir, but we're preparing to leave," the attendant said in her best official voice.

"My wife left her bag somewhere on the seats in the waiting area," David told the woman in a concerned tone. "It's got her meds in there, and she can't travel without them."

Emma was still trying to register what he was up to but remembered his question. "Can you do crazy?" For whatever reason, David expected her to perform. She gave the attendant her best expression of benign insanity.

The attendant considered the situation and decided towards policy. Well sir," she said with a tight smile, "we can help your wife find her seat while you run and find her bag."

David shook his head and leaned in to speak quietly with the woman. "Look, she's not capable of being left alone. She's mentally unstable, and unless you want to witness a major meltdown, you're going to have to let her come with me."

Both the attendant and David turned to assess Emma, whose panic-stricken face made the threat real enough for the now tight-lipped attendant.

"Fine," she said tersely, "but you'll have to hurry. We can't hold the plane for you."

"I don't expect you to," David remarked as he squeezed Emma between the attendant and himself. "We can grab another flight."

Emma had just enough time to glance back at the seats behind her. The woman who had smiled at her was no longer smiling. She and the man remained standing and glaring as the other passengers began to buckle in, ignoring another attendant's instructions that they take their seats.

Then they were off the plane and heading back out of the tube they'd navigated minutes before. When they reached the boarding area David went directly to retrieve the waiting tote.

"Run," he said, as if it was the most natural request in the world, and yanked Emma's hand so hard she felt her wrist snap. She didn't look back to see if the couple was following them. It took all of her concentration to match David's agile movement through the crowd, as if it were an obstacle course. Fighting for breath she held on tightly to his hand down one terminal hallway and into another, the gift and duty free shops a blur mingled with the scent of fast food and coffee. They whisked past every United Airlines gate until finally making it to British Airways. Emma bumped into David when he stopped to once again stare at a screen of entirely different flights. Then it was off at a run once again until David led them to a gate where a trickle of passengers was performing yet another boarding routine.

David drew Emma up beside him and pulled from his pocket a brand-new ticket. "Your name is Clara Edwards," he said as he thrust the paper into her damp hand. "Clara. Right. Whatever." Emma wheezed, struggling to catch her breath. David only smiled, handing his own ticket to the unsuspecting woman in a crisp blue uniform. "Welcome Mr. Edwards," the attendant said with her own generic smile. She waited expectedly for Emma, who stared back, ticket in hand.

"Let me get that honey," David gently cooed, and passed her ticket to the attendant. "We almost missed the flight," he explained. "My wife took too long packing for our honeymoon."

"Oh congratulations!" the attendant beamed. "Where are you headed?" David pulled Emma behind him, returning command of the tote as a distraction.

"The Middle East," he called out over his shoulder to the smiling attendant as the boarding door closed behind them.

Chapter 29
Heads Together

David glanced over at the woman sitting quietly beside him on the plane. Emma was spending the second half of their flight looking out her window. After take-off she began to demand answers. "Where are we going?" How did you know we were being followed? Where did you get those tickets?" She kept the most pressing questions to herself. "Do you have a plan?" "What did you learn about my father that you're not telling me?" She would have to wait for the right moment. David seemed hesitant to answer even her most immediate queries.

"We're flying straight to Istanbul. If they managed to follow us to the airport, that means they know about me, and they'll no doubt be waiting for us in Geneva."   As for his recognition of being tailed, he offered very little.

"I noticed that couple in the gift shop," he said as he rearranged his wallet and pulled out a passport for Emma. "It's a temporary," he explained when she flipped through it looking for a photo. "It's something Tony and I arranged. It means you're on official business with me, sort of like my secretary." He then closed his eyes and tried to fall asleep.

Emma's continued prodding tired him out, and he felt he'd told her all she needed to know. The truth was, he was going primarily on the instinct that had served him well throughout his career. Anthony encouraged him to use that sixth sense in mustering up the various possibilities they might encounter.

"I believe the answer to Emma's dilemma lies in Iran," Anthony had said before they parted ways.

"It's still a long shot," David countered, "and how are you going to get her there?"

That was when Anthony gave him a brown envelope with all the necessary paperwork. "I'm not going to get her there," he'd slyly remarked. "You are."

David looked at the papers. One set of tickets was for Geneva, the other for Istanbul.

"Why two sets of tickets?" David had asked as Anthony headed to his car. "Even if she accompanies me back to Geneva, we can arrange a flight to Turkey from there. And look, I haven't even agreed to take on Emma and her problems."

Anthony turned and smiled at him. "You're a good man David," he said, gesturing a thumbs up. "I know you'll do the right thing."

Resigned to the fact that Anthony was putting him in charge of the Wood's woman, he looked down again at the tickets. Calling out to his friend once again he asked, "But why the two sets?"

"Because you never know," was the only explanation his mentor offered.

'Sonofabitch,' David fumed. Reliving Anthony's assumption he'd take over pissed him off. It was also keeping him from falling asleep. His friend was devious in his efforts to get him involved. He'd somehow managed to draw up the tickets and passport, no doubt pulling strings and calling on old associates for favors. His disappearance didn't surprise David. It was probably his way of forcing the younger officer to do what Anthony felt he could not, find out what happened to Carter Woods, and keep Emma alive in the process.

When David opened his eyes, he was disturbed to find Emma staring at him.

"I know you're not sleeping," she said, tilting her head in a way that made those damned curls fall over one eye. "Could you please stop avoiding the fact that we need to talk? I mean really talk!"

So, during the rest of the flight, David made Emma give up every detail she could remember about events leading up to her father's death. The family had traveled through Europe, "sightseeing," according to Emma's dad. The final destination of Iran included a stopover in Turkey where they languished four days without leaving the hotel, seemingly due to the Turkish invasion of Cyprus. "Is that why we're going to Turkey?" Emma asked, nursing a much-needed glass of wine the flight attendant had handed her with a cheery, "congratulations!" Word must have traveled amongst the attendants about the honeymooners.

"Your dad's real purpose in traveling to the Middle East was already sketchy leading up to your stopover in Turkey. And then his time in Iran culminated in him losing his life. I want to retrace his steps as closely as possible. It might give me someplace to look more deeply into what he really was doing over there."

Emma accepted his explanation, but David didn't tell her about his connections in Istanbul that were already searching for any old-timers who might have known or encountered her father. Mustafa Arslan had been a reliable go-between for David during the time he worked as a NOC. They connected over a love of adana kebabi, the spiced minced beef kebabs sold on the streets that David frequented, while gathering what information he could on possible corruption within the Turkish government. Thanks to a father who was a prominent government official, Mustafa had his finger on the pulse of every local politician as well as those who could benefit from bribing them. "I'll see what I can find out from my friend," he had promised when David called from the airport, "I have an uncle who was in the thick of things back in the seventies. He's old but still very sharp. I'll let you know if anything comes up when you get here."

"I appreciate it, you know that," David told his former contact. Mustafa brushed him off with a laugh. "No problem. It gives me something to do. Just like old times." David had a few more contacts that he was certain would be aching to get back into the thick of things, if just to relieve the boredom of the everyday life they'd settled back into. It wasn't much, but casting out nets in this manner had yielded gold in the past.

As he mulled things over, he glanced again at Emma. She was looking out the window at nothing again, just dark sky and the occasional puff of clouds. She must have felt his eyes on her because she asked without looking away from the window, "Why are you helping me?" She did her best to mask the suspicion in her voice, but David knew she was wary of him and of his motives. Whatever had happened to her in the past had set in hard and fast.

"I understand that it's difficult to trust anybody in your current situation Emma," he explained. "But seeing as I'm all you've got right now, I think it would be helpful if you gave me the benefit of the doubt."

Her features softened as she absorbed the meaning of his words. The possibility that he was putting her mind at ease gave him an unexpected rush. Why was he helping her? He struggled to make sense of it himself.

"I can't say that I was actually pleased when Tony put me in place to help you." He might as well be honest. "Anthony is my friend, for one thing. And I do owe him. I'm also intrigued by the way your father died, and how any real information about his killing has disappeared." He left out the other reason. The one he couldn't admit to himself. He was drawn to her.

Emma nodded and offered David a grateful smile. "I hope you know that I didn't want to screw up anyone else's life because of this obsession I have. Even before the threats and violence, I wanted to know more about my dad. Now it seems I have to keep it up if I want that violence to stop. I never meant to drag you and Anthony into this mess."

For once Emma wasn't angry. And the way she looked at him made David want to pull her close, hold her just long enough to feel her heartbeat. He liked this side of Emma, but his attraction to her made it difficult to concentrate on his next move.

"I'm not doing anything against my will Emma," he said, placing his hand on hers without thinking. It was a natural gesture that he regretted as soon as he felt her reaction to his touch, a jolt of electricity seemed to run between them. Their eyes met, both trying to read the other's intent. He quickly released his hold, and the moment was gone, the memory of it lingering in the air between them. David made a process of reclining his seat, crossing his arms, and finally closing his eyes.

"We have a long flight ahead of us," he said, settling in. "Let's get some sleep while we can. Maybe I'll dream up a way of getting you out of *'this mess'* as you call it."

Emma placed her plastic wine glass in the seat pocket in front of her and wadded up her sweater to make a pillow. She leaned it against the window and closed her eyes as well. Both of them took a long time pretending to sleep before finally drifting off.

Chapter 27
Karl's Game

Vice President Magnus filed away a stack of reports. He liked to keep things orderly, and he couldn't think clearly if the slightest thing was out of place. This compulsion for order had made his childhood difficult. He was constantly teased for the way he fussed over his desire for straight lines and perfect corners. But as an adult he'd turned the compulsion into what most people now viewed as a quality. In his twenties he served in the army as a Ranger. The late seventies was an exciting time for Karl, who was chosen out of a handful of young officers to assist in covert operations in Iran. At that time, the CIA was closely watching things unfold between the Shah and the burgeoning Revolutionary movement. Hoping to hedge their bets, the men on Karl's team cozied up to the revolutionaries, offering them assistance and support should they be successful in their attempts to overthrow the Shah. At the time this appeared to be a well-played move.

The Shah's corrupt government crumbled and was replaced by the Islamic theocracy under Ayatollah Ruhollah Khomeini. Karl and his team were praised for maintaining connections with the new Iranian government. Shortly thereafter, when fifty two U.S. diplomats and citizens were held hostage by the Muslim Student Followers, Karl and his team were able to keep the lines of negotiation open, using their revolutionary contacts. Karl was able to extricate himself from what he considered a "shit show" by the 1980s. His father, then the Chairman of the Center of Intel Commission, managed to place Karl in a cushy position where he could advance quickly. Ultimately, he was politically appointed into the Department overseeing all Covert Action.

Karl quietly maintained his relationships with the Iranians who provided him with juicy details about the new government, until eventually he became acquainted with their associates, working within a number of other Middle Eastern countries. Things had gone blissfully along until the bombing in Beirut. That little mishap had taken him by surprise, particularly when the terrorists were discovered to have been one of the groups with which Karl maintained contact.

He began to panic when those groups were silent to his urgent requests to clarify their future intentions. If any link between him and the terrorists was discovered, Karl's political career was over.

His ambitions drove him to reach for the stars. The way he'd conducted himself during a relatively short political career jettisoned him into an inner circle of powerful allies, and marrying Debra had been a well-calculated move. She came from a large family of wealth and prestige, peppered with Washington attorneys and judges. Becoming part of her clan effectively led him right to the man campaigning for the presidency three years ago. President Stanford liked Karl Magnus and his impeccable record. John Stanford ran on a platform of honesty and exemplary moral conduct. Without a speck of scandal on his record, Magnus made for the perfect running mate. Karl's own crusade against terrorism was a strategy he concocted just after becoming vice president. He imagined using his insight and experience with the revolutionaries, who paved the way for later terrorist ideology, would serve him well as he championed his proclaimed cause. Karl tapped into the current climate of fear that gripped the nation, hoping to use his anti-terrorism platform in his own bid for the presidency, once Stanford's term was up. They easily won the election and had served, as far as the public knew, a productive, if somewhat boring, first term. President Stanford was then granted another four years by the American people, and V.P. Magnus appeared content to come along for the ride.

Karl kept himself in shape with workouts that had recently become more regular at the local gym. In his late sixties, the life of a government official on the rise had given him the incentive to maintain his good looks, though he'd allowed his hair to turn a distinguished gray. He pulled open a desk drawer and extracted a bottle of Hugo Boss Cologne, dabbing just a touch of it onto his hand and running it across his face. He was waiting on his next appointment, and soon a few taps at the door announced her arrival. "Hello," Karl answered the knock in a sing-song voice. A pretty brunette let herself in and then quietly closed the door behind her. She smiled and walked confidently toward the V.P., tossing a large manila folder on top of his desk, allowing its contents to spread onto his desk in disarray. Bracing her hands on the far side of the desk, she leaned the front of her body over, saying "I guess Jeanette went to the bathroom. I hope I'm not interrupting." Karl couldn't help smiling back. They both knew he'd made sure they would be alone. Karl shifted the papers back in place. He would never allow anyone else to disrupt his perfectly ordered world, but Allison was special. Petite, with eyes that danced with mischief whenever they were D.C.together, Karl was smitten by the young woman from the day they met. Early in their working relationship he made his interest known, and at first she'd rejected his advancements. It wasn't long, however, before she gave in to his charming ways. At least that was what Allison led him to believe.

"What's this?" He asked, the smile remaining on his face.

"The numbers you asked for. They're all there." Allison Becker was made Secretary of the Treasury just as soon as President Stanford was sworn into office. A brilliant and determined woman, she'd come from a military family, but managed to put herself through a prestigious college funded primarily from scholarships. Her story was the epitome of pulling oneself up from the bootstraps, and she quickly became the darling of certain D.C. circles. Allison was one of the first members of Stanford's cabinet, and strongly endorsed by V.P. Magnus.

Karl brought his eyes up from the paperwork. "Will there be enough?" He asked her with a gleam in his eye. Other than his wife, only Allison knew of his plan to run for President after Stanford was done. But his campaign would need funding, more than what the usual efforts could raise by traditional means.

Allison sashayed around Karl's desk and opened the folder. She placed a hand on his shoulder and bent down to whisper in his ear. "Plenty," she said in a conspiratorial tone. He could faintly smell the perfume she always dabbed behind her ears. "A woman's signature scent should be discovered, not announced," his mother had always said. It made him feel special to know only he enjoyed the particular pleasure of Allison's scent. He looked down at what she had compiled for him, but the figures swam before his eyes. All he could think about was how Allison would feel beneath him, later that night. He closed the file and pushed it back toward her.

"We'll go over it this evening…together." It wouldn't be long before Jeanette came back, and it would take a minute for him to calm down the business going on in his trousers. Allison smiled knowingly, and pulled the folder close to her chest. "What about Debra?" she asked, lifting one eyebrow up in a way that drove him crazy. "Won't she be mad that you're coming home late again?"

Karl didn't like to think of his wife while speaking with Allison. It made him uncomfortable, which may have been why Allison always brought her up. She seemed to revel in his discomfort and teased endlessly about his flawed marriage.

"Don't you worry about Debra," Karl assured her, "she knows working late is all part of the job. She wants to be First Lady just as much as I want to be…"

"…the most powerful man in the world?" Allison cut him off. It was meant to turn him on, and it worked. Karl smiled slyly. "Now stop messing with me and get your sweet ass out of here," he chuckled.

Allison headed toward his office door but stopped and whipped her hair around to confront him once again.

"I have to tell you about the other thing," she said with a pout. She wasn't quite done tormenting the V.P. She wanted to dangle some kind of snag in front of him, and then make it appear as if only she could fix the problem. She knew how much he disliked dealing with loose ends. Karl's smile dropped and his eyebrows drew together to create a crease in his forehead.

"Did you communicate with Tarlino?" he asked, dreading the very thought of the man and all the complications he presented.

"Yes," Allison answered, pretending to absent-mindedly flip through the folder. "He contacted me via that e-mail address you gave me, so he still doesn't know who I am."

Karl grew impatient, "Well, what did he say?!"

Allison realized she'd gone too far and would have to calm him down. "He said not to worry. There was a slight hitch in things, but they think they know where that woman is headed. That's how he referred to her. He didn't give a name so I'm assuming that's who you were worried about. Apparently, she's obtained some kind of bodyguard, but it looks like he's an officer within the agency, so he'll be able to track them both down well before anything is discovered."

Karl sighed with relief. If the Woods girl stumbled upon a clue that led to him it would cost him more than the candidacy. It could land him in jail. "I hope that slob knows what he's doing," he lamented, rubbing a hand over his eyes.

Allison moved back toward the door to leave the office. "That slob," she said with a snicker, "is someone who can find and hide money better than either of us. I'll see you later, Mr. Vice President."

The last part of her sentence she said loud enough for Jeanette to hear as she opened the door. Allison turned to Karl, "Unless there's anything else?" She asked in her most professional tone.

"No," Karl answered with a wink, "I think I have everything I need." When she left, he looked down at his pants and saw that word of Tarlino had erased the thrill of Allison's presence. Everything down there was back to normal.

Chapter 28
Istanbul

Emma meandered through the gift shop of the hotel where David took them in Istanbul. While he was checking in, he'd given her a small handful of bills. She looked at him in confusion, and he explained.

"Get whatever little things you need to keep you sane. I know it's been a long trip here, and it's not the last of our cash, so don't worry."

Now browsing through the shop, she wondered what there could possibly be that might restore her sanity. She kept her eyes on David just feet away at the reception desk, still nervous that at any moment they would again be on the run. She stopped at a clothes rack and fingered a lace blouse. It felt soft and foreign to her fingers. She was so used to wearing tee shirts and jeans that the idea of owning such a garment seemed frivolous.

"Can I help you find something?" A woman approached her with a smile. Her accent brought back memories of her childhood in the Middle East, and she had to remind herself that she was the one with the accent here in Turkey.

"Oh, I'm just looking for something to make me feel better?" She laughed at her own answer, thinking how silly it sounded.

"Ah yes," the woman nodded, "I understand. Every now and then we need to feel like girls again." She said knowingly. "Come, I'll show you my favorite thing here."

Emma followed to a mirrored shelf where the sales lady pulled out a small glass bottle with delicate lettering etched upon it. She took Emma's hand and, turning it over, dabbed a tiny amount of liquid from the bottle onto her wrist. Emma lifted her hand to her nose and inhaled. It was pure heaven, light and refreshing, the scent began to revive her soul, just a little bit.

Seeing her reaction, the sales lady smiled. "Ah, so you like it?"

Emma returned the smile, "It's lovely." Then a look of concern crossed her face. "Is it expensive?" The sales lady looked around slyly and tucked the bottle of perfume into Emma's hand. "I'll include it in the price of that blouse you were looking at," she whispered and walked to the clothing rack. Emma stood dumbfounded at the woman's suggestion.

"Oh, I couldn't possibly let you do that," she began to protest, but the woman held up her hand to shush her.

"I will just mark it as something I purchased for myself," she said, and set about placing the blouse in a bag. "As an employee I receive a tremendous discount."

Emma looked gratefully at the sales lady, moved by the kind gesture. *'I guess there really are some good people in this world,'* she thought to herself.

She handed the woman all the money David had given her along with the bottle.

"Are you sure?" she asked, praying the woman wouldn't change her mind.

The sales lady counted Emma's bills and put an imaginary number into the register. "Perfect!" she exclaimed. "You have just enough." She handed Emma the bag and gave it a pat. "It is my gift to you, welcome to Istanbul."

Emma left the shop and walked back to David feeling better than she had in weeks.

By the time they made it to their room the feeling of elation was replaced with exhaustion. She felt dead on her feet and waited impatiently for David to unlock the door. He chose the Holiday Inn within the older part of Istanbul for several reasons. To begin with, it was affordable. He managed to get by using the company credit card up to this point. But with no real "official business" in Turkey he wouldn't be able to justify any more purchases. He wasn't struggling financially, faring well on his government salary. But he hadn't expected to be spending his savings on Emma and her quest. He decided during the flight that he would take things day by day, hoping there would be a way to recoup expenses somewhere down the line. He was familiar with the Holiday Inn, having stayed at the old hotel whenever he was in town, working under NOC. He liked that the place was well managed, and that, despite its age, it offered clean and comfortable lodging. He was especially attracted to the low profile he could keep while there. No jet setters or wealthy oil Saudis strolled through the lobby of the Holiday Inn. It was a place where one could remain anonymous, and this appealed to him the most.

David opened the door and stepped aside to allow Emma in first. She had balked at the idea of sharing a room, but there didn't seem to be an alternative.

"I'm sorry you've had to spend your own money on everything," she had said to David in the elevator, assuming this was the reason they would be bunking together. "As soon as I can figure out a way to draw money from my account at home, I'll pay you back." She was used to carrying the load. All her boyfriends in the past ended up relying on her ability to earn and manage money. Having David foot the bill didn't sit well with her.

"That's not really the issue," David said, staring at the floor numbers lighting up inside the elevator as they made their way to the seventh floor. "I mean, yes. We don't have money to burn, but we're fine for now. It's just that, with all that's happened I think it's better if I remain as close to you as possible."

Emma felt a sudden and strange camaraderie with this man, who referred to them as a unit. "*We* don't have money to burn, but *we're* fine." She'd been feeling alone for so long, even with Anthony's help. It was nice to finally have an advocate. She hoped he didn't disappear on her like all the other men in her life.

Then she thought about his other comment, and a familiar sense of dread made her ask, "Do you think the people trying to kill me will find us here?"

In answer to her question David stepped out when the elevator doors opened and looked around before allowing her to follow. They made their way to the room, and once they entered, he immediately closed the curtains.

Emma stood and waited for the latest theory, assumption or snippet of explanation he might offer. She was learning to keep her expectations low. There were no bags to unpack, just the tote that she left on the floor by a plain desk and chair.

David threw his coat on a loveseat in the corner. "I'll sleep here," he said. "You can have the bed."

The idea of David's long body scrunched up on the small sofa seemed utterly ridiculous.

"It's cool," she laughed, "I don't mind taking the couch."

She sat on the bed and watched him as he went around the room, moving the phone, looking behind the television and mirror.

"Are you looking for something?" she asked.

David gave the room another once over, then sat down hard on the desk chair. He was tired too. "No," he sighed, "it's just a habit."

Emma wasn't sure what that meant, but she'd long ago formulated the notion that both David and Anthony were active in the CIA. In what capacity she could only guess, but she meant to find out more about David.

"So, what can you tell me now that we're safe in a hotel room, where I'm assuming there are no bugs on the phone or cameras in the mirror?"

David looked at her and smiled, then brought his hands up to rub weary eyes.

"Okay Super girl," he sighed, "here's what I think. We managed to ditch the men following us in the car. The fact that they picked up our trail at the airport means they have resources, and a pretty damned good line of communication. They probably know by now who I am, and that I'm involved with protecting you. If they're not fellow CIA officers then they have links to them. Otherwise, they wouldn't have been able to track us down so quickly. This place was never on the agency radar, because while I worked in the Middle East I intentionally kept certain places and people to myself. 'Kind of an insurance policy if you know what I mean?"

"Not really," Emma said, shaking her head, "but go on anyway."

"With a little bit of luck and the help of my old contacts here, we'll be able to do some research on your dad without being discovered by the people following you. But make no mistake, they want you dead."

Emma went white as the blood drained from her face. The lack of control, the utter hopelessness that came with knowing she'd been relentlessly pursued by unseen forces, tugged at her insides. She felt dizzy, and a buzzing started up in her ears growing louder as David continued to speak.

"I'm surprised they didn't take you out when they could," he was saying, "maybe, for some reason, they want to keep you around, possibly to interrogate you, find out what you've uncovered about your dad. Afterwards, they plan to quietly kill you in a way that would…."

She willed herself to stop listening, instead thinking back to a time on the farm when she was catching squirrels that had gotten into the chicken feed. There was a cage she purchased from the hardware store that made it easy to catch the destructive creatures. One could either shoot the squirrel or take it elsewhere and release it. That seemed like a waste of time, but when the moment came for Emma to place the pellet gun to its head, she found she couldn't bear to pull the trigger. The squirrel, quivering in fear, its eyes bright and nose working to smell out some kind of escape, was all too much for her. The power she had to determine whether the animal lived or died left her feeling awful. She ended up just letting the squirrel out and finding someplace else to put the feed. She felt like that shaking little rodent now, powerless and vulnerable. She lay on the bed pillows to block out the sound of David's voice.

He finally noticed how quiet she'd become and turned to see her hunched over on the bed. "Shit," he muttered, then rising from the chair, went to sit beside her. He put one arm around her shoulders. He hadn't been really close to a woman in a long time. It felt wonderful and awkward at the same time.

"I'm sorry," he said in a soft voice. "I'm an asshole. I just get caught up in trying to figure out the details. I think out loud and forget I'm not speaking to a hardened colleague, someone like Tony."

Emma looked at him sideways, allowing herself to lean into him. "Yes," she agreed, "describing the manner in which I might be kidnapped and killed won't do much for my confidence."

He moved to take her hand in his. "I guess I just started believing the words on your shirt." They both laughed, but Emma self-consciously pulled her hand from his, pretending she had to move her hair off her neck.

"Look, David," she murmured, "I don't know what kind of work you and Anthony are involved in, but I have a pretty good idea at least some of it would be considered dangerous to someone like me. That's why I appreciate your help, I really do. But try to remember I'm not you, okay? I'm tough, and I can handle myself, but I'm not you."

"Okay," he said and stood up. He'd made her uncomfortable. But at least she didn't seem as frightened, and that was something.

"I'm going to need you to toughen up even more if you want to go through with this," he explained. "Things could get intense and you'll have to follow directions. There's just no way around it Emma." He put his hands on his hips and gave her a stern look. "I have to be able to depend on you not to fall apart at a crucial moment. It's not fair, I know. But if you let those fuckers who are after you get under your skin, well…then it's all over anyway."

Emma nodded and hugged herself, then stood extending her hand to him. "I am a willing trainee," she said with a smile, though she wasn't joking. "I realize I'm no use to you as a helpless female. And they piss me off too."

David took her hand, and they shook in agreement, both smiling like life-long friends making a pact. Emma looked into David's eyes, searching for what might lay hidden behind the professional exterior, the entire premise of being capable and in control. Was there anything vulnerable about him, or had he tamped it all down with whatever training was required in his role of…what?

David stared back at Emma, returning her interest with the same intensity. He didn't look away, even though he knew he should have. He met her gaze feeling it was some sort of challenge. It was as if she was daring him to let go of her hand, and he found that he didn't want to. His expression softened, and he took in the way the light fell on her hair, the slight dark circles of fatigue under her eyes, and the fullness of her lips. Emma noticed the energy had changed between them, and in that moment she didn't see a CIA man, or spy, or even a mundane government worker. There was someone looking back at her who was as lonely as she was.

David realized too much time had passed. He couldn't just walk away from her as if nothing had happened. And so, against his better judgment, he kissed her.

It wasn't a tender kiss, but one of urgency, an instinct to connect with the woman he'd been attracted to from the first day they met. The kiss happened before he could think it through. Then, when he felt her lips parting, he was glad he hadn't.

Emma wasn't thinking either, just drifting down into the delicious warmth of his mouth on hers, and slowly returning his kiss. It was such a strange sensation, to be suddenly taken by a man she believed had merely tolerated her. It was easy to keep him at arm's length when she saw him that way. The man kissing her now had passion she could never have anticipated, and he was bringing the same out in her. It made him more dangerous.

Emma drew back, but he pulled her closer, not wanting the moment to end. He could feel her breasts against him as she let out a sigh. She smelled faintly of something he couldn't define. Was it citrus, or Honeysuckle? He was lost, all of his senses focused on her, until she pulled back again. This time he allowed her to move away, as awful as it was to release her. David and Emma stared at each other in wonder, and for a moment, time stood still. Emma was first to break the spell.

"I'm sorry," she stammered, "I didn't mean for that to happen."

"No," David objected, "it was my fault. I just…"

Emma put her hand up. She didn't want an explanation as to why he shouldn't have kissed her.

"Let's forget it, okay?" She walked toward the bed to gather her jacket and purse.

David felt he couldn't leave things hanging. He was confused by his own actions, but he certainly wouldn't admit it.

"We're both tired, and stressed," he went on. "It's only natural that we should express that to each other."

Emma went to the door indicating she was ready to leave. "David, will you please just shut up? I'm ready to go."

"Okay, good," David said, and moved to open the door for her. "Let's get to work."

Chapter 29
Shaking the Bushes

Anthony strolled down the pristine street of an upscale neighborhood in Solana Beach, California. Wearing dress shorts and a Tommy Bahama shirt, he looked like any other wealthy retiree who lived in the quiet seaside town. Every so often he glanced up at the address displayed on a gate or over a garage. Some houses sported the Mediterranean look so popular in Southern California. Others were more of a glorified bungalow design, but they all were immaculately kept up and surrounded by lush landscaping. He didn't stop when he spied the address he was looking for. Instead, he walked to the next house and turned the corner into an alley running along the back of each stately house. This was where the well-heeled, or their staff, lugged out garbage and recycling bins for collection. This area was also well maintained, though not as eye-catching as the front of the homes. Anthony slowed his walk, glancing up at the second story window of the house he sought. It was a residence as fine as the others, but in an understated way, with muted colors and unimaginative architecture, as if the owners wished to go unnoticed. The shades were drawn on all of the windows, signaling that no one was home. Anthony tried the back gate, but found it locked. He moved to the side of the garage, keeping close to the shade provided by palm trees and bougainvillea. There at the side of the garage he found another locked door, but after pulling out a pick gun, Anthony opened it in seconds. He was in.

He'd discovered the name of Zanders while searching Emma's room at the D.C. house. Before joining David and Emma for their fireside chat, he'd taken a moment to look for the mysterious binder she always carried. It was in the very first place he looked, under the bed mattress. *'Oh Emma,'* he thought at the time, *'such a lack of imagination.'* The binder held little information he hadn't already collected himself or learned through Emma's own admission. The only unfamiliar name was one in bold penciled print, block letters around which Emma had doodled, but very clearly reading **Zanders.** When David mentioned the name as one in the list of NOC Grumman employees, Anthony recognized a link. He kept it to himself however.

David had his own path to follow, and he didn't need the distraction of tracking down the man Anthony knew would lead to Frank Nirody. Of course, he had been listening to Emma's conversation with Charlotte, and he'd heard the name Andrew Zanders. But without knowing exactly where in California that man might live, he'd simply filed the information away. After learning of the Grumman connection, he'd pulled some strings and found Zanders' last known address in half the time it had taken Emma to work with HR. Now he shuffled through the dark garage, hoping he found Frank before anyone else did. He also hoped that Zanders, whoever he was, wasn't there to stop him.

There were no vehicles to bump into in the garage, so he ran his hand along the wall in the darkness until it fell upon the coolness of a doorknob. He turned the knob slowly, quietly pushing the door open with no resistance. It was early, the sun had only just come up, but no light penetrated the kitchen due to the drawn shades. The room looked clean and unused. Nobody had cooked in the kitchen for some time. He made his way down the hall to where he expected to find the living area. Anthony could make out the sound of a television, where some news anchor was relaying yesterday's events and tragedies. He entered the room silently, much as he had so many times at Emma's farm house. Other than the T.V., the room was sparsely furnished and uninspiring. The function of this home was not to exhibit the tastes of its owner. Anthony thought that even a home for sale had better staged furniture. This place had no heart and soul but was merely a way station for anyone wishing to anonymously pass through. Somewhere upstairs there were footsteps marching back and forth amidst the slamming of dresser drawers. 'Somebody's packing,' mused Anthony. He felt for his gun, welcoming the security of it in his hand as he approached the carpeted stairs that helped in his desire to proceed undetected.

A room presented itself to his left when he reached the landing. There, still wearing his pajamas, stood Frank Nirody, in a frenzy throwing clothes toward a duffle bag. "Hello Frank," Anthony pleasantly greeted the disheveled man, his gun pointed almost casually at his side. Frank jumped and turned to stare at the intruder.

"Who are you?!" His words came out in a high-pitched and barely suppressed scream. "How did you get in?" Frank began to step toward a bathroom just off the room where his clothes were strewn. Anthony wondered if there could be a window, and if this man might attempt jumping out of it. He looked to be in his seventies, and still in relatively good shape, except for a small paunch poking out from the buttons on his pajama top.

"Don't worry Frank," Anthony spoke soothingly to the skittish man, "I'm one of the good guys. Though, by the looks of things you're expecting the other type very soon."

Frank's eyes darted from the duffel bag back to Anthony's gun in a desperate attempt to gauge his options. Seeing none, he decided to bet on the intruder who, so far, hadn't attempted to hurt him. "What do you want?" he pleaded.

"I want to help you Frank," Anthony said with a smile. "All you need to do in exchange is answer a few questions. Right now, I need you to get dressed so we can leave. There's no time to pack."

Frank didn't know if he could trust the stranger with a gun trained on him. But if he could get him away in one piece he had no other choice. He tore off his pajama top and reached for a tee shirt lying on the bed. "I don't even have time to grab a few things?" he asked while pulling the shirt over his head.

Anthony plucked a pair of jeans from the floor and threw them at Frank, who scrambled to catch them with his free hand.

"Frank," he said matter-of-factly, "if I found you so easily how long do you think it will be before everyone else does?"

Frank pulled the jeans over his pajama bottoms. Anthony scooped up a pair of flip-flops from the duffel bag and escorted him out while he fumbled to button his jeans.

It was a nice restaurant, with high ceilings from which hung glimmering chandeliers. Their light bounced off mirrors that alternated between dark panels of oak and opulent wainscoting. David and Emma sat in one of the plush booths that offered views of the Bosphorus Sea. They'd only been served drinks so far, David telling the attentive waiter they were expecting another diner. "This restaurant looks expensive David," Emma whispered. "Can we afford it?" David kept his eyes on the ornate entrance of the restaurant, his glass of wine sat untouched on the white linen table. "I have a feeling we won't be paying for this particular meal," he said in a distracted way. "My friend chose the restaurant, and he prides himself on his hospitality." Emma took a sip of her own wine, wondering who this friend of his was, and how he figured in their mission. Taking in her surroundings she couldn't put her finger on what bothered her about the beautiful room. Ever since they were seated, she'd had a strange feeling of déjà vu.

"What's the name of this place?" she asked him, feeling stupid that she hadn't paid attention when their taxi pulled up to the luxurious building.

"Konyali," David answered, glancing back at her, "this building is the Topkapi Palace."

The memory rushed back to her. They were sitting at a booth like this one, her whole family. She and her sister squirmed in their seats, nervously eyeing the individual servants standing behind each family member. Any time so much as a crumb fell on the table, these uniformed men swooped in with a tiny dustpan and scraper to make it disappear. They were "taking in the sights," as her dad called it. Their journey to Iran was interrupted by some war between the Greeks and Turks. They were only stranded for three days, but her father was livid with the inconvenience, Anne trying in vain to calm him down and suggesting they go out together while leaving the girls to eat in their hotel room. Her father made some calls and got them a table in this very same restaurant, Emma was sure of it.

The weird thing about it was that her father insisted Emma and Leena come along. Their mother seemed disappointed, but she got the girls dressed up for the event. Halfway into the meal a man who "happened to know" her dad showed up at their table, inviting only her father to come meet his wife. Carter spent the remainder of the meal sitting with this couple while her mother fumed. Emma remembered them arguing about it once they finally got back to the hotel. She remembered the heated discussion, but not how it ended. It seemed strange that she would end up at the same restaurant, so many years later.

"I remember this place," Emma quietly said, more to herself than to David.

"What?" David asked, startled enough to tear his eyes from the entrance. "Did you come here with your dad?" It seemed unbelievable to him as well. "And you remember it? That's remarkable!"

Emma liked the way he was looking at her now, as if she had some hidden quality he hadn't previously noticed. She was wearing the new lace blouse, and he looked handsome in black pants and a button-down shirt. The opportunity to spend time with him, looking their best, made this feel like a date. For once she felt comfortable with a man, not annoyed or put down. They were just two people with the prospect of a delightful evening in front of them. It made her slightly giddy, and she laughed.

"Yes, well look around David," she murmured. "A place like this is hard to forget, especially when you're eleven. I'm still intimidated by it even though there isn't a waiter hovering behind me."

David gave her a quizzical look, then directed his eyes back to the entry, where a dapper man with a mustache had just entered.

"There he is!" David exclaimed and raised his arm to get the man's attention.

Mustafa Arslan nodded in recognition of his friend and made his way over to their table. David rose to greet him, and the two men embraced in genuine affection.

"So good to see you David!" Mustafa said with a hearty chuckle. "It really has been too long!"

"I miss our late-night political debates," David said, returning the smile. Then he turned to Emma, who was scrutinizing the two of them. They were acting like college buddies, and she wondered how they had forged such a close bond.

"Emma," David spoke politely with his hand on his friend's shoulder, "this is Mustafa Arslan. We got to know each other while I was working here some years back."

Emma regarded the man skeptically. David was being his usual vague self, and she didn't know what to make of the imposing man. Mustafa Arslan carried himself with blustering self-assurance. He was a big man, but in a muscular way. The way he moved reminded her of a retired boxer, no longer paid to fight, but ready to do so if needed. His smile exposed the whitest teeth she'd ever seen, and he smelled like cloves.

She smiled faintly but did not extend her hand. "Nice to meet you, Mister Arslan," she said with restraint. Mustafa didn't seem to notice her reserve.

"No beautiful lady," he crowed, "you must call me Mustafa! Scoot over and I will sit next to David. David you sit next to your pretty friend"

Emma made room for David who slid closer to Emma as he was told. The three of them adjusted themselves in the booth, then Mustafa heralded a waiter. Emma thought Mustafa must be a regular, because the waiter was instantly at his side producing larger wine glasses for the three of them, and proceeding to pour from a bottle of fine burgundy.

"I shall order for all of us," he directed, and rambled off a litany of Turkish dishes Emma didn't recognize. *'He's certainly used to getting his way,'* she thought with some resentment. The evening no longer felt like a date.

Mustafa locked eyes with Emma. "Now tell me young lady," he said in a lower voice, "are you truly the daughter of Carter Woods?"

Emma didn't answer. She was unprepared to discuss her father so soon. David broke in when he saw her hesitate.

"I filled Mustafa in on your background Emma. His father worked for the Turkish government, and his uncle was familiar with negotiations between the U.S. and Iran back in the seventies. He rubbed elbows with a lot of the contractors providing military equipment, including people at Grumman. I didn't think you'd mind if I shared your story with him."

This made Emma view David's burly friend in a new light. If he had relatives who knew her father, that could bring her closer to the truth behind his death. It made her hungry to listen to whatever Mustafa had to say. "Have you heard of my father?" she asked him, almost frightened about what she might learn. "Is there anyone in your family that remembers him? I realize it was a long time ago, but any piece of information would be helpful."

Mustafa reached across the table, coming dangerously close to knocking over David's wine. He grabbed both of Emma's hands and focused his deep brown eyes on her. Normally she would have been embarrassed by this stranger's sudden intimacy. Instead she felt as if this man truly cared for her, that he somehow knew the torment she'd been experiencing wondering about her father.

"Emma," Mustafa said, giving her hands a squeeze, "my Uncle Amir knew your father very well."

A connection beyond the clasping of hands grew between the two. Could Mustafa resurrect her father with his story? He was at least someone willing to speak about her father's past. Mustafa appeared equally moved and willing to share what he knew. David looked at both of them, and saw Emma transformed from a bitter and angry woman to one radiant with hope.

"What can you tell me?" she whispered.

Mustafa released her hands, took a large swig of the fine red wine, and then leaned in toward her.

"Your father was a good man. This is what my uncle said. My Uncle is Iranian, you see, and he was involved in the negotiations that took place between the Shah's government and your father's company, Grumman. Uncle Amir said that the Iranian government was quite corrupt at the time, and your father worked very hard to keep things fair when dealing with them."

It was difficult for Emma to envision her father as anything but a strict and sometimes abusive father. David had made it clear that Carter Woods was working in some way with the CIA. But that meant they had all lived under the lie that he was a retired Navy man working under contract. How could such a liar, and abuser, be "a good man"?

Mustafa went on. "The problems began with SAVAK. They were the Shah's equivalent of the CIA, only with much more freedom to repress any opposition. Their methods were brutal, involving unjust imprisonment, torture and execution of which the Shah was well aware. Most of those unfortunates were groups who represented the poor, such as the mullahs and the communists. The CIA either turned a blind eye or was terribly out of touch as to who the monarchy's real opponents were. The CIA only wished to gain information and analysis on those with anti-western sentiments, the middle-class "nationalists" who spoke from both sides of their mouths. They claimed to be against foreign intervention but wanted the U.S. to help them achieve social and political reform. Some of these people befriended your father."

Emma thought again of the "chance meeting" that took place in this restaurant so many years ago. Was the man who pulled her father from their table one of these nationalists Mustafa spoke of?

"What did these people want with Emma's father?" David asked. "As a CIA operative working under Non Official Cover he wouldn't have access to anything that would sway his higher ups one way or the other"

Mustafa shook his head. "That is where you are wrong my friend. My uncle told me Carter Woods learned of some kind of under-the-table side deals that were taking place within your organization at the time. Emma's father had been approached for assistance in these deals. He obtained… how do you say it? He had 'the dirt' on one or two of these guys doing the side deals. My uncle says this is how Carter ended up with a target on his back."

Emma paled at the reference, and Mustafa noticed. "I am sorry miss. That was insensitive, but you should know the truth." David still wasn't completely sold on the theory of Carter becoming involved in such a scheme. "Mustafa," he asked his friend, "how does your uncle know all this? How does he even know Emma's dad was in contact with these nationalists?"

Mustafa smiled and leaned back with obvious pride. "Because," he beamed, "my Uncle Amir was one of them."

Chapter 30
Frank

Frank Nirody nervously attempted lighting a cigarette, his hand shaking so badly, the quivering match failed to meet its goal, forcing him to blow it out as it threatened to burn his fingers. Before he could make another attempt, Anthony snatched the matches from Frank's hand and offered up a suitable flame. Trying to control the cigarette with one hand, Frank cupped the flame with his other, until successfully drawing in a deep and welcome mouthful of nicotine. He glanced up in appreciation to Anthony, but inside he wondered if this man was savior, or assassin. For his part, Anthony had already grown tired of the man sitting before him. They were peers, in a sense, but couldn't have been more different in the way they navigated the agency. Frank, for all intents and purposes, had used his brief stint working for the CIA as a conduit toward a cushy life. Anthony, on the other hand, had thoroughly enjoyed the excitement and purpose that working within the Agency gave him. If not for Patricia, he wouldn't have thought of ever giving it up. In Anthony's mind, Frank had broken the rules, possibly tarnishing the agency for his own personal gain. And it didn't appear Frank was the only one willing to do this. It made Anthony wonder if he was playing for the wrong team.

He shook out the flame and tossed the spent match on a cheap table provided at the Motel 6 where they were staying. Anthony had paid for a room before setting out to collect Frank. It was just off the freeway, and minutes away from Solana Beach, making it a convenient spot to settle in for a conversation with the increasingly skittish Frank. Pulling one of two cheap chairs from the table, Anthony positioned himself directly across from the man he meant to interrogate.

"Well now," Anthony spoke with a conciliatory approach, "however shall we pass the time?"

Frank cast his eyes down and took a deep drag from his cigarette, then maneuvered it to rest between his fingers so that he could clasp his hands together on his knees. It didn't help the shaking. "I don't want any trouble..." he began. Anthony said nothing in response. God, how he hated the smell of cigarettes! He felt that people who succumbed to the vile habit of smoking were intrinsically weak. Suppressing the urge to rip Frank's cigarette from his hands and throw it out the window, he instead pushed the glass hotel ashtray toward the trembling man. If smoking made him relaxed enough to talk, he was willing to put up with the stench.

Frank looked up to see Anthony sitting back in his chair, legs casually crossed and chin resting in his hand in a pensive manner. The silence was unnerving, and he was happy to speak, if only to fill the awkward void between them.

"It wasn't supposed to be this way," Frank pleaded in a whiny voice. "Everybody got what they wanted, and all I had to do was go home with a little something in my pocket."

Anthony let Frank catch his breath, then watched him pull from the cigarette once again. "Go on," he encouraged.

"It was all part of a business plan cooked up by this Ahmadi guy," Frank explained. "At least, he was the one who came to me. I think there were some people above him pulling the strings, but I didn't want to know who."

"And what was this business plan?" Anthony guided the frantic man.

Frank sighed, releasing a long stream of smoke into the air and placing the cigarette again between his lips with a quivering hand.

"Ahmadi said he was part of a group of government officials who didn't like the direction the Shah was taking their country. This guy somehow knew my position in Grumman was just cover."

"Did he really? And how do you suppose he knew that? What exactly was your directive, and who else could have known about it?" Anthony was thinking back on the tape Emma shared with him while in D.C. "Supplying intel to these people for money is dangerous, Ahmadi." Carter's words came back to him, and at the time he presumed the "people" Carter referred to were revolutionaries. This was the line fed to him and his team regarding Carter's treason. There had never been any mention of people within the Shah's government causing trouble.

Frank rubbed his forehead with the hand that held his cigarette.

"I don't know how Ahmadi knew, but he did. He made it very clear that he would expose us to Anti-American Iranians if we didn't give him what he wanted. All he asked was to be kept informed on whatever we found out about his own people. He said they didn't trust the U.S. government to keep in mind the best interests of regular Iranian citizens. It was all very weird."

Frank took yet another drag from his cigarette before continuing. "It didn't seem like too much of a compromise to comply, and his people were willing to pay for any information….handsomely."

"And so you gave Ahmadi what he wanted?" Anthony asked.

"Well of course I did!" Frank was becoming defensive. "I only gave up a few things I discovered over the course of my time there, groups I was supposed to watch, university students we were keeping an eye on, that sort of thing; nothing of any consequence."

Anthony regarded Frank with disdain. "Well, when you say no consequence, you mean not to your knowledge. There's no telling what may have happened to the people you named."

Frank flashed a startled look at Anthony. "These were the very people Ahmadi was protecting. Why should anything happen to them?"

Anthony's smile held no warmth. "How do you know that Ahmadi was what he claimed to be?"

Frank was silent, not comprehending Anthony's words. Anthony was compelled to fill in the blanks.

"Frank, Ahmadi could very well have been working for the Shah, for SAVAK. And I guarantee that the organization had free reign to do whatever was necessary to come down hard on anyone opposing the Shah and his policies."

The realization hit Frank hard. He began to shake his head. "I never heard anything about SAVAK. I was just trying to maintain my cover…"

"And making a pretty penny along the way," Anthony wryly finished Frank's sentence for him.

Frank threw his head down into his hands, a ruined man. "I left as soon as I could. I wanted out of there after hearing of what happened to Carter."

This was what Anthony was waiting for. Letting Frank introduce the subject had been almost too easy. "Yes," he coaxed, "let's talk about Carter Woods."

"Ahmadi said he wasn't cooperating, that he broke away on his own, looking for people he could sell information to. Apparently, he got the idea from Ahmadi, and then tried to drum up deals on the side. Our team leader said Carter got involved with the wrong people, probably revolutionaries. So, he'd have to be taken out. When I heard Carter was killed, I no longer wanted any part of the operation, legitimate or otherwise. I left and settled in with my wife back in the states. We had a good life until Carter's daughter called. That's when I contacted Zanders."

'So, at last we learn about the elusive Andrew Zanders,' Anthony thought. Without revealing his intense interest, he gently prodded Frank further.

"Zanders was the other man working under NOC?" When Frank nodded Anthony went on. "And what was his take on all of this? Was he helping Ahmadi as well?"

Frank shook his head, "no," he sighed, "According to Zanders he was never even approached. He stayed working within Grumman as a financial administrator. But his real job was the same as Carter's and mine."

Frank looked up woefully and went on. "Andrew Zanders is straight up. I told him what I was involved in right before I left. I wanted somebody to know in case I got eliminated like Carter. I didn't have anyone else to turn to, and Zanders promised to keep his ear to the ground if he heard any talk about me."

Frank stood, extinguishing his half-smoked cigarette in the ashtray before pulling out another. Glancing at Anthony he shrugged apologetically. "You know, I'd given these things up once I got back to the States. I only started up again after speaking with my wife."

"What was it that Charlotte said that got you back in the habit?" Anthony asked.

Frank did a double take and cocked his head. "How did you know my wife's name?"

'Whoopsie-daisy,' Anthony chided himself, before quickly recovering. "I've been following the Woods girl. I know about her phone call to your wife."

This flimsy explanation seemed to satisfy Frank, who was distracted by ensuring his own survival. He nodded and went to the window, drawing back the curtain to peer out at the parking lot below. "So, you're with the Agency," he said. It wasn't a question. And Anthony had no desire to provide details.

He redirected Frank back to the subject at hand. "What did your wife say?"

Frank dropped his hand from the curtain and lit his cigarette, successfully this time. The room was getting cloudy with smoke.

"I called her a few days after hearing Emma's message, once I had a safe place. Charlotte told me that a few of my old associates from Grumman came by. Supposedly they were at some conference in town and wanted to look me up. Luckily, she was able to convince them she hadn't heard from me. She said they were persistent, asking when I might be back. They left without hurting her, but those men obviously weren't buddies from Grumman. I didn't make any friends when I worked there. I don't even think Carter liked me. Anyway, Zanders said it was a good idea that I'd contacted him."

Anthony did his best not to cough from the smoke. It was time to wrap this up. "How did you manage to contact Zanders?"

"We stayed in touch over the years," Frank explained, walking across the tiny room and plopping himself at the end of a sagging bed. "Zanders was as good as his word. He'd call every year, just to check up on me. He gave me a number to reach him, in case of emergencies. I called him right after the Woods girl left a message, and he told me to meet him here in San Diego. He took me to his place in Solana Beach, asked me a bunch of questions, then left. He didn't say where he was going, but he told me if he wasn't back in three days I should leave. I waited longer than the three days. I didn't know where else to go, but then I figured something happened to him and I'd better run. That's why I was packing when you came in."

Frank stared at his lit cigarette, and then looked back up at Anthony. "How did you find me?"

Anthony ignored the question. "So, it was Zanders who was heading up your team in Iran?"

Frank looked at him, confused. "No. Andrew was just one of us, but he'd worked with the team leader before, I guess. He didn't like the man; said he was fussy and always acted above his station. He questioned his motives."

Anthony's eyes narrowed. "And the man heading up your team? Was he the one providing you information about what happened to Carter?"

"Yeah," Frank nodded, folding his arms, "it was a guy called Alberts."

"Theodore Alberts?" Anthony asked tersely.

"Yeah," Frank answered, "you know him?"

Anthony picked up the keys to his rented car, grabbed one of the door cards from the dresser, and tossed the other to Frank.

"I have to go out," he stated. "Bolt the door behind me, and of course don't let anyone in."

Frank stood and took a few steps toward the retreating Anthony. With a worried look on his face he asked, "You're coming back…right?!"

The only answer he received was the click of the motel door closing.

It was dark as Anthony descended the stairs. Lifting his shirt, he checked his belly band holster to ensure his gun was secure, and purposefully walked to the rental car he had waiting in the far corner of the parking lot. There were closer spots, but parking directly under his room would never have occurred to the seasoned officer. He pointed the key fob and the headlights blinked. Sliding into the driver's seat, he had little time to react to the sound of the car door opening and closing behind him. He reached for his gun just as a voice calmly said, "Don't shoot. My name is Andrew Zanders."

Anthony couldn't be sure if Zanders was friend or foe. For all he knew, this man might even be masquerading as Frank's ally, so he drew his gun anyway, and pointed it over the back of the seat, his left hand resting over the top of the weapon to secure his target. The Motel 6 sign faintly lit up the car's interior, illuminating the sanguine face of a man who looked to be in his seventies.

"You must be Newcastle." The man stated this as fact, and Anthony knew he'd been followed. "Who else is with you? Tell me now and be assured I will not hesitate to shoot you if we're surrounded."

Zanders only blinked, and then smiled even wider. "Anthony, it's just me. And you know it's just me. If anyone else knew where I was, I'd be dead by now."

Anthony lowered his gun, still not completely convinced this man was harmless. "Fair enough," he answered, "however I'll keep the gun handy if you don't mind."

"Not at all," Zanders agreed. "I'd do the same thing, under the circumstances."

The two men regarded each other, both senior officers with years of training and experience under their belts, both of them carefully considering the next move.

"It would be prudent for us to change locations, put a bit of distance between ourselves and Frank," Zanders advised. "I'm fairly certain of his safety, but one never knows."

"Agreed," Anthony nodded, "but I'll have to check you out first."

"Of course," Zanders said, raising his arms and clasping his hands over his head. With his gun aimed toward the back seat, Anthony frisked his passenger, never once letting his gaze leave the man's face. Satisfied that Zanders wasn't armed he considered his next problem. How could he be sure this man wouldn't assault him while he drove them to a safer location? As if reading his mind, Zanders spoke up.

"I could sit in the front seat, if you have something to restrain my wrists."

There had been no reason for Anthony to bring handcuffs, and there certainly wasn't any zip ties hidden away in the glove compartment of the rental.

Throwing the ball back in Zanders court, he asked, "What can you say that would convince me you're not a risk?"

Zander's smile faded, and his expression became grave.

"I want to save Emma," the sobering remark was clearly heartfelt. "Carter Woods was a friend of mine, and I owe him."

Any other time, Anthony would have required much more. But there was something about this man's words that rang true. Anthony decided to take a chance on this promising lead.

"Can you tell me anything about who is after Emma?" he asked. "I have a basic idea about the foot soldiers, but I have a notion there's somebody at the top pulling the strings."

Zanders nodded. "Good guess," he said with chagrin, "and it goes a lot further than our CIA colleagues."

Anthony frowned. This wasn't good news. Someone at the top could work the system in a way to make him, David, and even Emma, the enemy, just as he suspected they'd done to Carter Woods. Worse yet, a person at that level had more to lose if their crimes were discovered. And that made them dangerous, more willing to do whatever it took to keep their crimes from being exposed.

"Did Frank tell you everything he knew?" Zanders asked with a strange smile.

"He filled me in on certain details, regarding his work within Grumman and how he provided information regarding revolutionaries."

"Forget the Grumman thing," Zanders cut in, "it's all smoke and mirrors, something to distract from what Carter really found out. And the so-called revolutionaries were anything but. The real culprits are the ones who played around with bonafide revolutionaries. They have blood on their hands and would do anything to keep that secret, including killing Carter's daughter."

Anthony worked this latest revelation in his mind like a computer. His ability to quickly process information allowed his brain to adapt, clicking into place the latest facts and adjusting to a new reality. Now he needed to know only one more thing from Zanders. "How do you propose to help Emma, if the stakes are so high? He asked.

Zanders smiled and rubbed his chin. "Blackmail," he said the word slowly to let it sink in. "I have some very interesting information on the guy at the top. I even have someone on his side who's willing to turn. I just need to find a way to introduce the threat without exposing myself. That's where you come in, Officer Newcastle."

Satisfied, Anthony faced forward and turned the ignition. "Buckle in," he commanded. "Any ideas on a safer location?"

Zanders leaned back and drew his seatbelt across his shoulder. "Just drive southbound," he suggested. "towards the airport."

Anthony maneuvered the car out of the parking lot and turned toward the lights of the freeway. "What about Frank?" he asked Zanders. "He thinks I'm coming back."

Andrew Zanders looked out the window. "Yeah," he sighed, "I feel bad about leaving him on his own."

He and Anthony exchanged glances in the rear view mirror. They were both thinking the same thing, but Anthony voiced it. "He's no help to us now."

Zanders shrugged. "He knew what he was getting into a long time ago. He's lucky he made it this far. We don't have the time or the resources to protect him, and we have a plane to catch."

Anthony nodded, and quickly maneuvered the car through the streets of San Diego.

Chapter 31
Comrades in Arms

Emma looked over her shoulder to assess her appearance in the bathroom mirror. She hadn't thought to purchase sleepwear. In all the chaos and traveling, it simply never occurred to her that she might need something comfortable in which to sleep in a room she was sharing with a man she barely knew. Sensing her dilemma, David had offered his dress shirt, and it covered her just to her panties, making her feel even more exposed. How she longed for the sweatpants she'd so thoughtfully packed for the first leg of her trip, but was left at the house in D.C. She fastened one of the top buttons to make her outfit less revealing, but caught the faint scent of David in the process. Wearing his shirt felt as if he was wrapped around her, and it made her nervous. She'd pushed the memory of their kiss from her mind while dining with Mustafa. It was easier to focus on what the gregarious Turk had to say. But then she was distracted by David's suggestion, no…demand that they travel to Iran immediately.

Mustafa offered to arrange for the two of them to meet with his uncle Amir. They could take a commuter flight from Istanbul and travel as tourists. The anti-American sentiment had diminished quite a bit since the revolution. The recent oil embargo affected the Iranian economy to a point that tourism looked promising to the average Iranian. Western visitors excited to visit exotic places that had once been off limits were flocking to Iran, and visas could more easily be obtained. Mustafa had been adamant about Emma traveling to meet with his uncle.

"He remembers your father," the big man assured her, "and he is anxious to share his memories with you."

"Couldn't we just call him, or could he meet us here in Istanbul?" Emma asked. She wasn't eager about returning to a country that held only bad memories. Ever since returning from the Middle East as a girl, Emma saw Iran as a dark and threatening place, a country that would never give up its secrets, or even the body of her disgraced father. She was disappointed to hear David agree with Mustafa.

"No Emma, we should go," he pressed. When he caught sight of her disapproving glare, he explained. "If Mustafa's uncle is willing to talk to us then we should be respectful enough to meet him on his home turf."

They exchanged a long look, both understanding the inevitability of the trip. Deep down, Emma always knew that Iran was where she would have to go if she wanted to uncover the mystery of her father's death. But the idea made her uneasy, and she'd proceeded to drink perhaps a little more than she should. Mustafa wasn't much help. Ever the generous host, he encouraged the consumption of the fine wine he'd ordered for them. She wasn't drunk, but the heady atmosphere and fascinating conversation had left her feeling fuzzy. Listening to Mustafa and David banter, reminiscing over their past adventures and hearing the CIA officer actually laugh had helped her to relax. Now, wearing so little clothing and preparing to reveal her scanty attire to a virtual stranger, she wondered if she should have indulged in just a little more wine.

David lay scrunched up on the love seat, a thin blanket over his boxer shorts. A white V-neck tee shirt completed his night time apparel. Emma had insisted he use the bathroom first, and after brushing his teeth and leaving his shirt on the towel rack for her, he emerged to find her nervously sitting at the edge of the bed. Her eyes grew wide at the sight of him in only boxers and tee shirt, and she quickly ducked past him into the bathroom. He smiled at her shy response, but when he imagined her wearing only his shirt it made his stomach flip, so he turned over on his side to quell the desire rising up inside him. He heard the bathroom door open and closed his eyes to give her privacy. Instead of sprinting for the bed, Emma began to giggle.

"David," she laughed, "what are you doing squished up on that loveseat? Didn't I say you could take the bed?"

He opened his eyes to see Emma covered only with his dress shirt, red curls dancing as she shook her head at him.

"I wanted you to be comfortable," he said sitting up, the blanket still secure around his boxers. "I can fall asleep anywhere, really."

"Don't be stupid," Emma said, pulling a pillow from the bed before walking closer. "Just because I'm a woman doesn't mean you need to spoil me. Get your ass in the bed and let me take the love seat."

David tried to ignore the impossibly toned legs striding toward him. He stood up as a way of distracting himself, dropping the blanket from around his waist in the process. They stood facing each other in uncomfortable silence, until Emma glanced down at his boxers.

"Go on," she said softly, redirecting her eyes as she felt the blush come over her face. "I'm tired, and I'm sure you are too."

She moved past him and situated herself on the sofa, while David made his way to the bed. Throwing back the covers, he settled in and cast a look at Emma.

"Ready for me to turn off the light?" He asked.

Emma grabbed the blanket off the floor and flung it onto her legs. "Yup," she said, and buried her head in the pillow.

David reached for the lamp on the bedside table and pulled the cord, throwing the room into darkness. They both lay quietly for a few moments, until David broke the silence.

"Thanks for the bed Emma," he whispered.

"You're welcome," she whispered back. "G'night."

David soon sensed her sleeping. His natural instinct to stay awake and on guard was strong. But he was exhausted, and eventually he fell into a dreamless sleep.

He didn't know how much time had passed before he heard Emma screaming.

"Dad!" she cried out, and he leapt from the bed without turning on the light. His hand felt for the door, and after determining the lock was undisturbed, he rushed to Emma, falling upon her as she thrashed in another horrible nightmare.

"Dad!" she screamed once more, and David pressed his face against hers, speaking softly but firmly into her ear.

"Emma, wake up. It's okay. I'm right here."

He felt her jolt awake, and her breathing slowed, but her heart continued to beat rapidly under his shirt.

"Oh God," she sobbed lightly, "My dad was on fire. He was standing in front of me, burning. He reached out to hug me, but I didn't want to burn too…"

She was shaking, so David pulled her upright and closer to him.

"It's alright now Emma," he said soothingly. "It was just a dream." Although he could barely see in the darkness, he reached for the tears he knew would be there, wiping them gently from her face. She felt for his arms and clasped her hands around them.

"What am I doing David?" she pleaded. "I don't belong here. I can't go to Iran tomorrow. I'm so tired of this, and I want to go home!" She pressed her face to his chest, the soft cotton of his tee shirt growing wet from the tears that kept coming. David wrapped his arms around her and began to gently rock her.

"Shhh, Supergirl," he murmured. "You don't mean that. That dream just means you need to find out about what really happened to your dad. Once you do that, the nightmares will stop, I promise."

"How can you promise me something like that?" Emma's words were muffled against his chest, and she let out a small hiccup from crying so hard.

David put one hand on her head, stroking the sleek red hair he wanted to touch for so long. "I'll help you," he said calmly, "we'll figure it out together."

[handwritten note: it is always curly]

She wanted to believe him, and she knew he was right. There was no turning back now. She had no choice but to keep looking for answers about her father. For now, she was perfectly happy to have this man hold her and make assurances she was certain he couldn't keep. She took a deep breath and exhaled a ragged sigh. David sighed with her and pulled her from him just enough to trace his finger down her cheek. When he reached her chin, he tilted it slightly and placed a tender kiss on her lips. Emma kissed him back. It felt so natural and right, and she felt something rise up inside her, pushing aside the fear, and even most of the anger she'd felt for so many years.

They both pulled back in surprise, each wondering about the motivation of the other. Emma wasn't sure she could trust him, and David didn't know that he could trust himself. He didn't want to hurt her, but he was desperate to have her. The now familiar citrus and honeysuckle aroma fused with her own natural scent, and it was intoxicating. He swallowed hard, and then greedily breathed in more of her.

David kissed her again, only deeper, and she surrendered to him eagerly. His hands dropped to her waist, moving up inside the shirt. He marveled at the softness of her skin, like velvet. He moved up to her breasts, tentatively at first, then he stopped and looked into her eyes, questioning. Emma leaned into him, lightly kissing his neck. Her cheek encountered the mild stubble on his face, triggering some instinctive yearning she'd kept hidden deep within her. The closeness of his masculinity flooded over her, and she reached to unbutton the borrowed shirt, dropping it from her shoulders, she exposed her breasts. Her eyes sought his, silently inviting his touch.

Awkward at first, David shook slightly as he slowly moved one hand over her breast, then hungrily grasped at both. He felt as if he could hold her that way forever, but when she pressed the hardness of her nipples into his hands, he knew it was impossible to stop.

Pulling her close, he buried his face in her hair, which tickled his nose. He placed small kisses on her neck, making his way up to her ear, where he took a small nibble. She pulled back, laughing softly and, looking down at her naked breasts, appeared suddenly embarrassed. David held her face in his hands and breathing hard, he whispered, "I'll stop if you want me to. But you have to tell me now."

Emma brought her hands up to his and shook her head. "I don't want you to stop," she whispered back. David took hold of her hand and led her back to the bed, turning her toward him by the shoulders and kissing her again, his hand sliding down her back until it encountered her panties. He fumbled with the flimsy underwear until she pushed his hand away, and pulled them down herself. Stepping out of them, she moved her hands up his body. With his help, she pulled off the tee shirt, but she stopped him from removing his boxers. She wanted to do that herself, and it gave her a sense of power to slowly guide them down his legs, her hair brushing against his body and her fingers glancing against every muscle in his legs.

David couldn't wait any longer. He pulled her back up to his chest and grabbed a handful of hair, pulling her head back so he could kiss her deeply once more. He reached down between her legs, gently stroking and exploring to see if she was ready for him. Her answer came willingly, satiny and warm, and they crumbled together onto the bed, rolling with legs entwined until David found himself on top of her. It was dark, and she couldn't see the intensity behind his eyes as he pushed himself inside her. She let out a small cry, and, worried that he'd hurt her, David began to move away. But she reached around to his backside and pressed him in further, until they moved in some kind of primal rhythm, both of them holding back in anticipation of the other's pleasure. David took her arms up and over her head, pressing her wrists into the pillow with one hand and cupping one of her breasts in his other. He felt as if he were drowning in the miracle of Emma's body, soaking up her very essence. He did his best to move slowly, until he could feel the wave of her climax rushing up to meet his. With another tiny cry, she arched her back and met his last thrust, wrapping her leg around him and letting loose a shudder that matched his own. For a moment they were suspended in complete ecstasy, and then both sank their bodies down in utter release and fatigue, shivering in the aftermath.

They lay together, completely spent, reveling in the feeling of giving in to each other in every physical way. For Emma, it was almost uncomfortable to have allowed herself to be so vulnerable to a man. What did it mean now that he knew every part of her? Was she opening herself up to be hurt, as she had been every other time she'd given herself to a man? Regret began to set in, ruining the sense of peace and pleasure she'd enjoyed. She rolled over and pulled the covers up to hide her body from him, leaving David to wonder if he should move to comfort her, or leave her alone with her thoughts.

He was having more than a few of his own. Making love to Emma was magical and had felt right in every way. He thought he'd experienced love before, when he proposed to a young woman he met in college. But once he began attending the Academy, time and distance caused that relationship to disintegrate. Emma was different. His admiration for her was beyond what he'd ever felt for any woman. He wanted to save her, but she gave the impression that she really didn't need saving. She seemed to be a very strong and independent woman. But after learning her story he wondered if that was all a façade. Couldn't there be a frightened and wounded little girl behind all that confidence? He looked over at her, huddled on the other side of the bed and clutching the sheets. *'Shit,'* he thought to himself, *'have I made her happy or just made things worse?'* The fact that they'd had sex certainly complicated his efforts in helping her. And it definitely went against the unspoken rule he learned at the Agency; never become too close to someone you're trying to protect.

"Emma," he whispered, "are you alright?"

She said nothing, and he assumed she had fallen asleep. *'Just as well,'* he assured himself, rolling over and away from her. *'We have an early flight tomorrow.'*

He closed his eyes and soon was lightly snoring, leaving Emma to stare into the darkness.

Chapter 32
Patricia

Patricia had just about enough of this. Waiting to hear from her husband was one thing. Being stalked and threatened in his absence was quite another. She was used to Anthony's long "business trips" away from home. Well aware of his work in the Agency, she took things in stride and learned to appreciate the time Anthony carved out for her. It helped that he'd promised his retirement from the CIA was on the horizon, and that she would no longer spend sleepless nights wondering where he was and whether he was in danger. She looked forward to enjoying more time with him, and also living a truly authentic life. She became friends with Anne, and then with Anne's daughter Emma, as a favor to Anthony. He hadn't asked her to gain their confidence; he was far too good a husband to ask for that outright. But she knew that keeping an eye on her neighbor was a job he took as a favor to her. Far less exciting than past operations, the Woods case was considered practically mothballed. Her husband hated the boredom of his surveillance, but it would allow him to gradually back out of the business. Because of that, Patricia took it upon herself to foster a relationship with the Woods' women.

It hadn't been difficult. She truly enjoyed Anne's company and found her to be a sweet and engaging person. They shared a love of travel and were equally pleased to be settled down in their later years. When Anne died, Patricia truly mourned the passing of her friend and neighbor. She'd met Emma a handful of times. Anne's daughters didn't seem all that interested in visiting their mother on the family farm, once they'd struck out on their own. But when Anne passed and Emma decided to take on the property, Patricia got caught up in the younger woman's excitement over starting her new life.

They got on well, and Emma seemed to relish the company of another strong woman. After a while, Patricia felt compelled to support and comfort Emma. The bond between them grew, and their relationship became different from that of the one she'd had with Anne. Emma was intelligent, and she had a sharpness that intrigued Patricia. She sensed that the young woman had somehow been wounded by her upbringing. Stories emerged about some of the abuse suffered at the hands of Carter Woods, as well as the neglect of Anne.

But Emma was no victim, and she refused to complain about the rough childhood she had endured. Patricia knew the strong façade Emma presented hid a great deal of pain. This pain Emma kept firmly tamped down, but Patricia thought her friend was living a lie. And, in a way, so was Patricia. She hated that her initial move toward friendship was based on ulterior motives. This was another reason she looked forward to Anthony being relieved of Emma's case. With her husband's retirement, Patricia would be free to continue her friendship with Emma without the specter of the agency looming over her.

When Patricia was younger, working for the CIA seemed exciting, even though she was nestled safely in the administrative department. She loved her job, and the fact that she'd met her future husband there made her all the more loyal to the agency. She quit soon after they married, and lately he began to take on less work, preferring to spend his time with her. Everything seemed to be going in the direction of his upcoming retirement. Then Emma became a target, and Anthony felt responsible. He'd only called twice since leaving with their young neighbor. The first call asking her to care for the animals was short. The second call, in which he'd said his absence would be longer than anticipated, was shorter.

Looking after Emma's animals was no problem, a joy in fact. Patricia loved feeding the two remaining horses. They seemed appreciative of her affection after losing their brother. The chickens were cute, and Stella the dog followed her everywhere, constantly sniffing the property in search of Emma. She slept with the big ball of fluff every night, and it was a good thing. She awoke to Stella's barking one night when the canine alerted her to an intruder at the Woods' place. Patricia could see flashlight beams darting around the old farmhouse, and she called from her window, "who's there?!" Between Stella's barking and her shouting, the intruders must have gotten spooked. From what she could see there were only two men who emerged from the house. They jumped into a waiting car and sped away.

She thought about calling the police, but what good would that do? She had to trust that her husband would contact her as soon as he could. Then they could work out something together. Sure enough, the land line rang just as she was getting ready to take Stella on a walk. She'd already clicked on the panting dog's leash, with a plan of taking a little jog down the country road that ran in front of their home. She liked to cut over to a dirt trail that led to a creek, then gently flowing behind a cluster of willow trees. She'd taken Stella there a number of times since Emma's departure, and the sweet animal seemed to love the change of scenery. That morning Stella waited patiently by the door, while Patricia reached for the phone, praying it was her husband.

"Patricia?" It was Anthony's voice, prayers answered.

"Sweetheart, where are you?" she sighed in relief. "Are you okay?"

"I'm fine dear," he answered soothingly. "How about you?"

"Not so much," she confessed. "There were some men who broke into Emma's place. They left, but I'm afraid they'll come back"

There was a pause on the line, then Anthony calmly said, "they won't come back."

"How do you know?" Patricia said in disbelief. "I'm getting nervous Anthony, and I don't like just sitting here doing nothing."

Anthony chuckled on the other line. "That's my girl," he said, "always the problem solver." Then his tone became serious. "I know they're not coming back because they're looking for Emma, and by now they've probably found out she's out of the country."

"Okay," she said doubtfully. She couldn't imagine Emma making such a drastic decision. Then again, there was no telling what her husband was doing on his end to fix the situation.

"Can I help?" she asked. Anthony never involved her in his work, but this was different. Emma was her friend.

"Actually," Anthony's voice perked up, "you can, I think."

Patricia waited; excited to finally be a participant in her husband's other life. "Tell me more about your friend from college, the one who allows us to use her property in D.C."

They spoke at length, with Patricia writing down instructions and promising to do her best.

After her conversation with Anthony, Patricia pulled on her coat and gathered up Stella with her leash. Once again, the big dog panted with joy over the prospect of their walk. But the sound of the phone interrupted their plans once again. *'Anthony must have forgotten something,'* she thought.

"Hello," she answered. There was a pause, then a man's voice.

"Yes, is Anthony Newcastle there?"

Nobody called for Anthony on their land line. Patricia was the only one who got calls, from friends, family, or salespeople. She was immediately suspicious.

"May I ask who's calling?" She wasn't about to give up any information until she knew who was on the other line.

There was another pause, then, "is this Mrs. Newcastle?"

Thinking it must be some sort of sales call, she tried to blow the caller off.

"Look, I don't have time right now...." she began, exasperated.

"We were just hoping to speak with your husband Mrs. Newcastle. He hasn't been in touch with anyone here at the Agency. We were hoping he hadn't encountered some kind of accident or mishap."

Patricia's hand gripped the telephone receiver, and she tried to steady her breathing. The agency would never call looking for Anthony. If they'd lost contact with him there were other avenues they would explore before even thinking of notifying her. She knew this because Anthony had gone over it with her a multitude of times, after she quit working for the CIA.

"If I go missing darling," he told her, "you mustn't worry. I'm constantly monitored by the powers that be. You'll only receive notice if I'm injured or dead, and then it will be another officer who comes to your door to speak with you in person."

Having just spoken with her husband, Patricia knew the caller was not with the agency, not any part of the agency that looked after its officers anyway.

Patricia took a deep and quiet breath, and then continued in a calm voice.

"I'll need you to give me your name please," she spoke with what she hoped was a firm tone.

"So you haven't heard from your husband?" The man now appeared to be aggravated. He pressed on. "Does your husband often disappear without contacting you?"

She was disgusted by the manner in which the caller was desperately fishing, hoping she was stupid enough to give up any information on the man she loved.

"If you won't give me your name I can't help you," Patricia responded in a clipped response that was a little louder than normal. "I'll be calling my husband's contacts once I'm off the phone with you, to verify you are definitely not who you're claiming to be."

"I'm so sorry," the man on the line spoke politely, "I'm sure you're in a hurry to take your walk."

Patricia's blood ran cold. "What are you talking about?" She knew she shouldn't have risen to the bait, but the words escaped her lips before she had time to think about it.

"Your walk," the man went on, "with your neighbor's dog. You're taking care of it while Emma is gone, right?"

Patricia said nothing. Instead, she tried to remember Anthony's assertion that no one would come looking for Emma. In despair she thought that perhaps her husband hadn't thought they would come looking for him.

"You'll be taking the usual route, down to the creek, won't you?" The man didn't bother masking his threat. She was being watched, and he wanted her to know it.

Patricia decided she'd had enough. She was too old, and too smart to play this game.

"Kindly go fuck yourself," she said, before slamming down the receiver.

Then she pulled her cell phone from her coat pocket, and dialed the number of her friend in Europe, the one who allowed Anthony to stay at her place in D.C. She looked down at Stella, who remained waiting expectantly for the anticipated walk. Patricia bent down to unlatch the leash from Stella's collar. She ruffled the dog's soft, white head and rubbed under her chin.

"I'm sorry girl," she softly said, hoping to appease the now disappointed Stella. "No walk for us, not today."

A woman picked up on the other end, greeting her in French.

"Bonjour mon ami!" Patricia responded, "it's me! J'ai besoin de faveur."

Chapter 33
Uncle Amir

Emma and David walked down one of the older streets in Tehran, featuring intricate stone facades that loomed behind walled gardens. Persian pop music played loudly from one of the balconies where a woman wearing a chador peered down at them. Emma wore a head scarf and a modest blouse that covered her arms, along with long pants. But she still managed to attract attention from the locals, who stared intently, not bothering to hide their curiosity. David didn't seem bothered by any of it. He didn't exactly blend in with the general population, but the confident way in which he carried himself allowed him to make his way purposefully through the crowd. Emma nervously glanced from one side of the street to the other, wondering how the hell she'd ended up back in Iran after twenty-two years.

That morning, as they dressed and prepared to leave for the airport, an awkward silence stood like a wall between them. Neither of them seemed willing to discuss the passion of the previous night, and they both went to great lengths to avoid close contact. This had been difficult in the cramped hotel room, and as Emma packed up her meager possessions she'd accidentally bumped into David. She froze in place, holding her backpack between them like a shield.

"Come on Emma," David had quietly said, "I'm not going to bite you."

"Of course," she murmured, "I mean….I know you won't." She managed to finish getting ready without embarrassing herself further, and the plane ride took place in almost complete silence. Now that they were walking the streets of Tehran, she realized that the idea of coming back had lingered in her heart for years. She was tired of secrets, and tired of being hunted like some animal. If she were killed in Iran at least it would be while she was working on getting answers, finally, about her dad.

David stopped at a gate centered on one of the long walls. Together they stood staring up at the building. "That's weird," Emma said as she gazed at the red plaster of the wall surrounding what she assumed was a residence. "What's weird?" David asked. "I'm getting a little déjà vu here," Emma answered, "and I don't know why I would because I'm certain I've never been here before." David looked at his watch. "Well, this is where we're supposed to meet Mustafa's uncle and we're late, so...." Emma cut him off. "The pictures in my dad's envelope," she exclaimed. "This was one of the buildings in the photo's he left me." She smiled at David, proud of herself for having at last made use of one of her father's clues. Glancing at the top of the wall Emma could make out shards of glass that had been cemented in, protection from thieves and intruders. But looking beyond the gate she saw a lush garden bursting with color. Flowers and palm trees surrounded a burbling fountain, and an arbor shaded wicker chairs positioned around a wooden table. "I'm glad you were able to recognize the house from the photos Emma. It's cool that you put that together," David said with a small smile, and rang a bell at the side of the gate. She could hear a dog bark, and took it as a good sign. Emma never met a dog she didn't like, a sentiment she didn't have toward most people.

A man came out of a side door of the house and took the stone path leading to the gate, a wide smile on his face. He was a big man, like his nephew, but more refined in his movements. Dressed in a long, black robe and sandals, he called out to them before reaching the gate.

"You must be my nephew's American friends! Hello!" He placed one meaty hand on the gate while using the other to unlock the gate. Swinging it open he beckoned both of them in, but he extended his hand to David first. "I am Amir Asala, Mustafa is my sister's son. You are David, yes? Mustafa told me you have had many adventures together, but he didn't say exactly what those adventures were." Uncle Amir chuckled, then looked warmly towards Emma.

"And you must be Carter Woods' daughter! Welcome Emma, I knew your father well."

She immediately felt an odd sensation of relief. At last, someone was acknowledging not only the existence of her father, but making her feel welcome, like family. Emma had almost forgotten what it was like to acknowledge having a father, other than to defend him.

"Let's talk," Amir suggested, and led them to the arbor. David placed his hand on Emma's back, ushering her toward the wicker chairs. It felt very natural, but she warned herself not to become too dependent on a man whose business was cloaked in deception. Amir gestured to the seats on his left before taking one himself.

"Please sit," he said. "My wife is making us tea."

The cool of the arbor was a welcome sanctuary after walking the claustrophobic streets of old Teheran. Emma could smell jasmine, and she pulled at her headscarf to catch the breeze drifting through the arbor.

"You may take off your scarf if you like," Amir offered, "as an American woman I know you might be uncomfortable wearing it. There will be no problem while we're behind the walls of our garden."

Emma smiled gratefully and tugged the garment from her head, loosely folding it and placing it in her lap.

David spoke up, "Thank you so much for agreeing to meet with us Amir," he said. Emma and I understand your association with her father was many years ago."

Uncle Amir gave another wide smile. "Yes, it was long ago. But Carter Woods will forever be in my memory."

He turned to Emma, and nodded. "Looking at you reminds me of him. You have your father's eyes."

Emma was touched, and she was anxious to learn more. "How did you meet my dad Amir? Did you work with Grumman somehow?"

Amir smirked. "No, not at all, but I knew some people who did. Back then there was corruption running all through the government. Everyone had their hand out, and the Shah's people were the worst offenders."

He reached for a fragrant piece of jasmine hanging from a branch that framed the arbor. He rubbed it between his hands to release the fragrance, and then held it to his nose to inhale its fragrance.

Continuing to finger the blossom he looked thoughtfully at Emma. "I worked in the Shah's agency of finance," he continued, "and I could have become a very wealthy man if I'd gone along with some of the schemes run by a number of my colleagues. Instead, I helped to form a group that worked quietly to bring at least some power back to the Iranian people, the middle class, and some intellectuals. We were all very disenchanted with how the Shah was pushing Western ideals, but mostly we objected to the corruption. I believe your father was tasked with following me, as I was under suspicion of questioning certain government officials who were siphoning money from legitimate programs into their own pockets."

Amir sat up in his chair, leaning toward Emma.

"He was instructed to make note of who we were, and what kind of actions we were taking to disrupt the Shah's power. But, you see, our goal was not to overthrow the government. Some of the Shah's policies we saw as real improvements. Advancements in technology, education, even extending the rights of women were actions that pulled our country from being seen as backward to becoming one worthy of respect. The problem was the Shah's intelligence agency. He had his thugs rounding up anyone who dared to disagree with him, or even offer a different way of doing things. SAVAK was like your CIA, but without any restraints. Many innocent people were jailed, tortured, even executed without a trial. This is what we told your father. At the time, he was the only American we met who paid attention to our cause."

David had been listening intently. "At what point did Carter make contact with you Amir? Did he reveal his cover to you?" Such action was highly unusual for an officer, particularly a low level one like Carter who must have known he was being closely monitored. Making contact with a subject under surveillance could compromise an entire operation, and possibly cost the lives of other officers.

Amir shook his head. "At first he simply followed me, and asked about me to others in our circle. I had people in my agency working and socializing with the Grumman employees. He told me later that he became curious about my group. He sensed he was being lied to about our purpose. He didn't trust his boss, he said. Anyway, he eventually approached me at an associate's party, and said he wanted to speak with me privately. I wasn't sure I could trust an American who might be as corrupt as any of our people, but he seemed willing to open his mind about me and other Nationals. Once he learned the truth that we weren't rebel revolutionaries, well…let's just say he became nervous. He was, as he said, looking over his shoulder. There was only one man he said he thought he might trust, another CIA man working at Grumman. He had a strange name…Zanders, Andrew Zanders."

Both Emma and David sat straight up at the name. Now it was Emma's turn to ask questions. "Did my father have any information that might have made him a target, maybe someone he might expose? I mean, if corruption was the name of the game and my dad wasn't willing to play along, then wouldn't that make it easier to kill him, and then frame him as a traitor?"

David looked at Emma in surprise. He had underestimated her. She had been thinking things through, pulling clues together and apparently coming to her own conclusions. He considered the possibility of Carter's death being a set up for some time, but he'd had the advantage of viewing leaked information and conferring with Tony. Now he wondered what had become of his mentor, and why he seemed to have disappeared.

Amir pondered Emma's question for a moment. "He did ask me some very strange questions, very soon before his death. He wanted me to connect him with someone in our group whom he could trust. He spoke of perhaps staying with one of us so he could be safe, until he could find his way back home and set things straight. I introduced him to one of my very closest friends, a professor at the university. Unfortunately, that friend passed away some time ago. None of us are young men anymore." Amir chuckled, then looked up to see his wife bringing tea.

"Yasmin! Come meet Mustafa's friends!"

Amir's wife was slightly plump and beaming as she brought out a tray laden with cups, saucers, and a teapot.

"She doesn't really speak much English," Amir apologized, "but she is a wonderful hostess, and provides a very nice tea."

Yasmin happily set the tea out for her husband's guests, shyly casting her eyes at Emma and smiling. Everyone was quiet while she poured the tea, then she nodded to them all and hurried back to the house. Amir gazed lovingly at his retreating wife.

"She really is something, isn't she?" He turned to Emma, saying, "She is my second wife. She never met your father, but my first wife enjoyed making dinner for him. He was a real gentleman, and always made her laugh."

This was yet another image of her father that seemed so contrary to the man she knew. "What happened to your first wife?" Emma asked, hoping the question wasn't too intrusive.

A cloud crossed Amir's face. He looked down and stirred his tea. "She died," he softly said, "under suspicious circumstances."

Emma gasped at Amir's explanation. "Why!?" It was the only word that came to mind, and she hadn't meant to say it out loud.

Amir looked up, his face a hopeless expression of pain. "I think it was done in order to get to me."

Emma was horrified, and David put his hand on the man's shoulder. "I'm sorry," he said, because there was little else to say.

"Well, it's in the past, and a very long story that I won't share with you now. It happened after we learned of your father's death Emma. It was a very difficult time. After that I stayed out of things. I quit my government job and went to work for my sister's husband. Then of course the revolution happened and changed everything, so I moved back to Iran and took over this home from my father."

Emma nodded her head, feeling empathy for another who had suffered loss.

"I didn't mean to bring up a bad memory," she said apologetically.

"No," Amir responded, "thinking back on your father, and the fine dinners we shared with him, brings me joy. I only wish I could have protected him better. My professor friend was the one who told me he'd died in a car wreck."

Emma's heart skipped a beat. "Wait…what?! A car wreck? My mother was told he'd been shot!"

David reached over and took her hand, "Emma, we can talk about this later."

To their host he said, "Thank you so much for your time Amir. We should probably get going."

Now Emma was completely confused. Why should they leave after learning such conflicting information about her father's death?! What was going on?

David rose and pulled Emma up by her arm, the warm and natural rapport now gone from his demeanor.

"Oh, I'm sorry you have to leave so suddenly," Amir lamented. "Yasmin wanted to invite you to stay for our evening meal."

Emma glanced furtively from Amir to David in stunned silence.

David continued wrangling Emma toward the walkway leading out of the garden. "We're both very grateful for all the information about Carter," he said. "I'll let Mustafa know that you and your wife are well."

Amir nodded to David, then stopped Emma's retreat long enough to take her hand in both of his. "Your father would be very proud of you young lady. You are strong and smart, like him."

Emma smiled. She wanted desperately to stay, but David continued to tug annoyingly on her arm.

Amir followed them as far as the gate, stopping to wave to them as David hustled Emma out.

"Good luck," he called out, "Go with God!"

Chapter 34
Debra

Debra Magnus held the orange tightly in one hand, a sharp butcher knife in the other. She deftly sliced the fruit in neat corners, placed it in a hand-painted bowl from Italy, and then reached for another. Wearing the pajama bottoms and tee shirt that had become her morning uniform, she pressed her lips together, concentrating on her task, while a running dialogue coursed through her head. She would have to be careful about asking too much from her husband, poor thing was exhausted from overwork. Her hand stopped mid-slice and she stared straight ahead, thinking about what had occupied Karl's evenings during the last year that left him too tired for any intimacy with her. Hands poised over the orange, the image set her mouth in an even firmer line. Then the blade came down with such velocity it sent droplets of juice flying onto the tiled kitchen backsplash. Debra smiled to herself, collected the sacrificed orange pieces, and placed them neatly into the bowl alongside the other slices. Carrying the bowl with both hands through the kitchen, she bumped the swinging door open with her butt, and slid into the adjoining dining room, smile intact.

Karl was sipping on coffee, reading some kind of report in a binder, and not bothering to acknowledge his wife's entrance. He'd already finished the bacon and eggs Debra made to order especially for him. She gently placed the bowl of oranges on the table in front of him, and thoughtfully considered the man sitting in front of her. He was wearing a suit that complemented his strong physique, and for just a moment, Debra saw the man she married so many years ago. Then he spoke, and the moment was gone.

"Why did you bring me oranges?" Karl snarled at her. "You know I don't eat fruit in the morning."

Debra's smile faded, and she unnecessarily fiddled with the silverware on her own unused placemat. "I'm sorry dear," she purred.

"I just thought the vitamin C would be good for you. You've been working such long hours, I'm afraid you'll make yourself sick."

Karl snapped the binder closed and reached for the briefcase on the floor beside him. "I'll be fine," he quipped, dismissing her concerns. "All I need from you is to keep up your appearance. Lately you haven't looked much like the wife of a vice president."

Debra took her seat at the table and rested her chin in her hands. She no longer felt the sting of his words. She had her own little secret that kept her insulated from his increasingly cold remarks. Instead of reacting to his insult, she remained pleasant. "Will you be working late again?" she asked, not really caring if he was home for dinner. She had her plans, after all.

Karl buttoned his jacket and made to leave. "No, I have to catch a flight to New York. There's a fundraiser I need to attend. I told you about it last week!"

Debra smiled blandly up at her husband. "Oh right. Sorry honey, I forgot."

"Listen Debra," Karl complained, "if I'm going to run in a couple years, I need you to be a team player. Without financial backing I won't be able to fulfill our dream! I don't know what's distracting you lately but pull yourself together and get with the program."

'It's your dream, not mine,' Debra said to herself. Reaching for her husband's abandoned coffee cup, she took a sip and looked over the oranges for the biggest slice. "Okay, well I'll see you later, I guess. Good luck in New York."

Karl glared at her, irritated. Letting out a long sigh, he strode from the dining room. Debra listened to the front door open and close and took a bite from her orange slice as her husband peeled out of the driveway.

"Love you too," she said out loud, and took another sip of the lukewarm coffee.

A shrill ring interrupted her thoughts. She quickly rose and went to the hallway phone, lifting the receiver and uttering a polite "Hello."

"How did it go?" a female voice on the other end asked.

Debra smiled, a genuine smile, not the kind she pasted onto her face for Karl. "Oh the usual," she said with a shrug, placing herself on a hassock by the phone and crossing her legs. "He has no idea, of course. So that's good."

"Excellent!" the other woman came back. "Remember not to push the dumb-wife bit too hard. He's thinking with his dick right now, but we can't take anything for granted."

Debra pulled her free arm up above her head in a cat-like stretch. She felt like a cat right now, playing with a disgusting mouse.

"Oh don't worry," she said with a yawn. "I'm going to turn things around after he gets back from New York. He'll be greeted by the dutiful wife fully supporting his presidential run."

"Good girl," the woman laughed. "If we pull this off it's going to be sweet."

"Yeah," Debra agreed, getting to her feet. "Honey, I've gotta go. There's a million things to do before he gets back."

"Wait, there's one more thing," the caller said with urgency, "there's been a development. It's about our friend in the trenches. She has a request."

"Oh yeah?" Debra perked up, "when did you hear from her?"

"Recently," the woman came back, "she thinks there's someone in the line of fire that your lovely husband might be trying to roll over. She's not sure, but she says the way it's all playing out, well it has Karl's stink all over it."

"Oh really?" Debra grabbed a pencil and notepad she kept close to the phone. "You got a name?"

She listened as the caller read it off, and jotted down the name. Then she tucked the folded piece of paper in her bra.

"Is there anything we can do?" she asked.

"I don't know. But I'm going to try and find out. Just wanted to give you a head's up."

"Okay," Debra said, tousling her hair, "I'll keep it in mind. And hey, I'm sorry you have the crappier side of this deal."

"It's okay," Debra's caller demurred. "I can handle it, as long as I know where all of this will end up."

"He's going down, girl. He has to, and we have to make it happen," Debra's tone was all business.

"We will Debra," the woman softly said. "We will. Stay cool."

Debra pulled at her ear, thinking about the next few days. "You too honey," she said, "'bye….and good luck!"

Emma trailed David as he walked briskly away from Amir's home and down the street. Emma couldn't understand why he'd cut Mustafa's uncle off just as he revealed the manner in which her father was killed. And he hadn't seemed at all surprised with information that conflicted with what his own employers touted as fact. The trust she'd had in her companion was rapidly fading.

"Did you know my dad actually died in some kind of car wreck!?" She yelled at the back of David's head as he led the way down Amir's street to hail a taxi.

"Yes," was his curt reply, and nothing more.

"Well, *how* did you know?" She continued to badger. "And when the hell were you going to tell *me*?" She demanded.

David stepped to the curb and raised his arm toward a taxi coming toward them. "It was in your father's file," he said. "There hasn't been time to properly discuss it with you."

The taxi slowed, and David opened the door for Emma, placing her into the back seat with more force than necessary.

"Hey, take it easy!" Emma protested, as David slammed the door closed and moved to the other side of the vehicle to get in. Once inside he leaned toward the driver, giving instructions in what Emma presumed was Farsi. It never occurred to her he would know the language.

"So this isn't your first trip to Iran?" she asked, and then felt stupid for doing so. Of course, since he'd obviously worked before in Turkey, why wouldn't he have traveled to Iran at some point? It only solidified the fact that she really knew very little about David.

"I worked here briefly in a program that offered lessons in English within the rural communities."

"Sure you did," Emma muttered. "Are you going to answer my questions David?"

He started to answer, but was interrupted by a phone call. David pulled his phone from his jacket while Emma threw herself back on the car seat in a huff. He ignored her and flipped his phone open without looking to see who the caller was. "Hello," he said without hiding his irritation.

"Officer Jamison?" It was an older man's voice. "How is Miss Woods holding up?" The question had an underlying malice that was unmistakable.

"Who is this?" David said quietly so as not to alarm Emma who had her face turned away from him, angrily staring out the window.

"I'm someone who's interested in arranging a…..solution to Miss Woods' current situation," the man coldly stated. "I happen to know what you're up to Jamison. Did you not realize that looking up an unauthorized case, even an old one, would be flagged?" David tried to quell the sinking feeling in his stomach. "I acted alone," he said quickly, hoping to shift all the blame to himself. "Oh don't fret Jamison," the man said in a voice that was not at all reassuring. "I won't bother with Harriet, though I'm not so sure others would be so forgiving. Luckily for you I was the only person alerted to your inquiries. David let a quiet sigh of relief escape from his lips, and the man continued in a business-like tone. "I'm going to give you an address where you might find some answers."

"I'm listening," David responded while pulling out a pen and his notebook. Cradling the phone with his shoulder he quickly wrote the address down and tucked the notebook back into his jacket. "And what do you want in return?" He wasn't foolish enough to believe there would be no strings attached.

"I want your assurance that I'll remain untouched," the man stated flatly. "So long as I continue to feed you information leading you to this solution, you will arrange for my eventual immunity once things come to light. Do we have a deal?"

David paused, wondering if he had the ability, or even the desire to bargain with this dark entity. "I can't promise anything until I speak with my colleague," he began to debate. "Oh don't worry about Newcastle," the man said with a humorless chuckle. "He'll no doubt agree to my conditions."

David didn't have time to wonder how this man could be so sure of Anthony's reaction to such an open-ended deal. The voice on the phone interrupted his thoughts. "I want you to write down the number from which I've called. When you travel to that address in Tehran, call me. Do not enter the building without further instruction. Otherwise things could end badly. Goodbye Jamison."

David kept his expression neutral as he closed his phone and placed it back in his pocket. Emma was now glaring at him and he knew the questions were coming.

"Who was that?!" she demanded, expecting to be brushed off. "I don't know," David answered honestly, "but it appears somebody has been tipped off about our investigation."

Emma shook her head. "How is it our investigation when you insist on keeping things from me David? You can't expect me to just tag along here while you make all the decisions. And how can anyone know about what we're doing? Didn't you say I was safe while you were in control of things? Your credibility is turning to shit right now."

David let the sting of her words settle in. She was right, but there was nothing he could do to assure her now.

"Let's talk when we get back to the hotel." He calmly said, Maybe, when they got to their room there would be a word from Anthony. He stared straight ahead while Emma edged further away from him, leaning against the car door with arms crossed, fuming.

Once he opened the door into their room at the Laleh Hotel in Tehran David stepped aside for Emma to enter first. Whipping off her head scarf she looked around. It was the same hotel where her family had stayed back in '74, but then it had been called the InterContinental and was brand new.

Because her family had been waylaid in Turkey for three days, there was a mix up in reservations, and their room was rented out to some other family. Her dad raised such a stink about it that his boss at Grumman got them into the only other accommodations available, the Presidential Suite. It seemed strange when her father told them to be careful about what they said, because the room was bugged. The girls didn't care about that creepy fact, because the suite was huge and beautifully furnished. Emma and her sister felt like royalty staying there, and they took to calling themselves "Persian Princesses."

The room David secured for them was as far from that memory as possible. The furniture was dated, some of it no doubt from the hotel's debut, and the rug was thinning in places. But the air conditioning worked, and there were two double beds, one of which Emma now threw herself. With her hands linked behind her head on the pillow she stared at the ceiling and waited for David to close and lock the door. As soon as she heard him draw the bolt she sat up, resting on her elbows and studied his expression. As usual, it told her nothing.

"Okay," she said impatiently, "we're in the room. Talk to me David."

He threw the key card on the dresser and began his routine of scouting through the room for whatever surveillance devices might be hidden.

'Ridiculous,' Emma thought. "Stop checking out the room and answer me," she goaded him. "Nobody even knows we're in Iran David, let alone where we're staying."

He ignored her, continuing his routine assessment of the room. When he was finished he stood in front of the bed, pulled off his jacket and threw it on a nearby chair. "I wouldn't be too sure there aren't people looking for us here in Tehran Emma," he told her in a sobering tone. "Trouble seems to have a way of following you."

"Fuck you David," Emma responded, "you're just avoiding my question."

He sighed and sat on the chair, pushing his jacket aside. "Alright, what do you want to know?"

'Where to begin?' Emma wondered. She needed clarity about what Amir told them. "Is it true my dad died in a car wreck?"

David sat back in the chair and leaned his head on his hand. "It looks that way; however I only have a photo of the burned out car and, excuse me, a charred body to go by. This was in a file concerning your father that I unearthed back at the agency." Seeing Emma's pained expression when he mentioned the body, he quickly tried to redirect her thoughts.

"There's really no way we can confirm that was your dad, Emma. It was something I wanted to discuss further with Anthony, along with possible reasons why the agency might have lied about the case."

She wasn't going to let him off that easily. "You still could have told me David. I have a right to know how my dad died, particularly when it goes against what those sons-of-bitches told my mother. And where the hell is Anthony anyway?! I thought you two were friends. Is he in the habit of just dumping people like me on you and then scurrying away?"

David smiled a little at the thought. "No," he said firmly, "he has always been a conscientious person, and he seldom scurries."

"Well he certainly hasn't made an effort to keep in touch," Emma remarked, leaning forward and crossing her legs. "I trusted him to help me, and he disappears. He convinces me to trust you, and you lie to me! If you didn't tell me about the car wreck then there must be other things you're keeping from me as well." She rose from the bed and reached for the head scarf. "That's what you people do, right?" her voice rose in an accusing tone. "It's your job to lie to people like me! For all I know you're part of the plan to shut me up, or maybe just keep track of me until, what a surprise, the bad guys somehow find me and start shooting again!" She knew the accusation was ludicrous, but she'd had enough of being kept in the dark about her own life and death.

David stood and angrily gripped her shoulders. "That's bullshit Emma!" he said, giving her a little shake. "You know I've tried to protect you from the beginning. How would you explain my taking out the guy at the house in D.C., or the men shooting at us in the car? I've done nothing but help and help you, probably putting my own career on the line in the process."

David's sudden show of strength and emotion made her momentarily lose track of her thoughts. But she wouldn't let him bully her. "I didn't ask you to jeopardize your goddamn career David! That's on Anthony, and if you two think I'm going to go blindly along with this crap you've got another thing coming."

She was crying now, her nerves worn thin from being constantly on the move, from trying to remain tough, and from imagining her father being burned alive in a car so many years ago. Disappointment and fury welled up inside her, creating still more tears that she tried to wipe away. She wished she'd never gone to the bank, never gone to Anthony for help, and never given her father a second thought. Why did she even care about a man who transformed from hero to abuser all through her childhood? She wanted to go home, back to her farm and a normal life. She was done.

She tried to wrestle away from David, but his grip tightened.

"Let me go," she cried, "I'm out of here!"

David kept a firm hold. "Emma, you can't just walk out. It's dangerous. Where the hell do you think you're going?"

"Anywhere that's far away from you!" she yelled at him, knowing her anger was misplaced, but lashing out at the only person available.

"I won't let you go out there on your own," David said in the calm manner that was starting to drive her crazy.

"Why not David?" she demanded, "why the hell not?" Her face was inches from his, but she couldn't see him clearly through the tears. Crap, why was she still crying? She was being a baby when she wanted to prove to him she couldn't be pushed around. Emma wiped her nose with the back of her hand and moved to pull herself from his grip.

"What the fuck difference does it make anyway? I'm going back to Amir's place and find out what else he knows. You didn't give him a chance to finish. Maybe he can help me, someone who was with my dad the day he died."

She was rambling, and possibly grasping at straws. But she had to do something.

David still held her. "We have to wait for Tony. I know he's working things on his end. We just have to be patient. He'll contact us and let us know what direction to take from here."

Emma shook her head and gave an incredulous stare through her tears.

"Wake up David," she sobbed. "Anthony's long gone. He doesn't give a shit! He left me with you because he wanted out. Why don't you get out too? You're right. I'm nothing but trouble, so just let me go!"

David's eyes locked on to hers, searching for a way to reach her.

"I'm not letting you go," he said again, at a loss for any other words that made sense.

"Why?!" she pleaded. "Why don't you just go back to your nice job working for the government and let me screw things up on my own!?"

She sounded slightly hysterical now, beyond understanding her situation, or the man restraining her.

David searched for a way to get through to her, to somehow snap her out of feeling cornered and helpless. He was used to approaching problems in a practical manner, but there was nothing practical about Emma right now. No tactics or training in dealing with something like this came to mind.

She broke free from his grasp and snatched her purse from the bed where she'd thrown it. "You don't need to worry about protecting me David," she snapped. "I'm perfectly fine taking care of myself, and I have zero expectations of you."

"Don't be ridiculous," David shot back angrily. "You're overreacting and making decisions based on emotion." He turned away from her for only a moment, and Emma took that moment to fly out the door.

David moved to follow her, his efforts interrupted by the ringing of his phone. Assuming it was Anthony finally trying to reach him he answered while grabbing his coat and heading for the door once more. "Tony!" he practically screamed into the phone. "Where the hell are you?" There was a brief silence, followed by an insidious snickering that made his blood run cold.

"This isn't your beloved mentor Officer Jamison," the familiar voice snarled, "but it is your life line, yours and Emma's."

Chapter 35
Allison

Allison crossed the hotel room barefoot and wearing only a thin, black nightie. Pouring herself another glass of Bordeaux she became lost in thought, eventually lifting the goblet cradled in her hand to her lips. This moment had been a long time coming, and she couldn't blow it now. She thought back to when she was just a teenager, living in Beirut where her father was Counsellor. She and her mother didn't much like the lifestyle, but her father seemed pleased and committed to his position. Allison adored her dad, and she waited impatiently for him to come home from work, when he would insist she tell him about school instead of sharing details of his work. Allison was happy, until the day her father didn't come home. That afternoon she and her mother learned he had died at the hands of a suicide bomber. The Lebanese terrorist who drove a van into the embassy took out sixty-three people, seventeen of them Americans, including her father who worked at the embassy.

It was devastating to Allison, and she vowed to discover who had backed the terrorist and whatever group he represented, all the way to the top person. Her mother remarried, a captain in the army. He was a good stepdad, but not great with money. The family struggled financially, and Allison knew she was on her own if she wished to pursue college, and this she wanted very much. She busted her ass in high school and worked part time jobs to save up. Between that and the scholarships she'd acquired, it was just enough to enroll in Bryn Mawr, where she busted her ass some more. As a path toward her goal of understanding the machinations of terrorist activity she created a sort of club with other girls interested in modern history, focusing on Middle Eastern affairs. That was where she met her friend Lucy Champion. Lucy had the same intense interest in Middle Eastern history, engaged in her own research involving terrorism groups and how they evolved. Drinking beer in her dorm room, Allison learned that she and Lucy had a great deal in common. She had lost a boyfriend in the very same Embassy bombing.

"He was an officer, older than me so my parents didn't approve," Lucy divulged that night. "We were secretly engaged right before he was stationed in Beirut. We were going to get married after I graduated. I was planning a move to Lebanon, but the terrorist ended all that. I guess I never got over it." The two women forged a bond over the injustice of their shared loss, and both were determined to find out all they could about how the terrorist groups were funded and how they evolved. Lucy married well, a mover and shaker in the arms industry. She later divorced her husband and moved to France, but the marriage lasted long enough for Lucy to press her husband's associates for information regarding possible government ties to terrorist groups. What she learned she passed on to Allison.

Allison Becker graduated at the top of her class and eventually eased into top administrative positions in Washington. Lucy discovered there had been whispers regarding Karl Magnus among her husband's cronies. Magnus had played with fire back in his army days, mixing with Iranian revolutionaries in order to gain an intelligence foothold in the new regime. When Lucy let her friend know about Magnus, Allison put her laser focus on him. She worked her way up to the position of Secretary of Treasury, keeping her eye on Karl Magnus, and ensuring she caught him. Once she had his dick in her pocket the rest was easy. She found out all she needed to know about Karl and his role in her father's death. It made her sick to her stomach to have sex with Karl, but she gathered the dirt she needed, and eventually arranged a meeting with his wife. Debra didn't seem surprised by Allison's accusations regarding her husband. He'd cheated on her plenty of times before. Now she wanted out of the marriage, but not until she could be assured she would be financially independent. She and Allison worked together to patiently set a trap for the Vice President. Now it was game time.

Allison took another demure sip of the wine. *'Mustn't get too tipsy,'* she told herself, before turning to look at Karl. He was sprawled out on the king bed, eyes closed and clearly spent from the sexual romp that had just occurred. She turned back to the mini bar and poured Karl's glass full to the brim.

"I thought the meeting went well, don't you?" Allison asked in a conversational tone, as if she hadn't just made every part of him tingle and explode. *'Men can be so easy to manipulate,'* she thought. Now he would be pliable to whatever she suggested.

"With the budget approved you're free to begin work on those projects you hold so dear." She said this with more than a little sarcasm. Karl put his hand over his eyes in an exaggerated gesture.

"Do we have to talk business now Allison? I was feeling so relaxed."

She laughed and cozied up to him on the bed, nudging his arm in an effort to show him the full glass she brought. He sat up and took a giant swig, then leered at Allison before asking, "Wanna go again?"

She scoffed and placed her hand on his forehead, pushing him back on his pillow where he almost spilled his wine.

"We need to go over the game plan while we have time together," she chided him. "I've managed to tuck away some nice loopholes for you to gain access to funds, but it's up to you to squirrel it away and make it look like it's going to your pet projects."

Karl frowned and rose up to take another healthy gulp of the expensive wine.

"I'll have to skim a little off the top first," he grumbled. "I have a few paychecks to distribute to my people."

Allison sat across from him in an armchair, crossing her legs seductively and pretending to drink more from her own glass.

"What people are these?" she asked, as if she couldn't care less.

"Victor's guys," Karl said while swirling his glass to release the wine's aroma. "They're the ones put in charge of keeping that girl quiet."

Allison placed her glass on an end table by the armchair and made a production of pulling her hair up onto her head, effectively exposing her neck.

"Yeah, you never told me what that was all about," she said with a slight yawn. "Why do you have it in for her? What did that poor girl ever do to you?"

Karl shook his head. "Nothing directly. But her father, Carter, worked for Grumman as some kind of cover for a CIA operation when Iran purchased jets and other weapons back in the seventies."

"There were dirty dealings back then, some CIA officers with their hands in the honey pot. Tarlino's inside man was one of them, and this Carter guy was offered a cut of the pie. Unfortunately, he got to know some of the Iranians he was supposed to be watching, and they weren't even the real revolutionaries, not the hard core ones anyway. They were trying to make the regime more democratic, and they revealed some of the grift going on among the Shah's administration, which led him to the guys leading up his team who were also on the take. Anyway, he turned out to be too much of a boy scout. There was a real concern he would go to the head of the CIA and rat everyone out. I guess that's why they had him killed and pinned everything on him."

Allison played some more with her hair. "Again, what's that got to do with you?"

Karl grunted as he got up and, assuming that sex was done for the night, pulled on his pajama bottoms.

"Oh it's all so boring honey," he sighed. "It's all in the past."

Allison leaned back and smiled. "So bore me," she said quietly. "It turns me on."

Feeling hopeful Karl continued. "Carter Woods was a threat to me as well."

Seeing confusion on her face he went on to explain to Allison. "I was younger then, a Ranger in the army at the time and all fired up when I was recommended by my superiors to work in tandem with Carter's boss, a man named Theodore Alberts. He had a little thing going on the side, keeping an eye on the revolutionaries that were starting to make some noise about corruption in the Shah's government and such. These weren't the people already working within the government toward change. Those were the people Carter Woods became involved with. I was sniffing out the younger students and religious followers of Khomeini. My job was to meet with them and forge a relationship, just in case they did manage to take power. Then we'd have contacts within the new government and hopefully continue with business as usual."

Karl glanced at Allison to make sure he was still holding her interest. Her welcoming smile encouraged him to go on.

"Like I said, I was young, and I wanted to impress my superiors. I found it incredibly exciting that they put me in charge of tracking down the revolutionaries, the real ones, and offering them a deal. As a way to hedge our bet with Iran, the U.S. wanted to maintain contact with this group just in case things got out of control and the Shah was ousted, which is exactly what happened.

Allison's eyes grew wide. "You were associating with revolutionaries?! How did you manage to gain their trust? I thought they hated Americans."

Karl nodded. "They did, but I was able to convince them that our people working in Iran would be available to discuss terms with them if the tide turned in their favor. They believed the U.S. was quietly waiting to see how things turned out, and then would back whoever came out on top."

"And was that true?" Allison looked as if she found the story difficult to believe.

"Well," Karl shrugged, "it was, and it wasn't."

He let his mind wander back again to more heroic days.

"I received a lot of praise for my relationship with the people who took charge in Iran, so I kept the lines open. I even managed to generate dialogue between them and us during the hostage situation." Karl laughed, "They called me the Boy Wonder. I loved it!"

Karl paused to take another sip of wine. He was starting to feel buzzed from the alcohol, and set the glass down on his nightstand. If he was too drunk to perform for Allison then all of this chatter would be a waste of time. She was looking at him, waiting for more.

"The thing is," Karl continued, "I kind of embellished exactly what my commanders would be willing to supply in the way of support."

Allison's expression of disapproval made Karl nervous.

"I had to, sweetheart! These people meant business and never would have given me the time of day if I hadn't made big promises. Anyway, everything went to shit when Carter somehow found out about our activity. Alberts told me Carter was going to blow our covers, and tell the revolutionaries I was full of shit. The people on my team, headed by Alberts, took Carter out to save my ass. Anyway, I still got screwed because they never used my connections in any meaningful way. I was sent back to the States before the Shah even went into exile."

"Well," Allison sighed, "that's probably just as well. Being in bed with a group that paved the way for Islamic terrorists wouldn't look good. You wouldn't want that kind of history following you. Considering your current and very public anti-terrorist stance, your past could come back to haunt you. It's a good thing you broke off contact with them."

Karl shifted in bed and gave his mistress a sideways look, prompting Allison to gasp.

"You did break off contact with them, right?" she asked in disbelief. She smiled to indicate how intrigued she was with such a devious man.

Karl, sensing the truth would certainly arouse Allison, kept talking. "I continued relations with my revolutionary contacts on the sly and with Alberts' approval. We both felt it would benefit the U.S. to have somebody like me on the inside. And it didn't seem like a bad idea to know who was in charge in Iran."

A shadow crossed Karl's face, as he reflected on past mistakes.

"Then things got ugly," he said with a scowl. "Some of my contacts broke off and formed their own organizations. They came under the spell of Islamic fundamentalists who wanted nothing to do with the evil of Western ideals. I didn't realize they were focused on U.S. targets until it was too late. I'd already been mentioned by a number of them in messages intercepted by Alberts' superiors. He managed to put them off, saying I had ceased contact well before any terrorist activity. But the die had been cast, and I had to scramble to cover my tracks."

Allison did her best to hide the revulsion she felt toward the man beside her. She steeled herself to act naturally, placing a comforting arm around him in an act of support.

"So where does this poor woman you're hunting come in with all of this?" Allison asked in a soothing voice.

Karl fiddled with the drawstring of his pajama bottoms, wondering if this meandering conversation would result in more play time with his secret girlfriend.

"According to Tarlino, our Agency insider, Carter is believed to have had contact with another Grumman employee in Iran, another member of the team. This guy was asked to do the same kind of work, infiltrating the Revolutionary groups in order to gain Intel, and forge alliances. He wasn't nearly as effective as I was, but he knew what was going on. He knew I was doing the same kind of work. Maybe he was even a little jealous of me, because I was so much younger and hadn't paid any dues yet. Anyway, Carter met with this guy just before he was killed by Alberts' people. They suspect Carter tried to warn his colleague about what was going on. Tarlino says this dude got freaked out by Carter's murder and felt the need to share. He blabbed everything to a friend of Carter's who stayed with Grumman a long time after Carter was taken out. Both of these men are still alive, somewhere, and they both have the potential to expose me.

Allison rolled her eyes and began toying with the black silk nightie. "I swear to god Karl," she giggled, "if you don't tell me how this makes Carter's daughter your concern I'm going to fall asleep!"

Alarmed with the idea, Karl finally showed all his cards. "This girl has started to look into her father's death, honey! Her dad left her some kind of evidence, and it probably leads to his friends. If she joins forces with them, they could blame me and Alberts for all kinds of things, including her dad's death. If they take a closer look at the Grumman operation they might dig up shit on people like me, and maybe go public with it. I don't need that kind of publicity tarnishing my record now."

Allison crept seductively up to the bed, slowly pulling up the nightie. "And how far are you willing to go in order to shut this bitch up?" She asked.

Thinking the conversation was finally turning her on; Karl impatiently yanked at his pajamas and hopped into bed with a smile.

"That's the beauty of it," he said, flinging away the pillows to make room. "I'm leaving all of that to Tarlino and his people. I just told him to do whatever was necessary to get her out of the equation. He and his little band of assassins have a lot at stake too, so I'm pretty sure she's done."

He grabbed Allison's arm just as she discarded her nightie. Pushing her down roughly he hopped on top, kissing her roughly on the neck before allowing her to come up for air.

"Hey," she breathed heavily, "what's the doomed girl's name anyway?"

Karl lay on top of her, eager to go to work on round two.

"Emma," he panted, before pushing Allison's legs apart, "Emma Woods."

Chapter 36
Desperation

Emma ran blindly down the stairs and, upon reaching the lobby, right out the large, glass doors that opened up to the circular driveway where cabs lined up. There, she stopped and wondered how she could direct the driver to Amir's place. David knew the address, and on their trip out he'd given instructions to the driver in Farsi. She hadn't paid much attention at the time but spent most of the drive looking out the window. She remembered they passed the Grand Bazaar right before Amir's. David had even pointed it out to her.

"Pretty exotic really," he said as he directed her gaze out the window.

"I know," she'd answered. "We went there when I was a kid. I remember a boy carrying a big bundle of sticks on his back winked at me. Maybe he thought I was easy because I was obviously American, the way I was dressed. It was weird because I was only eleven. I hadn't even kissed a boy."

Amir's home was just around the corner from the bazaar. If she could get to the market, then she could make her way to his place easily. She walked quickly up to the nearest cab, where a man was leaning against the car door and talking to another driver. They both stood at attention when she stepped closer and said, "I'm sorry, I don't speak Farsi. Do either of you speak English?"

The nearest man nodded but said nothing. His friend laughed and gave him a push.

"He doesn't understand a word you said, miss. I speak English. Where would you like to go?"

Emma sighed with relief. "Can you take me to the Grand Bazaar?" She asked.

"Certainly," said the driver, and opened the back door.

"Who is this?!" David demanded into the phone while running down the hallway after Emma. "You don't need to know my name Jamison, not yet," the caller said. "Did you receive the photos I sent you?" In all the commotion with Emma David realized he hadn't checked his phone. "I don't know," he answered cautiously, "I'm currently engaged in something else." He didn't want to let this stranger in on anything that might indicate his location. He could hear a disgruntled murmuring from the caller. "You should have received them by now, Jamison. I suggest you take a good look at what I sent. As I said before, I want to make a deal. I can give you the major players in the Woods case, but I want immunity."

Just as Emma ducked into the cab, David appeared at the hotel entrance, cell phone to his ear. As the cab pulled away, he ran to the driver's friend who stood with arms crossed, disappointed at losing a fare. David barked a few words in Farsi to the startled driver and jumped in the cab. His driver scrambled to start up the vehicle, and they followed Emma's taxi until they were only another car's distance between them.

"Jamison!" The impatient voice brought David's attention back to his phone. "Are you still there?"

"Yes, "David answered, winded from his pursuit of Emma, "I'm interested in discussing the subject." He decided to come clean with the caller, at least about his current challenge. "Unfortunately I'm in the act of apprehending Miss Woods at the moment."

There was another brief pause. "You mean she's not with you?" David could make out a note of alarm in the caller's voice. "I'm following her…" David began to answer, but the caller cut him off.

"Under no circumstances should you allow her to be alone in Tehran," the caller commanded. "There are people watching both of you and they've been directed to take Emma out once I give the command. I'd hoped to warn you ahead of time, but I assumed you were capable of controlling her." The caller's tone was accusatory, but David only cared about what information he could obtain in order to save Emma. He yelled again in Farsi for the taxi driver to keep up with the car darting through traffic ahead of them, then turned his attention back to the caller.

"I'll have her back with me soon," he said confidently, "tell me what to watch out for."

"Look at the damned photos Jamison," the caller ordered. They show where the people coming for Emma have their base. They're local men, and not skilled, but they know enough about what's at stake, so they're motivated by greed. See that you gather up the Woods girl before they do and get somewhere safe. I'll call you again."

The phone went dead just as Emma's taxi maneuvered towards the bazaar.

Emma dug into her purse and found nothing in the way of money. *'Shit,'* she panicked, *'I'm going to have to run for it.'* She wondered what the jail time was, in Iran, for dodging cab fare. Eventually, the driver pulled up to the entrance of the marketplace that had been humming in business for over four hundred years. A multitude of shoppers milled about in the cool dusk air, looking to haggle over goods or simply take in the sights. Emma let herself out of the cab and made a pretense of searching through her purse. The idea of simply dashing from the cab as soon as it stopped had entered her mind, but the driver stepped out of his vehicle the same time she did. If she ran now, he most certainly would catch her. She decided to throw herself on the mercy of her driver. She looked up apologetically, hoping for the best.

"I'm sorry," she said, "I brought the wrong purse. I don't have the money to pay for the ride."

The man looked irritated, but not exactly vengeful. Maybe there was a way to make this right. She pulled out the pen and paper she kept in her handbag and began writing.

"Here," she said in desperation as she wrote. "This is my name, and the room number at the hotel where you picked me up."

She then tore the paper in half, giving the blank half and her pen to the driver.

"You write your name and number down, and what I owe you for the ride. I promise I'll get the money to you."

The driver gave her a doubtful look. Then, shaking his head he wrote down the information she needed and handed it back to her. She exchanged her information in kind, and they stood staring at each other.

Emma lowered her head, ashamed. "I'm really so sorry. I absolutely swear to you that you'll get paid," she said, looking up to see if he would believe her, or throw her back into the cab for a ride to the local police station. He was stone-faced for a moment, and then gave a little laugh.

"You're an American, yes?" he asked.

"Yes," she answered, "I'm afraid so."

The driver shook his head and headed back to the cab. "Well American girl," he said loudly, "I am trusting you. So you don't let me down, okay?"

"Okay," Emma replied, waving in appreciation, "I won't."

As he drove away, she hoped she lived long enough to make good on her promise. Making her way to the market's entrance, she failed to notice the cab that had pulled up some distance from her own. David threw some bills at his driver and jumped from the cab. But Emma was already rapidly disappearing amongst the throngs of people jamming the market's entrance. He hurried to catch up, doing his best not to lose sight of her in the crowd.

Chapter 37
Hostage

The market hit Emma's senses hard with a riot of color and commotion. As she drew near, the crowd of people became denser. A cacophony of many different conversations rose as one long babble in a language she didn't understand. She held her purse tightly against her body, and pushed ahead into the melee. The smell of bodies, animals and cooking food filled the air in an intoxicating blend. Emma pressed past vendors holding up their wares and did her best to stay in the middle of the crowd. If she went straight through the market she believed it would spit her out on the other side and into Amir's neighborhood. She tried to keep her eyes forward, willing herself not to get turned around in these unfamiliar surroundings, but occasionally something would catch her eye. A store front featuring vibrant women's clothing to wear under their chadors, another where freshly butchered chickens hung from the window, and a gaggle of young girls, their head scarves bouncing as they giggled over some private joke, all competed for her attention.

Once, as she hugged a corner wall to avoid a boy pulling at the harness of his goat, she nearly stumbled over a man crouched against the stones. He gazed up at her, one eye gray and blinded. He stirred a copper-colored kind of soup, and he held up a ladle brimming with the strange liquid, his smile revealing a limited amount of teeth. Emma remembered seeing this "soup" when she visited the market as a child. Locals paid for and gulped down the concoction with relish, but she never learned what it was. Now the sight brought back memories of her family navigating the bazaar, as out-of-place as she was now. Everything then had caught her by surprise, like the bedraggled bear wearing a muzzle. Her father told her that for so many drachma she could pet it, but she'd only felt pity for the poor animal. She blinked at the memory, and turned from the half-blind man to get her bearings.

Suddenly, she felt something hard poking into her lower back, and a hand tight around her arm. "If you shout, or cause trouble, we will shoot you," a voice whispered into her ear. Before she could react, another hand clasped the arm holding her purse. For a moment, she froze. Then, with heart beating, she turned her head to the first anonymous voice. "What do you want?" she hissed. "I don't have any money." She must have attracted attention as a westerner who might be carrying cash, or credit cards. She prepared to have her purse ripped from her shoulder, but the men on either side only guided her through the market, increasing their pace whenever they hit a pocket somewhat vacant of shoppers. Emma tried to catch the eye of anyone who might help her, but every shopper was intent on his or her own business. Sandwiched between two men who looked as if they were safely escorting her didn't help. Walking alone as a woman alone brought attention. With her two companions, she could have been any lady accompanied by male family members.

There was no time to figure out how to escape, and no one to save her this time. Shit! Why had she run off without David? She'd taken for granted the protection he provided, and had thought it wasn't enough. He told her not to assume they weren't being followed, but she stupidly ignored him and put herself in this position. These men weren't interested in robbing her. These were the people her father warned her about. *'I'm sorry dad,'* she thought to herself in anguish, *'I wasn't careful, and I failed you.'* There would be no more searching for the truth behind what she knew now was her father's murder. She would be just another casualty in whatever he discovered, caught up in it as well, and dying for her efforts.

Emma and her captors emerged from the bazaar and into the night where the crowd thinned, then fell away completely. Just as she suspected, Amir's neighborhood loomed ahead, but she was led further right, to an older and darker section of buildings. This neighborhood showed buildings in decay, some with crumbling stairs and rusting gates. The men kept her at a brisk walk, pulling her toward a narrow building that sat between two taller structures, giving it the appearance of being squeezed on either end. Practically carrying Emma up the steps leading to the front of the building, the two men stopped long enough for one of them to knock sharply on the splintered front door wood. Seconds ticked by as she tried to catch her breath. *'So this is where I'm going to die,'* she thought, a pragmatic acceptance of her fate causing her to feel an odd calm.

Chapter 38
Emma's Proposal

Footsteps could be heard from inside the building, until finally the door opened just a sliver. An obscured face regarded them dolefully. A few words were exchanged in what she assumed was Farsi, and the door swung open. She was ushered in and, with the door soundly bolted behind them, pulled further into the dark recess of another room. The room was nearly empty, where a dim light burned. There was only a weathered table at its center surrounded by two equally worn chairs. Emma was unceremoniously dumped into one of the chairs, a glass of water placed in front of her. She turned to catch a glimpse of her abductors, guessing there were two others in the room with those who had brought her. But before she could get a good look at any of them, they abruptly left; the sound of a bolt sliding into place reverberated around the room. Emma stared at the glass of water, thirsty, but unwilling to take a chance that it wasn't laced with poison. There was no way she was going to make it that easy for them. She would go out fighting, perhaps scratch some of them on the face to mark their crime and get some kind of satisfaction for herself.

She moved from the chair and began to explore her surroundings. The dark corners of the room yielded nothing but cobwebs and dust. In one corner musty smelling drapes hung limply over a window, but when Emma tried to move the latch open she found it was rusted shut. She cupped her hands to peer out at what lay beyond. There were bars covering the window from the outside, and she could faintly make out a narrow street. At least she was on the ground floor. Maybe she could find something with which to break the window, and scream for help before they came back to kill her. She frantically looked around, seeing nothing but the chairs, which looked as if they would break into pieces before shattering the glass. Dejected, Emma slammed her back against the wall, and slid down to the floor. There, she pulled her knees in and rested her head on crossed arms, her mind blank with despair. There was nothing to do now but wait, wait for them to come back and shoot her, or perhaps torture her for any incriminating information they thought she was withholding.

This brought to Emma a moment of clarity. What if these men hadn't any idea about what she may or may not have found out? According to David, foot soldiers like these guys were merely working for other, more powerful men. No doubt the ones pulling the strings were anonymous figures within the CIA. It was entirely possible these locals were simply paid thugs. Why else would they risk getting caught kidnapping and murdering an American? If they were working for money, maybe they could be bought. Emma's mind began to work out a crazy plan. It was a long shot, but it was better than waiting around, docile and dying at their command. By the time she heard footsteps returning she had her script prepared. She scrambled from the floor and placed herself on one of the sturdier chairs, crossing her legs and folding her hands on her knees as if waiting to interview for a secretarial position. Two of the men entered, one with his gun drawn, the other holding a set of handcuffs. Hiding her fear with a complacent look on her face, Emma smiled at the men. They drew up in surprise. They were expecting to come upon a whimpering and frightened damsel, but were instead met with a strangely composed woman.

Emma smiled slyly. "Good evening gentlemen," she said in a brisk and businesslike voice, "do either of you speak English?"

The men exchanged glances. Then the shorter one nodded. "I speak English," he stated firmly, clearly proud of the fact. Suddenly, as if to gain control over the situation, he proclaimed. "You are Emma Woods."

"I am," she responded without flinching, "and I wonder which of you are stupid enough to shoot me before asking why your boss wants me dead."

The taller man kept his eyes on Emma, but rattled something off to the other, clearly asking about what was being said. The English speaking man looked confused, and after speaking harshly to his accomplice, turned his attention back to Emma.

"You are in no position to ask questions," he spat the words out, but she saw doubt behind his eyes. Yes, it would be interesting to try and beat these men at their own game. Even if she failed, she could die with the satisfaction of knowing they would wonder what secrets she took to the grave.

"I'm only wondering why you haven't asked any questions yourself," she said with a shrug. Her face became serious, and she placed her hands on the chair while leaning forward, a gleam in her eye.

"Don't you think it's strange they haven't told you why I'm to be murdered? This was a great assumption on her part. But her gut told her these grunt men were merely pawns, sent to do the dirty work, thus preventing their bosses from getting blood on their hands. She leaned back on the chair and crossed her arms in front of her, a smug expression on her face.

"They expect you to just do as they ask, don't they? But what they don't know is how much more money I can pay. They are paying you, aren't they?"

The taller man was getting frustrated, and he elbowed his friend for information. The English speaker held up his hand to quiet his partner and turned his attention once more to Emma.

"We weren't supposed to kill you right away," he admitted without a speck of shame. "We were to first extract information about your father."

Trying not to betray the horror she felt at the prospect of being tortured and murdered, Emma smiled even wider.

"Of course you were!" She pronounced as if she'd already won the game. "And then you pass along what I tell you about my father....and the money disappears into pockets other than your own. How nice for them, but rather a bad deal for you I suspect."

Now the tall man could no longer wait. He barked a question at his friend, who snapped back at him in a long line of Farsi. His explanation brought about a look of astonishment to the tall man, who looked at Emma with renewed interest. Then he seemed to prompt his

310

[Margin note: You changed the tone of your narrative.]

friend with another question. The English speaker turned once more to Emma, suspicion on his face.

"How can you prove to us you have this money? There was no mention of money to us. We were told to get the names of those helping you, and…"

Emma cut him off. "And to find out what my father left me." She reached for her purse and stood, slinging it over her shoulder.

"I brought it with me," she said flatly, like a school teacher speaking to dim-witted students. "Why else do you think I'm getting help? I can pay for it, and everybody likes to get paid. Do you think the man who got me here did so because he's a nice guy? Nobody puts their job on the line to help out the daughter of a dead traitor. And after giving up to you where I have the money, and believe me, they know I have money, why do you suppose they want me eliminated?"

The two men exchanged glances, but she didn't wait for them to discuss it. She looked at them as if providing the last piece of a puzzle, like the puzzles she put together with her father. Only this one was a complete fabrication.

"They want to shut me up because not only do I have money, but I know where they got theirs!"

The English speaking man's eyes grew wide. He threw his shoulders back at this revelation and looked sideways at his friend.

Emma kept going. "Don't you see? I'm a threat to their bankroll. I can pay you off, and I can cut the flow of their funding by alerting the authorities. The man helping me is with the CIA, and he has access to men who work above your bosses. Their lovely extra income is threatened by what I know about them. My father helped them get their money, but when he wanted a bigger cut they killed him. They didn't know he left me all I needed to frame them, along with a whole lot of cash he'd stashed away right under their noses. You see, my dad had his own business on the side. There was a reason they wanted him dead, and there's a reason they want me gone too!"

She didn't know how she managed to pile on this bullshit. Some of it was speculation after listening to David and Anthony. The rest was pure fantasy, but it sounded plausible, and she liked the effect she was having on her audience. She had their rapt attention now. Even the tall man was enthralled, assuming that whatever she was telling his buddy was important. Emma slowly walked closer to the men, until her belly pushed against the English speaker's gun.

"The question is," she whispered, "how loyal are you to the men who expect you to work for so very little, when I can pay you quite a lot….and take them out as well?"

English speaker licked his lips, and pocketed his gun. "How do you do that?" he asked. There was no attempt to mask his excitement and greed.

Emma looked from one man to the other. "First, I'll take you to the money. I'm not stupid enough to have it on me. Some of it is back at my hotel. The rest is stashed safely, and is none of your business." She waited for English speaker to relay her proposal, and then spoke as if they were now all co-conspirators.

"You'll have to give the others some kind of excuse for taking me away from here. The less we have to split the money the better."

English speaker turned to tall man and once again translated. Tall man nodded in agreement and began to brandish the handcuffs.

"I prefer we leave the handcuffs out of this," she commanded, pushing the cuffs back into his chest, "just in case bullets start flying."

The tall man nodded and put away the cuffs. They headed for the door, but Emma stopped before tall man could open it. She turned to English speaker.

"Both of you should hold my arms like before, so they think you're taking me somewhere against my will." She spoke as if they were missing the obvious.

English speaker rolled his eyes. "Of course," he said, shaking his head, and instructed tall man to do the same. The door opened, and the three went out to seek an imaginary fortune. For the time being, Emma was free.

Chapter 39
The Catch

David remained hidden from the trio exiting the building. He had gotten so close when he followed Emma into the bazaar. Only a few steps away, he'd been surrounded and jostled by a large family apparently shopping for an upcoming wedding. Babbling in glee they intercepted David's path to Emma, almost carrying him away with them as they headed toward a shop selling bridal dresses. David caught sight of what must have been the bride-to-be in the center of the loud clan, blushing and embarrassed by all the attention. With an uncomfortable distance now between him and Emma, he finally managed to extract himself from the boisterous group. So intent was he on maintaining sight of her, he didn't notice the two men who peeled away from the crowd of shoppers. They moved quickly, and as they flanked Emma, the words echoed in David's ears. "They're local men…"

His heart sank as he realized he'd let Emma fall right into the hands of those sent to kill her. By the way one held his arm to her back David could tell it held a weapon. It prevented him from doing more, other than to follow along as close as possible without being detected. For one sickening moment he lost sight of the trio. He frantically scanned the crowd of shoppers until he had the instinct to look at the photos that were presumably on his phone. He hurriedly flipped the device open and viewed the images left there by his mystery caller. He immediately noticed Amir's residence, though it appeared the photo was taken much earlier. Was this the photo Emma was speaking of when she recognized Amir's place. The second photo was of another building that showed what looked like a marketplace in the background. The bazaar! Could this be the base David's caller was referring to? If so, it was nearby. He raced toward the nearest archway until the crowd of shoppers thinned and the artificial light gave way to a black night sky. David breathed in the cool air and focused on the familiar neighborhood. He quickly made his way across the road and took to the sidewalk he and Emma had traversed just that afternoon. Within minutes he spotted Emma and her captors walking just ahead of him. He trained his eyes on the three, but kept his distance, trying to formulate a plan. Too late he came to realize they were in front of the building he'd seen on his phone. Just outside of Amir's neighborhood, it was now a decrepit building that looked as if it might crumble to pieces at any moment. David scoured the nearby streets for a back entrance, settling into a narrow causeway that ran adjacent to the structure. A lone square of light shone from a lower window, illuminating the grimy street. As he crept toward the window's side he could just make out Emma fumbling with the latch. His heart ached as he watched her throw up her hands in frustration and slide to the floor. Precious minutes passed while he tried to come up with a plan. It was agonizing to know she was within his reach, yet hopelessly alone. He thought of using his gun to break the glass and hand it off to her through the metal bars. But as he reached for his weapon the men returned. Then he witnessed something truly astonishing.

Emma had calmly seated herself and appeared to be having a discussion with the men. He saw her rising, animated, and walking confidently toward them. "Careful Emma," he murmured as she brought herself directly up against the shorter man's gun. He clutched his own, ready to fire through the glass. But the men seemed intensely interested in what she was saying. She walked away as they conversed, picked up her purse, and approached them again. *'Good Lord,'* David thought, *'she's negotiating with them!'* What could she possibly say that would entice them not to kill her? They left the room with something obviously in mind, and he would be ready for them. Pulling out his phone as he ran from around the back of the building, he placed a call, praying Amir would pick up. He had just enough time to give instructions, and then duck behind a car across the street as they emerged from the building. With the three of them moving back toward the bazaar David quickly positioned himself just feet away. He stepped in line behind the shorter man, who had tucked his gun into the back of his pants once they cleared the building. They were still in a dimly lit part of the neighborhood. David waited until they crossed the street closer to the bazaar. Allowing them to get nearer to the crowds could draw unwanted attention. With Emma no longer under threat of being shot, David made his move.

He held an adapted syringe in his left hand that contained Methohexital, a fast-acting sedative that would incapacitate, but not kill the man in front of him. Reaching up to his left side, he firmly pressed the syringe into the shorter man's neck. His victim had no time to react and crumpled neatly to the ground just as David placed his gun into the back of the man on Emma's right.

"Stop where you are or you will be shot," he said in Farsi. Both Emma and the remaining captor turned to the sound of his voice. The tall man stood very still, eyeing Emma as if she might have the answer to this latest turn of events. She only stared at the scene before her in disbelief.

David knew he had to act fast. With his gun still pressed firmly into the back of the taller man, he searched for weapons.

"Step away from him Emma," he instructed, pulling a gun from his astounded captive and thrusting it into his own jacket. Both confused and relieved, Emma stepped back from the two standing men, but she bumped into the lifeless form at her feet and stumbled a bit. The tall man said something to David, who ignored him. He cast a quick glance at Emma. "Stand behind me," he told her, "Amir is on his way."

Sure enough, a car with only its parking lights on pulled up, and her father's friend jumped out. He immediately went to Emma. "Are you alright my dear?" he asked, compassion in his voice. She nodded, nearly weeping at the sight of him. They'd only just met, and now she felt as if he was her best friend.

David grabbed the tall man by both arms, pinning them behind his back, and then securing them with a zip tie he'd pulled from his pocket. Leading him to the back of the car, he yelled out to Amir.

"We need to take the other one too. Can you get him into your trunk?"

Amir nodded and managed to gather up the sedated man and pull him toward the vehicle, dumping him for a moment while he opened the back. Coming to her senses, Emma ran to help, and together they stuffed English speaker into the trunk. Amir slammed it closed, then motioned for Emma to get in front. They both quickly joined David and the tall man, and Amir pulled away, heading toward his house, car lights still on low.

Theodore Alberts breathed a sigh of relief. He'd just gotten off the phone with Jamison, who'd managed to retrieve the girl that had caused him so much trouble, who had been on his radar all these years. Now, with a little maneuvering, he could arrange for his own amnesty and, while he could no longer call himself an Agency man, he would be at least a free one. It seemed odd to think that the Woods girl no longer posed a threat, and he wasn't comfortable with the notion yet. He'd lost a sense of purpose, and he wondered what he could replace it with. Theodore moved away from his desk and looked out from the glass partition that separated him and the other officers busily working on other cases. They had no idea how much he'd put into his own operation. He had to abandon any hope of advancing further within the Agency, but no matter. He would be spared jail time, and could live handsomely off the funds hidden in an overseas account. It was a shame he couldn't have acquired more, maybe even toppled Newcastle from his high horse in the process. But sacrifices had to be made in order to ensure his own well-being. He had no qualms about throwing Tarlino and Magnus under the bus.

For now, his two superiors were under the impression that Emma Woods had been apprehended and would be held for interrogation followed by elimination. Alberts scoffed to his reflection in the glass partition. "Superiors," he sniffed, "nothing superior about those idiots." After learning the Woods girl and David Jamison were in Tehran he let Tarlino know, complaining he was spread a bit thin. This prompted Tarlino and Magnus to deem it unnecessary for Alberts himself to fly out and see to the business of Emma's execution. He'd even caused them to question the amount of funds available for the operation, so much so that they were not willing to dispatch additional resources to the Middle East.

"You've already overspent on this operation," Tarlino had admonished him. "That woman has always been your own personal vendetta. If you're so certain as to where she is then see that she's taken care of. And you'll have to make do with whoever you can find, dicker down the price if you can."

Alberts had long ago realized the operation was under threat of exposure. Antony Newcastle's interference troubled him, and after Officer Jamison's interest had been revealed to him a plan of self-preservation took hold. Soon the idea of helping the young officer along and revealing certain aspects of the case crept into his brain. When things really started to unravel, he diligently began to play both sides, jockeying into a position that allowed for a little wiggle room. He got in touch with his Iranian contacts. "It won't be necessary to send your best men," he'd advised, "just people that will work for the least amount of money." He smiled to himself before giving out an additional phone number. "Make certain you call my superior. Let him know you're under my employ and tell him you've already taken out our target." His contact had questioned this, forcing Alberts to further explain. "No, wait until I give the final order to pursue her. I just want you to assure the main man, in order to take some of the heat away from me you understand."

After putting the faux abduction into place he made the decision to call Newcastle and then Jamison. He hated the idea of partnering with a man he so openly despised and envied, but if it saved his own skin it would be worth the humiliation. He was actually surprised over how well he was received by Anthony. Perhaps this was due to Newcastle's growing attachment to the Woods girl, but Alberts didn't care either way. He hadn't been made to grovel, and Newcastle all but guaranteed immunity if it meant saving her and rounding up the bad players. He obtained Jamison's phone number, and everything seemed to be going smoothly, until he discovered from the young officer that Emma had fled. It took longer than expected for Alberts to contact his people in Tehran in order to ensure they would wait for his signal to go ahead, a signal he never intended to give. Unfortunately, his contact had indeed put in place a few men to carry out the mission. They were not his best men, and they didn't wait for Theodore's signal. His calls to David Jamison went unanswered, and he'd had to wait and see if his bargaining tool, the life of Emma Woods, was still available.

That afternoon he'd received a call from Tarlino, congratulating Theodore on having the girl apprehended, but wondering if she knew anything. "Our patron wants to know if the Woods woman spoke about anything involving Beirut," Victor wheezed. By the sound of it, the conversation between him and the boss had caused a great deal of stress.

"Beirut?" Theodore repeated back to Victor, "No, as far as I know they got nothing from her before she perished," Theodore hoped he was lying. "I'm waiting to hear back on the details. Why would our man want to know anything about Beirut?" Theodore knew full well the Vice President's dalliance with fledgling terrorists, but it was safer to play dumb.

"Never mind," Tarlino dismissed the question. "Just keep us posted on anything she may have given up."

"Don't you want to know how it was done? You did approve her termination, did you not?" Theodore wanted confirmation that both Tarlino and Magnus signed off on the operation.

"I told you to do what you have to do," Tarlino responded, further irritated by having to spell everything out. "That girl was a threat to all of us. She had to be eliminated."

Theodore smiled with satisfaction. "So I have it on your authority that our man is pleased we've taken her out?"

"Yes, yes," Tarlino huffed, "why are you making me repeat myself?"

"Just covering my ass," Theodore said sarcastically, "like you advised."

"Our patron doesn't give a shit what happened to the Woods girl," Tarlino shot back. "Just clean it all up so we can all move on. Do your job Alberts!" Victor Tarlino unceremoniously ended the call, and Theodore smiled in satisfaction. Recording his own phone calls was always a good habit.

Chapter 40
Setting the Snare

"Shit!" Karl rolled over in bed at the sound of his pager going off.

"What is it?" Allison said as she tucked a spotless pink blouse into her skirt. She went into the closet to retrieve a jacket that went along with her business suit. There were still more meetings for her to attend, and the little recorder she used to take notes went into a pocket for easy access.

Karl glanced at his pager and swore again. "Tarlino wants me to call," he grumbled. "Can't these people do anything without bothering me about every detail?"

Allison smiled, "That's your guy inside the Agency, right? Well, you'd better call him back. He's on a mission you care about. You're lucky he's keeping you informed."

Karl scowled at the professional looking woman standing before him. "I'm sorry I told you anything. Now you'll be nagging me just like a wife!"

Allison feigned an innocent and hopeful look. "Oh, if only!" She mocked and began to slip on sensible pumps.

Karl grabbed his cell phone from the bed stand and punched in a number. Allison leaned against the headboard, hands in her pockets.

Karl only waited a few seconds for the other party to answer. "Yeah, what's going on?" He demanded, panic in his voice. "I swear to god Victor, if I go down you're going down with me! I could pin everything on you and Alberts and don't think I wouldn't!" A voice could be faintly heard from Karl's phone, letting out a long stream of sentences.

"Is it Tarlino?" Allison whispered. "Yes," Karl snapped, impatiently waving her away. He then answered back into his phone, "So that's it? She's done?" He glanced up at Allison who waited expectedly.

"Okay, good," Karl continued nodding his head and glancing up at Allison with raised eyebrows, "Yes, I'll make sure it's deposited into your account...goodbye." He finished the call and threw his phone on the bed.

Turning back to Allison he clapped his hands. "Our worries are over!" he proclaimed with glee.

"So that was Tarlino?" Allison asked, to Karl's irritation.

"Yes, my dear. I told you it was!"

"Well, what did he say?" Allison plopped down on the bed and cuddled next to Karl like a child waiting for her bedtime story.

"The girl was taken in Tehran, brought to a safe location, interrogated and...taken care of." Karl flatly stated.

"Emma Woods?" Allison exclaimed, eyes wide. "They killed her?"

Karl couldn't understand why his brilliant girlfriend was asking such stupid questions.

"Honey," he said in a condescending tone, "try to keep up. Of course I'm talking about Emma Woods."

Allison shook her head in wonder, then slyly cast a lowered eye at Karl. "I can't believe you have men that will kill for you."

Karl wondered if a quickie was out of the question. She was already dressed, but it looked like she wouldn't take much convincing.

"Yeah, and the best part is it can never be traced back to me." Then he remembered the other part of his conversation with Victor. "Unfortunately, they couldn't get anything out of her, though I can't be sure how hard they tried."

Allison stroked his thigh with a firm hand, looking down to hide her disgust. "And can you trust that other guy? What was his name...Alfred?"

Karl placed his hand on hers and moved it onto his crotch. "Alberts sweetheart, and he's been paid enough to stay quiet as has Tarlino. That's where a small chunk of our funds have been funneled, to keep their mouths shut and to fight for the team. Thankfully nobody knows about that but you and me." He stroked her cheek with his free hand and lifted her chin to read her eyes. They told him nothing. Suddenly a sly smile played upon her lips.

"So you'll never know if she was aware of your affiliation with terrorists?" She let the words sink in and reveled in his look of panic.

"Shut up about that stuff, Allison!" She clearly had him rattled. "I told you about that in strictest confidence," he went on angrily, "if any of that got out before I run, it could ruin my chances for the presidency!"

Allison dismissed his concerns with a wave of her hand. "Oh relax, Karl," she laughed, "I wouldn't dream of spoiling your childhood dream. After all, you're going to compensate me for my loyalty and hard work, right?"

Karl regarded her with just a moment of suspicion, and then decided the idea of her betrayal was ridiculous. She was as ambitious as he was.

"I told you I'd make you a top member of my cabinet," he assured Allison, "how does the position of Vice President sound to you?"

She shrugged and pouted sweetly. "Okay I guess."

"Okay?!" Karl shouted incredulously. "Becoming the first woman vice president is just okay?!"

Allison laughed again. "Yeah, it would be awesome, thank you dear." She didn't care if he believed she was truly appreciative of his offer. Then, much to his disappointment, she stood and continued to prepare to leave, picking up her briefcase and heading for the door.

"Wait a minute," Karl called after her, "I thought this stuff turned you on!"

Allison pulled on the door knob and turned to face the Vice President, who was in the bed on his knees, wearing only his tighty-whiteys.

"Oh honey," she cooed, "there's no time for that now."

She blew him a kiss and left Karl Magnus, along with his erection, all alone.

Chapter 41
A Pause in the Madness

Emma sat staring out the bedroom window, a cup of tea growing cold in her hands. The smell of jasmine drifted up from the garden below, its scent calming her jagged nerves. Amir had offered her the use of his charming "guest cottage" while he and David interrogated her two captors. Once they arrived at Amir's the would-be kidnappers were spirited off somewhere unknown to Emma. She was escorted to the safety of the cottage by Amir's wife, who spoke very little English.

"Try sleep," the smiling woman urged her guest, leading her into the bedroom and showing her a clean kaftan on the bed.

"Your man working now. I come later with tea."

"Thank you Yazmin," Emma said gratefully, fingering the silk kaftan. It would be wonderful to finally lay her pounding head down on the mountain of pillows waiting on the inviting bed. She changed into the soft garment, wondering if she could cease the replaying of events in her head long enough to drop off to sleep. But a dreamless sleep had come, deep and heavy like one of the thick blankets under which she lay. She didn't stir until the next morning, awakened by the sound of doves cooing softly outside the open window. Yazmin came soon after with the promised tea, the ubiquitous smile indicating her pleasure that Emma had slept through the night. She slipped out the door without uttering a word, and Emma wondered if she was going to attend to the men with their own tea. Had they interrogated her captors all night? She gazed out at the garden, enjoying the rare luxury of a clear mind. For the first time in a very long while she realized she wasn't afraid. There was no telling what kind of success Amir and David would have extracting information from the two men who had held her captive. But somehow David would make things right, she was sure of it, and the certainty she felt came as a surprise. 'When have I ever been certain of anything?' she wondered.

At that moment, the door to the cottage swung open, and in walked a weary looking David. Emma set down her cup and stood to face him.

He stopped in the middle of the room and ran his hand through his hair in a way Emma now recognized as an attempt to gather his thoughts.

"Are you alright?" she ventured.

He looked awful. Dark circles under his eyes announced his own sleepless night, and she felt a pang of guilt over how rested she felt. His clothes were wrinkled and something had stained the front of his shirt. Was it tea, or perhaps blood? Emma didn't want to know. Her only concern was for the man who had saved her life.

"Jesus, David," she whispered, "you look like shit!"

He laughed and eliminated the space between them in three great strides, gathering her in his arms in a rejuvenating hug. Emma returned his embrace. He no longer smelled like soap, he was clearly exhausted, and he needed her. How wonderful.

"Come sit down," she ordered, "let me pour you some tea."

David eased into the chair by the window and used both hands to rub his eyes while she went to the little kitchenette just off the bedroom to empty her cup and refresh it using the ceramic pot left by Yazmin. When she turned back to David she found him staring at her.

"I like your dress," he said quietly, "you look like a local."

Emma walked back and placed the warm cup in his hands.

"A red-headed Iranian?" she giggled. "That's unlikely, but thanks for the compliment."

David used one free hand to ruffle his hair in the way she'd grown used to seeing when he was distracted. "Actually," he said in a voice gravely with fatigue, "it's not that unusual to see an Iranian with red hair. Statistically speaking they have more redheads here than in some European countries." She ignored his contradiction, and sat on the bed while he sipped the tea, the cup nearly disappearing within his long fingers. He finished it in several gulps and placed the empty cup on the window sill. Their eyes met, and nothing was said for what seemed to Emma a long time.

"Want some more tea?" she finally asked.

"No," David answered, shaking his head. "I want to tell you a few things."

Emma scooted back onto the bed and tucked her legs under the kaftan. "Okay," she murmured.

Breaking his gaze from her he looked out the window, considering what he could and could not reveal.

"There's only so much I can tell you about what went on last night, but we got some answers."

"Was it just you and Amir?" Emma asked. She didn't know why, but it bothered her to think of two very honorable men torturing her captives, no matter how much they deserved it.

"No," David answered to her relief, "Amir had some friends, and I called in for some help. You don't need to know any of that."

Emma was silent, not bothering to tell him she had no desire to be privy to those particular details.

"It turns out that the men who took you were directed by a terrorist group we've known about for some time. How they were connected to you is what Tony and I have been trying to figure out. That's why I wasn't worried about the way he went quiet on me for a while. I knew he was doing his own investigating back in the States. We were able to follow the money and link it up with the chain of command beginning here in Iran. I'm sorry to say that all that led back to some of our own people, one in particular who was in a deeply compromising position."

Emma didn't hide her confusion. "What has any of that got to do with me?" she asked, shaking her head.

David rose from the chair and joined her on the bed, wincing slightly from the soreness he began to feel traveling up his back. Emma noticed, and moved behind him to rub his shoulders. David let his head fall back against her chest.

"God, that feels good." He sighed. "Okay," he continued with his eyes closed, "where was I?"

"You were going to tell me everything," Emma teased, working her way down his back.

"Well, I'll do the best I can," David sighed again.

"While working in Iran your dad was approached by a colleague with information regarding a side operation headed by their shared commander. Money funding your dad's operation was redirected toward the purchase of weapons for the revolutionaries. Your father was going to blow the whistle on his commander, and this would expose a man who holds a position in our current administration. Your dad was targeted, causing his colleague to feign ignorance and lay low. Another operative, who made the mistake of doing the commander's bidding, freaked out when your dad was killed. That man was Frank Nirody. Tony tracked him down and found Zanders in the process."

"Zanders!?" Emma asked in amazement. At last she was learning the connection between the mysterious man and her father.

David lay down on the bed, weary from the last forty-eight hours. "The funding handed out to the revolutionaries turned out to be a bad move. They used the money to purchase weapons enlisted in the takeover of the U.S. Embassy, and later they funded the terrorist groups that began to pop up in the Middle East more and more. All of this made the people who targeted your dad very nervous. When you started digging into your father's history it made one of them, an elected official who painted himself as very anti-terrorist, extremely vulnerable."

Emma held up her hand. "Wait a minute," she interrupted, "somebody working for President Stanford wanted me dead!?"

David sat up and gave her a hard look. "I'm not prepared to answer that directly," he said purposefully. "There are still some things being put in motion that will bring that person to justice. But it has to be done delicately, so as not to implicate the President in any way. There are people working on it as we speak."

David turned to Emma and placed his hands on her shoulders.

"The important thing is, you won't have to be looking over your shoulder anymore Emma. We've cast a very wide net to cover all of those involved in this shit. There's not one person who will be left to come after you. It will be as if you were never involved, and your name will effectively be erased from the entire mess."

Emma looked down, bewildered. "I don't know how I feel about that," she said, "what about my dad?" She looked back up at David. "His name sure hasn't been erased from all of this. He's still a scapegoat for these assholes. It's not fair."

David brushed a stray curl from her eyes. "I know it's not fair Emma, but it's the best I can do….for now."

She could see he was entirely spent. If it weren't for her and her need for answers he would be getting the rest he so desperately needed.

"It's okay, David," she said, putting her own hand on his cheek. "It's enough for me to know I'm safe, and I thank you for that. Really, you've done so much and I owe my life to you."

"No!" He said it so forcefully she drew back in surprise. He pulled her closer. "I didn't do all this just for you, Emma."

Seeing her look of disappointment he went on to explain. "I've come to care about you through the investigation of your father, that's true. And I don't regret that. But as a CIA officer, I made an oath to serve and protect my country. For people like me and Tony, that means something. Finding out some of our own people were involved with terrorists, and consequently responsible for the deaths of U.S. citizens…well, that was hard to bear. It had to be remedied, and those people had to be held accountable."

Moved by his passion, Emma nodded. "I understand," she murmured.

David lay back on the bed, hopeful he'd gotten through to her. He would drift off to sleep soon, but not before setting her straight on one more thing.

"Anyway," he muttered, laying one arm over his eyes to block out the sun streaming in from the window, "I didn't save you. Not really. You saved yourself Emma. You truly are Super Girl."

Emma smiled softly and rose from the bed. She took the tea cup from the window sill and pulled the lace curtains, casting the room in a warm but muted glow. David was asleep before she'd pulled off his shoes and repositioned his legs onto the bed.

When he awoke the room was cast in shadows. The feeling of Emma cuddled up nearby reminded him of where he was. He lay still, matching her breathing and reveling in the way her body fit into his like two perfect pieces of a puzzle. And wasn't it a puzzle that had brought them together? He thought of the note Emma's dad had left for her. There was mention of a puzzle then, and now everything would soon be falling into place. He would have to fly back tomorrow, and oversee the culmination of many man hours filled with twists and turns. And he would be sending Emma back as well, but he wouldn't tell her about the last piece of the puzzle. She wouldn't like being kept in the dark, but in the end it would all come down to her and what she wanted.

Emma stirred next to him, her lips moving against his neck as she said something in her sleep. David hoped it wasn't another bad dream.

"Shhhh," he whispered, shaking her gently, "wake up Super girl. You're dreaming."

Her eyes flickered open, and when she realized who was speaking she smiled and threw her arm across his chest.

"Hey," she said sleepily.

"Hey," David said back, turning his body to meet hers.

They lay together, eyes closed and both thinking the same thing. "You're wearing too many clothes," David mumbled, moving his hand down the silk fabric.

"I'm only wearing a kaftan," Emma corrected him. "You're the one wearing too many clothes."

She opened her eyes and pulled his face closer to hers, "And to be honest, you're kind of smelly."

They both broke into laughter. It was the release they both needed. "I know," he said apologetically, "I haven't showered in a couple days."

Emma allowed her smile to fade, and looked at him thoughtfully. "I really don't care, David," she admitted. "I'm just happy you're here."

He took a moment to study her, memorize her face before closing his eyes once more and pulling her into a kiss. She kissed him back and it felt like surrender, not just for her but for David as well. They had struggled together and come out on the other end of madness. Now, like it or not, they had bonded, as if they'd survived some kind of war.

She kept her lips on his as she unbuttoned his shirt, but he had to let her go in order to pull it from his body. He threw it to the floor where it was met with the rest of his clothing in a dirty clump. His hands went to the silk dress, and Emma lifted her arms so he could peel it from her like a cloud. They knelt on the bed, naked and exploring each other slowly, while time stood still. David was first to lay back onto the bed, with Emma lowering herself slowly on top of him. He moaned and put his hands on her hips as she rocked him gently into her.

He looked up to see the sunset filtering through the curtains and turning her hair into a mass of shiny curls. She threw her head back and moved against him more urgently, bringing his hands up to her breasts. David held back, doing his best to wait for her. He let one hand travel from her breast to her face, tracing her mouth and then gently pushing his finger between her parted lips. She reached behind and stroked his thigh, causing him to grab her hips and guide her into the final throes of lovemaking that became a glorious eruption of warmth and united pleasure. It left them both quivering and serene, staring in astonishment before collapsing into each other's arms.

It was fully dark outside now, and Emma swore the beating of their hearts could be heard by the night birds singing in the garden outside. She rolled over toward David, pushing him onto his side so that she could spoon against him. He took her free arm and wrapped it close around his waist.

"Do you think you could sleep some more?" David asked dreamily.

"I can now," she giggled.

"Good," he whispered, clasping her hand and pressing it into his chest where his heart was still beating fast. "We'll talk more in the morning."

She wanted to say that she loved him then, but a tiny bit of doubt remained, and so she said nothing.

"Emma?" David whispered again.

"Yes?" she asked.

He paused for a beat. "Nothing," was all he could muster.

She waited, but decided she could no longer stay awake.

"Good night," she spoke softly into the back of his neck.

"Good night, sweetheart," David answered.

It was enough.

Chapter 42
House of Cards

Karl sat at his desk and stared at his computer, tapping on the mouse impatiently. The screen showing an empty bank account glared back at him. *'Where the fuck did the money go Allison?'* he thought to himself. He'd already placed several calls to her, but she wasn't picking up. He and Debra were supposed to meet at his office and then drive to yet another fundraiser. Karl was shocked she'd finally agreed to attend a function with him. Lately it seemed she was content to be a kept woman with little to no involvement in her husband's political aspirations. But last night she'd called him and agreed to accompany him to this afternoon's luncheon. This pleased Karl, because he was planning on hinting at a run for the presidency to some of the wealthier attendees. "I thought you hated these things," he had responded to his wife's declaration she would arrive at the White House before noon the next day. Debra only laughed; the first time he'd heard her laugh in almost a year. "Oh I don't enjoy the hand shaking and sucking up, but I suppose it's time I help you along in your....endeavor." It was a strange term in which to coin his bid for the presidency. But Karl brushed it aside, elated that his wife was finally on board.

Now he wished he could put off the luncheon and send his wife home while he figured out the financial mystery presenting itself to him on the screen. He'd left only one short message on Allison's phone, pleading with her to call him about "an urgent matter." He was so wrapped up in viewing the empty columns on his screen he jumped at the knock on his office door. "Come in!" he shouted, assuming it was Debra. Allison sashayed in as if she hadn't a care in the world. "Hey there, honey bun!" she chimed while Karl looked at her darkly. "Allison! Where have you been?!" he scolded. He stood to meet her and glanced into the connecting office. "For God's sake be careful how you address me when somebody might hear!" He walked past Allison to shut the door, then turned to grab her arm. "Why haven't you called me back? There's something wrong with our account and I need to know what's going on!"

"Hey!" Allison complained, "Take it easy Karl, you're hurting me!" She yanked her arm from his grip and went to sit at his desk, presumably to review the depressing information on his screen. She drew closer to the screen, and then let out a whistle.

"Jeez Karl," she said in a mocking tone, "what did you do with all the money?"

He stared at her, stunned. "What are you talking about?!" he sputtered. "This is no laughing matter, Allison. Please tell me you've moved the funds to a safe place!"

She looked away from the screen and let out a chuckle. "Yes, Karl. Worry not. I've moved everything to a very safe place."

He let out a sigh of relief, shaking his head. "That's my girl," he said, ambling toward her with renewed confidence. After clicking his mouse to shut down the computer screen, Allison leaned back in his office chair and regarded him with unveiled disgust.

"I don't think you understand Karl. When I say the money is safe, I mean it's safe from you getting your greedy paws on any of it."

Her words brought Karl up short, and Allison enjoyed the look of confusion and hurt on his face. A moment passed before the Vice President managed to speak.

"Allison, you're not being rational. You know I need access to those funds in order to make our plan come together." He changed his tone, speaking to her as if she were a willful child. "Withholding those funds will only slow down what we both want to happen. We want the presidency, don't we? What is it that you're up to?"

Allison put her elbows on his desk and rested her chin on her hands. "No Karl," she said quietly, "You wanted the presidency. I don't give a fuck about riding your coattails. I have a much bigger plan for you, a more satisfying one."

She stood and walked from behind his desk toward the door, coldly passing her former lover without a glance.

"Why are you doing this, Allison?" It was all he could manage to say.

She ignored him and pulled the tiny tape recorder from her briefcase. Karl looked at it in horror.

"Oh honey," she laughed, "you needn't be concerned. It's not on. I already have everything I need on previous recordings."

Dipping into her bag once again, she produced a small cassette and inserted it into the player. With a press of the play button the conversation between them about Emma came back to haunt him. Karl began to visibly sweat. He lunged at Allison in an attempt to grab the recorder. Anticipating his reaction she took a quick step to the side, causing him to fall clumsily onto the office sofa.

She turned off the recorder and regarded him with disdain. "It's no use Karl. I've made copies, lots of them. And they've been widely circulated amongst the proper authorities. Not everyone, you understand, but a select few who are eager to help me out."

The realization that he was effectively screwed came over Karl like a chilly wave. "Bitch!" he shouted, wild-eyed at Allison. "You fucked me over for money?! I could've given you the vice-presidency, and you tossed the opportunity away for money?!"

Allison shook her head. "No, Karl. I fucked you as a way of distracting you. I did what I had to do in order to gain your trust. I wanted to get as close to you as possible, find your weaknesses and exploit them when the time was right. So yeah, I fucked you, or should I say I let you fuck me. And believe me it wasn't easy. You're a lousy lay, Karl, did you know that?"

Now seething, Karl stood and grabbed Allison by her shoulders. "You cunt!" He spit the words at her with such velocity that, fearing he would strike her, she turned her face away. Karl gave her a shake while continuing his rant. "You tell me where the fucking money is right now, or I'll…"

Allison turned back defiantly. "You'll what Karl? What is it you think you could do to me? Are you going to have me killed like Emma? Well, guess what? That sweet girl is alive and well, and your cronies in that botched scheme are getting rounded up as we speak."

Stunned, Karl released her and stood, speechless.

Allison continued her assault. "You think this was all about the money?! Jesus Karl, you're so clueless. Taking you down was never about the money. That was just a byproduct of destroying you. The money's going to a good cause and you can bet you won't need it. People who aided and abetted terrorists make very bad candidates."

It dawned on Karl that the woman he believed he had wrapped around his finger intended to throw him to the wolves. "This is about my work in the Agency?!" He asked incredulously. "Why would you ruin me over something that never touched you? It never hurt anyone!"

"Oh really Karl?" she scoffed, "and how do you know that? How could you know for sure who you hurt by mingling with terrorists?"

She moved for the door, opening it and calling out. "Come on in, Lucy."

A tall and serious-looking woman stepped inside the office. Her hair pulled back in a slick ponytail, she wore designer fashion head to toe. Lucy gave Allison a peck on the check then turned to Karl. "Hello Mr. Vice President," she murmured and delivered him a scathing look.

Karl was befuddled, casting his eyes from Lucy to Allison and back again. His mouth agape and questions clearly formulating in his brain, Allison answered them before he could speak.

"This is Lucy Champion, Karl, a friend from Bryn Mawr. Back in school we discovered we had a lot in common. Do you know what the motto of that particular college is Karl?"

Seeing he was mute with shock she went on. "Veritatem Dilexi….I Delight in the Truth. The truth was very important to both Lucy and me. Something else we had in common was the fact that we both lost loved ones in the embassy bombing of Beirut."

Upon hearing this, Karl's face turned gray. He was starting to connect the dots, and Allison was going to help him along.

335

"Lucy lost her fiancé, and I lost my dad." To Karl's confused expression she explained, "Yeah, I was sixteen when the terrorist drove a van into the embassy lobby. Lucy and I bonded over our loss, determined to find out who backed the terrorist. Lucy was lucky enough to marry someone with connections, just as I was climbing the political ladder. With a little elbow-rubbing and research, we were able to track you down as the one who inadvertently funded our terrorist. So please don't say you didn't hurt anyone with your smarmy wheeling and dealing, Karl. It insults our intelligence."

Karl remained dumbfounded, slowly processing Allison's revelation. "So all of this….the chance introduction to me, the political maneuvering, pretending you supported my running…it was all…"

"Bullshit." Allison shot back. Hands on her hips she delivered another blow. "You didn't really think I found you attractive, did you?!"

She haughtily regarded her former, now clearly crushed, lover. "Oh Karl, I'm so sorry dear. But it had to be done. I felt you must be stopped, and Lucy and I were quite pleased to be the ones to stop you."

Lucy glanced at her very expensive Patek watch. "It's getting late honey," she said to Allison, "she'll be here soon."

"Who will be here soon?" Karl demanded, his head spinning now from an overload of bad news.

"Our compatriot, Karl, our inside gal. You didn't think we could do all this ourselves, did you? Oh no, we had help. We actually couldn't have done this without someone working behind the scenes, letting us know your schedule, your schemes, someone to pull your strings without you knowing they were being pulled. She lined you up perfectly for the kill sweetheart."

As if on cue, there was a gentle tapping, and Allison pushed the office door fully open. Debra Magnus stepped in, sporting slimming jeans and a sweater. The frumpy look had been erased, however, and replaced with a vibrant-looking and well-coiffed woman. "Hi Karl," Debra chirped cheerily, "I hope you don't mind my casual attire. I didn't see any sense in dressing up, since we won't be attending the luncheon." All three ladies stood together, an improbable army of women intent on toppling Vice President Magnus from a pillar of lies and false promises. He stared at his wife in disbelief. "You helped them Debra?! How could you? I'm your husband dammit. Where is your loyalty?"

Debra's expression was one of cool indifference. All she really wanted to do was get on with her life, one in which Karl would be completely absent. "Our concepts of loyalty are quite different, Karl. I see no reason to remain loyal to a husband who has been cheating on me pretty much since the day we got married." In answer to Karl's questioning look, Debra explained. "I knew about all of them, Karl. I was just biding my time until I could arrange a lucrative divorce. When Allison came to me with her plan I gave her all the help she needed, and in turn she funneled a lot of that money of yours into my private bank account. Daddy has already drafted the divorce papers for me so I won't be implicated in any of your crimes."

She walked up to Karl and delivered the final blow, just inches from his face. "I hope they lock you up somewhere horrible, Karl, maybe you can become someone's girlfriend."

Turning from her soon-to-be ex she waved goodbye to Lucy and Allison before treating Karl to a parting remark. "Don't worry honey," she laughed, "wherever you're going, I'll tell them you don't like fruit in the morning."

And with that, she left Karl forever. Allison smiled. "Debra's a badass, Karl. You didn't deserve her."

The shattered Vice President sat down hard on a neighboring chair, placing his head in his hands. "You can't do this to me," he sobbed, "I'm the Vice President of the United States. I have protections…"

Allison rolled her eyes. This was becoming tedious, and not nearly as fun as she imagined it would be. It was time to be done with Karl and embrace a life of her own. She linked arms with Lucy. "Okay sweetie, I'd like to wrap this up. Is there anything else you'd like to say to this asshole?"

Lucy shook her head. "No, his ruined career won't bring back my fiancé. So long as he's been stopped from hurting anyone else, I'm satisfied." She gave Allison a hug. "I'll tell Patricia it's done. Her husband and the other officer were staying at my townhouse before all this. She can fill them in, and hey, you and I have to share a spa weekend. Give me a call when you want to visit me in Biarritz." After one last hug for Allison, Lucy left without a word to Karl, who was left to ponder what the future would bring.

Through the open door Lucy passed three men who seemed to have appeared from out of nowhere. By the way they were dressed, Karl could only assume they were FBI agents. Sure enough, one of them brandished a badge. "Could you come with me Mr. Vice President? We have some questions for you. Your wife has already contacted your lawyer so that he could be present."

Allison walked to the edge of Karl's desk and looked down at the shell of a man he'd become. "If you go quietly Karl, they won't take you out in handcuffs."

Then she gathered her coat and made for the door. Without turning around she addressed Karl Magnus one final time. "The President doesn't want any scandal sullying his name, so you'll be put on ice for the remainder of his term. They want you kept out of the picture with some unknown illness until things can be sorted out. Good luck Karl."

The Secretary of Treasury strode out with a skip in her step and her head held high.

Chapter 43
The Takedown

Victor Tarlino shuffled up to a warehouse located a half hour's drive from CIA headquarters. It was a warm spring day, and he'd already begun to perspire, sweat stains showing under the armpits of yet another formerly white shirt. He agreed with Theodore Alberts it would be best to meet up outside of the workplace, away from colleagues and prying eyes.

"Why did our team want to meet in person for payment?" He'd asked when Alberts contacted him the morning after their mission was accomplished.

"My contract workers in Tehran were sending family members to collect their cut," Alberts complained. "They're nervous about getting anywhere close to the Agency, being of Middle Eastern descent. The others wanted to meet in person for their final pay-off. I suppose they want the all-clear from you that the operation is finished. Everyone wants to move on Victor, including me."

Victor could have argued with Teddy Alberts that the two of them would always be in the thick of this thing, a potential stain on their records. But he decided to let it go, and let the senior officer live under the misguided belief that his part in the operation would go undetected. Alberts didn't have to know that Victor had entrusted a file to the Vice President detailing all of Teddy's crimes, including the dirty deals he did back in 1974. That was Tarlino's insurance, just in case Alberts turned on him.

"Just covering my ass," Victor chuckled to himself, and unlocked the warehouse door.

Still, he was nervous. When he went to withdraw funds from the account provided by Magnus and his people, there was only enough to pay the men Alberts hired in Iran. Luckily, they came cheap. In fact, Victor was surprised to hear how little they wanted for their illicit work. Alberts also was expecting to pay more, but when they called to confirm Emma had been dealt with they quoted a much lower price. 'Perhaps they knocked it down a bit because things didn't go exactly as planned,' Victor thought. After all, they claimed they weren't able to get anything from the Woods girl because she couldn't withstand the "questioning." Consequently, paying off the contract killers would be easy. What to tell the rest of the team about their final cut would be tricky. He'd put in another call to Magnus, and explained the situation.

"Impossible!" the V.P. had blustered, "my partner has managed that account from the beginning. She knows it down to the penny and monitors all the activity. There must be some kind of bank error."

Victor had assured the V.P. that he'd followed all the proper procedures to obtain the funds, to no avail.

"I'll check it out when I hear back from my partner." Magnus promised. "I'm waiting for her to return my call. Tell your men we'll pay them as soon as things get sorted out."

Victor wasn't looking forward to the push back he was sure to receive from his team of shady employees. They had been paid in healthy increments up to now, with the lump sum coming after he and Magnus had done some creative financing, all of it illegal, yet skillfully covered up by his partner, whose name Karl kept secret. All in all, Victor lumbered toward the warehouse wishing the briefcase he carried was just a little bit heavier.

The others were already there. Theodore held court over the group, speaking with them in a low murmur, sporting his usual tailored suit. Surrounding him in a half circle were the men they'd hired for the rogue operation, the four men who'd killed Jeremy and Emma's horse and goats. Matthew Kealty from Science and Technology stood to one side, distancing himself from what he considered men of lesser intelligence. Nine or ten men stood to the right of Matt, talking in subdued Farsi. They all turned to look at the panting Tarlino coming in, carrying a briefcase. Everyone knew it contained cash, and Tarlino enjoyed the moment of rapt attention paid to him. He took his time to cross the floor of the warehouse, virtually empty except for a pile of unlabeled boxes stacked along the back wall. He finally reached the unlikely fraternity of murderers, liars and opportunists, and placed the briefcase on a lone card table, set up in front of the men. He turned to Theodore and nodded.

"Alberts," he curtly greeted the man he looked forward to not doing business with any longer.

"Tarlino," Theodore acknowledged his boss, without using any official title or showing the least amount of respect.

Victor ignored the snub. "Nice location you found us Alberts," he smiled, his eyes darting along the line of assembled men. "Not a bad drive from work and secluded enough to afford us some privacy."

Theodore wanted nothing more than to slap the smile off Tarlino's face, but the sooner they wrapped this up, the sooner he could take the opportunity to disappear. "I didn't choose this place," he coolly informed Tarlino, "this warehouse belongs to our esteemed colleagues from Iran."

Victor squinted at the group of men, quiet now and eyeing him cautiously. "Do they all have to be here?" he complained to Alberts.

One of the Middle Eastern men stepped forward. "We are originally from Iran, but are now American citizens" the man said, extending his hand toward Tarlino, who remained unmoved, rejecting the gesture.

The man recovered quickly, placing his hand in the pocket of his jacket. "We are here on behalf of family members still living in our homeland. This warehouse belongs to us. We are in the business of fine carpets…beautiful Persian rugs."

"Of course you are," Tarlino scoffed, unimpressed. "'Must be a very large family. Well, let's get down to business then, we'll pay you first. I believe my associate here offered your family members five-thousand each?" He accentuated the term "family," and moved to open the briefcase. With a loud click echoing throughout the warehouse, Tarlino exposed stacks of bundled bills, counting as he pulled them into his sweaty hands, and silently marveling how Alberts had gotten men to commit murder for such a low price. *'Yes,'* he mused, *'the oil embargo is probably hitting everyone hard over there.'*

The Iranian extended his hand once more, this time palm up. "I suppose you want some kind of guarantee that the girl is dead." He said.

Tarlino looked up in surprise, exchanging a look with Alberts who merely shrugged.

"I wasn't aware of that particular requirement for payment, but yes. Any kind of proof you can provide would be helpful."

The Iranian took his hand from his pocket and reached inside his jacket, pulling out a grainy photograph and handing it to Tarlino. With the photo in hand, Victor handed four neatly banded stacks to the man, who passed it back to his fellow expatriates. They sank back behind Matthew and the others, appearing to distribute the cash amongst them. Tarlino looked down at the picture of Emma, eyes staring and a dribble of blood clotting at the corner of her mouth. Red curls lay wet and plastered against her forehead. He appeared unmoved, and handed the photo off to Alberts, who took a longer look, a thin smile forming on his mouth.

"My nephew informed me they were unable to extract any worthwhile information from her. She claimed not to know anything about her father's death. She wouldn't give up the names of the people who were helping her either."

Tarlino looked again at Theodore, who only shook his head. "That's unfortunate," Victor sighed, "how long did she last?"

"Not long," the Iranian responded, "my nephew said they were careless, they were too rough..."

Tarlino cut him off, "Alright, well there's nothing we can do about it now," he said, waving the man away. "See that your nephew and the others get paid."

"This Emma Woods," the Iranian continued, "you did want her murdered, yes?"

Tarlino was already fumbling around in the empty case, formulating how he would break the bad news to the others, who were milling around impatiently. "Yes," he quipped, "we needed her taken out."

"Why?" the Iranian asked, causing Tarlino's head to snap up and scrutinize the man who still stood asking questions, irritating him.

"Not that it's any of your business, but she was on the verge of discovering things best left buried. There was quite a lot of money at stake. The person I work for believed that she got in the way."

"We know," said the Iranian, drawing a gun from his jacket and pointing it at Tarlino. Victor Tarlino's eyes grew wide, and he shot a look of desperation at Alberts. Nobody had noticed the Iranian's companions quietly positioning themselves around those still waiting for their cut. Every one of the Iranians had a firearm pointed, cocked and ready.

"What the fuck is this?!" Tarlino demanded, his eyes beseeching Theodore for an explanation. His cohort only stood silently, eyes darting from Victor to the Iranian.

Victor reached for the gun he kept in his pocket, an old habit from his younger days in the Agency. "I'd advise you not to try it," the Iranian said. In that instant Victor realized that this man who claimed to be from the Middle East didn't hold a trace of his former accent. Everything crumbled around him after that.

The door where Tarlino had entered was kicked down, and a team of armed officers began streaming in and shouting orders. A large garage door behind the boxes rolled up and still more officers flooded in, with David Jamison taking up the lead. Tarlino's team was quickly cuffed and placed face down on the warehouse floor. But David wanted Victor Tarlino to himself. He walked up to the Deputy Director of Operations, and slapped on a pair of handcuffs, metal circles cutting into the man's plump wrists. He looked past Tarlino at his accomplice.

"Hello Teddy," David said, unsmiling.

Theodore Alberts remained still, observing the action in a nonchalant fashion, his hands in his pockets.

"A pleasure to finally meet you Jamison, face to face," he said languidly, as if they were sharing cigars at a gentlemen's club.

"David Jamison," David responded, "Deputy Station Chief."

Alberts smirked, "Yes, however I'm quite certain that position will change after this little victory. Congratulations Jamison. You've climbed farther and faster up the ladder than I, and with much less effort may I say."

Victor Tarlino glared at Teddy. The fact that his partner remained standing without handcuffs settled in his mind. He looked at David in disbelief. "Why aren't you taking Alberts in?! He headed up this whole operation! You can speak to the Vice President. He'll vouch for me. God dammit, get him on the phone."

David shook his head. "I'm afraid the Vice President is indisposed at the moment. He can't help you Tarlino. As for Alberts, let's just say he struck a better bargain than the one he had with you."

Tarlino's glare returned to Teddy. "You sonofabitch," he fumed, "you turned on us?! You little shit; you won't get away with this! I'll have your ass and you'll go down with the rest of us, you can be sure of it!"

Theodore only smiled wickedly. "Oh no my friend, I've been granted immunity. As for my ass, well I was just following your orders. My ass is quite well-covered."

David then passed Tarlino off to an agent waiting nearby. The disgraced officer left a flurry of profanities in his wake.

Teddy and David stood face to face, sizing each other up.

"The information you gave up helped tremendously, but make no mistake, we all know you would have been just as pleased to have

Emma Woods eliminated if it served you. You're being allowed to live quietly under supervision Teddy, and your days as an Officer are, of course, over."

Teddy shrugged. "I did what I had to do. You'll find that there are players in this world. Eventually you'll have to play with them, and do your best to survive just as I have. As for Operation Nequitia, well I recognized it was doomed when my fellow players reached too high. They were stupid, and careless. You, on the other hand, were quite quick on your feet. How you managed to extract information from the hapless crew I contracted, well it must have been intense. I can only imagine what sort of interrogation techniques you used. You see, we're not much different, you and I."

David gave a smile that put Alberts off kilter.

"No brutal techniques were necessary Teddy. It's amazing how you can hire people right out from under their shitty employers. When you offer them a better deal, they switch loyalties very quickly. The best part was that we used your money to do it."

Alberts let a moment of defeat cross his face, and then went on sarcastically.

"It really is astounding how you were able to feed false information to Magnus and Tarlino, rummaging up those men to play Iranians. I tip my hat to you."

He stooped to pick up the photo of Emma that had been dropped by Tarlino. Studying the image, he gave a nasty snort of a laugh. "However, you never would have fooled me with this nonsense Jamison." He handed the photo back to David and reached for the briefcase that had been left on the table. David beat him to it, slamming the case closed and nearly damaging Teddy's fingers in the process.

"No tampering with the evidence, Alberts," David remarked evenly. He was all business, and dealing with Teddy made him want to take a bath, wash the filth of this dirty agent from his body. "Aren't you even going to ask about Emma?"

Teddy drew his hand back and tucked it back into the pocket of his jacket. "She was never meant to be harmed by the men I lined up. Her abduction is on you, Jamison. You let your guard down there I'm afraid. Anyway, I'm sure she's well and good under the protection of your mentor. Where is Newcastle by the way? I would have thought he'd delight in witnessing my downfall."

"Anthony sends his regrets. He had a former engagement," David said, anxious to send Alberts on his way. Signaling to the agent behind him he handed off the briefcase and took Alberts by the arm. "Your ride is here Teddy. Try to stay invisible in your crappy new life."

He allowed this announcement to settle in with Alberts before nodding to officers who hustled him away into a waiting armored van. He had one final conversation that needed to take place. He turned to his old friend Matthew, sulking and cuffed, standing alone amidst the last of the remaining officers. David slowly approached Kealty, shaking his head.

"Matt, Matt, Matt," he lamented, "how the fuck did you get mixed up in all this?"

Matthew shrugged, "What can I say Davy? They wanted to know what you saw in the file I brought up for you. The money was damn good. Well…the money I initially got anyway. They still owe me a lot more but…"

"But that's not coming, Matt," David said looking disappointed and disgusted.

"Dude," Matthew said sheepishly, "it was nothing personal."

"Right," David said, and then turned and walked away.

Chapter 44
The Ghost

Anthony stood with Zanders in a crowded plaza just inside Greenwich Village. Neither seemed particularly interested in the people passing by. Anthony observed the sky, while Zanders checked his watch.

"What time did you tell your man to have her here?" Zanders asked.

Anthony kept his attention on a flock of pigeons rising up from in front of them in a fluttering gray wave. "What time is it now?" He asked, the sparse hair on his head fluttering in the breeze created by the birds.

"Just past three," Zanders commented with disinterest.

"We call that fifteen hundred," Anthony scoffed. "You've really fallen away from your training Andrew."

Zanders shrugged. "It no longer serves me. Anyway, I enjoy being a civilian. Life is so much more predictable."

"Don't you find it somewhat sedentary?" It was a question that had nagged at Anthony ever since considering retirement.

"No," Zanders shook his head. "But everyone reacts to the lifestyle differently."

He scanned the street running along the plaza, watching as taxis drifted by.

"She'll be here soon," Anthony said confidently. "David put her on a flight direct from Turkey. That's where they ended up, and then he continued on to D.C."

"How did that go?" Zanders asked.

"Perfectly," Anthony declared, moving to face his cohort. "My wife let me know her college mates did a good job. Once she called her friend Lucy in France everything fell in place. She and Allison were able to find out what was planned for Emma, and then used the information to frame Magnus and Tarlino. It was touch-and-go there for a while, however. Emma was in real danger." Anthony turned his head away from Zanders in order to hide his shame. "I should have been there for her, Andrew. I was supposed to be watching her. She could have been killed."

Zanders placed a reassuring hand on Anthony's shoulder. "Don't blame yourself Newcastle. There were things going on right under our noses. And there was no way you could have known Emma would skip out on David like that…such an impetuous young woman. She really is so like her father in that way." He laughed at the idea. "Anyway, I'm glad it went well. It's a shame about Nirody though."

Anthony looked down, examining his shoes. "Yes," he coughed, "unfortunately we couldn't get anyone to him in time. Apparently they caught him going for ice in the hallway. That's where he was found. Damn dirty business and I feel sorry for whoever has to tell his wife."

Zanders nodded in agreement, and both men were lost in thought for a moment. A tan Dodge pulled up to the curb of the plaza, and a man emerged from the front passenger side. After a brief survey of the area, he moved to open the back door. Anthony and Zanders focused their attention on the woman stepping out from the back of the vehicle. Emma spotted Anthony immediately. She hesitated and looked for assurance from the man holding the door, a worried expression on her face. Anthony approached the front of the car and shook the officer's hand.

"Thank you," he said, "I can take it from here." Then he turned to face Emma.

"You don't look happy to see me," he said, smiling. "Didn't David fill you in on what I was doing?"

Emma stared at him, confused and weary from the flight home. When she and David parted ways she believed she was only meant to wait for him in New York, while he did the dangerous work of pulling in and arresting those who were after her. "Why New York?" she'd asked him as Mustafa drove them to the airport.

"I have people there who will keep you safe, and I don't want you too close to D.C. while shit's going down," he'd said. True to his word, a man approached her as soon as she got off the plane at LaGuardia. "Hello Miss Woods," he'd politely said, "David Jamison sent me. He said to mention the name Mustafa, just to reassure you that you're safe."

And quickly she'd been whisked away, assuming she was headed to a safe place. Now she regarded Anthony with suspicion, her expression tense. "No" she said while gathering her purse and sweater from the car and closing the door. "David left me in the dark, as usual."

"Don't be too hard on him," Anthony said. "He probably thought you wouldn't come if you knew I would be meeting you."

Emma didn't try to hide her irritation. "I was kind of hoping we were done with all the damned secrecy, but it seems like that bullshit is too difficult for you guys to shake off."

Anthony looked to the officer who nodded and got back into the car. As it pulled away, Emma continued to berate him.

"Really Anthony, you can't blame me for not trusting you. You pretty much disappeared on us. You never even bothered to contact David. For all we knew you'd gone over to the other side. I mean, David never doubted your integrity, but I know people fold all the time, and for lesser things than money."

"My dear, my brief absence had nothing to do with a lack of allegiance to you, David or the Agency," Anthony said firmly. "I understand your anger, but what I did was necessary and, in the end, contributed to your ultimate safety. Both David and I were committed to getting to the bottom of your father's case and doing so could have done considerable damage to our positions within the Agency. It was, by no means, a secure situation, but we managed it with the best possible outcome. You may now go back to a peaceful life on your farm, if that's what you wish."

He wasn't exactly apologizing, but Emma couldn't argue the fact that the work he and David had done seemed to have saved her neck.

She looked around and sighed, "So much has happened. I don't know what's real anymore."

Anthony gave an empathetic smile. "You've had a peculiar and taxing experience Emma. Most people would have broken under the strain of it all, but you behaved brilliantly. You were very brave, and I hope this doesn't sound condescending, but I am proud of you."

He offered Emma his hand, and after consideration, she took it and they walked toward the plaza where Zanders was waiting. "And now we must move on," he said briskly, wrapping her arm under his. "But you're going to have to trust me just one more time. I have someone I want you to meet."

They walked together toward Zanders, who offered Emma a bright smile. Anthony stopped in front of him and made the introductions.

"Emma Woods, Andrew Zanders. He has something to tell you about your father."

Emma stared in shock at Zanders. The mystery man, the person who'd eluded her from the very beginning of discovering her father's clues, now stood before her. How strange to finally be looking into his eyes. A million questions rushed to her mind, but they all seemed unimportant now. She could only muster the one that had plagued her from the beginning.

"Mr. Zanders, did my father die an innocent man?" She asked so quietly he had to lean in to hear her.

Zanders drew back and grinned. "Yes, and no," he said, taking her arm and leading her away from Anthony. "Let's take a walk," he suggested in a benign way that alarmed her. She looked desperately at

Anthony who had released her to Zanders. It didn't appear he would be coming along.

"It's alright Emma," he called after them confidently. "You're perfectly safe. I'll wait here."

Intensely curious about what Zanders might reveal about her father, Emma pushed aside her misgivings and walked with him. She wasn't sure about this stranger, but since they were in a crowded place, she decided to trust Anthony, as he'd requested, one last time. They proceeded, arm in arm, through the plaza and past a fountain where children played, balancing on the rim just above the water and worrying the grownups. When they made it to a path shaded with trees on either side, Zanders pointed to an empty park bench and they sat.

Emma could no longer bear the uncertainty of his answer. "What do you mean, yes and no," she asked. "Was my father innocent or not? Did you even know him well enough to be certain either way?"

Zanders leaned back, placing his elbows behind him on the bench and closed his eyes, as if he were going back in time. "I knew your father fairly well. We met at the Agency before going off to work for Grumman. I liked your dad, and I felt he was reliable, certainly more than the others on our team. Nirody struck me as a rather weak man, and Alberts was…"

Zanders paused, searching for the proper word. "Well," he chuckled, "Alberts was always a bit of an asshole."

Emma turned toward him, her posture stiff with anticipation. "I don't understand a word of what you're saying, and I don't care about any of that anymore," she said sharply. "I just want to know the truth about my father."

Zanders turned and looked at her intently. "Yes Emma," he said softly. "Your father was innocent."

She let out a sigh, not realizing she'd been holding her breath. She felt her body release all the tension held there for years. The utter relief was so foreign it left her feeling empty. Fighting to clear her father's name had been all she'd known for so long. It was what defined her. If she was no longer the daughter of a wronged man, then what was she? What was there to fight for, now that she knew?

Zanders watched her closely, wondering if she was ready for more. When she looked up he went on.

"Your father was approached by a man claiming to be part of the Shah's SAVAK forces. He was told they needed information on a particular group working within the government, but secretly backing the Ayatollah."

"I know all that," Emma said dully. She was still numb from the revelation of her father's innocence.

Zanders smiled in understanding. "Yes, and so you know that he was able to find out the truth, that this man was sent by an officer within the Agency by the name of Theodore Alberts. Theodore was doing what many men in the Agency did back then, hedging his bets. He could continue to work to keep the Shah in power, or he could gain access to revolutionaries who might someday take control. He worked closely with another officer, a younger man who was plucked from the army. This man's father used his political influence to place him somewhere he could prove himself, and the young man did advance in rank due to his ability to cozy up to the revolutionaries. Unfortunately, he kept his alliances for too long, and ended up exposing himself to the very terrorist groups that threaten the U.S. now. When he became an important member in the current administration things became….awkward. Your inquiries regarding your dad made this man immensely uncomfortable. If you had stumbled upon his dealings with revolutionaries, some who later became terrorists, it would look very bad, particularly since the President had run on an anti-terrorist platform."

"There's nothing to fear," Zanders said to Emma's look of alarm. "Anthony and David have taken care of the men involved. They've been exposed and dealt with."

In spite of the doubting look he received from Emma he returned to the subject of her father.

At any rate, your dad became a risk to these men when it became clear he wouldn't play ball. That's when Carter came to me, asking for help. Alberts thought I was in the dark, because I hadn't been approached to do what Nirody agreed to. I was the only one who your dad could trust. He sensed they would try to kill him, and make it look as if he'd flipped for personal gain. So I came up with a way to….extract him from the situation."

Zanders smiled again, while Emma regarded him with doubt. "Except it didn't work," she snapped. "He died anyway, and they got away with it."

Zanders looked away, the smile never fading from his face. "Who says it didn't work?"

Emma stared at him in confusion. "What are you talking about?" She wanted to scream at Zanders, but kept her voice low to avoid attracting attention from the occasional passersby.

He gazed back at her, with a curious expression. "Emma, you asked me if your father died an innocent man, and I said yes, and no. Your father was indeed innocent of the crimes they accused him of."

He looked away once more, nodding in the direction of the trees. "But he didn't die."

Emma blinked, and followed the direction of Zanders' gaze. There, just beyond the path, a man stood watching. He stepped away from the protection of the trees and stared back at her.

"He's still very nervous about revealing himself. That's why we chose a public place but with plenty of cover," Zanders explained. "I told him that a successful sting operation was done, and there was nothing to worry about. But I suppose old habits die hard."

Emma looked back at Zanders in wonder. She knew he was referring to the man standing in the trees, but she didn't dare believe it could be true.

"Go to him Emma," Zanders said, sensing her anxiety. "He's been waiting a long time."

She turned back to the man, a stranger with a familiar face. He looked to be in his seventies, with graying hair but in good physical shape. Emma stood and began walking toward him. As she got closer, she could see that his eyes were blue, like hers. She felt as if she were floating toward the man, nearly bumping into a couple in her path on her way. The stranger backed away, further into the trees, eyes darting left and right, then back at her. His expression was one of complete anguish. It was her father.

Emma caught her breath and felt as if she might faint. She stumbled and would have surely hit the pavement if her father hadn't rushed up to catch her.

"Emmers," he said as his arms enveloped her, "it's okay honey. I'm here."

She held on to her father and tried to catch her breath, fighting the urge to collapse into the dark comfort that fainting would provide. How could it be possible that the man who held her was the very reason she had lived an uncertain and tormented life? The shock she felt at seeing a dead father she'd idolized all her life gave way to indignation. How could he have been alive all these years without letting her know? Why had he left her mother to the hard work of raising two young girls on her own, and with no way to provide for them? Could he have known about his wife's terminal illness, and the burden placed upon Emma to care for her in those final days? She looked up into her father's eyes and asked the question burning in her mind.

"Dad…why?!"

Carter gathered his daughter up into a long-awaited embrace. He felt her stiffen, as if she were being held by a stranger. In fact, wasn't that what he was to her now?

"I'm sorry Emmers," he choked out the words, "I had no choice."

He stepped back and held her at arm's length. "Will you come with me, so I can explain?"

She lowered her head and began to cry, softly at first. But once the tears began to flow it became impossible to hold back. Great, big sobs wracked her body, releasing years of doubt and pain. Carter hated to see his daughter this way. And he couldn't bear the thought that she would be angry with him for his deceit, though he knew he deserved it. He half-walked, half-carried her away from the path and coaxed her deeper into the line of trees. Soon they were in a clearing that opened up into what looked like a Japanese garden. Cherry trees were just starting to flower, and a few blossoms fell onto their shoulders as they made their way to a stone bench perched alongside a little stream. Carter gently guided her to the bench where he sat beside her. Emma's weeping had subsided, but she still held herself tight and away from the man she'd believed to be dead for most of her life. They sat quietly, Emma wiping her eyes and Carter giving his daughter time to adjust to this new reality. He was desperate to be close to her, but he didn't attempt holding her hand. After a few moments he spoke.

"Emmers, I missed you and your sister every day, and I wanted to contact you and your mom so badly. But if I had, it would have put you all in danger."

Emma tried to untangle the multitude of questions this simple statement created. She wiped her nose with the back of her sleeve and shook her head.

"Then how did your note get to me? If looking for you meant I'd be targeted then why set up the note, and all the clues?"

Carter folded his arms and sighed. "I thought that if I let enough time pass, they'd assume the case was as dead as I was. I never believed for a minute that people from the Agency would have you under surveillance. I suggested you might be in danger just to scare you into being extra careful. I underestimated Theodore Alberts and his way of manipulating things. I learned later from Andrew Zanders that you were being harassed. He's been my eyes and ears from the very beginning. He stayed in touch with Frank Nirody, and that's how I knew you were working toward finding out the truth."

Emma didn't know what feeling to hold on to. She was ecstatic to be in the presence of her father at last. But now she saw him for the flawed creature he was and had always been. She was beyond disappointed in him. She felt pity for him, which was quite unfair considering the damage he'd done. Ever since she was a little girl, he had bullied her, Leena and their mother. He had put himself first in all things and disappeared from their lives in order to save his own. The final act of encouraging her investigation into his death at her own peril seemed incredibly self-serving.

"Dad," she said, looking him in the eye, "I love you, but I don't know if I can forgive you."

Carter hung his head and clasped his hands together, miserable in the knowledge he'd failed her. "I know Emma, I know."

She turned toward him and placed her hand on his shoulder. "No dad," she calmly but firmly stated, "you don't know! You don't know how much I needed you when I was a kid, and at the same time I was afraid of you. And you don't know how hard it was to take care of mom when she was dying of cancer. And you sure as shit don't know how much I lost in the process of finding out about you! So don't sit there and tell me you're sorry. I love you because you're my father."

She let her hand slide from him and plopped her back against a cherry tree that stood behind the stone bench, resigned to the ultimate truth about her father, "but I gotta say…you were kind of a shitty dad."

Carter looked at his daughter in amazement. Here was his brave girl, going up against criminals, figuring out how to find him, and giving him the telling off he deserved. To Emma's surprise, he smiled.

"Well," he said with a wry laugh, "I may have been a shitty dad, but I created you. And I think that's the one thing I did right. I am in awe of you Emma. And even though it's meaningless to you now, I truly am sorry for what I've done, not only to you, but to your sister and mom too. So look, here we are, and I'd like to make it up to you. I could walk away; get out of your life again if that's what you want."

Was that what she wanted? It certainly would make her life easier not to have her dad in it. But the temptation to make up for lost time tugged at her heart.

"I don't know Da," she mused, thinking about how good it felt to use the old nickname she had for him "let me think about it, okay?"

"Sure baby," Carter put his hand over hers. "Take all the time you need."

They sat quietly once more, until a thought occurred to Emma.

"You know what I need dad? I need answers."

Carter perked up, ready to give his daughter whatever she wanted.

"Absolutely!" He proclaimed, "Ask me anything!"

Emma turned to him, eager to finally learn the details that were hidden from her for so long. "Well," she began, "how did you do it?! I mean, David, the man who helped me in all of this, he saw a photo of the wrecked car you were driving. And there was clearly a burnt body that was supposed to be yours. Please tell me you didn't arrange for someone to die in your place!"

Carter smiled and shook his head. "No Emma, the body my Iranian friends left at the scene was someone who had died of heart failure the day before. One of my rescuers worked at the morgue. They placed that body by the car and lit the whole thing on fire. It was already burning by the time I drove past it."

He could see the scenario working in his daughter's mind, and the attempts she was making to put the pieces of his puzzle together.

"Emma, Zanders helped me work out a way to make it look like I was running from the men Alberts sent to kill me. We both knew there was never any intention to arrest me. It was always going to be a hit. I knew what they were up to, and I couldn't be allowed to expose their plan."

Emma's eyes shone in fear, and Carter went on, pleased to finally tell his story.

"My Iranian friends provided two cars, one for me to drive in a prearranged route, and another of the same model that I could pass by shortly after they set it on fire. By the time Albert's men came upon that burning car and corpse, I was long gone."

The realization that her father had staged his own death in perfect fashion gave Emma a momentary feeling of pride for him. "Way to go dad," she smiled and gave his shoulder a light punch. "That was sort of brilliant."

Carter beamed, basking in the hard-won glow of his daughter's approval. "Well, I wasn't going to let those assholes get to me." His expression grew somber once more. "The hard part was living in Iran, hiding out until Zanders could find a way to smuggle me back into the States. I owe him a lot, and I owe a lot to Newcastle and your friend, Jamison. Without their help I'm afraid we wouldn't be sitting here today."

"David's not exactly my friend," Emma corrected her father. "But yeah, between him and Anthony I don't know how I would have survived all this, and found you." She sat regarding her father, seeing him in a new light. Like both Anthony and David, he was neither hero, nor villain. He was just a man, doing his job as best he could, working for his country.

"Da'?" she whispered, tears welling up in her eyes.

"Yes Emmers," Carter whispered back.

She reached for his hand and looked at the beauty of the cherry trees in blossom; a feeling of closure overwhelming her.

"I forgive you."

Chapter 45
A New Life

The dirt fell through her hands in soft clumps, and Emma worked to break it up, spreading it over the garlic cloves she'd planted in September. Compost would enrich and protect the tiny green stems emerging just beneath the soil. With any luck she'd have a healthy crop of garlic to harvest by July. She didn't wear gardening gloves. She liked the feeling of the soft, dark compost. The sky was overcast, threatening rain, and Stella sat watching her work, occasionally glancing at the horizon in protection mode. Ever since she'd returned from New York, Stella had refused to let Emma out of her sight. In spite of Patricia's efforts to spoil the dog, Emma's absence had taken its toll. After the first week she was gone, Stella began to eat less and less, until she finally ignored her food altogether. But when Emma returned so did the dog's appetite, and soon she was plumping up to her original size.

She reached for the hulking great Pyrenees, running her hands behind her ears, the favorite scratching spot. Her dog panted in appreciation and placed one big paw on her owner's arm. Emma wrinkled her nose and put her free hand in front of her face. "Wow Stella," she laughed, "we gotta do something about that doggy breath!"

It was October, seven months since the ordeal that led to finding her father. Seven months since she'd seen or heard from David Jamison. He'd called her just after the reunion with her dad, letting her know he was assisting within the Agency to absolve her father and convict those involved in the cover-up.

"Well, I'm glad it's all getting sorted out," Emma sighed over the phone. "It'll be good for my dad to literally have his life back again."

"Get to your hotel, and I'll call you when we're done," David said, clearly preoccupied with the task of conducting the sting operation.

She spoke at length with her father before leaving him in the park. Carter Woods had agreed to let his daughter have some time to work out how she felt about their relationship. He provided her with his phone number, and she promised to contact him once she was ready.

At first she was too busy to think of anything but putting the farm back together. Jeremy had never been much help to her, but he was at least another living, breathing presence. The first night she slept in the old farm house she felt utterly alone, even with Stella curled up at the foot of the bed. She held a small memorial service for both Jeremy and Patches, hammering a homemade plaque on the barn door commemorating their spirits, together in heaven and hopefully watching over her. She planted cool weather crops, to provide income and keep her mind off what she'd endured that past February. By October she had root vegetables and all manner of greens to take to the Farmer's Market, where she also sold her chickens' eggs, although those were slowing down with the shorter days.

 Anthony came home after being "read out" from the Woods case, and he settled back in with a very relieved Patricia. Together they were making plans for his imminent retirement, and they had Emma over for dinner whenever she accepted their frequent offers. "You don't have to keep me under surveillance anymore Anthony," Emma teased her neighbor. "I'm no longer your problem." He brushed her comment off with a wave of his hand. "My dear," he huffed, "I've become accustomed to keeping my eye on you, and you'll always be my problem." When she had coffee with Patricia they'd both laughed over his gruff rebuke. "He won't admit it, of course," Patricia said with a gentle smile, "but he's always going to want to look after you. And it's not just out of habit. He genuinely cares for you. And hey, watching after you gives him a sense of purpose. Men like my husband don't take to retirement well. He'll always need a project." Patricia was organizing an adventure for them, a country-wide visit to all the national parks. They were set to leave in the spring, but Anthony only agreed to go if Emma "stayed out of trouble" while they were gone. He told Emma that he owed his wife a decent vacation. "Actually," he revealed to Emma over one of their coffee breaks in the farm house, "We both owe a lot to Patricia. Without her assistance we might not have gotten to the main bad guy in Operation Nequitia." In answer to Emma's puzzled expression he explained. "My wife took it upon herself to contact some people she knew who could help your cause. She and her college friends formed a pretty tight group, and they had access to information that ended up pointing to the very person that brought on danger to you. I can't tell you too much about it, of course." Emma had grown tired of this phrase, but she refrained from complaining about it. Patricia had always been her friend and ally, and what Anthony told her was just further proof.

She had yet to tell her sister Leena about their dad. She couldn't be sure how Leena would take the information that he was alive. She temporarily shelved the idea of letting Leena in on the miracle of their dad's resurrection until she put her own emotions in order. Emma hadn't even used the phone number given by her dad. The piece of paper on which it was written lay untouched in her bedside table. One month had slipped into two, and she put off calling him until it became too awkward to do so. She felt that she would, one day, reach out. Now that she knew he was available to her, she wanted to wait to completely reunite. The strange and overwhelming desire to seek him out faded away. Little by little it turned into something else, something peaceful, and not as melancholy. She would call him before Christmas, and invite him to the farm. She knew he'd always hated his childhood home, but he would come for her sake. She would make them dinner, and afterwards they could work on a puzzle.

David Jamison was another matter. Over the months her curiosity over what had happened to him turned into a longing for his touch. She replayed the nights they spent together over and over in her mind, trying to remember his face, how he smelled, and the way he made her feel safe and special. She began to wonder if what they'd had was love, or just sex? There wasn't time to discuss their relationship when he put her on the plane to New York. Too much was at stake, he'd told her, and he was completely focused on overseeing the operation meant to capture and convict the people who wanted her dead. After she met with her dad, Anthony left to join David in D.C., and Zanders transported her to a hotel. Later that night, just as she was ready to fall into bed completely exhausted, she received one last call from David.

"It's done," he'd told her, "we got all of them in one place and took them down."

She breathed a sigh of relief; weak from knowing that finally there was nothing left to fear. "So that's it?" She'd hoped he would tell her more, and maybe give her the satisfaction of knowing exactly how the monsters that had made her life hell had reacted to being arrested.

"I can't really tell you much more than that," David said in businesslike fashion. "It's being handled by people within the Agency now."

"Well, that's messed up David," Emma complained, "Because without me those assholes would never have been caught. Don't they kind of owe me some kind of explanation? At the very least they should issue my dad an official apology." Remnants of the old anger began to flare up inside her. She led the Agency to the bad guys, and they were dumping her without as much as a thank you. And now David appeared to be washing his hands of her as well.

"Your dad is going to be absolved of any wrongdoing, and he'll be given full restitution in the way of pension and back pay," David explained. "And as far as the Agency is concerned, you're a goddamned hero."

The words were meant to give Emma some kind of vindication, but it only left her feeling abandoned. Hers had been a horrendous experience, but she'd also felt empowered; amazed at how, throughout all of the trauma and danger, she'd emerged as a warrior. 'What now?' she wondered, and what about David? He hadn't even asked how she was, or how things had gone with her father.

"I met with my dad," she offered cryptically.

"I know," David answered, "Tony told me. I found out about your dad just after we arrested the bad guys. I'm happy for you Emma. I really am."

This only made her angrier. "So you knew about my father before I did?!"

"That's just how it went down Emma," David bristled at the familiar anger in her voice. "Everything came together so quickly and we had to perform in a precise manner. Anyway, Tony and Zanders thought it would be best if you met your dad as quietly and privately as possible. Everyone was concerned the shock might be too much for you."

"David," Emma said, incredulous at the notion, "I've been shot at, kidnapped and stalked. My boyfriend, my horse and my sheep [goat] were slaughtered. Who are they to decide if I can handle seeing my father? And who are you to keep things from me? That's bullshit!"

"It's what your dad wanted too," David murmured.

"Well it's not what I wanted!" She shouted into the phone. She was met with silence.

She wanted to ask if she'd ever see him again. She wanted to beg him to get on the next plane and find her in New York City. She wished he would break into her hotel room and slide under the bedsheets, making love to her for days. But she wouldn't be the one to speak first. It was his turn, and he wasn't saying anything.

"I have to go," she'd finally said, cutting through the silence.

"Emma, wait," David said, attempting to keep her on the line. "There are things we need to discuss, things I want to clear up with you…"

"Maybe later David," she said, unwilling to expose herself to anything hurtful he might say. "I'm really tired now. 'Bye."

It was the last words she spoke to him. And it threw her back into a crippling loneliness. She was, in fact, even more alone than after Jeremy died.

Considering everything that had happened, Emma thought it odd that her life hadn't really changed much. Yes, she had her father back, and getting to know him again would be healing. She'd suffered unimaginable loss, but she was still alive. And she still had the farm. In fact, other than becoming a stronger person, she was the same, and doing pretty much what she'd been doing before she received the envelope with the key.

"Fuck it," she muttered as she continued to work the soil. "I'm fine being by myself."

She looked up at Stella, who regarded her with the tilted head that always made her laugh. "You look just like the RCA Victor dog," she giggled as she reached to scratch the fluffy white head. "It's just you and me girl," she murmured to Stella. "'Hope you're okay with that."

Stella wagged her tail, but then snapped her head back to the horizon. "Woof!" the big dog proclaimed. She stood at attention and zeroed in on something behind Emma. Alarmed at the big dog's behavior, she turned to see what was coming. In blue jeans and a sweater, David walked through the field toward her. Emma slowly rose to her feet, self-consciously brushing the dirt off her coveralls. She let Stella run past her to bark some more at David, until he offered his hand for a sniff and the not-so-fierce guard dog decided he was okay. Stella led David back to her owner with a "look what I found" expression on her face. David stopped just inches from Emma.

"Hey," he said.

"Hey," Emma said back. Then, after a moment, "I didn't think I'd see you again."

David nodded. "Well, I wanted to call you a million times, but everything I thought I might say to you sounded lame. So I decided to just come see you in person"

He reached up to wipe some dirt that had found its way onto her nose. "You look good, Supergirl, as beautiful as ever."

Emma rolled her eyes and shook her head. "You can't just waltz back into my life David. It's not that easy."

David offered a contrite smile. "I thought maybe if I got down on my knees and begged forgiveness you might not kick me off the farm."

Emma stepped back and glared at him, unprepared for his sudden appearance, and unwilling to hear what he had to say. "I don't know

Officer Jamison," she taunted, letting the sarcasm seep in. "It seems as if we really don't have much in common. And I need someone in my life that I can depend on. I'm not going to put up with a guy who shows up one day, and then disappears on me the next. Am I supposed to believe you'll hang around here, helping me on the farm?"

She motioned her arm to indicate the place she loved. It had been the one constant in her life, the one thing she really could rely upon to be there every morning when she awoke. And for months it had been the only solid thing surrounding her when she went to bed alone at night.

David caught her arm and pulled her back into him.

"If Anthony and Patricia could manage it, then maybe we can too," he said with hope in his voice. "We can figure all that out later. We have time. Anyway, I'm pretty sure I'm in love with you, and I thought I'd come back to see if you felt the same about me."

He didn't wait for her to respond. Bringing her in close, he kissed her gently. Then, in her ear he whispered, "And I don't know how to waltz."

He kissed her again, more passionately until she responded, and they melted into each other, oblivious of the figure of Anthony, standing by an upstairs window, observing them in the field below his house.

A jealous Stella pushed her way between them, and David released Emma, laughing. The two of them stared at each other, until David ran his hand over his mouth, suppressing a smile.

Emma examined the dirt under her fingernails. How long would it take her to erase the evidence of a hard day's work? It seemed as if, lately, the dirt never washed away.

"I was angry at Anthony for a long time," she murmured. "I wouldn't speak to him when I first got home."

She cast a glance behind her and saw the upstairs curtain move in the Newcastle house. Turning back to David, she smiled and shrugged her shoulders.

"He was patient with me though, and kept trying to explain that he was only doing his best to help me all along. I suppose, in a way, he became a mentor to me. I came to understand that everything he did ultimately led me to my dad."

David brushed an errant curl from Emma's forehead and smiled.

"He's been a mentor to me too," he said softly. "And though he rarely lets his guard down, it's clear that he's a very kind man. The spook business is hard on his kind. I think retirement will suit him well."

Emma nodded in agreement, and they both stood silently regarding one another, a sense of anticipation ebbing between them. Suddenly, David realized there was another reason for his visit. He shook his head and ran his hand through his hair in a gesture now familiar to Emma.

"I almost forgot. I have a message from your dad."

Emma folded her arms, smiling at him with skepticism. "Oh really?! And what might that message be?"

"I told him how great you were to work with, and he wondered if you'd like to help him out on a small…project. He said something about you enjoying a new puzzle? He thought you might have turned into an adventure junky like him, and that maybe you were bored with farm life. What do you think?"

Emma bent down to pet Stella's soft head while her dog looked up at her adoringly. She let her eyes wander, taking in the countryside, the old farmhouse and barn. The horses and chickens grazed contently. Two new lambs frolicked in the field below. There were so many memories here, and so much to do. Emma shook her head, and gave a short laugh.

"I might consider it," she said.

The End

Colette Waddell's love of history and the study of other cultures began as a child, when her father's Navy pilot career took her family throughout the US, Europe and the Middle East. In the past, Colette pulled from her background in Anthropology and History, applying them to her non-fiction work.

Her previous books include "Through the Eyes of a Survivor," the memoirs of her dear friend, Nina Morecki's Holocaust experience, and "Shade House Conversations," the life history of a Navajo family.

In her spare time Colette enjoys singing and playing the violin. She lives on a small farm in Ashland, Oregon with her husband Ross, caring for twenty chickens, two dogs and three horses, all of whom feel woefully neglected.

Made in the USA
Las Vegas, NV
08 June 2023